Volume 38

ELLERY QUEEN'S SECRETS OF MYSTERY

Edited by

ELLERY QUEEN, *pseud.*

The Dial Press
DAVIS PUBLICATIONS, INC.
380 LEXINGTON AVENUE, NEW YORK, N.Y. 10017

A-1

COPYRIGHT NOTICES AND ACKNOWLEDGMENTS

Grateful acknowledgment is hereby made for permission to reprint the following:

The Clue of the Screaming Woman by Erle Stanley Gardner; copyright 1948, 1949 by The Curtis Publishing Company, copyright renewed by Jean Bethell Gardner; reprinted by permission of Thayer Hobson & Company.
A Stroke of Genius by Victor Canning; © 1964 by Victor Canning; reprinted by permission of Curtis Brown, Ltd.
Out of the Dream Stumbling by Florence V. Mayberry; © 1964 by Davis Publications, Inc.; reprinted by permission of the author.
A As in Alibi by Lawrence Treat; © 1965 by Davis Publications, Inc.; reprinted by permission of the author.
The Last One To Know by Robert Edward Eckels; © 1974 by Robert Edward Eckels; reprinted by permission of the author.
Jericho and the Studio Murders by Hugh Pentecost; © 1975 by Hugh Pentecost; reprinted by permission of Brandt & Brandt Literary Agents, Inc.
The Man Who Never Did Anything Right by Robert Bloch; © 1968 by Davis Publications, Inc.; reprinted by permission of Scott Meredith Literary Agency Inc.
The Killer with No Fingerprints by Lawrence G. Blochman; © 1964 by Lawrence G. Blochman; reprinted by permission of Curtis Brown, Ltd.
Blood Money by Phyllis Ann Karr; © 1974 by Phyllis Ann Karr; reprinted by permission of the author.
Have You a Fortune in Your Attic? by Lloyd Biggle, Jr.; © 1963 by Davis Publications, Inc.; reprinted by permission of the author.
The Lonely Habit by Brian W. Aldiss; © 1966 by Davis Publications, Inc.; reprinted by permission of Scott Meredith Literary Agency, Inc.
Just Like Inspector Maigret by Vincent McConnor; © 1964 by Davis Publications, Inc.; reprinted by permission of the author.
Operation Bonaparte by James M. Ullman; © 1963 by Davis Publications, Inc.; reprinted by permission of the author.
The Raffles Bombshell by Barry Perowne; © 1974 by Philip Atkey; reprinted by permission of Curtis Brown, Ltd.
Uncle from Australia by Ellery Queen; © 1965 by Ellery Queen; reprinted by permission of the author.
Captain Leopold Gets Angry by Edward D. Hoch; © 1973 by Edward D. Hoch; reprinted by permission of the author.
The Theft of Nick Velvet by Edward D. Hoch; © 1973 by Edward D. Hoch; reprinted by permission of the author.
The Spy at the End of the Rainbow by Edward D. Hoch; © 1974 by Edward D. Hoch; reprinted by permission of the author.

4

CONTENTS

1 SHORT NOVEL

17 NOVELETS AND SHORT STORIES

(CONTINUED ON NEXT PAGE)

5

CONTENTS   *(CONTINUED FROM PAGE 5)*

Dear Reader:

Every mystery has its secret.

Its innermost secret.

Let us divide the crime-mystery story into two all-inclusive categories–the tale of crime with detection and the tale of crime without detection.

In the first category–crime with detection–there are subdivisions: deductive, intuitional, and procedural detective stories, dealing with both realistic and bizarre situations, the latter including the locked room, the miracle problem, and the impossible crime; all these subgenres contain a detective, amateur or professional, or a law-enforcement agency whose common purpose is to discover the culprit and uncover the secret of the mystery.

In the second category–crime without detection–there is obviously no sleuth, no man or woman hunter; but even when the reader knows the identity of the criminal from the beginning, there is still a secret to be penetrated and disclosed. If it is not the secret of who, it could be the secret of how, or of when or where, and often of why–why did the criminal commit the crime, why did the victim invite or cause the crime?

In the 18 stories chosen for this collection you will be challenged by many different secrets–who did it, how was it done, when did it occur, where did it take place, why did it happen? The secrets are in the hearts of the stories, in the hearts and minds of the characters, and it is for you to investigate at the side of the detective or the author, matching wits wit for wit–or to be your own detective, probing, questing, examining . . .

"Nothing is secret which shall not be made manifest." So saith Luke, and so, in the 18 stories which follow, you can look behind the scenes, pull aside the curtains, push away the screens, peer through the veils, remove the masks, break the seals, open the doors—expose the deep, dark secrets of mystery. You will have the help of some of the greatest mystery writers and detectives of the past and present—Erle Stanley Gardner's Sheriff Eldon; Edward D. Hoch's Captain Leopold, Jeffery Rand, and Nick Velvet; Hugh Pentecost's John Jericho; Lawrence G. Blochman's Dr. Daniel Webster Coffee; Lloyd Biggle, Jr.'s Grandfather Rastin; Barry Perowne's A. J. Raffles; Lawrence Treat's Homicide Squad; Ellery Queen's E.Q.—they won't let you down, they won't fail you.

ELLERY QUEEN

Erle Stanley Gardner

The Clue of the Screaming Woman

This short novel, complete in this anthology, has been "lost" for 30 years. So far as we have been able to check, "The Clue of the Screaming Woman" has never been reprinted since its original appearance in "Country Gentleman," issues of January through April 1949, and has never been included in any of Erle Stanley Gardner's books, hardcover or paperback. The story features Sheriff Eldon, a modern Leatherstocking in a contemporary setting.

Erle Stanley Gardner is claimed to be "the best-selling American author of all time," and his sales figures substantiate that claim. His 96 books, most of them about lawyer-detective Perry Mason, have sold 185,000,000 copies in the United States alone, and approximately 225,000,000 worldwide. That's popularity!

Now, read about Frank Ames who came to the mountains to get away from people, to recuperate from the ravages of a prisoner-of-war camp, and learn how his solitude was shattered by a woman's scream . . .

Detective: SHERIFF BILL ELDON

Frank Ames surveyed the tumbling mountain torrent and selected the rock he wanted with great care.

It was on the edge of the deep water, a third of the way across the stream, about sixty feet below the little waterfall and the big eddy. Picking his way over half-submerged stepping stones, then across the fallen log to the rounded rock, he made a few whipping motions with his fishing rod to get plenty of free line. He knew only too well how much that first cast counted.

Up here in the high mountains the sky was black behind the deep blue of interstellar space. The big granite rocks reflected light with dazzling brilliance, while the shadows seemed deep and impenetrable. Standing down near the stream, the roar of the water kept Frank Ames' ears from accurately appraising other sounds, distorting them out of all semblance to reality.

The raucous abuse of a mountain jay sounded remarkably like the noise made by a buzz saw ripping through a pine board, and some peculiar vagary of the stream noises made Frank Ames feel he could hear a woman screaming.

Ames made his cast. The line twisted through the air, straightened at just the right distance above the water and settled. The Royal Coachman came to rest gently, seductively, on the far edge of the little whirlpool just below the waterfall.

For a moment the fly reposed on the water with calm tranquillity, drifting with the current. Then there was a shadowy dark streak of submerged motion. A big trout raised his head and part of his body up out of the water.

The noise made by the fish as it came down hard on the fly was a soul-gratifying "*chooonk.*" It seemed the fish had pushed its shoulders into a downward strike as it started back to the dark depths of the clear stream, the Royal Coachman in its mouth.

Ames set the hook and firmed his feet on the rock. The reel sounded like an angry rattlesnake. The line suddenly stretched taut. Even above the sound of the mountain stream, the hissing of the wire-tight line as it cut through the water was plainly audible.

The sound of a woman's scream again mingled with the stream noises. This time the scream was louder and nearer.

The sound knifed through to Frank Ames' consciousness. It was as annoying, as much out of place, as the ringing of a telephone bell at four o'clock in the morning. Frank desperately wanted that trout. It was a fine, big trout with a dark back, beautiful red sides, firm-fleshed from ice-cold, swift waters, and it was putting up a terrific fight.

That first time there had been some doubt as to the sound Ames had heard. It might have been the stream-distorted echo of a hawk crying out as it circled high in the heavens. But as to this second noise there could be no doubt. It was the scream of a woman, and it sounded from the trail along the east bank of the stream.

Ames turned to look over his shoulder, a hurried glance of apprehensive annoyance.

That one moment's advantage was all the trout needed. With the vigilance of the fisherman relaxed for the flicker of an eyelash, the trout made a swift rush for the tangled limbs of the submerged tree trunk on the far end of the pool, timing his maneuver as though he had known the exact instant the fisherman had turned.

Almost automatically Ames tightened on the rod and started reeling in, but he was too late. He felt the sudden cessation of the surging tugs which come up the line through the wrist and into the arm in a series of impulses too rapid to count, but which are the very breath of life to the skilled fisherman. Instead, the tension of the line was firm, steady and dead.

Knowing that his leader was wrapped around a submerged branch, Ames pointed the rod directly at the taut line, applied sufficient pressure to break the slender leader, and then reeled in the line.

He turned toward the place from which the scream had sounded.

There was no sign of animation in the scenery. The high mountain crags brooded over the scene. A few fleecy clouds forming over the east were the only break in the tranquil blue of the sky. Long sweeps of majestic pines stretched in a serried sequence up the canyons, their needles oozing scent into the pure, dry air.

Ames, slender-waisted, long-legged, graceful in his motions, was like a deer bounding across the fallen log, jumping lightly to the water-splashed stepping stones.

He paused at the thin fringe of scrub pine which grew between the rocky approach to the stream and the winding trail long enough to divest himself of his fishing creel and rod. Then he moved swiftly through the small pines to where the trail ran in a north and south direction, roughly paralleling that of the stream.

The decomposed granite dust of the trail held tracks with remarkable fidelity. Superimposed over the older horse and deer tracks that were in the trail were the tracks made by a woman who had been running as fast as she could go.

At this elevation of more than seven thousand feet above sea level, where even ordinary exertion left a person breathless, it was evident either that the woman could not have been running far, or that she had lived long enough in this country to be acclimated to the altitude.

The shoes she was wearing, however, were apparently new cowboy boots, completely equipped with rubber heels, so new that even the pattern of the heel showed in the downhill portion of the trail.

For the most part, the woman had been running with her weight on her toes. When she came to the steep downhill pitch, however, her weight was back more on her heels, and the rubber heel caps made distinct imprints. After fifty yards, Ames saw that the tracks faltered. The strides grew shorter. Slowly, she had settled down to a rapid, breathless walk.

With the unerring instinct of a trained hunter, Ames followed those tracks, keeping to one side of the trail so that his tracks did not obliterate those of the hurrying woman. He saw where she had paused and turned, the prints of her feet at right angles to the trail as she looked back over her shoulder. Then, apparently more re-assured, she had resumed her course, walking now at a less rapid rate.

Moving with a long, lithe stride which made him glide noiselessly, Frank Ames topped a rise, went down another short, steep pitch, rounded a turn in the pine trees and came unexpectedly on the woman, standing poised like some wild thing. She had stopped and was looking back, her startled face showing as a white oval.

She started to run, then paused, looked back again, stopped, and, as Ames came up, managed a dubious and somewhat breathless smile.

"Hello," Ames said with the casual simplicity of a man who has the assurance of complete sincerity.

"Good afternoon," she answered, then laughed, a short, oxygen-starved laugh. "I was taking–a quick walk." She paused to get her breath, said, "Trying to give my figure some much-needed disci-pline."

Another pause for breath. "When you rounded the bend in the trail, you–you startled me."

Ames' eyes said there was nothing wrong with her figure, but his lips merely twisted in a slow grin.

She was somewhere in the middle twenties. The frontier riding breeches, short leather jacket, shirt open at the front, the bandanna around her neck, held in place with a leather loop studded with brilliants, showed that she was a "dude" from the city. The breeches emphasized the slenderness of her waist, the smooth, graceful con-tours of her hips and legs. The face was still pale, but the deep red of sunburn around the open line of the throat above the protection of the bandanna was as eloquent as a complete calendar to Frank's trained eyes.

The sunburned skin told the story of a girl who had ridden in on a horseback pack trip, who had underestimated the powerful actinic rays of the mountain sun, who had tried too late to cover the sun-burned V-shaped area with a scarf. A couple of days in the mountains and some soothing cream had taken some of the angry redness out of the skin, but that was all.

He waited to see if there would be some explanation of her scream or her flight. Not for worlds would he have violated the code of the mountains by trying to pry into something that was none of his business. When he saw she had no intention of making any further explanation, he said casually, "Guess you must have come up the trail from Granite Flats about Sunday. Didn't you, ma'am?"

She looked at him with sudden apprehension. "How did *you* know?"

"I had an idea you might have been in the mountains just about that long, and I knew you didn't come up from this end because I didn't see the tracks of a pack train in the trail."

"Can you follow tracks?" she asked.

"Why, of course." He paused and then added casually, "I'm headed down toward where your camp must be. Perhaps you'd let me walk along with you for a piece."

"I'd love it!" she exclaimed, and then with quick suspicion, "How do *you* know where our camp is?"

His slight drawl was emphasized as he thought the thing into words. "If you'd been camped at Coyote Springs, you'd need to have walked three miles to get here. You don't look as though you'd gone that far. Down at Deerlick Springs, there's a meadow with good grass for the horses, a nice camping place and it's only about three quarters of a mile from here, so I–"

She interrupted with a laugh which now carried much more assurance. "I see that there's no chance for me to have *any* secrets. Do you live up here?"

Frank wanted to tell her of the two years in the Japanese prison camp, of the necessity of living close to Nature to get his health and strength back, of the trap line which he ran through the winter, of the new-found strength and vitality that were erasing the disabilities caused by months of malnutrition. But when it came to talking about himself, the words dried up. All he could say was, "Yes, I live up here."

She fell into step at his side. "You must find it isolated."

"I don't see many people," he admitted, "but there are other things to make up for it–no telephones, no standing in line, no exhaust fumes."

"And you're content to be here always?"

"Not always. I want a ranch down in the valley. I'm completing arrangements for one now. A friend of mine is giving me a lease with a contract to purchase. I think I can pay out on it with luck and hard work."

Her eyes were thoughtful as she walked along the trail, stepping awkwardly in her high-heeled cowboy riding boots. "I suppose really you can't ask for much more than that—luck and hard work."

"It's all *I* want," Frank told her.

They walked for some minutes in the silence of mutual appraisal, then rounded a turn in the trail, and Deerlick Meadows stretched out in front of them. And as soon as Frank Ames saw the elaborate nature of the camp, he knew these people were wealthy sportsmen who were on a de luxe trip. Suddenly awkward, he said, "Well, I guess I'd better turn—" And then stopped abruptly as he realized that it would never do to let this young woman know he had been merely escorting her along the trail. He had told her he was going in her direction. He'd have to keep on walking past the camp.

"What's your name?" she asked suddenly, and then added laughingly, "Mine's Roberta Coe."

"Frank Ames," he said uncomfortably, knowing she had asked him his name so abruptly because she intended to introduce him to her companions.

"Well, you must come in and have a cup of coffee before you go on," she said. "You'd like to meet my friends and they'd like to meet you."

They had been seen now and Ames was aware of curious glances from people who were seated in folding canvas chairs, items of luxury which he knew could have been brought in only at much cost to the tourist and at much trouble to both packer and pack horse.

He tried to demur, but somehow the right words wouldn't come, and he couldn't let himself seem to run away. Even while he hesitated, they entered the camp, and he found himself meeting people with whom he felt awkwardly ill at ease.

Harvey W. Dowling was evidently the business executive who was footing the bills. He, it seemed, was in his tent, taking a siesta and the hushed voices of the others showed the fawning deference with which they regarded the man who was paying the bills. His tent, a pretentious affair with heating stove and shaded entrance, occupied a choice position, away from the rest of the camp, a small tributary stream winding in front, and the shady pine thicket immediately in the back.

The people to whom Ames was introduced were the type a rich

man gathers around him, people who were careful to cultivate the manners of the rich, who clung tenaciously to their contacts with the wealthy.

Now these people, carefully subdued in voice and manner, so as not to disturb the man in the big tent, had that amused, patronizing tolerance of manner which showed they regarded Frank Ames merely as a novel interlude rather than as a human being.

Dick Nottingham had a well-nourished, athletic ease of manner, a smoothly muscled body and the calm assurance of one who is fully conscious of his eligibility. Two other men, Alexander Cameron and Sam Fremont, whose names Ames heard mentioned, were evidently downstream fishing.

The women were young, well-groomed and far more personal in their curiosity. Eleanor Dowling relied on her own beauty and her father's wealth to display a certain arrogance. Sylvia Jessup had mocking eyes which displayed challenging invitation as she sized up Frank's long, rangy build.

Conscious of his faded blue shirt and overalls with the patched knees, Frank felt distinctly ill at ease, and angry at himself because he did. He would have given much to have been articulate enough to express himself, to have joined in casual small talk; but the longer he stayed the more awkward and tongue-tied he felt, and that in turn made him feel more and more conspicuous.

There was good-natured banter. Sylvia Jessup announced that after this *she* was going to walk in the afternoons and see if *she* couldn't bag a little game, veiled references to open season and bag limit; then light laughter. And there were casually personal questions that Ames answered as best he could.

Whenever they would cease their light banter, and in the brief period of silence wait for Frank Ames to make some comment, Frank angrily realized his tongue-tied impotence, realized from the sudden way in which they would all start talking at once that they were trying to cover his conversational inadequacy.

Sam Fremont, camera in hand, came into camp almost unnoticed. He had, he explained, been hunting wildlife with his camera, and he grinningly admitted approaching camp quietly so he could get a couple of "candid camera" shots of the "sudden animation."

He was a quick-eyed opportunist with a quick wit and fast tongue, and some of his quips brought forth spontaneous laughter. After one particularly loud burst of merriment, the flap of the big tent parted and Harvey W. Dowling, scowling sleepily at the group, silenced them as effectively as would have been the case if some grim apparition had suddenly appeared.

But he came down to join them, a figure of heavy power, conscious of the deference due him, boomingly cordial to Frank, and with regal magnanimity saying nothing of the loud conversation which had wakened him.

A few moments later Alexander Cameron came stumbling up the trail, seeming to fall all over his heavy leather boots, boots that were stiff with newness. He seemed the most inexperienced of them all, and yet the most human, the one man who seemed to have no fear of Dowling.

There were more introductions, an abrupt cessation of the banter, and a few minutes later Ames found himself trudging angrily away from the camp, having offered the first excuse which came to his tortured mind, that he must inspect a site for a string of traps, knowing in his own mind how utterly inane the reason sounded, despite the fact that these people from the city would see nothing wrong with it.

Once clear of the camp, Frank circled up Deerlick Creek and cut back toward the main trail of the North Fork, so that he could retrieve his rod and creel.

He knew that it was too late now to try any more fishing. The white, woolly clouds had grown into great billowing mushrooms. Already there was the reverberation of distant thunder echoing from the high crags up at the divide and ominous black clouds were expanding out from the bases of the cloud mushrooms.

The thunderstorm struck just as Ames was crossing the top of the ridge which led down to the main trail.

The first patter of heavy raindrops gave a scant warning. A snake's tongue of ripping lightning dissolved a dead pine tree across the valley into a shower of yellow splinters. The clap of thunder was almost instantaneous, and, as though it had torn loose the inner lining of the cloud, rain deluged down in torrents until the sluicing streams forging their way down the slope were heavy with mud.

Knowing better than to seek shelter under a pine tree, Ames ran along the base of a granite ridge until he found the place where an overhanging rock, sandblasted by winds and worn by the elements, offered a place where he could crawl in and stretch out.

The lightning glittered with greenish intensity. The thunder bombarded the echoing crags and rain poured in cascades from the lip of the rock under which Ames had taken shelter.

Within ten minutes the heaviest part of the rain had ceased. The thunder began to drift sullenly to the south, but the rain continued steadily, then intensified into a clearing-up shower of cloudburst proportions and ceased abruptly. Half a minute later a venturesome shaft of afternoon sunlight explored its way into the glistening pines.

Ames crawled from under his protecting rock and resumed his way down the slippery slope to the main trail.

The soaking rain had obliterated the tracks in the trail. In fact, the ditchlike depression in the center of the trail still held puddles of water, so Ames, so far as he was able, kept to one side, working his way between rocks, conscious of the sudden chill in the atmosphere, conscious also of the fact that the clouds were gathering for another downpour, one that could well last all night.

Ames found his fishing rod and creel where he had left them. He slipped the soggy strap of the creel over his shoulder, started to pick up the rod, then stopped. His woodsman's eyes told him that the position of the rod had been changed since he had left it. Had it perhaps been the wind which accompanied the storm? He had no time to debate the matter, for once more raindrops began to patter ominously.

Picking up his rod, he swung into a long, rapid stride, the rain whipping against his back as he walked. He knew that there was no use trying to wait out this show. This would be a steady, sodden rain.

By the time Frank Ames reached his cabin he was wet to the skin. He put pine-pitch kindling and dry wood into the stove, and soon had a roaring fire. He lit the gasoline lantern, divested himself of his wet clothes, took the two medium-sized fish from the creel and fried them for supper. He read a magazine, noticed casually that the rain on the cabin roof stopped about nine-thirty, listened to the news on the radio and went to bed. His sleep was punctuated with dreams of women who screamed and ran aimlessly through the forest, of shrewd-eyed city men who regarded him with patronizing cordiality, of snub-nosed, laughing-eyed women who pursued him with pronged spears, their mouths giving vent to sardonic laughter.

Ames was up with the first grayness of morning. The woodshed yielded dry wood, and, as the aroma of coffee filled the little cabin, Ames poured water into the jar of sour dough, thickened the water with flour, beat it to just the right consistency and poured out sour-dough hot cakes.

He had finished with the breakfast dishes and the chores, and was contemplating the stream which danced by in the sunlight just beyond the long shadows of the pine trees, when his eyes suddenly rested with startled disbelief on the two rounded manzanita pegs which had been driven into holes drilled in the wall of the log cabin.

The .22 rifle, with its telescopic sight, was missing.

The space immediately below, where his .30-.30 rifle hung suspended from pegs, was as usual, and the .30-.30 was in place. Only the place where the .22 should have been was vacant.

Ames heard steps outside the door. A masculine voice called, "Hello! Anyone home?"

"Who is it?" Ames called, whirling.

The form of Sheriff Bill Eldon was framed in the doorway.

"Howdy," he said. "Guess I should drop in and introduce myself. I'm Bill Eldon, sheriff of the county."

Ames took in the spare figure, tough as gristle, straight as a lodgepole pine, a man who was well past middle age, but who moved with the easy, lithe grace of a man in his thirties, a man who carried not so much as an ounce of unnecessary weight, whose eyes, peering out from under shaggy eyebrows, had the same quality of fierce penetration which is so characteristic of the hawks and eagles, yet his manner and voice were mild.

"I'm camped up the stream a piece with a couple of head of pack stock," the sheriff said, "just riding through. This country up here is in my county and I sort of make a swing around through it during the fishing season. I was up here last year, but missed you. They said you were in town."

Ames stretched out his hand. "Come right in, sheriff, and sit down. Ames is my name. I'm mighty glad to know you. I've heard about you."

Bill Eldon thanked him, walked over to one of the homemade chairs built from pine slabs and baling wire, settled himself comfortably, rolled a cigarette. "Been up here long?"

"Couple of years. I run a trap line in the winters. I have a small allowance and I'm trying to stretch it as far as possible so I can build up health and a bank account at the same time—just enough for operating capital."

Eldon crossed his legs, said, "Do you get around the country much?"

"Some."

"Seen the folks camped down below?"

"Yes. I met some of them yesterday. I guess they came in the other way."

"That's right. Quite an outfit. Know any of the people camped up above?"

"I didn't know there were any."

"I didn't know there were either," the sheriff said, and then was quiet.

Ames cocked an eyebrow in quizzical interrogation.

"Seen anybody up that way?" Eldon asked.

"There are some folks camped up on Squaw Creek, but that's six miles away. A man and his wife."

"I know all about them," the sheriff said. "I met them on the trail. Haven't seen anything of a man about thirty-five, dark hair, stubby, close-cut mustache, gray eyes, about a hundred and sixty pounds, five feet, eight or nine inches tall, wearing big hobnail boots with wool socks rolled down over the tops of the boots—*new* boots?"

Ames shook his head.

"Seems as though he must have been camped up around here somewhere," the sheriff said.

"I haven't seen him."

"Mind taking a little walk with me?" the sheriff asked.

Ames, suddenly suspicious, said, "I have a few chores to do. I—"

"This is along the line of business," the sheriff answered, getting up out of the chair with the casual, easy grace of a wild animal getting to its feet.

"If you put it that way, I guess we'll let the chores go," Ames said.

They left the cabin and swung up the trail. Ames' long legs moved in the steady rhythm of space-devouring strides. The sheriff kept pace with him, although his shorter legs made him take five strides to the other man's four.

For some five minutes they walked silently, walking abreast where the trail was wide; then as the trail narrowed, the sheriff took the lead, setting a steady, unwavering pace.

Abruptly Bill Eldon held up his hand as a signal to halt. "Now from this point on," he said, "I'd like you to be kind of careful about not touching things. Just follow me."

He swung from the side of the trail, came to a little patch of quaking asp and a spring.

A man was stretched on the ground by the spring, lying rigid and inert.

Eldon circled the body. "I've already gone over the tracks," he said. And then added dryly, "There ain't any, except the ones made by his own boots, and they're pretty faint."

"What killed him?" Ames asked.

"Small-caliber bullet, right in the side of the head," the sheriff said.

Ames stood silently looking at the features discolored by death, the stubby mustache, the dark hair, the new hobnail boots with the wool socks turned down over the tops.

"When—when did it happen?"

"Don't rightly know," the sheriff said. "Apparently it happened before the thunderstorm yesterday. Tracks are pretty well washed out. You can see where he came running down this little slope. Then he jumped to one side and then to the other. Didn't do him no good. He fell right here. But the point is, his tracks are pretty indistinct, almost washed out by that rainstorm. If it hadn't been for the hobnails on his new boots, I doubt if we'd have noticed his tracks at all.

"Funny thing is," the sheriff went on, "you don't see any stock. He must have packed in his little camp stuff on his back. Pretty husky chap but he doesn't look like a woodsman."

Ames nodded.

"Wouldn't know anything about it, would you?" the sheriff asked.

Ames shook his head.

"Happened to be walking down the stream yesterday afternoon just a little bit before the rain came up," the sheriff said. "Didn't see this fellow's tracks anywhere in the trail and didn't see any smoke. Wouldn't have known he had a camp here if it hadn't been for—"

Abruptly the sheriff ceased speaking.

"I was fishing yesterday," Ames said.

"I noticed it," the sheriff said. "Walked by your cabin but you weren't there. Then I walked on down the trail, caught the glint of sunlight from the reel on your fishing rod."

Eldon's silence was an invitation.

Ames laughed nervously and said, "Yes, I took a hike down the trail and didn't want to be burdened with the rod and the creel."

"Saw the leader was broken on the fishing rod," the sheriff commented. "Looked as though maybe you'd tangled up with a big one and he'd got away—leader twisted around a bit and frayed. Thought maybe you'd hooked on to a big one over in that pool and he might have wrapped the leader around some of the branches on that fallen tree over at the far end."

"He did, for a fact," Ames admitted ruefully.

"That puzzled me," the sheriff said. "You quit right there and then, without even taking off the broken leader. You just propped your fishin' rod up against the tree and hung your creel on a forked limb, fish and all. Tracks showed you'd been going pretty fast."

"I'm a fast walker."

"Uh-huh," Eldon said. "Then you hit the trail. There was tracks made by a woman in the trail. She was running. I saw your tracks following."

"I can assure you," Ames said, trying to make a joke of it, "that I wasn't chasing any woman down the trail."

"I know you weren't," Eldon said. "You were studying those tracks, kind of curious about them, so you kept to one side of the trail where you could move along and study them. You'd get back in the trail once or twice where you had to and then your tracks would be over those of the woman, but for the most part you were sort of trailing her."

"Naturally," Ames said, "I was curious."

"I didn't follow far enough to see whether you caught up with her," the sheriff said. "I saw the rain clouds piling up pretty fast and I hightailed it back to my camp and got things lashed down around the tent. Of course," the sheriff went on, "I don't suppose you know how close you were to that running woman?"

"The tracks looked fresh," Ames said.

"Thought you might have seen her as she went by," the sheriff said. "Thought that might have accounted for the way you went over to the trail in such a hurry. You were walking pretty fast. Then I went back to the place where you must have been standing on that rock where you could get a good cast, up by the eddy below the waterfall, and darned if you could see the trail from there! It runs within about fifty yards, but there's a growth of scrub pine that would keep you from seeing anyone."

Ames was uncomfortable. Why should he protect Roberta Coe? Why not tell the sheriff frankly what he had heard? He realized he was playing with fire in withholding this information, and yet he couldn't bring himself to come right out and say what he knew he should be saying.

"So," the sheriff said, "I sort of wondered what made you drop everything in such a hurry and go over to the trail and start taking up the tracks of this woman. Just a lot of curiosity. Sort of felt I was snooping, but, after all, snooping is my business."

Once more the sheriff's silence invited confidence from Frank Ames.

"Well," the sheriff went on after a few moments, "I got up this morning and thought I'd stop down and pay you a visit, and then coming down the trail I saw a long streak down the side of the hill. It had been rained on but you could see it was a fresh track where someone had dragged something. I looked over here and found this camp. He'd dragged in a big dead log that he was aiming to chop up for firewood. Thought at first it might have been a sort of a tenderfoot trick because he only had a little hand ax, but after looking the camp over, I figured he might not have been quite so green as those new boots would make you think. Evidently he intended to build a fire under the middle of this log and as the two ends burned apart he'd shove the logs up together—make a little fire that way that would keep all night. He didn't have any tent, just a bedroll with a good big tarp. It's pretty light weight but it would turn water if you made a lean-to and was careful not to touch it any place while it was raining."

"You—you know who he is?" Ames asked.

"Not yet, I don't," the sheriff admitted. "So far I've just looked around a bit. I don't want to do any monkeying with the things in his pockets until I get hold of the coroner. Too bad that rain came down just when it did. I haven't been able yet to find where the man stood that did the shooting."

"How long ago did you find him?"

"Oh, an hour or two, maybe a little longer. I've got to ride over to the forest service telephone and I thought I'd go call on you. Now that you're here, I guess the best thing to do is to leave you in charge while I go telephone. You can look around some if you want to, because I've already covered the ground, looking for tracks, but don't touch the body and don't let anyone else touch it."

Ames said, "I suppose I can do it if—if I have to."

"Isn't a very nice sort of a job to wish off on a man," the sheriff admitted, "but at a time like this we all of us have to pull together. I've got to go three, four miles to get to that ranger station and put a call in. My camp's up here about three quarters of a mile. I've got a pretty good saddle horse and it shouldn't take long to get up there and back."

"I'll wait," Ames said.

"Thanks," the sheriff told him, and without another word turned and swung silently down the slope to the trail and vanished. . .

Ames, his mind in a turmoil, stood silently contemplating the scenery with troubled eyes that were unable to appreciate the green pines silhouetted against the deep blue of the sky, the patches of brilliant sunlight, the dark, somber segments of deep shadow.

A mountain jay squawked raucously from the top of a pine, teetering back and forth as though by the very impetus of his body muscles he could project his voice with greater force.

The corpse lay stiff and still, wrapped in the quiet dignity of death. The shadow of a near-by pine marched slowly along until it rested on the dead man's face, a peaceful benediction.

Ames moved restlessly, at first aimlessly, then more deliberately, looking for tracks.

His search was fruitless. There were only the tracks of the sheriff's distinctive, high-heeled cowboy boots, tracks which zigzagged patiently around a complete circle. Whatever previous tracks had been on the ground had been washed out by the rain. Had the murderer counted on that? Had the crime been committed when the thunderheads were piled up so ominously that he knew a deluge was impending?

Ames widened his circle still more, suddenly came to a halt as sunlight glinted on blued steel. He hurriedly surveyed the spot where the gun was lying.

This was quite evidently the place where the murderer had lain in ambush, behind a fallen pine.

Here again there were no tracks because the rain had washed them away, but the .22 caliber rifle lay in plain sight. Apparently the sheriff had overlooked it. He doubted that he himself would have seen the gun had it not been for that reflecting glint cast by the sunlight.

The fallen log offered an excellent means of approach without leaving tracks.

Ames stepped carefully on the dead roots which had been pulled up when the tree was blown over, worked his way to the top of the log, then moved silently along the rough bark.

The gun was a .22 automatic with a telescopic sight, and the single empty shell which had been ejected by the automatic mechanism glinted in the sunlight a few feet beyond the place where the gun was lying.

Ames lay at length on the log so he could look down at the gun.

There was a scratch on the stock, a peculiar indentation on the lock where it had at one time been dropped against a rock. The laws of probability would not admit of two weapons marked exactly like that.

For as much as five minutes Ames lay there pondering the question as to what he should do next. Apparently the sheriff had not as yet discovered the gun. It would be a simple matter to hook a forked stick under the trigger guard, pick the gun up without leaving any trace, put it in some safe place of concealment, then clean the barrel and quietly return it to the wall of his own cabin.

Ames pondered the matter for several minutes, then pushed himself up to his hands and knees, then back to his feet and ran back down the log, afraid that the temptation might prove too great for him. He retraced his steps back to a position where he could watch both the main trail and the spot where the body lay.

Some thirty minutes later Ames heard the sound of voices, a carefree, chattering babble which seemed oddly out of place with the tragic events which had taken place in the little sun-swept valley.

Ames moved farther back into the shadows so as to avoid the newcomers.

Ames could hear a voice which he thought was that of Dick Nottingham saying quite matter-of-factly, "I notice a couple of people are ahead of us on the trail. See the tracks? Let's wait a minute. They turn off right here. They look like fresh tracks—made since the rain. Hello, there!"

One of the girls laughed nervously. "Do you want reinforcements, Dick?"

"Just good woodcraft," Nottingham said in a tone of light banter. "Old Eagle Scout Nottingham on the job. Can't afford to lead you into an ambush. Hello, anyone home?"

Ames heard him coming forward, the steps alternately crunching on the patches of open decomposed granite and then fading into nothing on the carpeted pine needles. "I say," Nottingham called, "is anyone in here?"

Ames strove to make his voice sound casual. "I wouldn't come any farther."

The steps stopped, then Nottingham's cautious voice, "Who's there?"

"Frank Ames. I wouldn't come any farther."

"Why not?"

"There's been a little trouble here. I'm watching the place for the sheriff."

Nottingham hesitated a moment. Then his steps came forward again so that he was in full view.

"What happened?" he asked.

"A man was shot," Ames said in a low voice. "I don't think it's a good place for the women and I think your party had better stay on the trail."

"What is it, Dick?" someone called softly, and Ames felt a sudden thrill as he identified Roberta Coe's voice.

"Apparently there's some trouble in here. I guess we'd better get back to the trail," Nottingham called out. "A man's been shot."

Eleanor Dowling said, "Nonsense. We're not babies. The woman who needed her smelling salts went out of fashion years ago. What is it?"

Ames walked over to the trail. "Hello," he said self-consciously.

They acknowledged his salutation. There was a certain tension of awkward restraint, and Ames briefly explained what had happened.

"We were just taking a walk up the trail," Nottingham said. "We saw your tracks and then they turned off. There was someone with you?"

"The sheriff," Ames said.

Nottingham said, "Look here, old man, I'm sorry, but I think you owe us a little more explanation than that. We see the tracks of two men up the trail. Then we find one man standing alone and one man dead. You tell us that the sheriff has been with you, but we should have a little more than your word for it."

"Take a look for yourself," Ames said, "but don't try to touch the body. You can look at the dead man's shoes. They're full of hobnails."

Roberta Coe held back, but Nottingham, Eleanor Dowling and Sylvia Jessup pushed forward curiously.

"No closer than that!" Ames said.

"Who are you to give *us* orders?" Nottingham flared, circling the body.

"The sheriff left me in charge."

"Well, I don't see any badge, and as far as I'm concerned, I–"

He stepped forward.

Ames interposed himself between Nottingham and the inert figure. "I said to keep back."

Nottingham straightened, anger in his eyes. "Don't talk to me in that tone of voice, you damned lout!"

"Just keep back," Ames said quietly.

"Why, you poor fool," Nottingham blazed. "I used to be on the boxing team in college. I could—"

"You just keep back," Ames interrupted quietly, ominously.

Sylvia Jessup, acting as peacemaker, said, "I'm sure you'll understand Mr. Ames' position, Dick. He was left here by the sheriff."

"He *says* he was. I'm just making certain. Where did the sheriff go?"

Ames remained silent.

Sylvia pushed Nottingham to one side. "Where did the sheriff go, Mr. Ames?"

"He went to phone the coroner."

"Were you with him when the body was discovered?"

"No, the sheriff found the body, then came and got me, and then went to the ranger station to telephone."

Nottingham's voice and manner showed his skepticism. "You mean the sheriff discovered the body, then he walked away and left the body all alone to go down and get you at your cabin, and then after all that, went to notify the coroner?"

"Well, what's wrong with that?" Ames asked.

"Everything," Nottingham said, and then added, "Frankly, I'm skeptical. While I'm on vacation right now, I'm a lawyer by profession, and your story doesn't make sense to me."

Ames said quietly, "I don't give a damn whether it makes sense to you or not. If you don't think the sheriff's actions were logical, take it up with the sheriff, but don't try to argue with me about it because in just about a minute you're going to have to do a lot of backing up."

Nottingham said, "I don't back up for anyone," but his eyes were cautious as he sized up Frank Ames as a boxer sizes up an opponent in the ring.

There was contrast in the two types; Nottingham well-fed, heavily muscled, broad of shoulder; Frank Ames slender, lithe with stringy muscles. Nottingham had well-muscled weight; Ames had rawhide endurance.

Abruptly the tension was broken by steps and H. W. Dowling called out from the trail, "What's everyone doing over there?"

"There's been a murder, father," Eleanor said.

Dowling pushed his way through the scrub pines. "This damned altitude gets me. What's the trouble?"

Eleanor explained the situation.

"All right," Dowling said, "let's keep away from the place." He paused to catch his breath. "We don't want to get mixed up in any of this stuff." Again he paused for breath. "Who's the sheriff?"

"Bill Eldon," Ames said. "I think he visited your camp."

"Oh, yes," Dowling said, and his patronizing smile was as eloquent as words. "Dehydrated old coot. Where's he gone?"

"To notify the coroner."

"Well, I want everyone in my party to keep away from that body. That includes you, Dick. Understand?"

"Yes, H. W.," Nottingham said, suddenly meek.

"And," Dowling went on, "under the circumstances, I think we'll wait." He paused for two or three breaths, then added, "Until the sheriff gets back." His eyes swiveled to glower at Ames. "Any objection, young man?"

"Not in the least," Ames said. "Just so you don't mess up the evidence."

"Humph," Dowling said, and sat down, breathing heavily.

More voices sounded on the trail. A carefree, casual, man's laugh sounded garishly incongruous.

Dowling raised his voice and called out, "We're in here, Sam."

Crunching steps sounded on the decomposed granite, and Alexander Cameron and Sam Fremont came to join the party.

The abrupt cessation of their conversation, the startled consternation on their faces as they saw the body seemed to revive the shock of the others. A period of uncomfortable silence spread over the group.

Alexander Cameron, his equipment stiff and new, from the high-topped boots to the big sheath knife strapped to his belt, seemed about to become ill. Sam Fremont, quickly adjusting himself to the situation, let his restless eyes move in a quick survey from face to face, as though trying to ferret out the secret thoughts of the others.

Roberta Coe moved over to Frank Ames' side, drew him slightly away, said in a whisper, "I suppose it's too much to ask, but—could you—well—give me a break about what happened yesterday?"

"I've already covered for you," Frank Ames said, a note of anger showing in his voice, despite the fact that it was carefully lowered so the others could not hear. "I don't know why I did it, but I did. I stuck my neck out and—"

"Roberta!" Dowling said peremptorily. "Come over here!"

"Yes, H. W. Just a moment."

Dowling's eyes were narrowed. "Now!" he snapped. "I want you."

The tension was for a moment definitely noticeable to all. Roberta

Coe's hesitancy, Dowling's steady, imperative eyes boring into hers, holding her in the inflexible grip of his will.

"Now," Dowling repeated.

"Yes, H. W.," Roberta Coe said, and moved away from Frank Ames.

Sheriff Bill Eldon, squatting on his heels cowboy fashion on the side of the ridge, kept to the concealing shadows of the pine fringe just in front of the jagged rock backbone. John Olney, the ranger, sat beside him.

Here the slope was carpeted by pine needles and deeply shaded. Fifty yards back the towering granite ridge reflected the sunlight with such blinding brilliance that anyone looking up from below would see only the glaring white, and unless he happened to be a trained hunter, could never force his eyes to penetrate into the shadows.

The sheriff slowly lowered his binoculars.

"What do you see?" Olney asked.

Bill Eldon said, "Well, he ain't going to walk into our trap. He found the gun all right, looked it over and then let it lay there. Now all these other folks have come up and it looks like they aim to stick around."

"It's his gun?"

"I figure it that way—sort of figured that if he *had* been mixed up in it, he'd try to hide the gun. He wouldn't know we'd found it and he'd figure the safest thing to do would be to hide it."

"I still think he'll do just that," Olney said.

The sheriff said, "Nope, he's lost his chance now. Somehow I just can't get that gun business straight. If Ames had done the killing and it's his gun, you'd think he'd either have hidden it or taken it back home. The way it is now, somebody must have wiped it clean of fingerprints, then dropped it, walked off and left it. That someone had to be either pretty lucky or a pretty fair woodsman; knew that a storm was coming up and knew a heavy rain would wash out all the tracks. Hang it, I thought Ames would give us a lead when he found that gun. Guess we've got to figure out a new approach. Well, let's go on back and tell him we've phoned the coroner."

"When do you reckon Coroner Logan will get here?"

"Going to take him a while," the sheriff said. "Even if he gets a plane, he's got a long ride."

"We just going to wait?"

"Not by a damn sight," Eldon said cheerfully. "We ain't supposed to move the body or take anything out of the pockets until the coroner gets here, but I'm not going to sit on my haunches just waiting around. Let's be kind of careful sneaking back to our horses. We wouldn't want 'em to know we'd been watching! There's a lot more people down there now."

"City guys," Olney said, snorting.

"I know, but they all have eyes, and the more pairs of eyes there are, the more chance there is of seeing motion. Just take it easy now. Keep in the shadows and back of the trees."

They worked their way back around the slope carefully.

Bill Eldon led the way to the place where their horses had been tied. The men tightened the cinches and swung into their saddles.

"We don't want to hit that trail too soon," Sheriff Eldon announced. "Some of those people might be smart enough to follow our tracks back a ways."

"Not those city folks," Olney said, and laughed.

"Might not be deliberately backtracking us," Bill Eldon said, "but they might hike back up the trail. If they do, and should find they ran out of horse tracks before they got very far, even a city dude might get suspicious. Remember when they came walking up the trail, that chap in the sweater stopped when he came to the point where the tracks led up to the place we found the body. He's probably been around the hills some."

"Been around as a dude," Olney said scornfully, "but perhaps we'd better ride up a mile or so before we hit the trail."

"How do you figure this Ames out?" asked the sheriff.

Olney put his horse into a jog trot behind the sheriff's fast-stepping mount. "There's something wrong with him. He broods too much. He's out there alone and—Well, I always did think he was running away from someone. I think maybe he's on the lam. I've stopped in on him a few times. He's never opened up. That ain't right. When a man's out here in the hills all alone he gets lonesome, and he should talk his head off when he gets a chance to visit with someone."

Sheriff Eldon merely grunted.

"I think he's running away," Olney insisted.

The ridge widened and the ranger put his horse alongside the sheriff.

"Sometimes people try running away from themselves," the sheriff said. "They go hide out someplace, thinking they're running away. Then they find—themselves."

"Well, this man, Ames, hasn't found anything yet."

"You can't ever tell," Bill Eldon rejoined. "When a man gets out with just himself and the stars, the mountains, the streams and the trees, he sort of soaks up something of the eternal bigness of things. I like the way he looks you in the eye.

"When you're figurin' on clues you don't just figure on the things that exist. You figure on the people who caused 'em to exist." And Bill Eldon, keeping well to one side of the trail, gently touched the spurs to the flanks of his spirited horse and thereby terminated all further conversation.

The sheriff reined the horse to a stop, swung from the saddle with loose-hipped ease, dropped the reins to the ground and said easily, "Morning, folks."

He was wearing leather chaps now, and the jangling spurs and broad-brimmed, high-crown hat seemed to add to his weight and stature.

"This is John Olney, the ranger up here," he said by way of blanket introduction. "I guess I know all you folks and you know me. We ain't going to move the body, but we're going to look things over a little bit. Coroner's not due here for a while and we don't want to lose any more evidence."

The spectators made a tight little circle as they gathered around the two men. Sheriff Eldon, crouching beside the corpse, spoke with brisk authority to the ranger.

"I'm going to take a look through his pockets, John. I want to find out who he was. You take your pencil and paper and inventory every single thing as I take it out."

Olney nodded. In his official olive-green, he stood quietly efficient, notebook in hand.

But there was nothing for the ranger to write down.

One by one the pockets in the clothes of the dead man were explored by the sheriff's fingers. In each instance the pocket was empty.

The sheriff straightened and regarded the body with a puzzled frown.

The little circle stood watching him, wondering what he would do next. Overhead an occasional wisp of fleecy white cloud drifted slowly across the sky. The faint beginnings of a breeze stirred rustling whispers from the pine trees. Off to the west could be heard, faintly but distinctly, the sounds of the restless water in the North

Fork, tumbling over smooth-washed granite boulders into deep pools rippling across gravel bars, plunging down short foam-flecked stretches of swift rapids.

"Maybe he just didn't have anything in his pockets," Nottingham suggested.

The sheriff regarded Nottingham with calmly thoughtful eyes. His voice when he spoke withered the young lawyer with remorseless logic. "He probably wouldn't have carried any keys with him unless he'd taken out the keys to an automobile he'd left somewhere at the foot of the trail. He *might* not have had a handkerchief. He could have been dumb enough to have come out without a knife, and it's conceivable he didn't have a pen or pencil. Perhaps he didn't care what time it was, so he didn't carry a watch. But he knew he was going to camp out here in the hills. He was carrying a shoulder pack to travel light. The man would have had matches in his pocket. What's more, you'll notice the stain on the inside of the first and second fingers of his left hand. The man was a cigarette smoker. Where are his matches? Where are his cigarettes? Not that I want to wish my problems off on you, young man. But since you've volunteered to help, I thought I'd point out the things I'd like to have you think about."

Nottingham flushed.

Dowling laughed a deep booming laugh, then he said, "Don't blame him, sheriff. He's a lawyer."

The sheriff bent once more, to run his hands along the man's waist, exploring in vain for a money belt. He ran his fingers along the lining of the coat, said suddenly to the ranger, "Wait a minute, John. We've got something here."

"What?" the ranger asked.

"Something concealed in the lining of his coat," the sheriff answered.

"Perhaps it slipped down through a hole in the inside pocket," Nottingham suggested.

"Isn't any hole in the pocket," Eldon announced. "Think I'm going to have to cut the lining, John."

The sheriff's sharp knife cut through the stitches in the lining with the deft skill of a seamstress. His fingers explored through the opening, brought out a Manila envelope darkened and polished from the friction of long wear.

The sheriff looked at the circled faces. "Got your pencil ready, John?"

The ranger nodded.

The sheriff opened the flap of the envelope and brought out a photograph frayed at the corners.

"Now, what do you make of that?" he asked.

"I don't make anything of it," Olney said, studying the photograph. "It's a good-looking young fellow standing up, having his picture taken."

"This is a profile view of the same man," the sheriff said, taking out another photograph.

"Just those two pictures?" Olney asked.

"That's all. The man's body kept 'em from getting wet."

Ames, looking over the sheriff's shoulder, saw very clear snapshots of a young man whom he judged to be about twenty-six or twenty-seven, with a shock of wavy dark hair, widespread intelligent eyes, a somewhat weak vacillating mouth, and clothes which even in the photograph indicated expensive tailoring.

Quite evidently here was a young man who was vain, good-looking and who knew he was good-looking, a man who had been able to get what he wanted at the very outset of life and had then started coasting along, resting on his oars at an age when most men were buckling down to the grim realities of a competitive existence.

The picture had been cut off on the left, evidently so as to exclude some woman who was standing on the man's right, but her left hand rested across his shoulder, and, seeing that hand, Ames suddenly noticed a vague familiarity about it. It was a shapely, delicate hand with a gold signet ring on the third finger.

Ames couldn't be absolutely certain in the brief glimpse he had, but he *thought* he had seen that ring before.

Yesterday, Roberta Coe had been wearing a ring which was startlingly like that.

Ames turned to look at Roberta. He couldn't catch her eye immediately, but Sylvia Jessup, deftly maneuvering herself into a position so she could glance at the photographs, caught the attention of everyone present by a quick, sharp gasp.

"What is it?" the sheriff asked. "Know this man?"

"Who?" she asked, looking down at the corpse.

"The one in the picture."

"Heavens no. I was just struck by the fact that he's—well, so good-looking. You wonder why a dead man would be carrying his photograph."

Sheriff Eldon studied her keenly. "That the only reason?"

"Why, yes, of course."

"Humph!" Bill Eldon said.

The others crowded forward.

Eldon hesitated a moment, then slipped the photographs back into the envelope.

"We'll wait until the coroner gets here," he said.

Frank Ames caught Roberta Coe's eye and saw the strained agony of her face. He knew she had had a brief glimpse of those photographs, and he knew that unless he created some diversion her white-faced dismay would attract the attention of everyone.

He stepped forward calmly. "May I see those photographs?" he asked.

The sheriff turned to look at him, slipped the Manila envelope down inside his jacket pocket.

"Why?" he asked.

"I want to see if I know the man. He looked like a man who was a buddy of mine."

"What name?" Bill Eldon asked.

Frank Ames could see that his ruse was working. No one was looking at Roberta Coe now. All eyes were fastened on him.

"What name?" the sheriff repeated.

Ames searched the files of his memory with frantic haste. "Pete Ingle," he blurted, giving the name of the first man whom he had ever seen killed; and because it was the first time he had seen a buddy shot down, it had left an indelible impression on Frank's mind.

Sheriff Eldon started to remove the envelope from his jacket pocket, then thought better of it. His eyes made shrewd appraisal of Frank Ames' countenance, said, "Where is this Pete Ingle now?"

"Dead."

"Where did he die?"

"Guadalcanal."

"How tall?"

"Five feet, ten inches."

"What did he weigh?"

"I guess a hundred and fifty-five or sixty."

"Blond or brunette?"

"Brunette."

"I'm going to check up on this, you know," Bill Eldon said, his voice kindly. "What color eyes?"

"Blue."

Eldon put the picture back in his pocket. "I don't think we'll do anything more about these pictures until after the coroner comes."

Ames flashed a glance toward Roberta, saw that she had, in some measure, recovered her composure. It was only a quick fleeting glance. He didn't dare attract attention to her by looking directly at her.

It was as he turned away that he saw Sylvia Jessup watching him with eyes that had lost their mocking humor and were engaged in respectful appraisal, as though she were sizing up a potential antagonist, suddenly conscious of his strong points, but probing for his weak points.

By using the Forest Service telephone to arrange for horses, a plane, and one of the landing fields maintained by the fire-fighting service, the official party managed to arrive at the scene of the crime shortly before noon.

Leonard Keating, the young, ruthlessly ambitious deputy district attorney, accompanied James Logan, the coroner.

Sheriff Bill Eldon, John Olney the ranger, Logan the coroner, and Keating the deputy district attorney, launched an official investigation, and from the start Keating's attitude was hostile. He felt all of the arrogant impatience of youth for anyone older than forty, and Bill Eldon's conservative caution was to Keating's mind evidence of doddering senility.

"You say that this is Frank Ames' rifle?" Keating asked, indicating the .22 rifle with the telescopic sight.

"That's right," Bill Eldon said, his slow drawl more pronounced than ever. "After the other folks had left, Ames took me over here, showed me the rifle, and—"

"*Showed* you the rifle!" Keating interrupted.

"Now don't get excited," Eldon said. "We'd found it before, but we left it right where it was, just to see what he'd do when he found it. We staked out where we could watch."

"What did he do?"

"Nothing. Later on he showed it to me after the others had left."

"Who were the others?"

"This party that's camped down here a mile or so at the Springs."

"Oh, yes. You told me about them. Vacationists. I know Harvey W. Dowling, the big-time insurance man. You say there's a Richard Nottingham with him. That wouldn't be Dick Nottingham who was on the intercollegiate boxing team?"

"I believe that's right," the sheriff said. "He's a lawyer."

"Yes, yes, a good one too. I was a freshman in college when he was in his senior year. Really a first-class boxer, quicker than a streak of greased lightning and with a punch in either hand. I want to meet him."

"Well, we'll go down there and talk with them. I thought you'd want to look around here. There was nothing in his pockets," the sheriff said. "But when we got to the lining of the coat—"

"Wait a minute," Keating interrupted. "*You're* not supposed to look in the pockets. You're not supposed to touch the body. No one's supposed to move it until the coroner can get here."

"When those folks wrote the lawbooks," the sheriff interrupted, "they didn't have in mind a case where it would take hours for a coroner to arrive and where it might be necessary to get some fast action."

"The law is the law," Keating announced, "and it's not for us to take into consideration what was in the minds of the lawmakers. We read the statutes and have no need to interpret them unless there should be some latent ambiguity, and no such latent ambiguity seems to exist in this case. However, what's done now is done. Let's look around here."

"I've already looked around," the sheriff said.

"I know," Keating snapped, "but we'll take *another* look around the place. You say it rained here yesterday afternoon?"

"A little before sundown it started raining steady. Before then we'd had a thunderstorm. The rain kept up until around ten o'clock. The man was killed before the first rain. I figure he was killed early in the afternoon."

Keating looked at him.

"What makes you think so?"

"Well, he'd been hiking, and he was trying to establish an overnight camp here. Now, I've got a hunch he came in the same way you did—by airplane, only he didn't have any horses to meet him."

"What makes you think that?"

"Well," the sheriff said, "he brought in what stuff he brought in on his back. There's a pack board over there with a tumpline, and his roll of blankets is under that tree. His whole camp is just the way he'd dropped it. Then he'd gone up to get some wood, and the way I figure it, he'd wanted to get that big log so he could keep pushing the ends together and keep a small fire going all night. He didn't have a tent. His bedroll is a light down sleeping bag, the whole thing weighing about eight pounds. But he had quite a bit of camp stuff, maybe a thirty-five pound pack."

"What does all that have to do with the airplane?" Keating asked impatiently.

"Well, now," Eldon said, "I was just explaining. He carried this stuff in on his back, but you look at the leather straps on that pack board and you see that they're new. The whole outfit is new. Now, those leather straps are stained a little bit. If he'd had to bring that stuff in from up the valley, he'd have done a *lot* of sweating."

"Humph," Keating said. "I don't see that necessarily follows. Are there no roads into this back country?"

The sheriff shook his head. "This is a primitive area. You get into it by trails. There aren't any roads closer than twenty miles. I don't think that man carried that camp outfit on his back for twenty miles uphill. I think he walked not more than three or four miles, and I think it was on the level. I've already used Olney's telephone at the ranger station to get my under-sheriff on the job, checking with all charter airplanes to see if they brought a man like this into the country."

Keating said, "Well, I'll look around while the coroner goes over the body. There's a chance you fellows may have overlooked some clues that sharper—and younger—eyes will pick up."

Logan bent over the body. Keating skirmished around through the underbrush, his lean, youthful figure doubled over, moving rapidly as though he were a terrier prowling on a scent. He soon called out.

"Look over here, gentlemen. And be careful how you walk. The place is all messed up with tracks already, but try not to obliterate *this* piece of evidence."

"What have you got?" Olney asked.

"Something that has hitherto been overlooked," Keating announced importantly.

They bent over to look, and Keating pointed to a crumpled cloth tobacco sack which had evidently been about a quarter full of tobacco when the drenching rain had soaked through to the tobacco, stiffening the sack and staining it all to a dark brown which made it difficult to see against the ground.

"And over here," Keating went on, "just six or eight inches from this tobacco sack you'll find the burnt ends of two cigarettes rolled with brown rice paper, smoked down to within about an inch of the end and then left here. Now *I'm* no ex-cattleman," and he glanced meaningly at Bill Eldon, "but *I* would say there's something distinctive about the way these cigarettes are rolled."

"There sure is," Bill Eldon admitted ruefully.

"Well," Keating said, "that's my idea of a clue. It's just about the same as though the fellow had left his calling card. Here are those cigarettes, the stubs showing very plainly how they're rolled and folded. As I understand it, it's quite a job to roll a cigarette, isn't it, sheriff, that is, to do a good job?"

"Sure is," Bill Eldon observed, "and these were rolled by a man who knew his business."

"Don't touch them now," Keating warned. "I want to get a photograph of them just the way they were found, but you can see from just looking at this end that the paper has been rolled over and then there's been a trick fold, something that makes it hold its shape when it's rolled."

"That's right," Olney said—there was a new-found respect in his voice.

"Let's get that camera, coroner," Keating announced, "and take some pictures of these cigarettes. Then we'll carefully pick this evidence up so as not to disturb it. Then I think we'd better go check on the telephone and see if there are any leads to the inquiries Sheriff Eldon put out about someone bringing this chap in by airplane. I have an idea that's where we are going to get a line on him."

"What do you make of this evidence, Bill?" the ranger asked Eldon.

It was Keating who answered the question. "There's no doubt about it. The whole crime was deliberately premeditated. This is the thing that the layman might overlook. It's something that shows its true significance only to the legal mind. It establishes the premeditation which makes for first-degree murder. The murderer lay here waiting for his man. He waited while he smoked two cigarettes."

"How do you suppose the murderer knew the man was going to camp right here?" Bill Eldon asked.

"That's a minor matter," Keating said. "The point is, he did know. He was lying here waiting. He smoked two cigarettes. Probably the man had already made his camp here and then gone up the hill for firewood, dragging that log down the hill along the trail that you pointed out."

Eldon's nod was dubious.

"Don't you agree with that?" Keating demanded truculently.

"I was just wondering if the fellow that was killed wasn't pretty tired from his walk," Eldon said.

"Why? You said he only had to walk three or four miles from an airfield and it was pretty level ground all the way."

"I know," Eldon said, "but if he'd already established his camp here and then gone up the hill to get that firewood and dragged it down, the murderer must have moved into ambush *after* the man went up to get that log."

"Well?"

"The victim certainly must have been awfully tired if it took long enough getting that log for the murderer to smoke two cigarettes."

"Well, perhaps the murderer smoked them after the crime, or he may have been waiting for his man to get in just the right position. There's no use trying to account for all these little things."

"That's right," Eldon said.

"This evidence," Keating went on significantly, "would have been overlooked if I hadn't been prowling around, crawling on my hands and knees looking for any little thing that might have escaped observation."

"Just like a danged bloodhound," Olney said admiringly.

"That's right," Bill Eldon admitted. "Just like a bloodhound. Don't see anything else there, do you, son?"

"How much else do you want?" Keating flared impatiently. "And let's try and retain something of the dignity of our positions, sheriff. Now, if you've no objection, we'll go to the telephone and see what we can discover."

"No objection at all," Eldon said. "I'm here to do everything I can."

Information was waiting for them at the Forest Service telephone office.

The operator said, "Your office left a message to be forwarded to you, sheriff. A private charter plane took a man by the name of George Bay, who answers the description you gave over the telephone, into forest landing field number thirty-six, landing about ten o'clock yesterday morning. The man had a pack and took off into the woods. He said he was on a hiking trip and wanted to get some pictures. He told a couple of stories which didn't exactly hang together and the pilot finally became suspicious. He thought his passenger was a fugitive and threatened to turn the plane around and fly to the nearest city to report to the police. When George Bay realized the pilot meant business, he told him he was a detective employed to trace some very valuable jewels which had been stolen by a member of the military forces while he was in Japan. He showed the pilot his credentials as a detective and said he was on a hot lead, that the jewels had been hidden for over a year, but the detective felt he was going to find them. He warned the aviator to say nothing to anyone."

Bill Eldon thanked the operator, relayed the information to the others.

"Well," Keating said, "I guess that does it."

"Does what?" the sheriff asked.

"Gives us our murderer," Keating said. "It has to be someone who was in the Army during the war, someone who was in Japan. How about this man Ames? Isn't he a veteran?"

"That's right. I think he was a prisoner in Japan."

"Well, we'll go talk with him," Keating said. "He's our man."

"Of course," Eldon pointed out, "if this dead man was *really* a detective, it ain't hardly likely he'd tell the airplane pilot what he was after. If he said he was after Japanese gems, he's like as not looking for stolen nylons."

"You forget that the pilot was calling for a showdown," Keating said. "He forced this man's hand."

"Maybe. It'd take more force than that to get *me* to show *my* hand on a case."

"Well, I'm going to act on the assumption this report is true until it's proven otherwise," Keating said.

Sheriff Bill Eldon said, "Okay, that's up to you. Now my idea of the way to really solve this murder is to sort of take it easy and . . ."

"And *my* idea of the way to solve it," Keating interrupted impatiently, "is to lose no more time getting evidence and lose no time at all getting the murderer. It's the responsibility of your office to get the murderer; the responsibility of my office to prosecute him. Therefore," he added significantly, "I think it will pay you to let me take the initiative from this point on. I think we should work together, sir!"

"Well, we're together," Bill Eldon observed cheerfully. "Let's work."

Roberta Coe surveyed the little cabin, the grassy meadow, the graveled bar in the winding stream, the long finger of pine trees which stretched down the slope.

"So *this* is where you live?"

Frank Ames nodded.

"Don't you get terribly lonely?"

"I did at first."

"You don't now?"

"No."

He felt at a loss for words and even recognized an adolescent desire to kick at the soil in order to furnish some outlet for his nervous tension.

"I should think you'd be lonesome *all* the time."

"At first," he said, "I didn't have any choice in the matter. I wasn't physically able to meet people or talk with them. They exhausted me. I came up here and lived alone because I *had* to come up here and live alone. And then I found that I enjoyed it. Gradually I came to learn something about the woods, about the deer, the trout, the birds, the weather. I studied the different types of clouds, habits of game. I had some books and some old magazines sent me and I started to read, and enjoyed the reading. The days began to pass rapidly and then a tranquil peace came to my mind." He stopped, surprised at his own eloquence.

He saw her eyes light with interest. "Could you tell me more about that, and aren't you going to invite me in?"

He seemed embarrassed. "Well, it's just a bachelor's cabin, and, of course, I'm alone here and—"

She raised her eyebrows. Her eyes were mocking. "The conventions?"

He would have given much to have been able to meet the challenge of her light, bantering mood, but to his own ears the words seemed to fairly blurt from his mouth as he said, "People up here are different. They wouldn't understand, in case anyone should—"

"I don't care whether they understand or not," she said. "You were talking about mental tranquillity. I could use quite an order of that."

He said nothing.

"I suppose you have visitors about once a month?"

"Oh, once every so often. Mr. Olney, the ranger rides by."

She said, "And I presume you feel that your cabin is a mess because you've been living here by yourself and that, as a woman, I'd look around disapprovingly and sniff. Come on, let's go in. I want to talk with you and I'm not going to stand out here."

Silently he opened the door.

"You don't even keep it locked?"

He shook his head. "Out here I never think of it. If Olney, for instance, found himself near this cabin and a shower was coming up, he'd go in, make himself at home, cook up a pot of tea, help himself to anything he wanted to eat, and neither of us would think anything of it. The only rule is that a man's supposed to leave enough dry wood to start a fire."

"What a cute little place! How snug and cozy!"

"You think so?" he asked, his face showing surprised relief.

"Heavens, yes. It's just as neat and spick-and-span as—as a yacht."

"I'm afraid I don't know much about yachts."

"Well, what I meant was that—well, you know, everything ship-shape. You have a radio?"

"Yes, a battery set."

"And a gasoline reading lamp and a cute little stove and book-shelves. How wonderful!"

He suddenly found himself thoroughly at ease.

Abruptly she said, "Tell me more about this mental tranquillity. I want some of that."

"You can't saw it off in chunks, wrap it up in packages and sell it by the pound."

"So I gathered. But would you mind telling me how one goes about finding it? Do you find it at outcroppings and dig it up, or do you sink shafts, or . . .?"

"I guess it's something that's within you all the time. All you do is relax and let it come to the surface. The trouble is," he said, suddenly earnest, "that it's hard to understand it because it's all around you. It's a part of man's heritage, but he ignores it, shuts it out.

"Look at the view through the window. There's the mountain framed against the blue sky. The sunlight is casting silver reflections on the ripples in the water where it runs over the rapids by the gravel bar. There's a trout jumping in the pool just below the bar. The bird perched on the little pine with that air of impudent expectancy is a Clark jay, sometimes called a camp robber. I love him for his alert impudence, his fearless assurance. Everything's tranquil and restful and there's no reason for inner turmoil."

Her eyes widened. "Say, when you warm up to something, you *really* talk, don't you?"

He said, "I love these mountains and I can talk when I'm telling people about them. You see, lots of people don't really appreciate them. During hunting season, people come pouring in. They come to kill things. If they don't get a deer, they think the trip has been a failure. What they see of the mountains is more or less incidental to killing.

"Same way with the fishing season crowd. But when you come to *live* in the mountains, you learn to get in time with the bigness of it all. There's an underlying tranquillity that finally penetrates to your consciousness and relaxes the nerve tension. You sort of quiet down. And then you realize how much real strength and dignity there is in the calm certainty of your own part in the eternal uni-verse.

"These mountains are a soul tonic. They soothe the tension out of your nerves and take away the hurt in one's soul. They give strength. You can just *feel* them in their majestic stability. Oh, hang it, you can't put it in words, and here I am trying!"

The interest in her eyes, the realization of his own eloquence made him suddenly self-conscious once more.

"Mind if I smoke?" she asked.

"Certainly not. I'll roll one myself."

He took the cloth tobacco sack from his pocket, opened a package of cigarette papers.

She said, "Won't you try one of mine?"

"No thanks. I like to roll my own. I–" He broke off and said, "Something frightened those mountain quail."

He held a match for her cigarette, rolled his own cigarette and had just pinched the end into shape when he said, "I knew something frightened them. Hear the horses?"

She cocked her head to one side, listening, then nodded, caught the expression on Frank Ames' face and suddenly laughed. "And you're afraid I've compromised your good name."

"No. But suppose it should be *your* companions looking for you and . . ."

"Don't be silly," she said easily. "I'm free to do as I please. I came up here to explain to you about yesterday. I–I'm sorry."

The riders came up fast at a brisk trot. Then the tempo of hoofbeats changed from a steady rhythm to the disorganized tramping of horses being pulled up and circling, as riders dismounted and tied up. Ames, at the door, said, "It's the sheriff, the ranger, and a couple of other people.

"Hello, folks," he called out. "Won't you come in?"

"We're coming," Bill Eldon said.

Frank Ames' attitude was stiffly embarrassed as he said, "I have company. Miss Coe was looking over my bookshelf."

"Oh, yes," the sheriff said quite casually. "This is James Logan, the coroner, and Leonard Keating, the deputy district attorney. They wanted to ask you a few questions."

Keating was patronizingly contemptuous as he looked around the interior of the neat little cabin, found that the only comfortable chair was that occupied by Roberta Coe, that the others were home-made stools and boxes which had been improvised into furniture. "Well," he said, "we won't be long. We wanted to get all the details, everything that you know about that murder, Ames."

"I told the sheriff everything I know about it."

"You didn't see anything or hear anything out of the ordinary yesterday afternoon?"

"No. That is, I–"

"Yes, go ahead," Keating said.

"Nothing," Ames said.

Keating's eyes narrowed. "You weren't up around that locality?"

"I was fishing downstream."

"How far below here?"

"Quarter of a mile, I guess."

"And the murder was committed half a mile upstream?"

"I guess that distance is about right."

"You weren't fishing upstream at all?"

"No. I fished downstream."

Keating's eyes showed a certain sneering disbelief. "What are you doing up here, anyway?"

"I'm–Well, I'm just living up here."

"Were you in the Army?"

"Yes."

"In Japan?"

"Yes."

"How long?"

"I was a prisoner of war for a while and then I was held there a while before I was sent home."

"Picked up some gems while you were there, didn't you?"

"I had a pearl and–What do you mean I *picked up* gems?"

Keating's eyes were insolent in their contemptuous hostility. "I mean you stole them," he said, "and you came up here to lie low and wait until things blew over. Isn't that about it?"

"That's definitely not true."

"And," Keating went on, "this man who was killed was a detective who was looking for some gems that had been stolen from Japan.

He looked you up yesterday afternoon and started questioning you, didn't he?"

"No!"

"Don't lie to me."

Ames was suddenly on his feet. "Damn you!" he said. "I'm not lying to you and I don't have to put up with this stuff. Now, get out of here!"

Keating remained seated, said, "Sheriff, will you maintain order?"

Bill Eldon grinned. "You're doing the talking, Keating."

"I'm questioning this man. He's suspect in a murder case."

"*I'm* suspect?" Ames exclaimed.

"You said it," Keating announced curtly.

"You're crazy, in addition to the other things that are wrong with you," Ames told him. "I don't have to put up with talk like that from you or from anyone else."

Keating said, "We're going to look around here. Any objection?"

Ames turned to Bill Eldon. "Do I have to—"

Roberta Coe said very firmly and definitely, "Not unless you want him to, Frank; not unless he has a search warrant. Don't let them pull that kind of stuff. Dick Nottingham is an attorney. If you want, I'll get him and—"

"I don't want a lawyer," Ames said. "I haven't any money to pay a lawyer."

"Go ahead. Get a lawyer if you want," Keating said, "but I think I have enough evidence right now to warrant this man's arrest. Would you mind letting me see that cigarette, Mr. Ames."

"What cigarette?"

"The one you just put in the ash tray. Thank you."

Keating inspected the cigarette, passed the tray silently to the sheriff.

"What's strange about the cigarette?" Ames asked.

"The cigarette," Keating said, "is rolled in a peculiarly distinctive manner. Do you always roll your cigarettes that way?"

"Yes. That is, I have for years. I pull one edge of the paper over and then make a little crimp and fold it back before I start rolling. That helps hold the cigarette in shape."

Keating took a small pasteboard box from his pocket. This box was lined with soft moss and on the moss were two cigarette stubs. "Would you say these were rolled by you?"

Ames leaned forward.

"Don't touch them," Keating warned. "Just look at the ends."

"I don't think you'd better answer that, Frank," Roberta Coe said.

"I have nothing to conceal," Ames said. "Certainly those are my cigarettes. Where did you find them?"

"You rolled those?"

"Yes."

Keating stood up and dramatically pointed his finger at Frank Ames. "I accuse you of the murder of George Bay, a private detective."

Ames' face flushed.

"Will you take him into custody, sheriff? I order you to."

"Well, now," the sheriff said in a drawl, "I don't know as I have to take anybody into custody on the strength of your say-so."

"This man is to be arrested and charged with murder," Keating said. "A felony has been committed. There is reasonable ground to believe this man guilty. It is not necessary to have a warrant of arrest under those circumstances, and, as a member of the district attorney's office, I call on you as the sheriff of this county to take that man into custody. If you fail to do so, the responsibility will be entirely on your shoulders."

"Okay," Bill Eldon said cheerfully, "the responsibility is on my shoulders."

"And I want to look around here," Keating said.

"As long as you're halfway decent, I'm willing to do anything I can to cooperate," Ames told him, "but you're completely crazy if you accuse me of having anything to do with that murder."

"It was your gun that killed him, wasn't it?"

"My gun was at the scene of the crime—near the scene of the crime."

"And you don't know how it got there?"

Ames said, "Of course I don't. Do you think I'd be silly enough to go out and kill a man and then leave my rifle lying on the ground? If I'd killed him, I'd have taken my gun to the cabin, cleaned it, and hung it up on those pegs where it belongs."

"If you were smart, you wouldn't," Keating sneered. "You'd know that the officers would recover the fatal bullet and shoot test bullets from all the .22 rifles owned by anyone in these parts. Sooner or later you would have to face the fact that the man was killed with a bullet from your gun. You were smart enough to realize it would be a lot better to have the gun found at the scene of the murder and claim it had been stolen."

"I wouldn't let them search this cabin, Frank," Roberta Coe said in a low voice. "I'd put them all out of here and lock the cabin up and make certain that no one got in until they returned with a search warrant, and then you could have your attorney present when the search was made. How do you know they aren't going to plant something?"

Keating turned to regard her with hostile eyes. "You're doing a lot of talking," he said. "Where were *you* when the murder was committed?"

Her face suddenly drained of color.

"Were you up here yesterday in this cabin?"

"No."

"Anywhere near it?"

"No."

"Go past here on the trail?"

"I–I took a walk."

"Where did you walk?"

"Up the trail."

"Up to the point where the murder was committed?"

"No, not that far. I turned back. I don't know. Quite a bit down-stream from here."

"See this man yesterday?"

Roberta tightened her lips. "Yes."

"Where?"

"I met him on the trail. He was walking down toward the place where I was camped."

"Why was he walking down there?"

"I didn't ask him. He overtook me on the trail, and we exchanged greetings and then walked together down the trail to the place where I'm camped, and I introduced him to the others."

"And then he turned back?"

"No. He said he was going on."

"Well, now isn't that interesting! I thought you said he was fishing yesterday afternoon, sheriff."

"He'd been fishing. I found his rod and creel where he'd left it, apparently when he walked down the trail."

"Well, well, well, isn't *that* interesting," Keating sneered. "So he went fishing and then left his rod and creel by the water. Just laid them down, I presume, and walked away."

"No, he propped the rod up against the tree and hung the creel over a forked limb."

"And then what?"

"Apparently he walked on down the trail."

"What was the idea, Ames?" Keating asked.

Frank said, "I wanted to look over some of the country. I–I walked on down the trail and met Miss Coé."

"I see. Went as far as her camp with her?"

"Well, I walked on a ways below camp."

"How far?"

"Oh, perhaps two hundred yards."

"Then what?"

"Then I turned back."

"Back up the trail?"

"No, I didn't. I made a swing."

Roberta Coe, rushing to his assistance, said, "He was looking over the country in order to find a site for some traps this winter."

"Oh, looking for traps, eh?"

"A place to put traps," Roberta Coe said acidly.

"Which way did you turn, Ames? Remember now, we can check on some of this."

Ames said, "I turned up the draw, crossed over the divide and then the rainstorm overtook me, and I lay in a cave up there by the ridge."

"You turned east?" the ranger asked, suddenly interested, and injecting himself into the conversation.

"Yes."

"Looking for a trap-line site?" Olney asked, incredulously.

"Well, I was looking the country over. I had intended to look for a trap-line site and then–"

"What are you talking about?" Olney said. "You know this country as well as you know the palm of your hand. Anyhow, you wouldn't be trapping up there. You'd be trapping down on the stream."

Ames said, "Well, I told Miss Coe that I–Well, I was a little embarrassed. I wanted to walk with her but I didn't want her to think I–It was just one of those things."

"You mean you *weren't* looking for a trap site?" Keating asked.

"No. I wanted to walk with her."

"In other words, you lied to her. Is that right?"

Ames, who had seated himself once more on a box, was up with cold fury. "Get out of here," he said.

"And don't answer any more questions, Frank," Roberta Coe pleaded. "You don't have to talk to people when they are that insulting."

Keating said, "And I'm going to give you the benefit of a little investigation too, Miss Coe."

Ames, his face white with fury, said, "Get out! Damn you, get out of my cabin!"

Bill Eldon grinned. "Well, Keating, you wanted to do the questioning. I guess you've done it."

"That's it," Keating said grimly. "I've done it, and I've solved your murder case for you."

"Thanks," Bill Eldon said dryly.

They filed out of the cabin.

Once more Keating said, "I order you to put that man under arrest."

"I heard you," Bill Eldon said.

Keating turned to Olney. "What sort of title does this man have to this property?"

"Well, he's built this cabin under lease from the Forestry Service—"

"And the Forestry Service retains the right to inspect the premises?"

"I guess so, yes."

"All right," Keating said, "let's do some inspecting."

Frank Ames stood in the doorway, his heart pounding with anger, and the old nervous weakness was back, making the muscles of his legs quiver. He watched the men moving around in front of the cabin, saw the ranger suddenly pause. "This chopping block has been moved," Olney said. "It was over there for quite a while. You can see the depression in the ground. Why did you move it, Ames?"

Ames, suddenly surprised, said, "I didn't move it. Someone else must have moved it."

Olney tilted the chopping block on edge, rolled it back to one side.

Keating said, "Someone has disturbed this earth. Is there a spade here?"

Olney said, "Here's one," and reached for the shovel which was standing propped against the cabin.

Keating started digging under the place where the chopping block had been.

Ames pushed forward to peer curiously over Bill Eldon's shoulder.

Roberta Coe, standing close to him, slipped her hand into his, giving it a reassuring squeeze.

"What's this?" Keating asked.

The spade had caught on a piece of red cloth.

Keating dropped to his knees, pulled away the rest of the loose soil with his fingers, brought out a knotted red bandanna, untied the knots and spread on the ground the assortment of things that were rolled up in it.

Ames, looking with incredulous eyes, saw a leather billfold, a card case distended from cards and documents, a fountain pen, a pencil, a notebook, a knife, some loose silver, a white handkerchief, a package of cigarettes, a folder of matches and a small, round waterproof match case.

Keating picked up the card case, opened it to show the cards of identification, neatly arranged in hinged cellophane pockets.

The first card showed a picture of a man with thick hair, a close-clipped dark mustache, and, even in the glimpse he had of it, Frank Ames could see it was the photograph of the murdered man.

"Deputy license of George Bay," Keating announced. "Here's another one. Identification showing George Bay licensed as a private detective. Here's a credit card, Standard Oil Company, made out to George Bay. Some stuff that's been in here is missing. You can see this card case has been distended with cards that were in the pockets. They're gone now. What did you do with them, Ames?"

Ames could only shake his head.

"You see," Keating said triumphantly, turning to Eldon. "He thought he could keep anyone from finding out the identity of the murdered man, so he removed everything that could have been a means of identification."

The sheriff shook his head sadly. "This murderer is making me plumb mad."

"You don't act like it," Keating said.

"Thinking we'd be so dumb we couldn't find all the clues he planted unless he was so darned obvious about it," the sheriff went on sadly. "It's just plumb insultin' to our intelligence. He was so darned afraid we wouldn't find all that stuff he even moved the choppin' block. I'd say that man just don't think we've got good sense."

"You mean you're going to try to explain away *this* evidence?" Keating asked.

Bill Eldon shook his head. "I'm not explaining a thing. It's just plumb insultin', that's all."

Roberta Coe, her mind in a turmoil, followed a tributary of the main stream, walking along a game trail, hardly conscious of where she was going or of her surroundings, wanting only to get entirely away from everyone.

She could keep silent, protect her secret and retain her position in her circle of friends, or she could tell what she knew, help save an innocent man—and bring the security of her life, with all of its pleasant associations, tumbling down in ruins. After all, the sheriff had not specifically asked her to identify those photographs.

It was not an easy decision.

Yet she knew in advance what her answer was to be. She had sought the vast, rugged majesty of the mountains, the winding trail along the talkative stream, to give her strength.

If she had been going to take refuge in weakness, she would have been in camp with her companions, a highball glass in her hand, talking, joking, using the quick-witted repartee of her set to shield her mind from the pressure of her conscience.

But she needed strength, needed it desperately. Frank Ames had managed to get spiritual solace from these mountains. If she could only let some of their sublime indifference to the minor vicissitudes of life flow into her own soul.

Then it would be easy. Now it was—

Suddenly Roberta sensed something wrong with a patch of deep shadow to the left of the trail. There was the semblance of solidity about that shadow, and then, even as her eyes tried to interpret what she saw, the figure that was almost hidden in the shadow moved.

Roberta screamed.

Bill Eldon, who had been sitting motionless, squatting on his heels cowboy-fashion, straightened himself with sinewy ease.

"Now, don't be frightened, ma'am," he said. "I just wanted to talk with you."

"You—You—How did you—find me here?"

"Now, take it easy," Bill Eldon said, his eyes smiling. "I just thought you and I should have a little talk."

"But how did you know where I was—where you could find me—where I was going to be? Why, even I didn't know where I was going."

Eldon said, "Figure it out, ma'am. This game trail follows the stream. The stream follows the canyon, and the canyon winds around. When I cut your tracks back there in the trail, I knew I only had to walk up over that saddle and come down here to gain half a mile on you. Now, suppose you sit down on that rock there and we just get sociable-like for a little while."

"I'm sorry, sheriff, but I don't feel like—"

"You've got to tell me what frightened you yesterday," the sheriff insisted, kindly but doggedly.

"But I wasn't frightened."

Bill Eldon settled back on his heels once more. Apparently he was completely at ease, thoroughly relaxed.

With the peculiar feeling that she was doing something entirely against her own volition, Roberta sat down.

Bill Eldon said, "Lots of people make a mistake about the mountains. When they're out in the wilds with no one around they feel they're hidden. They're wrong. Wherever they go, they leave tracks."

Roberta Coe said nothing.

When Bill Eldon saw she was not going to speak, he went on. "Now, you take that trail yesterday, for instance. It carried tracks just like a printed page. I came along that trail and saw where you'd been running. I saw where Frank Ames had put down his fishing rod and his creel and hurried after you. The way I figure it, you must have screamed and run past the hole where he was fishing just about the time he had a big one on.

"By getting up on the bank, looking down in the pool, I could see the submerged branches of that dead tree. Sure enough, on one of those branches was part of a leader, just wrapped around the snag, and a hook was on the end of the leader. Because I was curious, I took off my clothes, worked my way down into the water and got that fly out. Gosh, it was cold."

The sheriff reached in his pocket, took out a little fly book, opened it, and showed a section of leader and a Royal Coachman fly.

"Same kind Frank Ames uses," he said. "You can see a little piece of the fish's lip still stuck on the hook. The way I figure it, Ames hadn't hooked him too solid, but he had him hooked well enough to land, but as soon as the fish got in that submerged tangle of branches and wrapped the line around a branch, he only had to give one jerk to tear the hook loose. Now, Ames wouldn't have let that fish get over in the submerged branches unless something had distracted his attention. That something must have been something he heard, because his eyes were busy looking at the water."

Abruptly Bill Eldon turned to look at her. "What made you scream?"

She pressed white knuckles against her lips. "I'm going to tell you," she said.

"I've known that, ever since I—ever since I left Frank Ames. I was just walking to—well, the mountains seem to do so much for him—I wish I could feel about them the way he does. Sometimes I think I'm beginning to.

"I was just out of college," she continued, "a naïve little heiress. This man was working for Harvey Dowling. He was both a secretary and general assistant. His name was Howard Maben. He was fascinating, dashing. Women simply went wild over him. And I fell in love with him."

"What happened?"

"We were secretly married."

"Why the secrecy?"

"It was his idea. We ran away across the state line to Yuma, Arizona. Howard said he had to keep it secret."

"Did you know Harvey Dowling then?"

"Yes. Harvey, and Martha, his wife. It was her death that caused the scandal."

"What scandal?"

She said, "I don't know if I can explain Howard to you so you'll understand him. He's a dashing, high-pressure type of man who was a great favorite with women. He loved to sell things, himself included. I mean by that he liked to make a sale of his personality. I don't think there's any question but what he'd get tired of home life within the first thirty days.

"Well, anyway, I guess—it's something I don't like to talk about, but—well, I guess Howard had been—Well, Martha Dowling was attractive. She was an older woman. Harvey was always busy at the office, terribly intent on the deals he was putting across, and—Well, they fooled H. W. and they fooled me.

"Apparently Howard started going with Martha Dowling. They were very discreet about it, pretty cunning, as a matter of fact. They'd never go except when Harvey Dowling was out of town, and—well, I guess they stayed at motor courts. It was a mess."

"Go ahead," Bill Eldon said.

"Harvey Dowling was on a two weeks' trip. He was in Chicago, and Howard made certain he was in Chicago, because he'd talked with him that morning on long-distance telephone. Then he and Martha went out. They looked over some property that Harvey Dowling wanted a report on, and then—well, they went to an auto camp. They didn't like to be seen in restaurants. Howard had brought a little camp kit of dishes and cooking utensils, one of those outfits that folds up to fit into a suitcase."

"Go ahead."

"Martha Dowling got sick, some form of an acute gastroenteric disturbance. Well, naturally, they didn't want to call a doctor until after she got home. She died in Howard's car on the road home. Of course, Howard tried to fix up a story, but the police began to investigate and put two and two together. Harvey was called from Chicago by his wife's death and talked with the servants and—well, you can see what happened."

"What did happen?"

"Howard knew the jig was up. It seems he'd been left in charge of Dowling's business. He was already short in his accounts. So he embezzled everything he could get his hands on and skipped out.

"Dowling left no stone unturned to get him. He spent thousands of dollars. The police finally caught Howard and sent him to prison. No one knows that I was married to him. I was able to get the marriage annulled. I was able to prove fraud, and—well, of course, I'd been married in Arizona, so I went there and I had a friendly judge and a good lawyer and—there you are. There's the skeleton in my closet."

"I still don't know what made you scream," the sheriff said.

"I saw Howard. You see, his sentence has expired. He's out."

"Now, then," Bill Eldon remarked, "we're getting somewhere. Where was he when you saw him?"

"In the deep shadows of a clump of pines, well off the trail. I saw just his head and shoulders. He turned. Then he whistled."

"Whistled?"

"That's right. Howard had a peculiar shrill whistle we used to have as a signal when he wanted me to know he was near the house where I stayed. I'd let him in by the side door. It was a peculiar whistle that set my teeth on edge. It affected me just like the sound of someone scraping his nails along rough cloth. I *hated* it. I asked him to use some other signal, but he only laughed and said someone else might imitate any other call, but that whistle was distinctively his. It was harsh, strident, metallic. When he whistled yesterday, I felt positively sick at my stomach—and then I turned and ran just as fast as I could go."

"You aren't mistaken?"

"In that whistle? Never!"

"See his face?"

"Not clearly. The man was standing in the deep shadows. It was Howard. He had a rifle."

"Who else knows Howard Maben—that is, in your party?"

"Mr. Dowling is the only one; but that girl, Sylvia–I *think* she went back to dig up some of the old newspaper files. She's made remarks about Mrs. Dowling's death–well, questions. You understand, it's a subject that's taboo in Dowling's crowd."

"How was your ex-husband dressed when you saw him?"

"I only had a quick glimpse. I couldn't say."

"Wearing a hat?"

"Yes, a big Western hat."

"Now, then, try and get this one right," the sheriff said. "Had he been shaved lately?"

"Heavens, I couldn't tell that. He was in the shadows, but he could see me plainly and that's why he whistled for me to come to him."

"I'm wondering whether he'd been sort of hanging around for a while, watching your camp, or whether he just came in yesterday. I'd certainly like to know if he was shaved."

"I really couldn't see."

"And you didn't tell anyone about this?"

"No."

"Now, how much did Dowling know about you and Maben?"

"He knew that we were going together. I guess that's one of the reasons Harvey Dowling didn't suspect his wife. It was a nasty mess–well, you know how Dowling would feel. We've never talked much about it."

"I know," Bill Eldon said, his eyes looking off into space, "but there's still something I don't get about it."

She said, "All right, I suppose I've been a sneak. I suppose I'm living a lie; but I didn't want anyone to know about my marriage."

"On account of Dick Nottingham?"

Her eyes snapped around in startled appraisal. "How did you–?"

"Sort of guessed from what I saw the other day. Having a little trouble?"

"You mean Sylvia?"

"Yes."

"Well, you guessed that too."

"How do you feel about Sylvia?"

"I'd like to cut her heart out. Not that I care about Dick any more. He's shown what a conceited boor *he* is. I'd like to have him at my feet just long enough to walk on him, though."

"Just to show Sylvia?"

"And to show Dick. Sylvia doesn't care about Dick. She's a love pirate, one of the girls who have to satisfy their ego by stealing some man. And I'm—well, I'm living a lie. I wish now I'd played my cards differently, but I can't do it now. I've made my choice. To tell anyone now would make me out a miserable little liar. I don't want to be 'exposed,' particularly with Sylvia to rub it in, and I think Sylvia suspects."

"Never told Nottingham anything about this?"

"Nothing. Should I have done so?" she asked.

"I don't think so," Eldon answered.

The defiance melted from her face. "I was afraid you were going to be self-righteous," she said.

Bill Eldon said nothing.

"The marriage was annulled," she said. "I'm living for the future. Suppose Dick Nottingham and I had married? Suppose I had told him? He'd have been magnanimous about it and all of that, but the thing would have been buried in his mind. Sometime, four or five years later, when I burned the biscuits or was slow in getting dressed to go to a bridge party, he'd flare up with some nasty remark about the grass widow of a jailbird. He'd be sorry the next day, but it would leave a scar."

She paused. "I suppose I'll have to repeat this to that deputy district attorney?"

"I don't think so," Eldon said. "He'd do a little talking and the first thing you know, you'd be reading all about yourself in the newspapers. What is now just a plain murder would suddenly get a sex angle, and the big city papers would send reporters up to get pictures of you and write up a bunch of tripe. You'd have your past 'exposed.' You'd better go right ahead just the way you're doing."

"You mean you're going to keep my secret?"

"I'm going to let you keep it."

She remained silent.

The sheriff pulled an envelope from his pocket, took out the pictures he had removed from inside the lining of the coat of the murdered man.

"These pictures are of Howard—the man you married?"

She barely glanced at them, nodded.

"You recognized them when I first found them?"

"Yes, and that's my hand on his shoulder. That ring is a signet ring my father gave me."

"Any idea what this detective was doing with those pictures?"

"Howard's sentence expired about two months ago. He's after Dowling—or me. And the detective somehow got on Howard's trail.

And Howard, with all that fiendish cunning of his—well, he got the detective."

The sheriff got to his feet, moving with a smooth ease. "Well, I've got work to do."

Roberta Coe moved impulsively forward, said, "I don't suppose you'd have any way of knowing that you're a dear!" and kissed him.

"Oh," she said in dismay, "I've ruined your face! Here, let me get that off."

She took a handkerchief from her pocket. The sheriff grinned as she removed the lipstick. "Good idea," he said. "That young deputy district attorney would think I'd been bribed. Hell, you can't tell, maybe I have!"

Bill Eldon reined his horse to a stop, swung his left leg over the horse's neck and sat with it crooked around the saddle horn.

"How are things coming?" he asked.

"As far as I'm concerned," Leonard Keating said, "it's an open-and-shut case. I'm ready to go back any time you're ready to pick up the prisoner."

Eldon said, "I want to look around the country a little bit before I start back. Got to check up on some of the homesteaders up here."

"What are we going to do with Ames?" Keating demanded. "Let him run away?"

"He won't get away."

Keating said indignantly, "Well, I'll tell you one thing, he isn't *my* responsibility."

"That's right," Eldon said. "He's mine."

John Olney, the ranger, looked at the sheriff questioningly.

"Now then," Bill Eldon went on, "we, all of us, have our responsibilities. Now, Keating, here, has got to prosecute the man."

"There's plenty of evidence to get a conviction of first-degree murder," Keating said.

"And," Bill Eldon went on, "part of the evidence you're going to present to the jury is the evidence of those two cigarette stubs. That's right, eh?"

"Those cigarette stubs are the most damning piece of evidence in the whole case. They show premeditation."

"Nicely preserved, aren't they?"

"They're sufficiently preserved so I can identify them to a jury and get a jury to notice their distinctive peculiarities."

"All right," Eldon said cheerfully, and then added, "Of course, that murder was committed either during the rainstorm or just before the rainstorm. The evidence shows that."

"Of course it does," Keating said. "That cloth tobacco sack which was left on the ground had been soaked with rain. The tobacco had been moistened enough so that the stain from it oozed out into the cloth."

"Sure did," the sheriff said. "Now then, young man, when you get up in front of a jury with this ironclad, open-and-shut case of yours, maybe some smart lawyer on the other side is going to ask you how it happened that the tobacco got all wet, while those cigarette ends made out of delicate rice paper are just as dry and perfectly formed as the minute the smoker took them out of his mouth."

The sheriff watched the expression on the deputy district attorney's face. Then his lips twisted in a grin. "Well, now, son," he said, "I've got a little riding to do. How about it, John? Think you got a little free time on your hands?"

"Sure," the ranger said.

"What?" the deputy district attorney exclaimed. "Do you mean—?"

"Sure," the sheriff said. "Don't worry, buddy. Ames is *my* prisoner. I'm responsible for him. You just think out the answer to that question about the cigarette ends, because somebody's going to ask it of you when you get in court."

"There's no reason why the murderer couldn't have returned to the scene of the crime."

"Sure, sure," Eldon said soothingly. "Then he rolled cigarettes out of soggy, wet tobacco, and smoked 'em right down to the end. But somehow, I reckon, you've got to do better than that, young fellow."

Bill Eldon nodded to the ranger. "Come on, John, you can do more good riding with me than—"

"But this is an outrage!" Keating stormed. "I protest against it. This man, Ames, was arrested for murder!"

"Who arrested him?" the sheriff asked.

"If you want to put it that way, *I* did," Keating said. "As a deputy district attorney and as a private citizen, I have a right to take this man in custody for first-degree murder."

"Go ahead and take him in custody then," the sheriff grinned. "Then he'll be your responsibility. Come on, John, let's go riding."

The sheriff swung his leg back over the horse's neck and straightened himself in the saddle.

"You'll have to answer for this," Leonard Keating said, his voice quivering with rage.

"That's right," Eldon assured him cheerfully, "I expect to," and rode off.

Bill Eldon and the ranger found a live lead at the second cabin at which they stopped.

Carl Raymond, a tall, drawling, tobacco-chewing trapper in his late fifties, came to the door of his cabin as soon as his barking dog had advised him of the approaching horsemen.

His eye was cold, appraising and uncordial.

"So, you folks are working together now," he said scornfully. "I haven't any venison hanging up, and I have less than half the limit of fish. As far as I'm concerned—"

Bill Eldon interrupted. "Now, Carl, I've never asked any man who lives in the mountains where he got his meat. You know that."

Raymond swung his eyes to the ranger. "You ain't riding alone," he said to the sheriff.

"This is other business," the sheriff said. "The ranger is with me. I'm not with him."

"What's on your mind?"

"A man's been murdered down here, five or six miles over on the Middle Fork."

Raymond twisted the wad of tobacco with his tongue, glanced once more at both men, then expectorated between tightly clenched lips. "What do you want?"

"A little assistance. Thought maybe you might have crossed some tracks of a man I might be looking for."

"The mountains are full of tracks these days," Raymond said bitterly. "You can't get a hundred yards from your cabin without running across dude tracks."

"These would be the tracks of someone that was living in the mountains, playing a lone hand," the sheriff said.

"Can't help you a bit," Raymond told him. "Sorry."

The sheriff said, "I'm interested in any unusually big fires, particularly any double fires."

Raymond started to shake his head, then paused. "How's that?"

The sheriff repeated his statement.

Raymond hesitated, seemed about to say something, then became silent.

At the end of several seconds Olney glanced questioningly at the sheriff, and Eldon motioned him to silence.

Raymond silently chewed his tobacco. At length he moved out

from the long shadows of the pines, pointed toward a saddle in the hills to the west. "There's a little game trail, works up that draw," he said, "and goes right through that saddle. Fifty yards on the other side it comes to a little flat against a rocky ledge. There was a double fire built there last night."

"Know who did it?"

"Nope. I just saw the ashes of the fire this morning."

"What time?" asked the sheriff.

"A little after daylight."

"Carl," the sheriff said, "I think that's the break we've been looking for. You've really been a help."

"Don't mention it," Raymond said, turned on his heel, whistled to his dog, and strode into his cabin.

"Come on," Bill Eldon said to Olney. "I think we've got something!"

"I don't get it," Olney said. "What's the idea of the double fire?"

Eldon swung his horse into a rapid walk. "It rained last night. The ground was wet. A man who was camping out without blankets would build a big, long fire. The ground underneath the fire would get hot and be completely dry. Then when the rain let up and it turned cold, the man only needed to rake the coals of that fire into two piles, chop some fir boughs, and put them on the hot ground. In that way he'd have dry, warm ground underneath him, sending heat up through the fir boughs, and the piles of embers on each side would keep his sides warm. Then about daylight, when he got up, he could throw the fir boughs on the embers and burn them up. He'd put out the fire, after he'd cooked breakfast, by pouring water from the stream on the coals."

"A man sleeping out without blankets," Olney said musingly. "There's *just* a chance," he added, "that you know something I don't."

Bill Eldon grinned. "There's just a chance," he admitted, "that I do."

Roberta Coe found Frank Ames in his cabin, pouring flour and water into the crusted crock in which he kept his sour dough. The door was ajar and from the outer twilight the illumination of the gasoline lantern seemed incandescent in its brilliance.

"Hello," she called, "may I come in? I heard you were released on your own recognizance."

"The sheriff," Ames said, "has some sense. Come on in. Are you alone?"

"Yes. Why?"

"But you can't be going around these trails at night. It'll be dark before you can possibly get back, even if you start right now."

"I brought a flashlight with me, and I'm not starting back right now. I just got here!"

"But, gosh, I–"

She crossed the floor of the cabin, to sit on one of the homemade stools, her elbows propped on the rustic table. "Know something?" she asked.

"What?"

"I told the sheriff about screaming and about how you came after me and all that. I realized I'd have to tell him sooner or later, but–well, thanks for protecting me–for covering up."

"You didn't need to tell them. They've got no case against me, anyway."

She felt that his tone lacked the assurance it should have.

"I told them anyway. What are you making?"

"Sour-dough biscuit."

"Smells–terrible."

"Tastes fine," he said, grinning. "A man must eat even if the State *is* trying to hang him."

"Oh, it's not that bad."

"It is, as far as that deputy district attorney is concerned."

"I hate him!" she said. "He's intolerant, officious and egotistical. But–well, I wanted you to know I'd told the sheriff and there's no reason why you should try to–to cover up for me any more."

"How much did you tell him?"

"Everything."

For a moment his look was quizzical.

"You don't seem to show much curiosity," she said.

"Out here we don't show curiosity about other people's business."

She said rather gaily, "I think I'm going to stay to supper–if I'm invited."

"You'd better get back to your folks," he said. "They'll be worried about you."

"Oh, no they won't. I explained to them that I'm going to be out late. I told them I was conferring with the sheriff."

"Look here," he said, "you *can't* do things like that."

"Why can't I?"

"Because, for one thing, I'm here alone–and for another thing, you can't wander around the mountains at night."

"Are you going to invite me to supper?"

"No."

"That's fine," she said. "I'll stay anyway. What else are *we* going to have besides sour-dough biscuit?"

Watching her slip off her jacket and roll up her sleeves, he surrendered with a grin. "*We're* going to have some jerked venison, stewed up with onions and canned tomatoes. You wouldn't have the faintest idea how to cook it, so go over there and sit down and watch."

Two hours later, when they had eaten and the dishes had been cleaned up and when they had talked themselves into a better understanding, Roberta Coe announced that she was starting back down the trail. She knew, of course, that Ames would go with her.

"Do you have a flashlight," she asked, "so that you can see the trail when you come back?"

"I don't need a flashlight."

He walked over to the wall, took down the .30-.30 rifle, pushed shells into the magazine.

"What's that for?" she asked.

"Oh," he said, "sometimes we see deer, and fresh meat is—"

She laughed and said, "It's illegal to shoot after sundown. The deer season is closed, and the hills are simply crawling with game wardens and deputy sheriffs. You must think I'm terribly dumb. However, I'm glad you have the rifle. Come on."

They left the cabin, to stand for a moment in the bracing night air, before starting down the trail.

"You're not locking the door?" she asked.

"No need to lock the barn door after the horse has been stolen."

"Somehow I wish you would. You might—have a visitor."

"I think I'd be glad to see him," he said, swinging the rifle slightly so that it glinted in the moonlight.

"Do you want me to lead the way with the flashlight or to come behind?"

"I'll go ahead," he said, "and please don't use the flashlight."

"But we'll need it."

"No we won't. There's a moon that will give us plenty of light for more than an hour. It's better to adjust your eyes to the darkness, rather than continually flashing a light on and off."

He started off down the trail, walking with his long, easy stride.

The moon, not yet quite half full, was in the west, close to Venus, which shone as a shining beacon. It was calm and still, and the night noises seemed magnified. The purling of the stream became the sound of a rushing cascade.

The day had been warm, but now in the silence of the night the air had taken on the chill that comes from the high places, a windless, penetrating chill which makes for appreciation of the soft warmth of down-filled sleeping bags. The moon-cast shadows of the silhouetted pine trees lay across the trail like tangible barriers, and the silent, brooding strangeness of the mountains dwarfed Roberta Coe's consciousness until her personality seemed to her disturbed mind to be as puny as her light footfalls on the everlasting granite.

There was a solemn strangeness about the occasion which she wished to perpetuate, something that she knew she would want to remember as long as she lived; so when they were a few hundred yards from camp, she said, "Frank, I'm tired. Can't we rest a little while? You don't realize what a space-devouring stride you have."

"Your camp's only around that spur," he said. "They'll be worrying about you and—"

"Oh, bother!" she said. "Let them worry. I want to rest."

There was the trunk of a fallen pine by the side of the trail, and she seated herself on it. He came back to stand uncomfortably at her side, then, propping the gun against the log, seated himself beside her.

The moon was sliding down toward the mountains now, and the stars were beginning to come out in unwinking splendor. She knew that she would be cold as soon as the warmth of the exercise left her blood, but knew also that Frank Ames was under a tension, experiencing a struggle with himself.

She moved slightly, her shoulder brushed against his, her hair touched his cheek, and the contact set off an emotional explosion. His arms were about her, his mouth strained to hers. She knew this was what she had been wanting for what had seemed ages.

She relaxed in the strength of his sinewy arms, her head tilting back so he could find her lips. Sudden pulses pounded in her temples. Then suddenly he had pushed her away, was saying contritely, "I'm sorry."

She waited for breath and returning self-assurance. Glancing at him from under her eyelashes, she decided on the casual approach. She laughed and said, "Why be sorry? It's a perfect night, and, after all, we're human." She hoped he wouldn't notice the catch in her voice, a very unsophisticated catch which belied the casual manner she was trying to assume.

"You're out of my set," he said. "You're—you're as far above me as that star."

"I wasn't very far above you just then. I seemed to be—quite close."

"You know what I mean. I'm a hillbilly, a piece of human flotsam cast up on the beach by the tides of war. Damn it, I don't mean to be poetic about it and I'm not going to be apologetic. I'm—"

"You're sweet," she interrupted.

"You have everything; all the surroundings of wealth. You're camped up here in the mountains with wranglers to wait on you. I'm a mountain man."

"Well, good Lord," she laughed, a catch in her throat, "you don't need to plan marriage just because you kissed me."

And in the constricted silence which followed, she knew that was exactly what he had been planning.

Suddenly, she turned and put her hand over his. "Frank," she said, "I want to tell you something—something I want you to keep in confidence. Will you?"

"Yes." His voice sounded strained.

She laughed. "I just finished promising the sheriff I'd never tell this to anyone." And then, without further preliminaries, she told him about her marriage, about the scandal, the annulment of her marriage.

When she had finished, there was a long silence. Abruptly she felt a nervous reaction. The cold, still air of the mountains seemed unfriendly. She felt terribly alien, a hopelessly vulnerable morsel of humanity in a cold, granite world which gave no quarter to vulnerability.

"I'm glad you told me," Frank Ames said simply, then jackknifed himself up from the log. "You'll catch cold sitting here. Let's move on."

Angry and hurt, she fought back the tears until the lighted tents of her camp were visible.

"I'm all right now," she said hastily. "Good-by—thanks for the dinner."

She saw that he wanted to say something, but she was angry both at him and at herself, thoroughly resentful that she had confided in this man. She wanted to rush headlong into the haven of her lighted camp, escaping the glow of the campfire, but she knew he was watching, so she tried to walk with dignity, leaving him standing there, vaguely aware that there was something symbolic in the fact that she had left him just outside the circle of firelight.

She would have liked to reach her tent undiscovered, but she knew that the others were wondering about her. She heard Dick Nottingham's voice saying, "Someone's coming," then Sylvia Jessup calling, "Is that you, Roberta?"

"In person," she said, trying to make her voice sound gay.

"Well, you certainly took long enough. What happened?"

"I'll tell you about it tomorrow," she said. "I'm headed for my sleeping bag. I'm chilled."

Eleanor Dowling said, "I'll bring you a hot toddy when you get in bed, honey."

She knew they wanted to pump her, knew they wanted to ask questions about the sheriff, about her supposed conference. And she knew that she couldn't face them—not then.

"Please don't," she said. "I'm all in. I have a beastly headache and I took two aspirin tablets coming down the trail. Let me sleep."

She entered the tent, conscious as she did so of Frank Ames' words about how she was waited on hand and foot. They had kept a fire going in the little sheet-metal stove. The tent was warm as toast. A lantern was furnishing mellow light. The down interior of her sleeping bag was inviting. Not only did she have an air mattress, but there was a cot as well.

"Oh, what a fool I was!" she said. "Why did I have to go baring my soul. The big ignoramus! He's out of my world. He—he thinks I'm second-hand merchandise!"

Roberta Coe's throat choked up with emotion. She sat on the edge of the cot there in her little tent, her head on her hands. Hot tears trickled between her fingers.

She realized with a pang how much that moment had meant to her, how much it had meant when Frank Ames' arms were around her, straining, eager and strong.

Sylvia Jessup's voice sounded startlingly close. "What's the matter, darling?" she asked. "Has something happened—"

Roberta looked up quickly, realizing now that the damage had been done, that the lantern was in such a position that her shadow was being thrown on the end of the tent. Sylvia, sitting by the campfire, had been able to see silhouetted dejection, to see the shadow of Roberta seated on the cot, elbows on her knees, face in her hands.

"No thanks, it's all right," Roberta said, jumping up and bustling about. "I just got a little over-tired coming down the trail. I think it's the elevation."

"You don't want me—"

"No, thank you," Roberta said with a tone of finality which meant that the conversation was terminated.

Roberta crossed over to the lantern, turned it out, and the tent was in warm darkness, save for little ruddy spots which glowed on the canvas where small holes in the wood stove gave shafts of red light from the glowing embers.

Sylvia hesitated a moment, then Roberta could hear her steps going back toward the campfire. Sylvia undoubtedly was bursting with curiosity. She realized that Roberta would hardly have walked back alone over the mountain trail at night, and Sylvia was a prying little sneak as far as Roberta was concerned.

But somehow that momentary interlude, that flare of feeling against Sylvia Jessup, made Roberta Coe reappraise herself and the situation.

She knew instinctively that Frank Ames would not be back. Perhaps his coolness had not been because he had learned of her prior marriage. Perhaps—it could have been that it had made no difference to him. His constrained attitude, his abrupt departure might have been merely the result of what he had said previously—that they were worlds apart.

The doubt, the reaction, left her with the most devastating loneliness she had ever experienced.

Almost without thinking, she put her coat back on, quickly glanced around the tent to see that she was leaving no telltale shadow, then she slipped to the flap and out into the night, detouring so that she kept the tent between her and the campfire until she had reached the circle of scrub pine which surrounded the camp.

Once or twice she stumbled in the shadows. There was no moonlight here in this little valley, and the light from the campfire served only to make the terrain more deceiving, but Roberta kept moving rapidly, heedless of the natural obstacles, stumbling over roots and little hummocks until she was able to skirt the sheltering rim of pines and come to the main trail.

The cold, crisp air of the mountain night seemed like a stimulus which enabled her to rush along the trail. In the starlight, the trail showed as a faint gray thread, and Roberta, feeling as weightless as some gliding creature of the woods, buoyed up by surging hope, moved rapidly along this faint thread.

But after a few minutes the strange exhilaration left her. All at once her body mechanism asserted itself, and her laboring lungs told her all too plainly that she needed air. The unaccustomed effort of running, the steady upgrade, the elevation, all contributed to a breathlessness which made the strength drain out of her legs.

She knew she couldn't make it. Frank Ames had had too much of a headstart on her, and his own hurt pride would make for an emotional unrest which would demand some physical outlet. He would be swinging along up the trail, with his long legs devouring the space.

"Frank!" she called, and there was desperate pleading in her voice.

She had not brought her flashlight. The moon had now settled almost to the mountains. Only occasionally, where there was a break in the pines, was there a field of weak illumination over the trail.

She could hear steps ahead of her. She wanted to call out again, but her laboring lungs had barely enough air for breath. Her pounding heart threatened to push itself out of her chest.

"Frank!" she called with the very last bit of breath that she could muster. And then her laboring heart gave a wild surge as she saw motion in the shadow ahead.

But the figure that stepped out to meet her was not that of Frank Ames. A shrill, metallic whistle, harsh as the strum of an overtaxed taut wire, knifed her eardrums. Cold horror gripped her.

"No–No!" she half sobbed.

She turned, but there was no more strength left for flight. Her feet were like heavy rocks, the legs limber.

The figure moved swiftly.

Sheriff Bill Eldon, down on hands and knees, poked slowly around the two parallel piles of ashes. Undoubtedly these two campfires marked the spot where some man had been camping the night before, a man who was a seasoned veteran of the woods, who had spent a cold night without blankets, yet without inconvenience.

John Olney, standing a little to one side, watching with keen interest, was careful not to disturb the ground so that any remaining tracks would be obscured. The long western slant of the sunlight built up shadows, gave a transverse lighting which made tracks far more easy to see than would have been the case during the middle of the day.

The sheriff's forefinger pointed to slight disturbances in the ground that would have escaped the attention of any except the most skilled tracker. "Now here," he said, "is where Carl Raymond came along. Raymond was hunting deer. You can see that he skirted the edge of the plateau, keeping in the shadows, hoping he'd catch something still feeding in this little meadow.

"Anything out there would have been most apt to be a doe with a fawn, a spike buck, or perhaps a good fat barren doe. So you can figure Raymond was hunting for meat.

"Now, he got to this place right here and then could see where the campfire had been, so he moved over to investigate. Now that accounts for Raymond's tracks."

Olney nodded. The ground to that point was to him as plain as a blueprint to an architect.

"Now then, these two fires," the sheriff went on, "tell quite a story. The man used wood from that dead pine over there. Then he cut fir boughs, raked the coals to one side, slept on the warm ground with a fire on each side of him, and early in the morning threw the fir boughs on the flames. You can see where the stuff caught into instant flame and burnt up until it left only the naked branches. Those were still green and didn't burn easily. The man didn't try to burn them at all. He simply brought water over here from that little spring and doused the fire and covered it up, so as to eliminate that much of the fire hazard. He certainly didn't want the faintest wisp of smoke to show when it came daylight."

Again Olney nodded.

"So the fir boughs must have been burned up pretty early, probably just as it started to turn daylight. Now, notice the way these boughs are cut. They're not cut through with a single clean stroke. Every one of them has taken two or three cuts, but the cuts are clean.

"Our man wasn't carrying a hatchet, but he was carrying a big knife and it was razor-sharp."

Again Olney nodded.

"You can see his tracks around here," the sheriff went on. "He's wearing a good sensible boot, a wide last, with a composition cord sole and heel. That man could move through the forest without making any noise at all. He could be as quiet as a panther. Now then, he had to have something to carry the water from the spring to put out this fire. What do you suppose it was?"

"His hat?" Olney asked.

"Could have been," the sheriff said, "but somehow I doubt it. Notice the number of trips he made here to the spring. He's worn a regular trail up there, and the place where the little trickle of water has carried the charcoal down from the fire shows that he was using something that didn't hold much water. Let's sort of look around over here in the brush. Wait a minute!"

The sheriff stood up by the edge of the blackened space, made throwing motions in several different directions, said, "Over here is the best place to look. There's no high ground here. He could have thrown a can farther this way than in any other direction."

The sheriff and the ranger moved over to a place where the brush was lower and the ground sloped away from the fire.

"Getting dark," the sheriff said. "We're going to have to move along fast if we're going to find what we—Here it is."

With the deft swiftness of a cat pouncing on a gopher, the sheriff dove into a little clump of mountain manzanita and came out triumphantly bearing a soot-covered can. The top of the can showed an irregular, jagged crosscut, indicating that it had been opened by a few thrusts with a wide-bladed knife.

"Well," the sheriff said, "we're beginning to find out something about him. He has a knife with a blade a little over an inch wide. It's razor-sharp, but he's using it for opening cans as well as cutting brush. Therefore, he must have some pocket whetstone that he's using to keep the edge in shape.

"Now this can has been on the fire. The label is all burned off, but from what you can see on the inside, it must have been a can of baked pork and beans. It doesn't look as though he had a spoon to eat it with but whittled himself out a flat piece of wood that he used for a spoon. I s'pose we'd better hold that can for fingerprints, but it tells me a story without using any magnifying glass. He didn't carry that can of beans in here with him, John. He must have stolen it someplace."

The ranger nodded.

"He's traveling light and fast, and he knows the mountains," the sheriff went on. "He can move as silent as a cat, and he's broken into a cabin and stolen a few provisions and a rifle."

"A rifle?" Olney asked.

"Sure," the sheriff told him. "Come on over here and I'll show you."

In the fading light, the sheriff took the ranger back to the place where a pine tree was growing straight and slim within some twenty feet of the place where the fire had been made.

"He put the rifle down here," Bill Eldon said, "while he was cutting the branches for his bed. You can see where the butt of the rifle rested in the ground. Now, John, just as sure as shooting that was *after* it had quit raining. You can still see the little cross-checks from the shoulder plate on the stock. The ground was soft and—well, that's the way it is."

"You don't suppose he could have made camp *before* it started to rain and then put the rifle here while he was getting breakfast, do you?"

"I don't think so," Eldon said. "This is the place where he would naturally have propped the rifle while he was getting those fir boughs. It's just about the right distance from the fire and a nice place to stand the rifle. When he was getting breakfast he'd let the fire get down to coals—of course, he could have had the canned beans for supper instead of breakfast. Anyhow, it was after it'd quit raining. I've had a hunch he made this camp after the rain had quit.

"Now, the rain didn't quit until after dark. A man wouldn't have blundered onto this little spring here in the dark, particularly on a rainy night. No, John, this is some fellow that not only knows the mountains, but he knows this particular section of the country. He's able to move around pretty well at night and when he left here early this morning he was smart enough to try and cover his tracks as much as possible. You see, he took off up that rocky ridge. My best guess is he kept to the rocks and the timber all day and kept holed up where he could watch, while he was waiting for dark."

The sheriff pursed his lips thoughtfully, looked at the streak of fading daylight over the Western mountains, said, "He's probably trying to get out of the mountains. But there just ain't any telling just what he has in mind. If he's the one that killed the detective, he planted that evidence by Ames' cabin. He might be intending to do another job or two before he gets out of the mountains—and he may be sort of hard to stop. Let's see if we can look around a bit before it gets slap dark."

The men reined their horses down the trail. Suddenly, Bill Eldon pulled up and urged his horse into the fringe of light brush. "Take a look at that, John."

The ranger peered down at a light-brown pile on the ground. "That's the beans," he said in astonishment.

Eldon nodded.

"Why did he open a can of beans, cook 'em over a campfire and then dump 'em all out?" the ranger asked.

Bill Eldon considered that question for a space of seconds, then said, "There has to be only one answer, John. He didn't want to eat 'em."

"But why?"

Bill Eldon touched the reins. "Now," the sheriff said, "we know where we're going. But we're going to have to sort of wait around after we get there, until this man we want makes the first move. Come on, John."

Trying her best to make time, Roberta fled down the trail. Her lungs were laboring, her heart pounding, and the trail pulled at her feet, making each step an individual effort.

She realized this man behind her was not trying to catch her. He was running slowly, methodically, as though following some preconceived plan.

Roberta tried once more to scream, but her call for help sounded faint and puny, even to her own ears.

Her heavy feet failed to clear an outcropping of rock. She stumbled, tried in vain to catch herself, threw out her arms and at exactly that moment heard behind her the vicious crack of a rifle.

The wind made by the bullet fanned her hair as she went down in a huddled heap on the trail. Lying prone, she simply lacked the strength to struggle back to her feet. She knew that the man behind her could reach her long before she could get up, and this dispiriting knowledge drained the last of her strength.

She heard Frank Ames' voice saying, "Drop that gun," then the sound of another rifle crack arousing echoes through the mountain canyon.

Roberta got to her hands and knees, and seemed unable to get the strength to rise to her feet.

She heard Frank Ames saying, "Darling, are you all right? You're not hurt? He didn't get you?"

She heard voices from the direction of the camp, saw flashlights sending beams which crisscrossed in confusion, making lighted patches on the boulders and the pine trees.

She turned from her knees to a sitting position, laughed nervously, and felt a touch of hysteria in the laugh. She tried to talk, but was only able to say gaspingly,

"I'm—all right."

She saw Frank Ames standing rigid, watchful, dimly silhouetted against a patch of starlit forest, then off to the left she saw an orange-red spit of flame, and another shot aroused reverberating echoes from the peaks. The bullet struck a tree within inches of Frank Ames' head, and even in the dim gray of starlight, Roberta

could see the swift streak on the trunk of the pine tree where the
bullet ripped aside the bark.

Ames merely stood more closely behind the tree, his rifle at ready.

"Keep down, Roberta," he warned, without even turning to look
at her.

Roberta remained seated, her head slightly back so that she could
get more oxygen into her starved lungs.

Lights were coming up the trail now, a procession of winding,
jiggling fireflies, blazing momentarily into brilliance as the beam
of some flashlight would strike her fairly in the eyes.

Frank Ames called, "Put out the lights, folks. He'll shoot at them."

The rifle barked again, twice, one bullet directed at the place
where Frank Ames was standing, the other at Roberta Coe, crouched
on the trail. Both bullets were wide of the mark, yet close enough
so the cracking pathway of the high-power bullet held vicious men-
ace.

Roberta heard the sound of galloping horses, realized suddenly
the precariousness of her position on the trail, and scrambled
slightly to one side. She saw Frank Ames move, a silent, shadowy
figure gliding through the trees, noticed, also, that the procession
of flashlights had ceased.

The sheriff's horse, which was in the lead, shied violently, as it
saw Roberta Coe crouched by the trail. Roberta saw the swift glint
of starlight from metal, heard the sheriff's voice, hard as a whiplash,
saying, "Get 'em up!"

"No, no!" Roberta gasped. "He's back there, over to the left. He—"

The man betrayed his location by another shot, the bullet going
high through the trees, the roar of the gun for a moment drowning
out all other sounds. Then, while the gun echoes were still reverberating from the crags, the dropping of small branches and pine
needles dislodged by the bullet sounded startlingly clear.

"What the heck's he shooting at?" the sheriff asked.

Frank Ames said cautiously, "I'm over here, sheriff, behind this
tree."

"Swing around, Olney," the sheriff said. "Cut off his escape. He's
up against a sheer cliff in back. We can trap him in here."

By this time the others were trooping up from camp, and the
sheriff stationed them along the trail. "I'm closing a circle around
this place," the sheriff said. "Just yell if you see him, that's all."

Bill Eldon became coldly efficient. "Where are you, Ames?"

"Over here."

Eldon raised his voice. "Any of you from the camp got a gun on you?"

"I have," one of the wranglers said.

"All right," the sheriff announced. "That's four of us. If we go in after that man, he can't escape. He could make his way up that high cliff if he had time, but he'll make a lot of noise doing it and expose himself to our fire. He's only safe as long as he stays in this clump of trees. We have men stationed along the trail who can let us know if he breaks cover in that direction. The four of us can flush him out. Anyone have any objections? You don't *have* to go, you know."

"Not me," the wrangler said. "I'll ride along with you."

The silence of the others indicated that the sheriff's question could have had significance for only the wrangler.

"Let's go," Bill Eldon said. "Keep in touch with each other. Walk abreast. We'll force him to surrender, to stand and fight it out, or to try climbing that steep cliff. When you see him, if he hasn't got his hands up, shoot to kill."

The sheriff raised his voice, said, "We're coming in. Drop your gun, get your hands up and surrender!"

There was no sound from the oval-shaped thicket at the base of the big cliff which walled it in as something of an amphitheater.

Bill Eldon said to the ranger, "We're dealing with a man who's a tricky woodsman. Be on your toes; let's go!"

A tense silence fell upon the mountain amphitheater where the grim drama was being played. Overhead the stars shone silent and steady, but within the thicket of pines was an inky darkness.

The men advanced for a few feet. Then Bill Eldon said, "We're going to need a flashlight, folks."

"Don't try it. It'll be suicide," Ames said. "He'll shoot at the flashlight and—"

"Just hold everything," the sheriff said. "Hold this line right here."

Eldon walked back to his saddlebags, took out a powerful flashlight which fastened on his forehead. A square battery hung over his back, held in place by a harness, leaving his hands free to work his rifle.

The sheriff said reassuringly, "If he starts shooting, I can switch this off."

"Not after you're dead, you can't," Frank Ames said.

"It's a chance I have to take," Eldon said. "That's a part of my job. You folks keep back to one side."

Eldon switched on the flashlight. The beam cut through the darkness, into the pine trees, a pencil of light, terminating in a splash of brilliance.

The sheriff kept slightly forward, away from the others, his rifle ready. He kept turning his head slowly, searching the long lanes of pine trees until at length he suddenly snapped the gun forward and held it steady.

The beam of the flashlight showed a gun, neatly propped against a tree.

"Now, what the heck do you make of that?" Olney asked.

"Reckon he's going to give himself up," the wrangler from the dude camp said, and called out, "Get your hands up or we'll shoot!"

There was no answer.

They advanced to where the gun was leaning against the tree.

"Don't touch it!" the sheriff said. "We'll look it over for finger-prints. He must have been standing right behind that rock. You can see the empty shells around on the ground."

"Have you got him?" a voice called from the trail.

"Not yet," Eldon said.

"What the devil's all this about?" stormed H. W. Dowling, crashing in behind the searching party. "I demand to know the reason for all these—"

"Get back out of the way!" Eldon said. "There's a desperate man in here. You'll be shot."

"A sweet howdy-do," Dowling said. "What the devil's the matter with the law-enforcement officers in this county? Can't I organize a camping trip into the mountains without having someone turn it into a Wild West show? My sleep's gone for the night now. I—The whole camp pulled out on me. I had to run—"

Sheriff Eldon said grimly, "We can't pick the places where mur-derers are going to strike. All we can do is try and capture the criminals so men like you will be safe. Okay, boys, let's go. I think he's out of shells. Do you remember, that last shot went high through the trees?"

"I'd been wondering about that," Ames said. "What was he shoot-ing at?"

"We'll find out," the sheriff said, "when we get him."

They moved forward. Then, as the thicket of trees narrowed against the perpendicular cliff, they closed in compact formation until finally they had covered the entire ground.

"Well, I'll be darned!" Olney said. "He's managed to get up those cliffs."

"Or out to the trail," Eldon said.

He moved out from the protection of the trees, moved his head slowly so that his beam covered the precipitous mountainside. "Don't see anything of him up there. Don't hear anything," he said. "I told you he was a clever woodsman. Let's get over and see if anyone saw him cut across the trail."

They moved back to the trail where the shivering dudes, the cook and the outfitter were spaced at regular intervals. "Anybody come through here?" the sheriff asked.

"No one," they said. "We could see well enough—"

"He might have been pretty clever," the sheriff said, "might have worked into the shadows."

He moved slowly along, looking for tracks on the trail.

"What this country needs is more efficiency!" Dowling growled sullenly.

"Well, I missed him," Eldon said resignedly. "Let's go on back to camp. If he got through our lines, and abandoned an empty gun, it's possible he's planning to go down and raid your camp for another gun."

Eldon untied his horse, swung into the saddle, said, "I'll go on ahead on a gallop so as to beat him to it."

Olney mounted his own horse, followed the sheriff.

"You folks come on," Bill Eldon called over his shoulder.

The huddled group watched the shadowy figures gallop on down the trail.

Dowling said, "I want you boys to organize a guard for our camp tonight. I don't like the idea of a murderer being loose. Come on, let's get out of here."

Roberta and Frank managed by some unspoken understanding to wait behind until the others had gone.

"You're not hurt?" Frank asked.

"No."

"What happened? How did you run onto him?"

"He was—I don't know, he was just loitering there in the shadows. I got a vague, indistinct glimpse of head and shoulders and—"

"I know," Ames said. "I heard that peculiar whistle you were telling about, so I turned and came back. He shot and I saw you fall—"

"I fell just before he shot," Roberta said. "I stumbled. The bullet grazed my hair."

"What I don't understand is how you happened to be out on the trail. You'd gone into your tent and blown out the candle," Ames said.

"You were watching?" she asked, almost before she thought.

He waited for some five seconds before he answered. "Yes," he said.

She said, "Frank, let's not let foolish pride come between us. I thought–I thought you were going away–out of my life–because of my prior marriage–I started up the trail after you. I had to find out–I–"

"I was leaving because I knew you were too far above me. For a minute I thought–well, you acted as though–Oh, shucks, I love you! I love you!"

Bill Eldon sat by the big campfire, drinking coffee.

"If you ask me," Nottingham protested, "this is about the fourth fool thing that's been done tonight."

"What?" Bill Eldon asked.

"Having us all gather around a campfire while we know there's a desperate killer out in the hills. He can see our figures silhouetted against the blaze and–"

"I know," the sheriff said, "but it takes a good man to shoot at night."

"Well, I think this murderer is what you'd call a 'good man.' Good enough to do just about as he pleases."

The sheriff ignored the insult. "Funny thing about that murderer, now," he said. "I've been sort of checking up with people about where everyone was when Frank Ames first came into this camp. It seems like there were two people missing, Alexander Cameron and Sam Fremont. Now, were you two boys together?"

"No, we weren't," Cameron said. "I went on downstream, fishing."

"*Down*stream?"

"That's right."

"And you?" the sheriff asked Fremont.

"I went downstream a ways with Cameron and then I left him and started hunting for pictures of wildlife," Fremont said. "I suppose you have the right to ask."

"You got those pictures?" the sheriff asked.

"Certainly. They aren't developed. I have two rolls of film."

"Of course," Nottingham pointed out, "those pictures wouldn't prove a thing, because he could have gone downstream *any* time and taken a couple of rolls of film."

"Don't be so officious," Fremont said, grinning. "When I came back the girls were all strutting sex appeal for the benefit of a newcomer. I stole a couple of pictures showing 'em all grouped around Ames. Those will be the last two pictures on the last roll."

"How about the guides?" Sylvia asked. "They weren't here. At least one of them was out—"

"Rounding up the horses," the wrangler cut in. "And unless horses can talk, I haven't any witnesses."

"I was in my tent taking a siesta," Dowling said. "The unusual chatter finally wakened me."

"Well, I was just checking up," the sheriff said. "Were you in bed tonight when the shooting started, Dowling?"

"Yes. I dressed and came barging up the trail as fast as I could. The others hadn't turned in; they got up there well ahead of me."

"You hurried right along?"

"Naturally. I was as afraid to stay in camp alone as I was to go up there where the shooting was taking place."

The sheriff regarded his toes with a puzzled frown.

"You folks do whatever you want," Dowling said indignantly, "but I'm going to get away from this fire."

"I don't think there's the slightest danger," the sheriff said.

"Well, I'm quite able to think for myself, thank you. I'm not accustomed to letting others do my thinking for me. You evidently didn't think fast enough to keep him from shooting at Roberta."

"That's right," Bill Eldon admitted. "I didn't. Of course, I didn't have quite as much to go on as I have now."

"Well, as far as I'm concerned," Dowling said, "*I'm* going to get away from this campfire."

"You seem to be pretty much of a woodsman," the sheriff said.

"I did a little trapping in my younger days," Dowling admitted.

"You know," the sheriff drawled, "I think I know how that murderer got through our cordon. I think he climbed a tree until we went past.

"And," the sheriff went on, "after we'd passed that tree a few steps, he dropped back down to the ground."

"And ran away?" Nottingham asked.

"No, just mingled with us," Eldon said. "You see, he was well known, so he only had to get through the line. I had that all figured out as soon as we came on the empty gun propped against the tree. That's why I brought you all down here and built up a bright campfire. I wanted to see which one of you *had pitch on his hands!*"

In the second or two of amazed silence which followed, one or two of the men looked at their hands.

The others looked at the sheriff.

"The man who did the killing," the sheriff went on, "went to a lot of trouble to make it appear that there was someone else running around the hills. He had practiced the whistle that was used by a certain man whose name we won't mention at the moment. He went to a lot of trouble to make a bed of fir boughs that hadn't been slept in, to open a can of beans that wasn't eaten. He tried to kill Roberta Coe, but Ames showed up and spoiled his aim. Then he jumped into the thicket of pine trees, did a lot of shooting, dropped the gun, climbed a tree, waited for us to enter the brush, then came threshing around, indignantly demanding an explanation."

"Indeed!" Dowling sneered. "I wonder if you're asinine enough to be trying to implicate me."

"Well," the sheriff said, "there are some things that look a little queer. You were in your tent when the shooting started?"

"Fast asleep. I jumped up, dressed, grabbed my six-shooter and ran up the trail to join the others. Here's my gun. Want to look at it?"

"Not right now," Eldon said, casually taking his cloth tobacco sack from his pocket and starting to roll a cigarette. "But if you'd run all the way up the trail, you'd have been out of breath. Instead of which, you took time to curse my bucolic stupidity and you weren't out of breath in the least. In fact, you strung quite a few words together."

The sheriff used both hands to roll the cigarette. "And you have pitch on your hands and on your clothes, and somewhere in your tent I think we'll find a pair of cord-soled shoes that will fit the tracks of—"

"Take a look at this gun now," Dowling said, moving swiftly. "And take a look at the *front* end."

The sheriff was motionless for a moment, then went on rolling his cigarette.

"I don't want anyone to move," Dowling said. "Keep right here in plain sight by this campfire and—"

Suddenly from the other side of the campfire came the swift flash of an explosion, the roar of a gun, and Dowling stood dazed, glancing incredulously at his bloody right hand from which the gun had disappeared.

The sheriff put the cigarette to his lips to moisten the paper, drew his tongue along the crease in the rice paper, and said in a low drawl, "Thanks for that, Ames, I sort of figured you'd know what to do in case I could talk him into making a break."

The eastern sun had long since turned the crags of the big granite mountains into rosy gold. The shadows were still long, however, and the freshness of dawn lingered in the air.

Frank looked up as he heard the sound of the horse's hoofs trampling the ground. Then Roberta's voice called, "Ahoy, how are the hot cakes?"

"All eaten up," Ames said, "and the dishes washed. Why don't you city slickers get up before lunch?"

She laughed. "We did," she said. "In fact, no one went to bed at all. The packers broke camp with daylight, and the sheriff has already taken Dowling out to stand trial. I thought you'd want to know all the latest. Bill Eldon certainly isn't the slow-thinking hick he might seem. Howard Maben was released from the penitentiary two months ago, but he got in trouble again over some forged papers and is awaiting trial in Kansas right now. The sheriff got all that information over the phone.

"George Bay was free-lancing to see if he couldn't clear up Mrs. Dowling's death. He had an idea he could collect a reward from the insurance company if he showed it was murder.

"Bay didn't have much to go on. But Bill Eldon has just about solved *that* case too. He found out that Howard and Mrs. Dowling had a picnic outfit in a suitcase. They carried powdered milk. She was the only one who took cream in her coffee.

"Dowling only had to put poison in the powdered milk and then leave on a business trip, where he'd have an alibi for every minute of the time. The picnic case, you see, was never used except when he was gone, and only his wife used the powdered milk.

"You should have heard Sheriff Eldon questioning Dowling. He soon had him floundering around in a mass of contradictory stories.

"He'd learned Bay was on his trail and decided to kill Bay so it would look as though Howard had done it. He knew Howard's term had expired but didn't know Howard had been rearrested and was in jail. Dowling had had his tent placed so the back was right up against that pine thicket. He'd pretend to be asleep, but he'd taken the pegs out of the back and he'd carry a change of shoes and prowl along the mountain trails. I guess he was pretty desperate, after getting all that wealth together, to be trapped by an old crime. He tried to frame it on you, of course, stealing your gun, then later even planting some of your cigarette stubs. He buried the things from his victim's pockets at your place where officers would be sure to find them. But because he thought Sheriff Eldon was a doddering old man, he overdid everything.

"Well, that's all the news, and I must skip. I'm supposed to be back in the main trail in ten minutes. The others are going to pick me up on the way out. I thought I'd just stop by and—leave you my address. I suddenly realized I hadn't told you where you could reach me."

She was standing in the door of the cabin, smiling, looking trim and neat in her leather riding skirt, cowboy boots and soft green silk blouse.

Frank Ames strode toward her, kicking a chair out of his way. "I know where to reach you," he said.

Five minutes later she pushed herself gently back from his arms and said, "Heavens, I'll be late! I won't know how to catch up with them. I don't know the trails."

Ames' circling arms held her to him.

"Don't worry," he said. "You have just left lipstick smears all over one of the best guides in the mountains."

"You mean we can catch up with the others?" she asked.

"Eventually," Frank Ames said. "You probably don't know it, however, but you're headed for the County Clerk's office."

"The County Clerk's office? Surely you don't mean—?"

"I'm leaving just as soon as I can get a few things together," he said. "You see, I want to record a claim. Up here in the mountains when we find something good, we file on it."

"You—you'd better have it assayed first, Frank."

"I've assayed 'it,' " he said. "Underneath that raspberry lipstick there's pure gold, and I don't want anyone to jump my claim."

"They won't," she assured him softly.

"Q"

Victor Canning

A Stroke of Genius

Lancelot Pike planned a little caper down to the smallest detail. It was really a simple affair, and should have worked. But the strangest thing happened . . . a tale of the Minerva Club . . .

Criminal: LANCELOT PIKE

The Minerva Club, in a discreet turning off Brook Street, is one of the most exclusive clubs in London. Members must have served at least two years in one of Her Majesty's Prisons and be able to pay £50 a year dues. In the quiet of its Smoking Room, under the mild eye of Milky Waye, the club secretary, some of the most ambitious schemes for money-making, allied of course with evasion of the law, have been worked out. But, although notoriety is a common quality among members, fame–real honest solid fame–has come to few of them.

Lancelot Pike is one of these few but, although he is still a member, he is not often seen in the august halls of the Minerva. However, over the fireplace in the Smoking Room, hangs one of his greatest works–never seen by the general public–a full assembly, in oils, of the Management Committee of the club; it shows thirty figures of men whose photographs and fingerprints are cherished lovingly by Scotland Yard.

Lancelot's road to fame was a devious one and the first step was taken on the day that Horace Head, leaning against a lamppost in the Old Kent Road and reading the racing edition, saw Miss Nancy Reeves. Without thinking, Horace began to follow her, some dim but undeniable impulse of the heart leading him. And, naturally, Lancelot Pike, who was leaning against the other side of the lamppost, followed Horace, because he was Horace's manager and was not letting Horace out of his sight.

Horace Head at this time was at the peak of his brief career as a professional middleweight fighter. He was younger then, of course but still a wooden-headed, slow-thinking fellow with an engaging smile bracketed by cauliflower ears. He was wearing a gray suit with a thick red line in it, a blue shirt, a yellow bow tie, and brown shoes that squeaked.

He squeaked away after Miss Nancy Reeves and there wasn't any real reason why he should not have done so. She was a trim slim blonde with blue eyes and a pink and white complexion that made Horace think—and this will show how stirred up he was—of blue skies seen through a lacing of cherry blossoms. It had been a good many years since Horace had seen real cherry blossoms too.

Lancelot Pike followed him. Lancelot was a tall, slim, handsome, versatile number, with a ready tongue, a fast mind, and a determination to have an overstuffed bank account before he was thirty no matter what he had to do to get it. At the moment, Horace—at one fight a month—was his stake money.

If Miss Nancy Reeves knew that she was being followed, she showed no signs of it. She eventually went up the steps of the neighborhood Art School and disappeared through its doors.

Horace continued to follow. He was stopped inside by an attendant who said, "You a student?"

Horace said, "Do I have to be?"

"To come in here, yes," said the attendant.

"Who," said Horace, "is the poppet in the green coat with blonde hair?" He nodded to where Miss Nancy Reeves was almost out of sight up a wide flight of stairs.

"That," said the attendant, "is Miss Nancy Reeves."

"She a student?" asked Horace.

"No," said the attendant. "She's one of the art teachers. Life class."

"Then make me a student in the life class," said Horace, the romantic impulse in him growing.

At this moment Lancelot Pike intervened. "What the devil are you after, Horace? You couldn't paint a white stripe down the middle of the road. Besides, do you know what a life class is?"

"No," said Horace.

"Naked women. Maybe, men, too. You've got to paint them."

"To be near her," said Horace, "I'll paint anybody, the Queen of Sheba or the Prime Minister, black all over. I got to do it, Lance. I got this sort of pain right under my heart suddenly."

"You need bicarbonate of soda," said the attendant.

Horace looked at him, reached out, and lifted him clear of the ground by the collar of his jacket and said, "Make me a student."

Well, it had to be. There was no stopping Horace. Lancelot helped
to fill out the form and, in a way, he was glad because he knew that
the classes would keep Horace away from the pubs between training.
Horace was the kind who developed an enormous thirst as soon as
training was finished.

So Horace became a student in the life class. It was a bit of a
shock to him at first. He came from a decent family of safe crackers,
holdup men, and pickpockets. He didn't approve of naked women
posing on a stand while a lot of people sat round painting them.

To do him credit, Horace seldom looked at the models. He sat
behind his easel and looked most of the time at Nancy Reeves.
Naturally he did very little painting–but he saw a lot of Nancy
Reeves.

She was a nice girl. She soon realized that Horace was almost
pure bone from the shoulders up; but she was a great believer in
the releasing power of art, and she was convinced that Horace would
never have joined the class if there had not been some deep-buried
longing in him for expression.

Now Horace, of course, had not the faintest talent for drawing or
painting; but, realizing that he could not sit in the class and do
nothing, he would just smack an occasional daub of paint on his
canvas in a way that loosely conformed to the naked shape of the
model before him. Nancy Reeves soon decided that Horace was–if
he was going to be anything–an abstract painter. She would come
and stand behind him at times and her talk went straight over his
head–but Horace enjoyed every moment of it.

After two weeks of this, Horace finally got to the point of asking
her if she would go to a dance with him. Surprisingly, she agreed,
and she enjoyed it because, whatever else he was not, Horace was
quick on his feet at that time and a good dancer.

Now, a week after the dance, Horace and Lancelot had fixed up
a little private business which Lancelot had carefully planned for
some time. This was to grab the payroll bag of a local building firm
when the messenger came out of the bank on a Friday morning.

Lancelot Pike had the whole thing worked out to the dot. Horace
would sit in the car outside the bank, and Lancelot would grab the
moneybag as the man came to the bottom of the steps and they
would be away before anyone could make a move to stop them. It
was a bit crude, but it had the merit of simple directness and nine
times out of ten–if you read your papers–it works.

It worked this time–except for one thing. The man came down the steps carrying the bag, Lancelot grabbed it and jumped into the car, and Horace started away; but at that moment the messenger shoved his hand through the rear window and fired at Lancelot Pike. But the gun wasn't an ordinary one. It was a dye gun full of a vivid purple stain. The charge got Lancelot full on the right side of the face, ran down his neck, and ruined a good suit and a silk shirt. Well, there it was. They got back to the Head house, where Lancelot had a room, without any trouble from the police. Lancelot nipped inside with the moneybag and Horace drove off to ditch the car.

When Horace returned he found Lancelot hanging over the wash basin trying to get the dye off. But it wouldn't budge. It was a good rich purple dye that meant to stay until time slowly erased it.

"You won't be able to go out for a while," said Horace. "Months, maybe. The police will be looking for a purple-faced man."

"Lovely," said Lancelot savagely. "So I'm a hermit. Stuck here for weeks. You know what that's going to do to a gregarious person like me?"

Horace shook his head. He didn't know what a gregarious person was.

"We got the money," he said.

"And can't spend it. Can't put it to work to make more. Cooped up like a prisoner in the Tower. Me, Lancelot Pike, who lives for color, movement, people, the big pageant of life, and golden opportunities waiting to be seized."

"I could go to the chemist and ask him if he's got anything to take it off," suggested Horace.

"And have him go to the police once he's read the story in the evening newspaper!"

"I see what you mean," said Horace.

So Lancelot—very bad-tempered—was confined to his room. For the first few days he kept Horace busy running to and from the public library getting books for him. Lancelot was a talented, not far from cultured type—things came easily to him and idleness was like a poison in his blood that has to be worked out of his system. But it was people and movement that he missed. Every evening Horace had to recount to him all that he had done during the day and, particularly, how he was getting on with Miss Nancy Reeves at the Art School.

Curiously enough, Horace was getting on very well with her. There was something simple, earthy, and engagingly wooden about

Horace which had begun to appeal to Nancy Reeves. It happens that way—like calling to unlike . . . think of the number of men, ugly as all get-out, with beautiful wives, or of dumb women trailing around with top intellects.

Anyway, Lancelot began to take a great interest in Horace's romance, and he knew that the time would come when Horace would ask the girl to marry him, and he was offering ten to four that she would not accept.

Horace wouldn't take the bet, but he was annoyed that Lancelot should think he had such a poor chance.

"What's wrong with me?" he asked.

"Nothing," said Lancelot, "except that you really aren't her type. To her you're just a big ape she's trying to educate."

"You calling me a big ape?"

"Figuratively, not literally."

"What does that mean?"

"That you don't have to knock my head off for an imagined insult."

"I see."

"I wonder," said Lancelot. "However, forget it. You ask her and see what answer you'll get."

Meanwhile Lancelot helped Horace with his homework from the Art School.

Each week each student did a home study composition on any subject he liked to choose. Lancelot got hold of canvas and paints and went to work for Horace. And then the painting bug hit him—and hit him hard.

He gave up reading books and papers, gave up listening to the radio and watching television, and just painted. It became a mania with him in his enforced seclusion—and it turned out that he was good. He had a kind of rugged, primitive quality, with just a lick of sophistication here and there which really made you stop and look.

Naturally, Nancy Reeves noticed the great improvement in Horace's work and her spirit expanded with delight at the thought that she was drawing from the mahogany depths of Horace's mind a flowering of his true personality and soul. There's nothing a woman likes more than to make a man over. They're great ones for improving on the original model.

Well, one week when Lancelot's face had faded to a pale lilac, Horace came back from the Art School saying that the home study that week had to be "The Head of a Friend," and Lancelot said,

"Leave it to me, Horace. Self-portrait by Rubens. Self-portrait by Van Gogh—"

"It's got to be a friend," said Horace. "I don't know no Rubens—"

"Quiet," said Lancelot, and he began to ferret for a canvas in the pile Horace had bought for him. As he set it up and fixed a mirror so that he could see himself in it, he went on, "How's tricks with the delicious Nancy?"

"Today," said Horace, "I asked her to marry me. A couple more good fights and with my share of the wages snatch, I can fix up the furniture and a flat."

"And what did she say?"

"She got to think it over. Something about it being a big decision, a reckonable step."

"Irrevocable step."

"That's it. That's what she said."

"Means she don't believe in divorce. If she says Yes, which she won't, you'll have her for life. When do you get your answer?"

"End of the week."

"Twenty to one she says No."

"You've lengthened the odds," said Horace, wounded.

"Why not? Deep knowledge of women. When they want time, there's doubt. Where there's doubt with a woman, there's no desire."

"Why should she have doubts? What's wrong with me?"

"You're always asking that," said Lancelot. "Some day somebody is going to be fool enough to tell you. Horace, face it—you're no Romeo like me. I've got the face for it."

"I love her," said Horace. "That's enough for any woman."

Lancelot rolled his eyes. "That anyone could be so simple! A man who has only love to offer is in the ring with a glass jaw. Now then, let's see." He studied himself in the mirror. "I think I'll paint it full face, kind of serious but with a little twinkle, man of the world, knowing, but full of heart."

Well, by the end of the week the self-portrait was finished and Horace took it along to the school. He set it up on the easel and pretended to be putting a few finishing touches to it. When Nancy Reeves saw it she was enraptured.

"It ain't," said Horace, who had learned enough by now to play along with art talk to some extent, "quite finished. It needs a some-thing—a point of . . . well, of something."

"Yes, perhaps it does, Horace. But you'll get it."

She put a hand gently on his shoulder. They were in a secluded part of the room. "By the way, I've come to a decision about your proposal. It's better for me to tell you here in public because it will keep it on a calm, sane, level basis—a perfect understanding between two adult people who considered carefully, very carefully, before making an important decision. I feel that by producing in you this wonderful flowering of talent that I've completed my role, that I have no more to give. Marriage after this would be an anticlimax, since my attachment to you is really an intellectual and artistic one, rather than any warm, passionate, romantic craving. I know that you will understand perfectly, dear Horace."

"You mean, no go?" asked Horace.

Nancy nodded gently. "I'm sorry. But for a woman, love must be an immediate thing. There must be something about a man's face that is instantly compelling. Now take this painting of yours—there's a man's face that is full of the promise of romance, of tenderness and yet manly strength. I'd like to meet your friend."

For a moment Horace sat there, the great fire of his love just a handful of wet ashes. That Nancy Reeves could go for Lancelot just by seeing his portrait filled Horace with bitterness—a bitterness made even blacker by the fact that Horace had taken Lancelot's bet at twenty to one, and now stood to lose £100.

"You mean," said Horace, "that you could go for him?"

"He's certainly got a magic. You've caught his compulsive personality and—"

"You should really see him," said Horace jealously. "One-half of his face is as purple as a baboon's—well, like this—"

In a fit of pique, Horace picked up his brush, squirted some purple paint onto his palette, and slapped the purple thickly over the right side of Lancelot's face.

From behind him Nancy Reeves's voice said breathlessly, "But Horace—that's just the defiant abstract touch it needed! The unconventional, the startling, the emphatic denial of realism . . . Horace, it's staggering! Pure genius. Don't do a thing more to it—not another stroke!"

Horace stood up, looked at her, and said, "There's a lot more I could do to it. But if you like it so much—keep him. Call it 'A Painter's Goodbye.' " He walked out and he never went back to Art School again.

A week later, while Horace was sitting dejectedly in Lancelot's room watching him work at a painting, the local Detective-Inspector and a Constable walked in unexpectedly.

The Inspector nodded affably and said, "Hello, Horace. Evening, Lance. Forging old masters, eh?" He was in a good mood.

Horace gave him a cold stare, and Lancelot kept his hand up to his face to cover his pale lilac cheek.

The Inspector went on, "Funny–I never connected you two with that wages snatch. Bit out of your line. Thought it was strictly an uptown job."

He leaned forward and looked at the painting on which Lancelot was working. "Nice. Nice brushwork. Fine handling of color. Bit of a dabbler myself. Bitten by the bug, you know. Great relaxation. Go to all the exhibitions. They had one at the Art School yesterday. Picked up this little masterpiece by Horace Head."

The Constable stepped forward and brought from behind him Lancelot's self-portrait with Horace's purple-cheeked addition.

"Fine bit of work," said the Inspector. "Sort of neo-impressionistic with traces of nonobjective emotionalism, calculated to shock the indifferent into attention. It did just that to me–so you can take your hand away from your cheek, Lance, and both of you come along with me."

And along they went–for a three year stretch.

But it didn't stop Lancelot painting. He did it in prison and he did it when he came out. Gets 500 guineas a canvas now, and his name is known all over the country.

But he's not often in the Minerva Club. His wife–who was a Miss Nancy Reeves–doesn't approve of the types there and rules the poor fellow with a rod of iron.

"Q"

Florence V. Mayberry

Out of the Dream Stumbling

*One of the oddest stories we've published in a long time—a strange
story that will get under your skin, skewer into your consciousness—and
perhaps into your subconscious . . .*

The man on the witness stand looked younger than he was. Thirty-
four, the papers said. In spite of the strain he was under, he had
an unused look. Not innocent. The facts of the case made that apparent, and they were underscored by the too-soft set of his mouth.
He just looked, simply, unused. The sob sisters were playing him up
as a struggling artist, Bohemian, tempted, all that sort of thing. But
as for tempting, some people tempt with a crook of the finger.

He was frightened. He kept staring at his sister, who sat in the
courtroom with her head down. The way he stared added to his
unused look—the way a child looks at its mother, helpless and be-
seeching. Hurt, too, as though he couldn't believe anyone could punish
him.

The sister was from a different cut of cloth. A thin, pale woman
with use all over her. Not ugly. Good features, if the observer went
beyond the strain on her face. She was obviously anguished by her
brother's trouble. Several of the newspaper stories had featured
her—how she had worked so many years to help her brother become
an artist, how she refused to believe he could murder anyone, in spite
of the evidence. All the broken, strained, understated words by which
she tried to tell how much she loved him . . .

Many a person in the courtroom was wrenched by pity because of
the sister. It gave the case a deeper perspective.

"Call my sister again, please call Lulie back!" the man on the
witness stand cried out, as the prosecuting attorney continued to
question him.

An embarrassed hush fell over the courtroom . . .

If they call me up there again, I'll break down, I know I will. I
wish I could just stay out of the courtroom until—poor Jack, he sounds

just as he did when he was three years old and fell down the stairs and cut his chin and wouldn't let anyone but me touch him. I can't believe we've grown up, and that this has happened to us.

If I didn't have to listen to all these questions! I think I know what happened, but with all these questions and the answers they think they ought to hear, what really happened becomes a secret that keeps running and hiding. When it hides, I have to search and search. And is it the truth when I find it? I don't know any more.

Like my dream last night. About the crystal house.

There, I won't listen to them. I'll just think about my dream, and Celia's crystal house. Maybe it will keep me thinking straight. Because the secret is there. I knew it all over again, the truth, when I went out of the dream house stumbling . . .

I went to the house that was built of crystal. No glass—Celia Hartman's house would never be built of common glass. I touched its door to enter. In the way of dreams the door swung back and the floor itself seemed to move, although I felt no movement, and without walking a step I was inside the house. I was looking for Celia.

Instead of wallpaper in the great entrance hall there were golden designs imbedded in the crystal walls. There were no lighting fixtures. A glow was in the ceiling and I wished I could see how it worked—it was so fabulous, so rich. Like Celia. Eighty millions, Jack said she had. Or maybe it was one hundred and eighty millions—a hundred millions from her family and eighty millions from her former husband. It doesn't matter. It was so much that it was shocking.

But the crystal house and its feeling of infinite luxury didn't shock me. Somehow I expected it to be this way. Anything less would have been a disappointment.

I wondered where the butler was. Because, by this time, everyone knows that Celia Hartman has a butler.

The instant I wondered, there he was, strutting toward me from a gold-fretted archway.

"Where's Celia?" I asked.

"Who knows?" he said. "She's probably hiding. And you haven't a key, so you can't hunt for her."

"My brother has a key," I said. "One key is quite enough for one family. And Celia must be here."

"In that case," he said, and turned and strutted ahead of me. He led me into a room, not quite as large as the auditorium of the San Francisco Opera House.

"Is this the living room?" I asked.

"Drawing room," he corrected primly. "It will be handy for your brother to paint in. Look at the beautiful divans. They've been freshly upholstered."

When I saw the divans, my throat swelled in the way it's been behaving lately. Nerves, the doctor says. I suppose he's right, but sometimes I can hardly breathe; it might as well be real instead of nerves. And for all its vastness this room was crowding, squeezing, choking me with its fat, stuffy divans.

"They're hideous," I said. "I can't imagine anyone with as much money as Celia putting towels on her furniture."

"Not towels," he said superciliously. "Toweling. Special hand-woven, deep-piled toweling. Clean and efficient. Look," he said, leading me to an immense table beside the crystal wall. It, too, was covered with toweling. "If one spills paint or blood or what have you," and he knocked over a vase with roses in it, "it sops up. Very handy, as you see."

I began to think that surely I was wrong in my taste, for Celia wasn't crazy—at least where physical things were concerned. The quick way she took Jack away from Gigi proved that. She knew the ultimates of clothes and jewels and cars and yachts and men, and, I suppose, houses. If she upholstered her furniture in toweling, it must be right.

"Perhaps it's fur," I suggested.

"Fur is for poor people," the butler said. "This was woven from Miss Celia's own design in Miss Celia's own mills."

My throat tightened over that queer lump again . . .

I remembered the only fur coat our family ever had. It was ten years ago, right after Jack and Gigi were married. Jack had sold a painting to a bar on Mission Street. I was upset because he sold it to such a vulgar place—spittoons, beer smell, and a juke box blaring. Especially when the painting was so sparkling, clean-lined, one I especially loved of San Francisco on a clear, sunshiny morning. Jack had it priced at $500. I had insisted that he put high prices on his paintings, even his first ones, because people take a second look when things cost a lot.

Then, when I found out Jack had sold it to the bar for $75, I was furious. I told him to take the money back and ask for his painting. But Gigi was so happy that he had actually sold one, he wouldn't do it.

Jack and Gigi should have used the money to pay the studio rent; I told them they ought to. I was afraid I wouldn't have enough money for everything. There was a big bill at the art supply store and the bill for clothes I'd bought for Jack so that he would look impressive when he called at the galleries—I had all those to pay.

But Gigi was only nineteen and so beautiful. And she was always threatening to go to Hollywood to earn the money they continually needed. So Jack bought her a fur coat, to prove he could give her what she wanted. Jack loved her. He really loved her very much. I don't think he ever loved Celia the same way.

They went to Market Street to a cut-rate store and paid $71.45, including tax, for a genuine seal-dyed Dymka. I never heard of such a thing before. I asked about it at my office—and they should know about such things there, it being the office of the biggest department store in San Francisco. The girls laughed like crazy and started playing around with the letters and came up with "d – m yak."

When I first saw the fur coat, with Gigi parading around their studio with the black fur clutched tight to her flat tummy and slim hips, it frightened me. It looked so expensive that I thought here would be one more bill for me to pay. When she took it off, it changed. Dymka was either rabbit-piled mouse, or mouse-sheared rabbit. Or yak. Still, on a person, even on me, it looked rich. I'm not as young as Gigi. And nobody was ever as beautiful as Gigi. But I am slim and tall, and all those years of ballet gave me a grace I'll never lose. After I got Gigi the job modeling at the store and she bought a camel's-hair coat, I could have used the Dymka. But she said she never thought I'd want her discards, so she gave it to a thrift shop.

When their studio rent came due, right after Jack bought the coat, I had to lend them $50. I always keep a hundred dollars or so ahead in the bank for Jack. He's my baby brother and I feel responsible for him. When we were children, I told him we would be famous together, rich and famous. I was studying ballet, and good at it. And after Jack began to copy cartoons out of the funny papers when he was only six, I knew he should be an artist. I planned it all for us.

But the doctor had to find that murmur in my heart. I'd rather he had let me die. Because he said I had to stop dancing. Mama was just sick about it; she was always sure I was the genius of the family. But after Mama died—well, anyway, there was the murmur. Besides, it takes two people to be a genius, one to push and one to do. The way things turned out, Mama was wrong. Jack was the genius . . .

"My sister-in-law had a fur coat," I told the butler. "She didn't look poor in it. She looked like a million dollars."

"We've got a million dollars in our refrigerator," said the butler, his nasty little face twisting all over itself. "Miss Celia keeps it on hand to serve with cocktails. That's what she intends to serve at Mr. Jack's exhibition."

"I want to see it," I said. "All my life I've wanted to see a million dollars."

"This way, madam," said the butler, drawing himself up, sticking out his stomach, making me notice for the first time that he was wearing red and white striped velvet pajamas. "They're liveried pajamas," he explained, smirking.

We walked—slowly and heavily, like wading through water—into the kitchen. There was the refrigerator, all done up in toweling too.

That idiot butler hopped into the kitchen sink, pajamas and all, and turned on the water. "Hand me the towel off the icebox," he said.

"Don't be such a fool," I said. "All the stories I've read about butlers, they didn't act like you. I've changed my mind, I don't want to see Celia's money, I want to see Celia. Where's she hiding?"

"She's in the courtroom," he said.

"Nonsense," I said. "If I know Celia, she'll be in the bedroom."

But I don't think it was I who said that. It was my voice, but I think Gigi said it . . . She could never quit dwelling on the time she found Celia in Jack's and her bedroom. Like a wildcat, she was.

Gigi was supposed to be at work. It was busy at the store—they were getting ready for a fashion tea. And it was stupid of me—I shouldn't have mentioned, while Gigi and I were eating lunch together, that Celia was coming to the studio that afternoon to talk over the one-man show Celia was sponsoring for Jack. In the middle of the afternoon Gigi told her boss she was getting appendicitis or something, and went home. It was a horrible mess. Gigi slapped Celia and kicked her as she ran downstairs. Celia had a bad fall. I was thankful she was so rich, else she might have sued.

Every time Jack came near Gigi, she scratched his face. Fighting was in her blood. She was beautiful and a good enough girl, but quite common on occasion. Malloy was her name before she married Jack.

The minute Jack called me, I rushed right from the office to her studio. "Georgiana Grace!" I scolded, using her real name instead of the pet name Jack liked. "Do you realize you may ruin Jack's chance to have this big exhibit? Celia's going to bring important critics. Maybe Jack will get a picture story in *Life*—Celia knows one of the editors. You know very well Jack's paintings are hanging all over this apartment, even in the bathroom. Would you spoil his career just because he showed his sponsor the paintings in the bedroom?"

Gigi said a filthy word. "Grow up!" she said. "Jack's too big to dress in doll clothes any more."

"Jack, will you give me your word that everything between you and Celia was–proper?" I asked. Jack never lied to me. When he was small and used to work coins out of my piggy bank, he would always admit it.

"Everything was proper," Jack said.

"I'll bet!" Gigi yelled, and scratched him again.

The madder she got, the more Jack tried to hold her and kiss her. At last she let him. When I went into their kitchen to start dinner, he was holding her on his lap explaining how it would be foolish to give up the exhibition when it would all be over in another week or so.

"Then I'll buy you another Dymka, baby!" he laughed. But not a word about the hundreds and hundreds of dollars that–oh, well . . .

Watching the butler splash himself and his velvet pajamas in the sink made me suddenly frantic to be clean and cool. I was drenched with perspiration. I was stifled by this house.

I tiptoed out and entered what seemed to be the dining room, with chairs arranged around a long rectangle. But the rectangle was not a table. It was a huge painting, a portrait of Jack, one I had never seen. He was dressed in evening clothes, and carried two cats by their tails. The cats had women's faces. One was mine, the other was Gigi's. Her face looked lovely and right, on the cat's body. Her long, slanted blue eyes–Jack always called them the eyes of a Celtic nymph–were feline, wonderfully exotic.

Beyond this room was a long hall. At the end of it, through a broad doorway, I saw the golden posts of what I thought must be a bed.

"Celia!" I called. A bathroom would be off her bedroom. And I was driven by the need to bathe myself.

My cry couldn't be heard, even by me. All the hall was padded with the soft, thick toweling. Every sound was absorbed. The soundless cry backed up in me. It created a rhythm, a bottled frenzy; it made my blood beat, beat, until it was like music. I began to dance, the way I used to. My head bent, my neck curved like Pavlova's in the pictures Mama collected for me.

Suddenly I knew why I was hunting Celia. I was going to ask her to sponsor me in a dance exhibition.

I went dancing down the long, muffled hall. Bending, leaping with a lightness I should have lost years ago. It would astonish Celia, with her superior veiled look. She'd not look at me now the way she did at that cocktail party she gave for Jack, wondering what part of me could possibly be like Jack.

I danced into the room with the golden bedposts. But there was no bed attached to the posts. They were slender, golden columns that spiraled so high they held up the blue sky. No, it wasn't the sky. Only a blue ceiling. In the blue ceiling were star shapes, outlined with tubed light. It was hideously ugly, because it was dead. It was a dead sky.

The golden posts formed a high, open circle. Celia stood within the circle. Her big dark eyes were lowered so I could not see the golden flecks in them that always reminded me of how rich she was. So I wasn't frightened of her any more.

It was wonderful not to be frightened of a rich person. Always before I had been frightened by her rich house and her rich thinking and her rich manners—even by the rich way she was put together, her round golden flesh, her lips like little red-satin cushions, her poured-honey hair, the golden flecks, all the smooth butter luxury of her.

"You're not as beautiful as Gigi," I told her confidently. "Gigi is a Celtic nymph. She's Irish, you know."

She still didn't look at me. "Yes, I know," she said. "Jack told me."

"I was always a nervous child," I explained. "If I had not been so nervous, I would have been as beautiful as Gigi—as beautiful as you."

"Not as Gigi," she said. "Gigi is a Celtic nymph."

"I'm tired of hearing that," I said. "Do you have a bathtub in your bedroom?"

"This is not a bedroom," she said. "This is the courtroom. I am standing in the middle of the court. Isn't it lovely the way I was able to buy heaven for its ceiling?"

She lifted her eyes, but so high that I couldn't see into them. She clasped her hands under her chin and gazed at the blue ceiling.

"Don't try to look saintly," I warned. "I know as much about your kind as Gigi does. I just pretended I didn't so I wouldn't hurt Jack's career. It's my career too, you know."

She smiled. She really looked quite kind. "Ever get fooled?" she asked softly.

My body burned, but at the same time I was cold with perspiration. The lump in my throat hurt. I began to cry. "I must have a bath, I'm filthy, and there's no tub here."

Celia moved beside me, her eyes once more directed toward the floor. I think she pressed a button on one of the golden posts–I was too disturbed to see. For the floor of the circular court slowly slipped aside, revealing a large pool of water with steps leading into it.

I walked slowly down the steps to the water's edge.

"But the water's dirty! It's full of old dead leaves," I said, weeping again.

"You've let it get stagnant," Celia sneered. "You should have drained it long ago."

What a terrible woman! Blaming me for her own dirty pool of water! I hated her terribly. I hated her with all the hate I had ever had for anyone throughout my life.

I turned, whirling, leaping up the steps, a nymph doing arabesques of fury.

Celia began laughing, raising her eyes toward me.

"Don't look at me!" I warned. "If you look at me, I'll kill you!"

But she was already looking. Staring, staring.

There was a towel in my hand–I must have picked it up somewhere in the house.

She waved her hand at me, as though in farewell, and turned her back. Then she lay on the floor and went to sleep.

Slowly, as though walking through water, I went to her, eased the towel beneath her cheek. Then I knotted it tightly over her face. She made no struggle. She was already sound asleep.

I left her and ran away. The house compressed, the way things do in dreams, and I was running out the door, stumbling, running again, the secret no longer hiding but pursuing me . . .

"Your sister's testimony was clear," said the prosecuting attorney to the defendant. "There is no need to call her back. Now, is it not true that you entered the bedroom where the deceased was sleeping, asphyxiated her with a chloroform-saturated towel, and–"

The defendant began to cry. "I wasn't there when she died!" he said wildly. "I was at Celia Hartman's house. Only she wasn't home. I had a key–that's why the butler didn't know I was there. But he thought he heard a voice calling in the hall–he testified to that."

*"He thought," the prosecuting attorney emphasized sarcastically.
"And a voice so unclear to him that it could be either male or female.
The butler had been sound asleep–he had retired early under bro-
mides because of a heavy cold. He believes he may have been having
a nightmare. But he arose at once, put on his bathrobe, and examined
the upper hall and the lower. No one was there."*

*"My sister sent me there! She sent me, but she won't tell you!" the
defendant said. He stood up and faced his sister. "Lulie, in the name
of God, tell them!"*

"Order!" demanded the judge, pounding his gavel . . .

I never intended to have Jack blamed. That just happened. One
thing built on another, and after it did, I began to think that Jack
ought to suffer a little. A person needs to suffer to learn how to take
care of himself. And after this Jack will have to take care of himself.

First, the police came. Jack had called them. I was across the
street with old Mrs. Bellingham–she reminds me so much of Mama.
And she isn't right any more–she didn't know when I came in, she
can't remember five minutes at a time. But even though Jack had
called the police, and swore he was innocent, his fingerprints were
all over the chloroform bottle. And there were the bruises on her
shoulders where he'd held her to keep her from scratching out his
eyes.

They were sure he did it. And I kept thinking: suffering toughens
a person, and Jack needs toughening. Just for a little while. So I
told them I wasn't there, that I didn't know anything.

After all, he intended to do it. That night, when I saw him fumbling in my medicine cabinet, I felt uneasy. He's always borrowing
things. But that night he had a queer, white look around his mouth.
Earlier I'd heard them fighting, too, that's when she got the bruises.
But he told me she was asleep and he needed antiseptic for a scratch.
As for her falling asleep right after a fight, that was natural. She
was a beautiful animal, and a good fight relaxed her.

He was gone a half hour or so. Then he came tearing back. "For
God's sake, wake her up! Get a doctor!" he said. "I think she's dead.
Lulie, I didn't mean it. But she swore she'd stop my exhibit, swore
she'd kill Celia–"

I ran next door to their apartment. The nasty smell of chloroform
hit me. I knew then what he had borrowed from my medicine cabinet. It was the chloroform I'd bought for my kitten when it had fits.

A towel hung from the bed beside Gigi. The chloroform smell

came from it. I examined Gigi. "You're always losing your head," I told Jack. "She's not dead. She's breathing and her heart's beating. You know how soundly she sleeps. But you idiot! How could this help us?"

"I don't know–I didn't want to lose the show–I don't know," he kept saying.

"Get out of here," I said. "Go see Celia. Stay there a while. But don't tell anyone, you hear?–about what you tried to do. I may have to call a doctor and I don't want you around here talking too much. Remember, keep your mouth shut."

He ran out.

I put cold water on Gigi's face. I blew my breath into her mouth. It was useless. Before I began, I knew it. There had been no breath, no heartbeat, when I examined Gigi. She was dead before I ever got to their apartment.

And already I knew what I had to do. I don't have a career, and Jack does. Besides, I want to take care of him–it's my life! What else have I got?

I fixed it so that Jack would believe I was the one who really murdered her. That way, he could go on living and working; he wouldn't have to hate himself so much. I picked up the towel, put it on her face, and poured the rest of the chloroform on it. My fingerprints were on the bottle, too. That was only natural. It was my chloroform.

Jack came back, found the towel on her face, and called the police. But when they questioned him, he just kept saying, "Talk to my sister, talk to my sister." He didn't know how to handle it. For what could he say that wouldn't make him guilty, too?

The police found me across the street with that dear old soul, Mrs. Bellingham. She kept muttering how I'd been there since I came home from work. I had run in to see her for a minute when I first came home, and she didn't remember I'd ever left. By then, with all those policemen and reporters around, I was almost numb. I didn't say anything. I let them talk and I just nodded. It was so clear they thought Jack had killed her. Well, I was scared, and I kept thinking I hadn't really done it. And Jack needed some sense scared into him. So I let it ride.

In those crazy dreams I always start to kill Celia. Then, like the girl beside the pool in the crystal house, when her eyes look directly at me they have no golden flecks. They aren't dark. They are Gigi's blue, slanted eyes.

I'll sit here, quiet, free, for just another minute or two. Then I'll tell them. I'll tell them I did it.

Everyone in the courtroom gazed at her as Lulie abruptly arose from her seat. "Please! Please!" she cried. "Let him alone! He didn't do it, I did it! But it wasn't Gigi, it was the butler I killed. He wouldn't take me to Celia. He was sitting in the kitchen sink, and I held his head under the faucet until he drowned!"

The judge pounded his desk with his gavel. "Bailiff," he ordered. "Remove that poor woman from the court!"

Lawrence Treat

A As in Alibi

A police procedural starring Lieutenant Decker, the Chief of Homicide himself, in one of the best stories in this fine series . . . Keep your eye on the clock—all the clues stare you in the face . . .

Detectives: HOMICIDE SQUAD

Lieutenant Decker, the lean, gray-haired, gray-eyed Chief of Homicide, sat behind the beat-up desk in his tiny office and felt old. Empty inside. Past his prime. Licked, washed up. Twenty years ago he'd have shot fire and brimstone, and blasted this overweight slob into a confession.

But now—what? Here was Frank London, a half-baked, itinerant bum of a folk singer, sneering at him, sneering at the police. Logic hadn't worked, threats hadn't worked, the tricks of the trade hadn't worked. Nothing had even dented the guy, and Decker had nowhere to go. Not up, not down. Not sideways. Just stay put and molder away. Call the case a bust, put it in the Unsolved File, and know in his heart that he'd failed.

There was only one thing that Lieutenant Decker was sure of: Frank London had killed her. Decker knew it and London knew he knew it—which was why London had that smirk on his face. A big, round, oversized face with large agate eyes, cheeks like little red balloons, and that impossible, twisted handlebar of a blond mustache decorating his lip.

It was a grotesque mustache, braided like a quoit or a pretzel or a wicker carpet-beater. The Beatles had their hairdo, Groucho had his cigar—but this joker had his mustache; and he was making a monkey out of Decker and the Homicide Squad and the whole police department. And when they released London, somebody would be the fall guy and his name was Decker. William B. Decker, a cop for 35 years and head of Homicide for the last 15. The smart thing was to hand in his resignation, then go home and tell Martha, his wife. And move to Florida or California and never work, never worry, never be alive again.

Yeah? Not me, brother, not me!

Decker stared at the beefy hunk of beatnik in front of him and said, "Okay, let's go over it once more. You got to the cottage around five, her folks were already gone, and so you and Jodie rehearsed for a couple of hours. You left her a little before seven, walked up the path to the top of the cliff where your car was parked, and nobody saw you. A damn freak like you, and nobody ever noticed you!"

"The invisible man," London said tauntingly. His deep, resonant, troubadour voice separated every word and enunciated it with care. "I left, didn't I? Or do you think I'm still there?"

Decker knew that the car had been driven away around seven, although nobody could identify London as the driver. "You got into your car," Decker said crisply, "drove home and took a shower. Presumably to wash off the blood."

"There was no blood."

"What did you do with the towel?" Decker asked. That was one of the few points he had. London's landlady was certain that a towel was missing from London's bathroom, and Decker was convinced the folk singer had used it to wipe off the blood and then had disposed of it, along with the white polo shirt he'd been wearing. "What did you do with the towel?" Decker asked again.

"I buttered it, put pepper and salt on it, and cut it into terrycloth canapés. My usual dinner."

That was the way the interrogation had been going. London kidding him, skating rings around him, and enjoying every minute of it. Always the showman, always putting on an act. And then London pulled a masterpiece of pure gall. He took the unbelievably long braids of that fancy mustache of his, pulled one ropy end straight up, over his nose, and stretched the other end at a right angle, to his right. With Decker facing him, the mustache now looked like the two hands of a clock, pointing to nine o'clock.

Nine o'clock—the crucial time.

He did it solemnly, deadpan, and then he twisted his mustache back into its usual pretzel shape, sat there with that maddening smirk on his face, and clammed up. That was his answer: nuts to you, Lieutenant Decker. And somehow, Decker felt he'd been given the clue to the puzzle—been given it by the man's brag and conceit; but Decker was just too dumb to figure it out.

Restraining an impulse to smack the guy, the Lieutenant thought-back to the first, futile interview between them. He'd been pretty sure, even then. He'd asked questions, listened to answers, then sent London back to a cell for the night, while the Homicide Squad checked up on what London had said.

Orthodox procedure, and Decker thought he had the guy cold. Duck soup, he'd told himself. London's alibi depended on the time when the murder had been committed, and so he had simply set a clock on the scene of the crime to the hour of his alibi. Which was a trick that had never fooled anybody, once a case was properly investigated.

Except this time.

Decker scowled. "Then you went to the Red Grotto for your evening performance. Jodie didn't come, and you went on stage alone."

"The show must go on," London said smugly.

Decker's adrenaline oozed out, and his face turned red. "You sang *Frankie and Johnny*," he said tightly. "Then you sang a new song, one you say you had just made up. A few people remembered some of the words. It started off—"

He picked up the sheet of paper on which he'd scrawled the beginning of the ballad, as some of the audience had recalled it. He read it off starkly, prosaically. " 'My love has gone to a far country, My love has gone away from me, Sing die, goodbye, Oh, sigh, sigh, sigh.' "

"Nice song," London said judiciously.

"Where'd you learn it?"

"I made it up as I went along. It came naturally." London gave Decker a self-satisfied grin and added, "That's genius for you."

"You were singing her requiem. How did you know she was dead?"

"I didn't. I felt sad. Maybe it was telepathy. Maybe her spirit was in me, for those few minutes. The audience was so touched that for a few seconds nobody even applauded. Then their cheers rang to the rafters. It was a great moment."

The folk singer cocked his head to one side and grinned like an overfed gargoyle. "It was nine o'clock, exactly."

Decker glared, then spun around in his chair. The swivel squeaked. He reached for the doorknob, twisted it. He swung the door outward and gave it a kick. "Okay," he said in a dead voice. "You can go. You're free."

London jumped up with a shout and held out his hand. "Lieutenant, that's great! Thanks, Lieutenant, thanks."

Decker turned away.

"Look," London said, "don't take it like that. So you were wrong. Forget it. Enjoy yourself. I'm going to throw a party at the Red Grotto that this town's going to remember for years. I'm going to have all my friends there, including you. Lieutenant, be my guest–the guest of honor."

"Get the hell out of here," Decker said, barely spitting out the words.

London shrugged, grinned, and left.

Decker frowned as he slid his finger along the pieces of paper on his desk–the sheets with the words of the song and the timetable of the murder.

It was years since he'd blown his top and let a suspect see how infuriated he could become. Alone now, Decker asked himself where he'd gone wrong.

His investigation had been thorough, he'd examined the facts exhaustively. There were no loose ends, no doubts in his own mind. Jub Freeman, lab man and forensic scientist and a damn good one, had gone over every inch of the cottage, and the Homicide Squad had spent days questioning everybody who had been in the neighborhood. The picture was clear enough.

The Dorkins and the Finleys lived together–they had lived together for 20 years in the big stone house on Dixon Heights. Hannah Dorkin and Natalie Finley were sisters–their relationship was close. In his own mind, Bill Decker called it beautiful, and they were beautiful women in the fullness of maturity. Prominent in social work, married to eminent men, Hannah Dorkin and Natalie Finley were kind, gentle, rich in forgiveness. Decker wondered whether they'd forgiven London. And whether they'd ever forgive him, Lieutenant Decker.

Jodie Dorkin was the only young person in the household, and the Dorkins told the Lieutenant that, as a child, Jodie had sometimes got mixed up as to who were her father and mother, and who were her aunt and uncle. She solved the problem by loving them all equally.

Her father and uncle were distinguished men. Judge Dorkin was gruff, blunt, rigorous in his honesty and rocklike in his adherence to high principle. Decker knew him professionally and respected him for his clear mind and incorruptible character. Dorkin's clipped wit and his firm, impartial administration of justice had made enemies. No upper court appointment for him. Politics couldn't take away his distinction, but it had kept him from the advancement he so richly deserved.

Dr. Richard Finley was a small gentle man, a world-famous cardiologist and surgeon. He was urbane, civilized, honored in his profession. You looked at him and wondered how such an unobtrusive little man could have risen so far. But when he spoke, you began to understand why, and when you noticed the delicacy and strength of his hands, you knew there was talent in them. He had the king's touch, which cured.

The four adults had gone down to their river cottage early that mild, summery Saturday afternoon. The cottage was at the foot of the river bluff, just within the metropolitan limits. A dozen other cottages were scattered along the bank of the river—pleasantly cool refuges in the heat, each of them with a dock and a boathouse built over the water.

Jodie was already at the cottage—she'd gone there the day before and stayed overnight. At 18, she was interested in folk singing and had performed here and there as an amateur; but she hadn't been serious about it as a career until she met Frank London. He had a good voice, he was an experienced performer, and on some level he and Jodie clicked. Their voices complemented each other, but more than that, they gave each other style. London's stature grew as some part of him softened and gained understanding, while Jodie acquired some of his confidence and bravura. They were a team, and fast becoming the sensation of the small hootenannies.

Jodie had told her family that Frank was meeting her at the cottage, that they wanted to rehearse some new numbers. The older people had never liked London, but they realized you don't have to like your colleagues in order to work with them. And Jodie had assured them there was nothing serious between her and Frank, and never would be.

"He likes me," she'd said. "Maybe a little too much, but I know he's a heel. Except the times we're singing together, he rubs me the wrong way. So you've nothing to worry about, any of you."

And they didn't. They loaded the picnic basket in their boat, and went upriver. They didn't take watches, didn't know what time it was. That was part of the fun, part of what made their outings so carefree.

"We go upriver," Dr. Finley said, "and land wherever we feel like, or else we just drift back. We do it every week-end. Sometimes we swim, sometimes we birdwatch, sometimes we just talk. We eat when we're hungry. Occasionally we stay out overnight. We never know. But we're free, we're completely emancipated from time."

Brother, Decker thought. What a day to be emancipated! They had returned after dark. They had no idea what time it was. Ten–twelve–two–they couldn't say. They'd been immersed in a dream world and their senses were drugged, suspended, heavy with sound and sight and the richness of their own living. Until they turned on the light in the living room of the cottage and saw Jodie. She'd been stabbed with a kitchen knife. There was blood. There had been a fight. She'd resisted. Her clothes were torn. In the course of the struggle her foot had apparently caught the cord of the electric clock, unplugged it, and sent it crashing down. The cord was still hooked around her leg.

What the four grownups had subsequently gone through, they themselves could hardly relate. Dr. Finley had examined Jodie. Respiration had not entirely ceased. The doctor took over, and with the help of the others he improvised emergency techniques. First-aid equipment and some of his basic instruments were in the cottage, so he tried to accomplish a medical miracle.

There was no phone, and even if there had been, no one would have bothered to summon the police. Time was too important–a transfusion and manual massage of Jodie's heart were the only possible hopes, and they had to be done immediately, without moving her.

Natalie Finley had formerly been a nurse. She assisted; she was familiar with the delicate and unusual operation that Dr. Finley had performed before, in hospitals. He made the incision and they stood by and did what he told them to. They gave blood, under primitive conditions.

How long Finley worked on Jodie, none of them could tell. An hour, three hours? They hadn't the slightest idea. But it was dawn when Finley finally gave up and told Judge Dorkin to trudge up the hill to the nearest phone and notify the police.

When Decker got the call from headquarters, he tumbled out of bed and drove to the scene. He saw the two women briefly, then got the basic facts from Judge Dorkin and Dr. Finley. Frank London had presumably been there. The clock had always kept accurate time. Decker didn't touch it. Jub Freeman would dust it for finger-prints and examine it and the cord for any possible physical evidence, no matter how minute. The hands pointed to nine o'clock.

Decker had four homicide men at the scene before he and Mitch

Taylor left to pick up London. London was the obvious suspect and Decker woke him up, heard him mutter sleepily that he'd rehearsedwith Jodie and left her around seven, maybe a little earlier, that she'd failed to show up at the Red Grotto, and so he'd gone on alone, and what the hell was this all about?

Decker told him and hauled him off to headquarters. Decker's grilling was expert. London was reticent about details and insolent in his general behavior, but Decker thought he had a pretty good case. London had stabbed her, then set the hands of the clock to indicate nine, and figured he had a pretty good alibi.

He spent the day in jail while Decker gradually learned how a man can come to hate a clock.

His first theory—that London had set the clock after the stabbing—ran into immediate difficulty. The time-set button was jammed and bent, and couldn't be moved. Decker decided it was jammed because, when the clock fell, the button had hit the arm of a wicker chair. Fragments of the wicker were wedged against the stem of the time-set, and there were clear marks on the chair to show where the clock had hit.

Microscopic examination made it seem highly unlikely that London had scraped off tiny bits of wicker and inserted them in such a way as to make the time-set inoperative. It was just one of those accidents. Therefore, London must have set the clock at nine *before* he committed the murder. That was Decker's first conclusion, in what he now thought of as his hours of innocence.

Medical evidence was consistent with placing the time of attack between seven and nine p.m. London had been there until almost seven, and everything in his background was against him. He'd been a juvenile delinquent in Chicago and had spent time in a reformatory. Later, he'd gone to New York and had become something of a Greenwich Village character. He sang and strummed in bars, drank too much, got into fights. He'd been arrested for assaulting a woman, but she'd refused to prosecute. There were rumors of other, similar incidents, although they hadn't got as far as a police blotter. He'd finally left New York, gone on tour, landed here, and met Jodie.

He was in love with her, according to everybody who knew the pair of them, but she would have no part of him. He'd made a few scenes at the Red Grotto, but she'd always managed to hold him off. To Decker, the picture of the murder was crystal-clear. Jodie and Frank London had been alone in that isolated river cottage. He'd tried to make love to her, she'd resisted, and he'd grabbed a kitchen knife and stabbed her in a violent rage.

So much for London. But granting him his nine o'clock alibi, it was reasonable to believe that a prowler had walked into the cottage after London had gone. The Homicide Squad combed the neighborhood for evidence of a stranger who might have assaulted and killed Jodie. No trace of an intruder had been found.

Which brought everything back to the clock.

It was an old battered clock, hexagonal in shape, and the numbers on the dial were indistinct. Nevertheless they were there, and the clock had stopped at nine. Decker bought two similar clocks and offered five bucks to any of his squad who could figure out how London could have jammed the time-set button in exactly the way it had been found. Nobody collected the five bucks.

It was a noisy clock, and the judge told him the family used to joke about it, referring to its death rattle. But it kept good time and they were sentimental about it, so they never replaced it.

"The electricity might have been cut off," the judge said.

"It wasn't," Decker said. "We checked that, for the last month. And we checked your fuse box. If it was keeping accurate time earlier in the afternoon, when you were still here, we have to assume it remained accurate."

The judge frowned. "I can't say that I really noticed."

But his wife had. "It was not only keeping time," Hannah Dorkin said quietly, "but the week before it had stopped making noises. I'm sensitive to sound, and I missed hearing the funny little rattle it always made. I mentioned it to Jodie, and she said she'd fix it, and she did."

"How?"

"She didn't tell me. We were making sandwiches and she was slicing some ham and she cut her finger. She went for a Band-Aid and we never finished the conversation."

Decker was still clinging to the idea that London had set the clock ahead to nine, and then murdered Jodie. Finally Dr. Finley scotched that theory.

"You couldn't set it," he said. "I tried to do something about the noise a few months ago, and I dropped it and bent that time-set button. Couldn't even turn it with a pair of pliers. But you couldn't hurt that clock. I checked it by my watch on Saturday, before we went out on the boat, and the clock was accurate."

The judge was philosophic in his point of view. "Lieutenant," he said, "we've both seen a lot of murders. The unbalanced man, the psychopathic killer without a motive—sometimes he commits a crime and isn't seen. Years later he's caught for something else and he confesses, and you just marvel at his luck, at the string of coincidences that made his escape possible."

"Not this time," Decker said. "London killed her."

"What does the D.A. say?" the judge asked.

"That he won't indict London until I can place him at the cottage at nine. And at nine—well—"

Decker turned away. At nine o'clock Frank London had been strumming a guitar at the Red Grotto and making public lament for Jodie Dorkin. He'd known she was dead, he'd practically advertised it. Therefore she'd been killed around seven—except that an unimpeachable clock said no.

Decker had traced Jodie's movements in detail; he had looked for a jealous suitor, for some clue that would provide a name, another person to question. Decker drew a total blank.

On Friday, the day before her death, Jodie had had an all-day swimming party at the boathouse. About a dozen teen-agers had come in the morning and stayed until after dark, but most of them hadn't even been in the cottage. Around 6:30, however, two or three of them had gone there with Jodie to get food from the refrigerator; but they hadn't even noticed the clock.

Nothing unusual had happened. Nobody had got drunk. There were no fights, no incidents. Decker obtained a list of everybody who'd been at the party and checked out their whereabouts on Saturday. They could all account for themselves, and so it came back to London. Every time it came back to Frank London.

What, then, had gone wrong? Where had Decker slipped up?

Grunting, he yanked open the drawer of his desk. His favorite pencil, his personal diary. There on the bookcase, the small stuffed crocodile that brought him luck—or used to. He wondered whether to take it home with him, or to leave it here for his successor.

Fifteen years as head of the Homicide Squad, and what would he leave behind? What was personal to him in this tiny cubicle of an office that had held so much drama, had seen so many killers break down, confess, and walk out the door to their inevitable fate?

He sighed morosely. Tonight, London was setting up a celebration. He'd get drunk and shoot off his mouth about how he'd put one over on the police. Maybe Decker ought to go to that party, after all. Maybe London would give himself away.

Decker stepped outside and told the receptionist he was leaving for the day. In the corridor, he thought of going upstairs to the lab. Jub Freeman was working on that robbery case. The clock would be over in the corner, on the workbench near the window; but if Decker set eyes on the thing now, he was liable to smash it to pieces. He went out to the parking lot, got in his car, and drove home.

Martha seemed to know. She'd suffered these many years through all his moods, all his triumphs and despondencies, all the tough cases that woke him up in the middle of the night and sent him down to his desk in the small book-lined den, where he might scrawl out an idea, put together some outlandish logic, or connect two bits of apparently unrelated evidence that finally solved the unsolvable.

Tonight, she seemed to understand. She was tender, quiet; she talked of small things in a low, comforting voice, while he sat on the couch and sipped at a double scotch. After dinner he stalked out, got in his car, and went driving.

Anywhere. Out to the river cottage. Past the Red Grotto. It didn't matter where. He just wanted to be moving, to get away from himself and his problem.

He had a dozen bright ideas to explain how, although London had stabbed Jodie around seven, the clock had stopped at nine. Maybe it had still been going after she'd been stabbed. Maybe London had removed the glass over the dial of the clock after stabbing her, pushed the hands to nine, and then replaced the glass.

Decker swore. He was kidding himself with wild theories that no jury would take seriously. What he needed was a simple, down-to-earth explanation that would undermine the evidence of the clock and blast the cockiness out of London. He'd confess then. No doubt about it. Lieutenant Decker knew the type—he could handle guys like London.

Still driving aimlessly, Decker found himself rolling past headquarters. There was a light on in the lab—Jub Freeman was apparently working late. On impulse Decker swung through the arched entrance of the building and parked in his regular spot in the courtyard. He got out of the car, strode through the lobby where a sergeant was seated at the long high desk, and went upstairs.

Jub, a stocky, cheerful, round-cheeked guy, dimpled up in a smile as he greeted Decker. "Just checking up on a soil precipitation test that I started this afternoon," he said, putting down a test tube. "Anything on your mind?"

"I got no mind," Decker said. "When I give up on a jerk like

London, I'm a nitwit. No brains. Low I.Q. Been lucky up to now, but I got found out."

Jub corked the test tube carefully and placed it in a rack. "He'll give himself away, some time. He'll get drunk. He'll brag about it to some dame. Just wait, Lieutenant. You'll get him."

"I can't wait. You know what the papers are going to say tomorrow, don't you? Then the Commissioner will have a little talk with me and—" Decker shrugged despondently, noticed the Dorkin clock lying on a workbench near the window, and stalked over to it.

"Who the hell left it at nine o'clock?" he demanded bitterly. "Somebody needling me?" He plugged the cord in, then picked up the clock.

Jub said, "You've been working too hard. Go away for a few days. Rest up. Things will blow over."

Decker whirled, twisting his body. "Jub, don't try to—" He broke off, aware that the clock had started making its distinctive rattling.

As the six-sided clock now lay in Decker's hand, it was tilted 60°, one side to the left—that is, counterclockwise. The numbers on the dial were faded and barely legible. If you told time simply by the position of the hands, they now indicated about ten minutes to seven.

The Lieutenant gasped. He shifted the clock back one side, clockwise. The dial now read nine o'clock. The barely visible numeral six was now at the base, and the rattling sound had stopped.

"So *that's* how Jodie 'fixed' it," Decker said in a low, somewhat awed voice. "She just turned it one side to the left. Look, Jub. Stand it up the way it's supposed to be, with six at the bottom, and it doesn't make any noise. But if you do this—"

He shifted it to the next left of the six flat sides, with the barely discernible numeral eight at the base. The noise started, and the dial now seemed to show ten minutes to seven. "And nobody noticed that she left the clock *standing on the wrong side*. After all, lots of clocks don't even have numerals and people tell time easily enough."

Jub nodded. "She must have done it on Friday, when she was there all day. Then on Saturday, after he stabbed her and looked down and saw the clock, London realized what a terrific break had been handed to him. Standing in the correct position, with six at the base, the clock showed the wrong time—not ten minutes to seven when he stabbed her, but nine o'clock—time enough for London to give himself an alibi!"

Decker, wonderment still on his face, patted the clock and broke into a broad grin. "Until now—but now we've got him," he said, "got him cold!"

Robert Edward Eckels

The Last One To Know

When the husband says, "Tonight I have to go back to the office," and then it develops that he has to work late "two, maybe three nights a week," should the wife become suspicious? ...

It was a big step for us, after all those years in the house, to move to an apartment, even a three-bedroom condominium only a few blocks inland from the lake. But we had both agreed—or said we did anyway—that it would be foolish to try to keep up that big old place just for the two of us now that the children were out on their own.

So an apartment seemed to be the answer. And actually once we made the move it wasn't too bad. A lot of the furniture had to go, of course. But the things we really wanted we kept. The third bedroom became Paul's study and was soon as cluttered with his books and papers as his den had been. And somehow the big walnut hutch with my good china and crystal was fitted into the dining area along with the old table and chairs.

We kept a lot of our old habits, too. Paul set up our portable grill on our little balcony, for example, so during nice weather we could continue our regular weekend cookouts.

I mention that in particular because, God help me, that's where it all started.

It was an ordinary Saturday in late May. We had company, I remember—the Smallwoods, George and Sheila. I'd never been particularly close to her, but he and Paul had similar jobs in different branches of the same company and office politics dictated that we exchange visits three or four times a year.

Neither of the men had worked that day, of course, and now they were out on the balcony nursing their drinks and getting the cookout fire "ready." Usually Paul has a great time poking and stirring the charcoal briquets until they're well burned down and covered uniformly with a fine coat of gray white ash. But this particular evening when I stuck my head out to see when they'd be ready for the food, both of them were ignoring the fire and staring bemusedly at the building opposite.

Curious to see what had caught their attention, I padded quietly up beside Paul and looked, too. And there in the apartment obliquely across from us a girl stood just inside her own balcony doors doing stretching and bending exercises. She was a stunning girl, tall and dark and clad in a black leotard.

"Now I've seen everything," I said. "The two of you ogling like moonstruck teen-agers."

Paul started and looked embarrassed, but George wasn't the least bit discomposed.

"We weren't ogling, Myra," he said. "We were admiring. And there's no age limit on that."

"Lucky for you," I said, "because at the age you two are that's about all you can do. Anyway, call me when the fire's ready. *If* you can bring yourself to think about mundane things like that." And, laughing and shaking my head, I went back into the apartment to share the joke with Sheila.

Paul finally got the fire burned down the way he wanted it, cooked the steaks, and the four of us settled down to eat. I forget what we talked about, but it wasn't anything serious or important. And the Smallwoods made their excuses shortly afterward and left.

"We'll have to do this sometime again soon," Paul said after he'd closed the door behind them. "When they can stay longer."

"We may not have the chance," I said. "It's only a matter of time before they break up."

"What makes you say that? Did Sheila tell you something?"

"No," I said. "But I saw the way they acted. Very strained and formal. *And*," I added significantly, "she got very uptight when I told her about you two 'admiring' that girl. If she was as sure of George as I am of you, she'd have found it as funny as I did."

Paul regarded me quizzically. "You really did think that was funny, didn't you?" he said. "You know, Myra, I'm not at all sure that's very flattering."

Flattering or not, I still thought it was funny two days later and couldn't resist needling Paul slightly when he came home that evening from work.

"I'm sorry to tell you this," I said. "But I saw that girl you 'admired' so much on the phone today. And from the way she kept playing with the cord and smiling a little cat's smile while she was talking, it had to be a man she was talking to. A special man, too, because afterwards she got out her ironing board and started to iron a party dress."

Paul paused in the middle of taking off his coat. "What did you do, Myra," he said, "spend all day spying on her?"

"No," I said, "of course not. But she practically lives in front of those glass doors and never draws her drapes. And I'm out on our balcony a lot. You know how I am about fresh air. So I couldn't help but see what she was doing."

"I see," Paul said. He finished taking off his coat, hung it up, and went into the living room, loosening his tie.

I followed him. "Anyway," I said, "seeing her getting ready for her date gave me an idea. I've got a special man, too. So I got out *my* iron and ironed *my* party dress, figuring we could make a night of it, too."

Paul hesitated and even before he spoke I knew it hadn't worked. "Gee, Myra," he said, "I wish we could. And maybe we can tomorrow. But tonight I have to go back to the office."

"Go back to the office? In heaven's name why? You haven't worked overtime since your last promotion and that was years ago."

"I know," Paul said. "But workloads are building up, and the old man thinks the senior staff should set an example by putting in the same hours as the troops. I don't like the idea, but unfortunately he's the boss."

"So you may be working other nights as well," I said, trying not to sound desolate.

Paul nodded slowly. "Possibly," he said. "It all depends on what happens tonight."

On the optimistic assumption we wouldn't be eating in, I hadn't laid anything out for dinner. But I threw something together out of a couple of cans plus a frozen entree that didn't turn out too badly—although from the way Paul gulped his down it might have been ashes.

He left almost as soon as he'd finished eating, giving me a peck on the cheek as he went out the door. "Don't wait up," he said. "God knows when I'll be done."

"Sure," I said and closed the door after him. Then I turned back to the empty apartment. God, alone here all day and now all evening, too. It was almost too much to bear. Still, there it was, and I might as well make the best of it.

The first thing I did was turn off the air conditioner and start opening up the apartment. I felt better after I'd done that, less as if I were living in a closed-in shell sealed off from the rest of the world. Fortunately, too, there was a cool breeze coming in from the lake, and I stepped out onto the balcony to savor it.

Without my really willing it, my eyes slid over to the girl's apartment. She still hadn't drawn her drapes and I could see her clearly through the balcony doors, perched on the edge of a sofa so she wouldn't wrinkle her dress, and leafing through a magazine while she waited for her date to call.

I smiled wryly into the night. Enjoy it while you can, dear, because it doesn't last long. And when it's over, there isn't much to look forward to.

I rolled over in bed and rose on one elbow as Paul came in. He didn't turn on the lights but began to undress quickly in the dark.

"Hi," I said.

He made a startled movement. "I didn't mean to wake you," he said.

"I wasn't really asleep," I said. "What time is it?"

"Late," Paul said and went on undressing.

"I tried to call you earlier," I said. "Around nine. But nobody answered the phone."

"That must have been while I was in the boss's office," he said. "Sorry. Why did you call?"

"I just wanted to talk," I said. We were silent a moment. Then I said, "Will you have to work more nights?"

"I'm afraid so. Two, maybe three nights a week."

"For how long?"

"For as long as it lasts. But not tomorrow, though. I said we had something planned and I couldn't possibly get out of it."

"Well, if that's the way you feel about it, forget it."

"That's not the way I feel about it," Paul said testily. "That's the way I *explained* it." He found his pajamas and started to put them on. "What did you do while I was gone?" he said.

"Nothing much," I said. "I *was* right about that girl across the way, though. Her boy friend picked her up shortly after you left for the office."

"Look, Myra," Paul said, getting into bed, "do me a favor, will you? Forget about that girl. A joke's a joke, but this one is beginning to wear a little thin."

"Sure," I said. I hesitated a moment, then moved closer to him. But he only groaned and rolled over on his side away from me. "God,

I'm tired," he said. And a few minutes later I heard his deep regular breathing.

After a while I slept myself.

The next morning the cleaning lady came in to do the heavy work. I could have done it myself, should have, in fact. But I'd always had her to help at the house, and sheer inertia kept me from letting her go now that I no longer needed her. In any case, she came and I went out on the balcony to be out of her way. And so it was that I came to see the girl across the way once more.

It was late when she rose—close to noon—and she padded out from her bedroom to stand just inside her balcony doors and stretch like a great cat. Even without makeup and with her hair in a disarray from the night's sleep, there was just one word to describe her and that's the one I used before—stunning. I couldn't blame Paul for staring at her. If I'd been a man, I wouldn't have been content with just staring; I'd have gone over and met her.

The cleaning woman called me inside then. But I saw her later in the day. She looked as if she'd just come in from shopping, because she was dressed for the street and carried a long flat box that she placed on the coffee table in front of her sofa and began to unpack carefully. It looked also as if things between her and her boy friend were going to get interesting before long, because what she held up to admire was a long filmy negligee.

So, of course, that evening while I was waiting for Paul to finish dressing, I couldn't resist going to the balcony and looking over at her. But the negligee was nowhere in evidence. She sat on the sofa again as she had the night before, but dressed this time in her bathrobe and with her hair in curlers.

What? I thought. No date tonight? Well, we can't be winners all the time, honey, and tonight's *my* night to howl.

But somehow the evening didn't turn out the way I'd hoped. We went to what had been our favorite restaurant, but it had been years since we'd been there last and it wasn't the same as we remembered. Or maybe we weren't the same. Or maybe it was just that the evening wasn't the spontaneous spur-of-the-moment affair I had intended. But whatever the reason, we didn't really enjoy ourselves and came home early.

More than a little disappointed, I slipped off my dress, pulled my robe over my slip, and went out onto the balcony to catch the last of the lake breeze. After a few moments Paul came out to stand beside me.

"Sorry the evening was such a flop," he said.

"It wasn't anybody's fault," I said. "It just happened that way. And," I added, nodding toward the other building where the dark-haired girl was visibly boredly watching TV, "at least I had a better evening than she did."

"Myra," Paul said, "I thought we agreed you weren't going to keep dragging that up."

"I'm not dragging anything up," I said. "I just commented that she didn't have a date tonight." After a moment I added thoughtfully, "And that's odd."

"Myra!"

"Don't 'Myra' me," I said. "It *is* odd, because a girl that good-looking shouldn't have any difficulty getting all the dates she wanted."

"Maybe she just didn't want one tonight," Paul said.

"No," I said, shaking my head, "that's not it. Because she's bored silly over there."

"Well, whatever the reason then," Paul said, taking my elbow firmly to lead me back into the apartment, "it's still no business of yours. Now come to bed. I've got a big day ahead of me tomorrow."

He was right, of course. It *was* no business of mine. But she'd piqued my curiosity, and I knew I wouldn't be content until it was satisfied.

I didn't see the girl at all the following day. I glanced over her way a couple of times, of course, but either she was out or our schedules didn't mesh. That evening, though, as I was opening up the apartment again after Paul had gone, I noticed her lights were on and that the drapes covering her balcony doors were unpulled. I hesitated a fraction of a second, then, flicking off the lights behind me, stepped out onto the darkened balcony for a better view.

For a while nothing stirred in the other apartment, but then just when I least expected it she moved in from the side outside my line of vision and began to rearrange things on the coffee table.

It was hard to tell what she had planned for the evening because she was dressed in a long housecoat, which could mean anything—or nothing. I felt a stir of encouragement, though, when she suddenly broke off what she was doing and moved purposefully out of my line of vision again. Obviously, she'd gone to answer the door. So the housecoat had to mean that they intended to spend the night in.

I was proved right a few minutes later when she reappeared behind the balcony doors, mussed and rumpled and laughing. I craned forward, waiting for her lover to join her so I could get a good look at him. But then suddenly she reached up and abruptly drew the drapes together.

I took an involuntary step backward as if physically affronted. A couple of seconds later, though, I realized there couldn't be anything personal in it. Looking out from the light, she couldn't possibly have seen me in the dark. Still, it was curious that she'd picked that particular moment to shut off her apartment. And it made me more curious than ever to get to the bottom of things over there.

It took me another two weeks of patient observation, but then I had my answer. And, of course, something this good I had to pass onto someone. Which is why I told Paul.

It was on another Saturday. He was back out on the balcony, fiddling with the grill, and the girl across the way was back doing her stretching and bending exercises where the whole world could see.

"Admiring again?" I said, stepping out to join Paul.

He had the grace to blush. I smiled and moved over to the railing. "It's taken a while," I said. "But I've finally figured her out. She's having an affair with a married man."

I wasn't prepared for the vehemence of Paul's response. "For God's sake, Myra," he exclaimed, "how can you say a thing like that about someone you've never met and don't know the first thing about?"

"Oh, I know quite a lot about her," I said. "I've been watching her. And she has a very strange on-again off-again love life. Three, sometimes four evenings a week she's given a terrific rush, but the rest of the time she's left to herself. And," I added significantly, "those dates are always on the same nights and never on a weekend. Now, how do you explain that those are the nights her boy friend has an excuse to be away from his family?"

"I wouldn't even try to explain it," Paul said, "because it's none of my business. What is my business, though, is that you seem to be spending all your time spying on a neighbor."

"That's not true," I said. "I was just curious and I did a little checking to satisfy that curiosity. But that's all."

" 'But that's all,' " Paul said. He shook his head. "Seriously, Myra, I've been worried about you ever since we moved here. You've had entirely too much time on your hands. And that's not healthy."

"It would help," I said bitterly, "if you spent a little more time around here yourself. For all I see of you I might as well not have a husband."

He looked away. "If I could change things," he said, "I would. But I can't."

I put my hand out to touch his arm. "I didn't mean that," I said. "I don't know what I'd do without you."

Paul still wouldn't look at me. "Please, Myra," he said, "just find something to get you out of the apartment once in a while. And keep your mind off that girl."

"Don't worry," I said. "I'll find something. I promise."

It's funny how things work out. Because if I hadn't made that promise to Paul it never would have occurred to me to call Sheila Smallwood. And if I hadn't called Sheila, none of the rest would have happened, either.

"I don't know why I didn't think of this before," I said to Sheila when I had her on the line. "But it's foolish for both of us to sit home alone. So why don't we take in a movie or something while Paul and George are working tonight?"

There was a long moment of silence from Sheila's end of the line. Then: "I don't know what you mean, Myra. George hasn't worked nights in years. Has Paul?"

"Yes," I said slowly. "I thought all the senior staff were."

"Well, that's the first I've heard of it," Sheila said. "Although," she added too hastily, "just because George isn't working, that doesn't mean others aren't. And we can still get together if you like. Even if only to talk—"

"No," I said, putting the phone down. "No."

God, what a fool I'd been! But isn't that what they say? The wife is always the last one to know?

More sick than angry, I mechanically went through the routine of opening up the balcony doors, then just sat out there and let the darkness settle around me.

Paul and another woman! Because, of course, what else could it be? Some chit of a girl probably, from the office or—

My attention was diverted despite myself by a sudden movement in the building across the way—the girl pulling her drapes closed to signal the arrival of her lover.

I started to look away, no longer interested. But then my eyes swung back to those closed drapes and I was caught by a sudden thought. Why was she always so careful to close them *the moment her lover arrived?* Was it modesty? Or was it that she knew someone was watching–someone who would recognize the lover and spoil their little game?

Because the lover was Paul.

No, I told myself, that was crazy. Things like that just didn't happen. But even then other thoughts were crowding in: hadn't the start of her affair coincided with the start of Paul's working nights? Hadn't she been stuck home alone the one night Paul had taken me out? And the other nights her lover had called, weren't those also nights Paul had "worked?" I was sure they were.

Until at last I sat there faced with the awful realization that for the last month I'd been watching another woman carry on an affair with my husband.

That night I lay stiff and still, pretending sleep when Paul came in. The next morning, too, I waited until I was sure he was gone before getting up. Sooner or later I was going to have to face him, I knew. But not just yet, not until I had planned what I had to do next. Because a night of thinking it over–and over and over–had convinced me that the last thing I wanted was to lose Paul.

Not that things could ever be the same between us. But a divorce would leave me with nothing but an empty apartment and an emptier life. And that, above all, was what I didn't want.

The big question, though, was how could I prevent it? There was always the chance, of course, that if I pretended not to have noticed anything, the affair would burn itself out. It was an awfully big maybe, though, and could I really sit here alone night after night knowing what was going on across the way? But what other choices did I have?

Not many, I'm afraid. I couldn't compete with the girl on her own terms. Even in my heyday 20 years before I'd have been no match for her, and I didn't have to look in a mirror to know that the years in between hadn't been altogether kind. I didn't dare risk an out-and-out confrontation with Paul, either. At this stage of the game, forced to make a choice, he was probably infatuated enough to choose her.

Bitterly I went to the balcony and stared across. The girl had risen early today and was out on her own balcony smoking a before-breakfast cigarette. Damn, damn, damn you, I thought, wishing her ugly or dead or both.

Almost as if the thought had reached across to her, she straightened with insolent grace, flipped away the cigarette, and strolled casually back into her apartment. Deliberately she left the drapes open and as I watched her move about it came to me. What I could do to beat her.

It was early that evening when I heard Paul come in. I got up from where I was sitting on the balcony and went back to our bedroom where he was in the process of unbuttoning his shirt.

"Hi," he said. "I didn't think you were home." He finished unbuttoning the shirt and pulled it off. "I just have time to change and run right back. There are some people in from Washington and I have to have dinner with them and then go over the final specs for a new contract." He broke off when he saw my face. "What's the matter?" he said. "Is something wrong?"

I shook my head and forced myself to smile. "No," I said. "I'm just disappointed. I'd hoped you'd be staying home tonight."

Paul mumbled something and turned to pick out a fresh tie. I came over, as I always did, found one that matched his suit and handed it to him.

"Would you like to hear something funny?" I said. "I was watching that girl across the way this afternoon—"

"Myra!" Paul said. "You said you were going to stop that."

"I know," I said. "And I really intended to. But then her lover showed up and I couldn't resist getting a peek at him."

Paul paused with his tie half knotted. "Her lover?"

"Well, it certainly wasn't her brother—not the way they carried on. But the funny part is that I must have been wrong about his being married. Actually he's quite young. And good-looking, too."

Paul didn't say anything, so I went on, as if the idea had just occurred to me. "But then maybe I wasn't wrong after all. Wouldn't it be something if she had a married lover to pay her bills and then was two-timing him with this younger one?"

"Yes," Paul said, and he pulled the knot in his tie tight with an abrupt, almost angry gesture.

After he had gone, I sat on the darkened balcony, waiting. Over across the way the girl waited, too. Then the by now familiar ritual began as she went to answer her door.

This time, though, it was quite a while before she came back into view, and there was now a tenseness and stiffness about her movements that had never been there before. She reached up to pull the drapes closed, then stopped abruptly in mid-act to turn and shout something back at her unseen companion. I couldn't hear the words, of course. But I could see the expression on her face, and it was angry. Good. This was even better than I'd hoped for when I'd deliberately sowed seeds of suspicion in Paul's mind.

Then as I watched, a hand lashed out from beyond the drapes to slap the girl savagely. She reeled back, stumbled, and fell toward the coffee table.

The story made quite a splash in the papers the next day: GIRL MURDERED IN LUXURY APARTMENT. I made a point of reading it to Paul at the table that evening.

"Good lord, Paul," I said, "it's that girl across the way! Look, here's her picture. And it says that the back of her head was smashed in—either from striking the edge of the coffee table or from a blow from some kind of club."

I looked up, pretending not to notice his white face and stricken expression. "I was right about her," I said. "She was two-timing somebody and he found out and killed her. I think I ought to go to the police."

"No," Paul said sharply. "What I mean is," he went on as I looked at him curiously, "you couldn't really tell them anything. Like names or who the men are. The police might even think you were making it up." He shook his head. "It's just better not to get involved."

I sighed. "I suppose you're right," I said and put the paper aside. "Do you have to work tonight?"

He shook his head again. "No. That's all over."

"I'm glad," I said. "It's good to have you back."

Paul nodded and mumbled an excuse to go over to the liquor cabinet and pour himself his third stiff drink of the evening.

Poor Paul. I hope he isn't going to turn into an alcoholic over this—especially since he has no real reason to. Because I sat there for a long time that night watching the girl's apartment after she'd fallen. And I saw her get up again. From the way she staggered though, it was obvious she was alone and either hurt or at least groggy.

So it had been a simple matter, while Paul was off somewhere walking out his anger and frustration, to slip over to the other building, find the girl's apartment, and just to make sure he was never tempted again, finish what he'd begun.

Hugh Pentecost

Jericho and the Studio Murders

John Jericho, painter by profession and detective by instinct and force of circumstance, investigates the Greenwich Village murder of a tycoon's son. But this murder has a dangerous, large-scale potential: if Jericho doesn't find the killer in a few hours, the waterfront will erupt like a volcano, explode like a bomb, in bloody violence ...

Detective: JOHN JERICHO

It was said of J. C. Cordell that he owned half of the world—oil, electronics, airlines, shipping, hotels, you name it. In an article about him Cordell was quoted as saying that he had the only three things in the world that could matter to any man. "I have my son, my health, and the wealth and power to live and do exactly as I please," he told his interviewer.

On a warm lovely summer day J. C. Cordell was deprived of one of those assets. His son lay dead in a small studio-apartment in New York's Greenwich Village, with three bullet holes in his head. "The police suspect gangland revenge," an early radio report informed the world.

It revived an old waterfront story—old by at least two years. Special guards in the employ of J. C. Cordell had trapped some men trying to steal a cargo of expensive watch mechanisms from the hold of one of Cordell's ships. The guards had opened fire and one of the thieves was killed. The dead man turned out to be Mike Roberts, son of the reputed czar of the waterfront underworld, Reno Roberts. The word was out at the time that Reno Roberts would even that score with J. C. Cordell, but two years had gone by without reprisals, and Roberts' threats were forgotten.

Now J. C.'s only child, Paul Cordell, was dead, and the waterfront and the Village were alive with police trying to pin a Murder One rap on Reno Roberts and his men.

It was almost overlooked in the heat of that climate that a second man had died in the Village studio, also of gunshot wounds. He was the artist who lived there. Richard Sheridan was considered to have been an innocent and unfortunate bystander. It turned out that J. C. Cordell indulged himself in the buying of paintings and sculpture. He had come across the work of Richard Sheridan in a Madison Avenue gallery, been impressed, and had commissioned Sheridan to paint a portrait of his son.

Paul Cordell had gone to Sheridan's studio in the Village for a series of sittings. Ever since the shooting of Reno Roberts' son on the waterfront and Roberts' threats, Paul Cordell had been accompanied everywhere by a bodyguard.

One had to assume that the tensions had relaxed after two years. The bodyguard, a private eye named Jake Martin, had grown fat and careless on his assignment. He had waited outside dozens of places where Paul was gambling or involved in one kind of party or another. Jake Martin's life was almost entirely made up of waiting for Paul Cordell to satisfy his various appetites.

On that particular summer day Paul had told Martin that his sitting for Sheridan would last a couple of hours. Certain that no one had followed them to Sheridan's studio, Martin had gone across the street to a bar to have himself a few beers. It was a hot day. While Martin was away from his post a killer had struck, wasting Paul Cordell and Richard Sheridan, the innocent bystander.

Telephone lines were busy with the story. J. C. Cordell was in touch with the Mayor, the Waterfront Commission, the F.B.I. Reno Roberts was going to have to pay for this. The Mayor, in turn, was in touch with the Police Commissioner. Unless a cap was put on this case, fast, bloody waterfront violence was facing them. A girl who had been with Paul Cordell only the night before called her friends. My God, did you hear what happened to Paul Cordell? And the news had spread like wildfire. . .

John Jericho was not in the habit of listening to the radio. He didn't own a television set. He had been working with a kind of burning concentration on a painting in his studio in Jefferson Mews at the exact moment when Paul Cordell and Richard Sheridan had been wiped out only a few houses down the block. When Jericho, six feet four inches of solid muscle, his red hair and red beard giving him the look of an old Viking warrior, got absorbed in a painting, the sky could have fallen in on Chicken Little and he wouldn't have been remotely aware of it.

Exhausted after the last brilliant strokes on his canvas, Jericho had thrown himself down on his bed and slept. An unfamiliar creak in a floorboard would have awakened him instantly. He heard the telephone ring, but it was a nuisance, so he ignored it. But the caller was persistent, dialing the number every five minutes over a long stretch of time. Finally, outraged, Jericho reached for the instrument on his bedside table and shouted an angry hello.

"Mr. Jericho?" It was an unsteady female voice. "This is Amanda Kent."

"Oh, for God's sake, Amanda." Jericho glanced at his wrist watch. "It's after one o'clock in the morning!"

"Did you hear what happened to Rick Sheridan?" the girl asked.

It was, perhaps, a notable question because all the people who had made all the phone calls during the evening had always asked: "What happened to Paul Cordell?"

Amanda Kent, Jericho had heard, had been desperately in love with Rick Sheridan. To her Paul Cordell was a nobody, a zero.

To Jericho, Greenwich Village was a small town in which he lived, not a geographical segment of a huge metropolis. He knew the shopkeepers, the bartenders and restaurant people, the artists and writers. He knew the cops. He knew the waterfront people who lived on the fringes of his "village." The ships and the men who worked on the docks had been the subject matter of many of his paintings. He ignored the new drug culture. He walked the streets at any time of day or night without any fear of muggers. He was too formidable a figure to invite violence.

A little before two o'clock on the morning of Amanda Kent's phone call Jericho walked into the neighborhood police station and into the office of Lieutenant Pat Carmody. Carmody, a ruddy Irishman with a bawdy wit when he wasn't troubled, was an old friend. On this morning he was troubled. He was frowning at a sheaf of reports, a patrolman at his elbow. He waved at Jericho, gave the patrolman some orders, and leaned back in his chair.

"I expected you'd be showing up sooner or later, Johnny," he said. "Young Sheridan was a friend of yours, I know."

"More than a friend," Jericho said. "A protégé, you might say. He mattered to me, Pat. What exactly happened?"

"He was painting a portrait of Paul Cordell, J. C. Cordell's son," Carmody said. "Damn good from what's there left to see. You remember the rumble between J. C. Cordell and Reno Roberts?"

Jericho nodded.

"Ever since Roberts' son was shot by Cordell's watchmen, Paul Cordell has had a bodyguard—followed him everywhere, like Mary's little lamb. He was a lamb this afternoon, all right, while Paul sat for his portrait. Wandered off to pour a couple. Hell, there hadn't been any trouble for two years. Anyway, someone persuaded Sheridan to open his studio door and whoever it was blasted Paul Cordell and him. No witnesses, nobody saw anyone. No one admits hearing the shots. Lot of neighbors at work that time of day. Clean hit and run."

"And you think it was Roberts' man?"

"Who else?" Carmody shrugged. "Roberts bided his time, then ordered a kill. Like always, when there's trouble on the waterfront, Reno was at his house on the Jersey coast with a dozen people to alibi him. Not that he would pull the trigger himself. He probably imported a hit-man from someplace out of the city, somebody who's long gone by now."

"No solid leads?"

"You mean something like fingerprints?" Carmody made a wry face. "Nothing. No gun. Meanwhile the town is starting to boil. J. C. Cordell isn't going to wait for us to solve the case. There's going to be a war, Cordell versus Roberts. There's going to be a lot of blood spilled unless we can come up with the killer in the next few hours."

Jericho pounded on the door of Amanda Kent's apartment on Jane Street. He could see a little streak of light under the door. Amanda, he told himself, would not be sleeping this night.

She opened the door for him eventually and stood facing him, wearing some sort of flimsy negligee that revealed her magnificent body. Amanda was a model, and stacked away in Jericho's studio were dozens of sketches of her body, drawn when she had posed for him professionally.

Amanda's physical perfection was marred now by the fact that she was sporting a magnificent black eye.

"Mr. Jericho!" she cried, her voice muffled, and hurled herself into his arms.

He eased her back into the apartment, her blonde head buried against his chest. The small living room was something of a shambles—liquor glasses and bottles upturned on a small coffee table, ashtrays overflowing with cigarette butts, sketch-pad drawings scattered everywhere. Looking down over the girl's shoulder Jericho recognized Rick Sheridan's distinctive technique. Rick had evidently made dozens of drawings of Amanda's perfections.

Jericho settled Amanda on the couch and passed her the box of tissues on the coffee table.

"What happened to your eye?" he asked.

She gave him a twisted little-girl smile. "I bumped into a door," she said.

Her face crinkled into grief again. "Oh, God, Mr. Jericho, he was so young, so great, he was going so far!"

"I haven't come here to join you in a wake," Jericho said. He was remembering that after you had savored Amanda's physical perfection you were confronted with a very dull girl who delighted in cliché and hyperbole. "Why did you call me, Amanda?"

"Because I thought Rick's friends ought to know what happened to him," she said. "The radio and television are only talking about this gangster who was killed—as if Rick hadn't even been there. I thought his friends—"

"You've got it wrong," Jericho said. "It wasn't a gangster who was killed, it was a gangster they think did the killing."

"Only Rick matters to me," Amanda said. "Oh, God!" She looked up at him through one good eye and one badly swollen one. "There's no reason any more for it to be a secret, Mr. Jericho. You see, Rick and I were having a—a—thing."

"Lucky Rick," Jericho said. "But spare me the details, Amanda. If you were that intimate with Rick you might be able to supply some information. Who would have wanted to kill Rick?"

Her good eye widened. "Nobody! It was this Cordell man they were after, wasn't it? Rick was shot because he could identify the killer. Isn't that the way it was?"

"Maybe," Jericho said. He appeared to be looking away into the distance somewhere. "But there's a chance it may have been some other way, doll. Did Rick have a row with anyone? Was there some girl who was jealous of the—the 'thing' you and Rick were having?"

"I was everything to Rick," Amanda said. "There hadn't been any other girl for a long, long time. Rick didn't have rows with people, either. He was the kindest, gentlest, sweetest—"

"He had the makings of a great painter," Jericho said. "*That's* the tragedy of it."

There was the sound of a key in the front-door lock. Jericho turned and saw a huge young man carrying a small glass jar in a hamlike hand.

"Oh, gee, you got company," the young man said. "How are you, Mr. Jericho?"

Jericho searched for the young man's name in his memory and came up with it. Val Kramer. He had grown up in the Village and was close to being retarded. There had been moves to exploit his size and extraordinary strength. Someone had tried to make a fighter out of him, but he proved hopeless. Much smaller but faster and brighter men had cut him to ribbons.

He'd been tried as a wrestler, but he was no actor, the key to success in the wrestling game, and his only thought was to crush and possibly kill his opponents. He couldn't get matches. He was now, Jericho remembered, a kind of handyman and bouncer for a rather disreputable saloon on Seventh Avenue.

"I couldn't find a meat market open noplace, love," the giant said to Amanda. He grinned shyly at Jericho. "For her eye, you know." He advanced on the girl, holding out the glass jar. "Friend of mine runs a drug store on Hudson Street. I got him up and he gave me this."

"What is it?" Amanda asked.

Jericho saw what it was. There was a wormlike creature in the jar. Long ago leeches had been used to bleed people—the medical fashion of the time—and particularly to suck the black blood out of bruised eyes.

"You must put this little guy on your eye," Val explained to Amanda, "and he sucks out all the blues and purples." He was unscrewing the lid of the glass jar, fumbling with his clumsy fingers for the slimy slug.

Jericho felt a faint shudder of revulsion run over him. He remembered hacking his way through a Korean swamp with those dreadful bloodsuckers fastened to his chest, his arms, his legs.

Somehow the giant boy-man had Amanda helpless on the couch, pinioned by the weight of his body while he held her head still with his left hand and aimed the loathsome leech at her black eye with his right. Amanda screamed at him.

"No, Val! Please! No, *no!*"

"It's for your own good, Manda," the giant crooned at her.

"No!"

Then Val Kramer did an extraordinary thing. He lowered his head and fastened his mouth on Amanda's, smothering her scream. For a moment she resisted him, kicking and pounding at him with her fists. And then, suddenly, she was just as eagerly accepting him as she had been resisting, her arms locked around his neck. Gently Val managed to release himself and without any further outcry from Amanda placed the repulsive leech on her swollen eye.

"Have you fixed up in no time," Val said.

He stood up. Amanda lay still, her eyes closed, the leech swelling and growing larger as it sucked her blood.

Val Kramer gave Jericho a sheepish grin. "It's hard to convince anyone what's good for them," he said. "I gave Manda that black eye, so I'm responsible for fixing it up."

"She said she bumped into something," Jericho said.

"This," Kramer said, grinning down at his huge fist. "She was acting crazy about this artist fellow that got shot. She was going to run over there, get mixed up with the cops and all. I had to try to stop her, and somehow, in trying, I kind of backhanded her alongside the eye. I didn't mean to, of course."

"Of course," Jericho said. "But it was natural for her to want to go to Rick, wasn't it? She tells me they were pretty close."

Val Kramer looked up and the smile was gone from his face. "She belongs to me, Jericho," he said. "I can turn her on or off. You saw that just now, didn't you? She belongs to me."

Jericho took a deep breath and let it out in a long sigh. "Well, I'm sorry to have interfered with your blood-letting, Val," he said. He looked at Amanda, lying so still on the couch, her eyes closed, the leech swelling like an obscene infection. "I came because she called me."

"That was before I told her she could only get in trouble with Roberts' people if she stuck her nose in," Kramer said. "We appreciate your coming, though."

"My pleasure," Jericho said. "When Amanda comes to, tell her that."

Jericho walked west from Jane Street toward the waterfront. The scene in Amanda's apartment was something out of Grand Guignol, he thought. The girl, grief-stricken for a lost love, suddenly turned on by that giant child, submitting to his kiss, and to the disgusting creature held fixed on her eye. Jericho supposed that reactions to the physical were Amanda's whole life.

There was a house near the abandoned West Side Highway which Jericho had visited before. During a longshoremen's strike some years ago Jericho had done drawings and paintings of the violence, and he had met Reno Roberts and been invited to an incredible

Italian dinner given by the crime boss. Reno Roberts had admired Jericho's size, his bawdy humor, and in particular his ability to draw extraordinary caricatures of the dinner guests. Jericho had earned a pass to the gangster's presence that night and he decided to use it now.

The security was unexpectedly tight. More than a block from the house Jericho was picked up by two of Roberts' men who recognized him.

"Better not try to see Reno this morning," they told him. "You heard what happened?"

"That's why I'm here," Jericho said. "I might be able to help him."

"He don't need no help," one of the men said.

"Everybody can always use help," Jericho said. "Ask Reno to let me see him for five minutes."

Reno Roberts was a short squat man, bald, with burning black eyes that were hot with anger when Jericho was ushered into his presence. A large diamond ring on a stubby finger glittered in the light from a desk lamp.

"Not a time for fun and games, Johnny boy," he said. "Pasquale says you want to help. What help? Can you turn off the cops?"

"Maybe," Jericho said.

"Can you turn off J. C. Cordell? Because he has his own army which won't wait for the police. A lot of us are going to die on both sides in the next forty-eight hours. I am supposed to have killed Paul Cordell."

"But you didn't," Jericho said.

"What makes you think I didn't?" Reno asked, his eyes narrowed. "J. C.'s people killed my boy Michael. We don't let such things pass in my world."

"But you did," Jericho said. "You let two years pass. You didn't strike when your anger was hot. Why? I'm guessing it was because your boy was involved in an unauthorized theft. The guards on Cordell's pier only did their duty. They didn't know whom they were shooting. You were filled with grief and sorrow, but there was no cause for revenge. Your boy pulled a stupid stunt and paid the price for it."

"Not a bad guess," Reno said.

"So why strike back now, after two years?" Jericho asked. "And why do it so stupidly? That's not your style."

"Why stupidly?" Reno asked, his eyes bright.

"It would have been easy to finger Paul Cordell without having a witness present," Jericho said. "Why do it when it was also necessary to kill a completely innocent man? Why do it in broad daylight in a building where there might be other witnesses? Why choose a moment when Paul Cordell's bodyguard might walk in on you before the job was done? All those risks, Reno, when it could have been done with no risks. Not your style. Not professional."

"Can you convince the cops and J. C. Cordell of that?" Reno asked.

"By producing the killer," Jericho said.

Reno leaned forward in his chair. "You know who it was?"

"A hunch, Reno. But I need your help."

"What kind of help?"

"I need you to persuade someone to talk to me without any holding back."

"Name him," Reno said. "And why are you doing this for me, Johnny boy? You don't owe me anything."

"Rick Sheridan was my friend. I owe him," Jericho said.

"I don't talk about my customers," Florio, proprietor of Florio's Bar & Grill, said to Jericho. He was a tall, thin, dark man who looked older than his 50 years. "You come into my place with some guy's wife and I don't talk about it. It's none of my business."

"But Reno has made it clear to you that you must talk," Jericho said.

"I would rather cut out my tongue than betray my friends," Florio said. "You are a friend of the cops."

"Didn't Reno tell you that I am also his friend?"

"The heat is on Reno. He would do anything to take it off."

"Maybe the people I want to talk about are not friends you would cut out your tongue to keep from betraying," Jericho said. "One of them works for you now and then. Val Kramer."

Florio's face relaxed.

"Poor dumb kid," he said. "Yeah, he fills in behind the bar when I'm shorthanded."

"Yesterday?"

"From five in the afternoon till midnight. My regular bartender was home with the flu."

"My friend Rick Sheridan was murdered at about four in the afternoon. Did you know Rick?"

"Sure, I knew him. He came in here three, four times a week. A great guy. Very bad luck for him he was there when they hit Paul Cordell."

"If that's what happened," Jericho said. "Did you know Rick's girl, Amanda Kent?"

Florio laughed. "Rick's girl? He couldn't stand the sight of her. He used her as a model, I guess. She fell for him. She's a crazy kid, but he wanted no part of her. Only a couple of nights ago he told her off, right here in my place. He told her to get lost, to leave him alone."

"What do you know about Amanda Kent and Val Kramer? Is Val one of her lovers?"

"Oh, he was gone on her. Over his head gone. He followed her around like some faithful collie dog. But she had no time for him." Florio's face clouded. "Funny thing. She came in here with Val yesterday—at five o'clock—when he came on the job. She stayed here all night, till he went off at midnight. She left here with him then. When they came in at five we hadn't heard anything about the shooting. The news came over the radio a little before seven. Amanda went into a kind of hysterics, but she didn't leave. Some of the customers sat with her, tried to console her. You want to know who they were?"

Jericho shook his head slowly.

"I don't think so," he said. "She had hysterics, but she waited for Val Kramer to finish his tour, some five hours after she heard the news on the radio?"

"Yeah. I suppose—well, I don't know exactly what I suppose. Maybe she was afraid to go home. Maybe she thought Reno's boys might be after anyone who might have been around Sheridan's place at the time of the shooting."

"Are you saying Amanda was around Rick's studio at four o'clock?"

Florio shrugged. "I don't know for sure, Mr. Jericho. When the news came on the radio she had, like I told you, hysterics. She kept saying, over and over, 'I just saw him a little while ago!' "

"Did she get potted while she waited for Kramer?"

"Funny you should ask," Florio said, "because I remember being surprised that she didn't. She usually drank a lot. I figured she'd really go overboard when she heard about Rick Sheridan. But she didn't. She stayed cold-sober."

"And waited for Kramer?"

"Val would make her a perfect bodyguard," Florio said. "He's too stupid to be afraid of anybody or anything."

The gray light of dawn was sifting through the city's canyons when Jericho again knocked on the door of Amanda Kent's Jane Street apartment. It was Val Kramer who opened the door.

"Gee, Mr. Jericho, you got some news for us?" he asked.

"Perhaps," Jericho said. "May I come in?"

"Sure. Come in," the childlike giant said. "Have some coffee? I just made a fresh pot of coffee."

"I'd like that," Jericho said, moving into the apartment. "How's Amanda?"

"She's fine," Kramer said, his smile almost jubilant. "That blood-sucker really did his thing."

"Would you believe it?" Amanda asked from the bedroom doorway. She was still wearing the see-through negligee, but the swollen and discolored eye had vanished. "That little sucker really sucked. You found out something, Mr. Jericho?"

Jericho took the mug of hot coffee Kramer brought him. "I found out who killed Rick and Paul Cordell," he said quietly.

"Who?" they asked simultaneously.

"One of you," Jericho said, very quietly. He took a cautious sip of the scalding-hot coffee.

The childlike giant giggled. "You gotta be kidding," he said.

"I was never more serious in my life, Val," Jericho said.

The room was deathly still. Kramer looked at Amanda who had suddenly braced herself against the doorframe.

"I don't think you should say things like that, Mr. Jericho," the girl said, her voice shaken. "Because it's crazy!"

"Oh, it's crazy enough," Jericho said. "Rick had turned you down, Amanda, and he had to be killed for that. How crazy can you get? I came here to get you to turn over the gun to me, whichever one of you had it. I can't put it off, friends. There is about to be a war on the streets in which dozens of innocent people will die. So hand it over."

Val Kramer made a slow hesitant move toward the pocket of his canvas jacket. He produced a small pearl-handled gun that was almost hidden in his massive hand. He pointed it at Jericho, clumsily, like a man unaccustomed to handling such a weapon.

"It's too bad you couldn't mind your own business, Mr. Jericho," he said.

"Amanda called me, asked me for help," Jericho said, not moving a muscle.

"No such thing!" Amanda protested. "You were Rick's friend. I thought you should know what happened to him."

"Six hours after you'd heard the news? Why didn't you call me from Florio's bar? You were there for five hours after you heard the news."

"I–I was hysterical. I didn't have my head together," Amanda said. "After I got home I began to think of friends of Rick's who ought to be told."

"You wanted me to nail Val, didn't you, Amanda? Because you were afraid of him. When he found out you'd called me he hit you. You didn't bump into any door, did you, Amanda?"

"So I killed him," Val said, in a strange little boy's voice. "He couldn't get away with what he did to Manda. I went to his studio and I told him he had to pay for what he'd done to Manda, so I killed him. And I killed the guy who was there, because he could tell on me. I didn't know it was Paul Cordell and that it would make a lot of trouble. And now I'm going to kill you, Mr. Jericho, because you can tell on me."

He lifted the gun a little so that it was aimed at Jericho's heart. Jericho threw the hot coffee full in the childlike giant's face. There was a roar of pain and Kramer dropped the gun as he lifted his hands to his scalded face. Then he lunged at Jericho.

It was a matter of strength against strength and skill. Jericho sidestepped the rush, and a savage chopping blow to Kramer's neck sent the giant crashing to the floor like a poled ox. He lay still, frighteningly still. Jericho bent down and picked up the little pearl-handled gun.

Then Amanda was clinging to him, weeping, "Oh, thank God, thank God!" she said. "I was so terrified of him!"

Jericho's fingers bit into her arms and held her away from him. "You scum," he said. It was more like a statement of fact than an angry expletive. "That poor guy would do anything on earth for you, including taking the rap for a murder you committed. Followed you around like a faithful collie dog, I was told. Followed you to Rick's studio yesterday afternoon. It was a habit with him—the faithful collie dog.

"He was too late to stop your killing a man who simply wasn't interested in what your body had to offer. 'Hell hath no fury—' He couldn't stop your killing, but he helped you get away. He took you to Florio's where he had to work. You stayed there for seven long hours. Why? Because you needed a bodyguard? Because you were grateful? No, because he had you cold and you knew you were going to have to do whatever he told you to do."

"No! No!" It was only a whisper.

"But you knew how to handle him, and you had to wait till it was possible. You knew that if you gave yourself to him he was yours forever, to handle as you pleased. You knew he would take the blame for you if the going got tough, no matter what. You waited for him all those hours in Florio's because until you could pretend that you cared for him he had you trapped. You took him home here and you offered him something he'd never really dreamed of having."

"I–I had no choice," Amanda said. "He killed Rick just like he said. I–"

"He hit you in the eye in some kind of struggle with you," Jericho said. "And because he really loves you, in his simple-minded and faithful way, he went out to find a piece of beef to put on your eye and when he saw there was no butcher shop open he found you that leech. While he was gone, you called me. You were already thinking of a way out. You would have fed me bits and pieces if I hadn't discovered them for myself. Unfortunately for you I found the right pieces and not the phony ones you'd have fed me."

"I swear to you–"

"It won't do, Amanda," Jericho said. "You're going out of here with me now, and just pray to God that your confession comes in time to stop blood from running in the gutters." He looked down at the unconscious giant. "And just pray that I can make that poor jerk believe that your body wasn't worth the price he was willing to pay. Get moving, Amanda."

"Q"

R o b e r t   B l o c h

The Man Who Never Did Anything Right

Wasn't it Gilbert K. Chesterton who asked, "Where hide a leaf?" And answered, "In a forest." And "Where murder a man?" And answered, "In a battle." Well, Robert Bloch goes further, much further—to the ultimate . . .

He came on duty promptly at ten o'clock.

Hanson was already waiting inside the door when he unlocked it, and Hanson was scowling.

"Late again," Hanson said. "I got a heavy date."

"But it's just ten now—here, look at my watch—"

Hanson brushed past him. "You never do anything right," he muttered. "Okay, into the cell, Shorty."

Hanson took the keys, locked him in, and went away.

And then he was alone in the room.

Hanson had called it a cell, and in a way it was. The room was too small, too hot, too bare. It had no windows, and the indirect lighting produced a constant glare. The only furniture was a table and one chair; there was no radio, no TV, nothing to read, not even a cot to rest on. He wasn't supposed to rest, of course: he was supposed to stay alert and wait for orders from the loudspeaker set high up in the wall.

That's all there was to it—just one hour of guard duty every night, from ten to eleven. All he had to do was wait for orders, and of course there never were any orders. It wasn't a hard assignment at all, but the button made him nervous.

It was just a small button, set in the wall under the loudspeaker. He could sit with his back to it if he liked and pretend it wasn't even there.

But it was there, and it made him nervous. One hour a night was about all he could take: one hour a night, sitting in that locked room with the little button.

The trick was to think about something else.

He sat down and reached for a cigarette, then remembered he didn't have any cigarettes. No smoking—that was one of the rules. No wonder Hanson had made that crack about it being a cell.

Maybe the routine was getting to Hanson too. Maybe he too was ready to flip. But no, Hanson wouldn't flip. He wasn't the flipping kind. Not handsome Hanson—that big ape, always talking about his heavy dates. He'd sure been in one hell of a hurry to get out tonight. And he'd had that nasty grin on his face, just as if he was still seeing Myrna.

But he wasn't, of course. Myrna wasn't Hanson's girl; she was *his* girl. She'd told him so last week, swore she was through with Hanson, said she'd given him the gate. From now on there'd be just the two of them, Myrna and himself.

And tonight, in just one hour, when he got out of here—

Then he remembered. Myrna had called and left a message for him. She couldn't see him tonight, she had a headache.

Headache. He had a headache, too. Particularly when he remembered Hanson's grin. Could it be that—?

No, she wouldn't doublecross him.

But Hanson would.

"You never do anything right," Hanson had said. And he'd grinned when he muttered it, grinned as though he had some kind of secret. He couldn't wait to lock him up, here in the cell.

"Okay, into the cell, Shorty."

Shorty. That was the part that really hurt.

Because he was short. He knew it, Hanson knew it, Myrna knew it.

But was it his fault he was a runt? Was that any excuse for being picked on, laughed at, tricked? He couldn't help being short any more than Hanson was responsible for being tall and good-looking. It wasn't fair.

He stood up, feeling the heat and the closeness in the little room. God, why didn't something happen? But there wasn't a sound. And he still had fifty minutes to go. Fifty minutes—that meant only ten minutes had passed. How could he stand it? How could he stand it, knowing that Hanson was out there, free? Hanson and Myrna, together, laughing at him in the cell, laughing at Shorty who never did anything right.

Think of something else, he told himself.

He found himself staring at the button.

The button, the small button in the wall.

He turned away, telling himself not to be nervous, to forget about the button. In a little less than fifty minutes he'd be out of here, he could phone Myrna, she'd tell him she loved him, and they'd laugh about his fears together.

Or was she laughing now? She and Hanson, together? Why try to fool himself—it was true, he was sure of it. That damned Hanson! He ought to be killed.

Think about that for a moment. Yes. Think about killing Hanson. The trouble was, he couldn't. Because he was Shorty. And Hanson was big and strong. There would never be a chance; none of them was ever allowed access to weapons, for obvious security reasons. Besides, he had never used a gun or a knife. He'd bungle the job for sure. "You never do anything right."

So Hanson would go on living and laughing and loving, while Shorty stayed here locked in the cell with the little button.

If only there was some way to kill Hanson, some way to commit the perfect crime!

But he wasn't smart enough to figure out anything like that, and he wasn't big enough or brave enough to carry it through.

He paced the tiny room, cursing under his breath. Perfect crime! There was no such thing. No matter how cleverly one planned it, there could always be a slipup somewhere along the line. The only perfect crime is one that nobody can ever possibly know about.

That's when he stopped, standing in front of the button, standing and staring.

There was a way. A way in which he could kill Hanson and nobody would ever know. Because nobody would ever be *left* to know.

He stood there for a moment, staring at the button, seeing it up close for what it really was. A little round world. But that didn't matter, as long as Hanson died.

He reached out, pressed

"Q"

Lawrence G. Blochman

The Killer with No Fingerprints

It was a knife job—a bloody one; and when the 64,000,000-to-1 fingerprint angle showed up, Lieutenant Max Ritter turned to his private medical examiner, Dr. Daniel Webster Coffee, chief pathologist and director of laboratories at Northbank's Pasteur Hospital . . . a modern medical detective story in the great tradition . . .

Detective: DR. DANIEL WEBSTER COFFEE

The place was almost a shambles when Max Ritter, Lieutenant of Detectives, arrived. All the living-room furniture was slashed or overturned. Chair legs and lamps littered the apartment. So many light bulbs had been broken that the police had to work by flashlights until more bulbs could be sent up. The bed was a rat's nest of bloody tatters, and a trail of gore led from the bedroom through the living room into the bathroom.

The dead man was lying in the bathroom in a pretzel-like posture that would have made a Ringling Brothers contortionist green with envy. He had one foot in the toilet bowl, one arm in the wash basin, and his head in the bathtub. The wood-handled long-bladed kitchen knife which had carved hieroglyphics into his torso had been left lying on the bathroom floor. So had a cheap plastic raincoat which the murderer had obviously worn to protect his clothing, as well as the crumpled bloody towels with which he had wiped his hands and probably his shoes.

The house phone was off the hook and lay on the floor—a fact which led to the early discovery of the crime. The desk clerk of the Westside Residential Hotel had plugged a jack under a signal light that had suddenly flared for Apartment 26. He had said "Office" several times, but got no response. He thought he heard curious sounds in the background and repeated "Office" three more times. When he heard what he thought was the sound of a door closing, he had run up the stairs—the self-service elevator was somewhere in the stratosphere—and had banged on the door of Apartment 26. When there was no response, he ran back down the stairs and called the police. He made no attempt to enter the apartment with his passkey until the squadcar cops arrived. Why should he, a law-abiding and unarmed citizen, usurp the unquestioned duty of the uniformed forces of the law?

While the print men, photographers, and other technicians were picking their way gingerly through the mess in Apartment 26, Lieutenant Ritter was collecting pertinent data. But the swarthy, lugubrious beanpole of a detective found the desk clerk, the manager, and the neighbors singularly uninformative. It seemed incredible to Ritter that such a desperate life-and-death struggle could have gone on without arousing some auditory interest; yet this appeared to be the case. The man and wife across the hall were addicted to loud television—the wife was rather deaf—and the people in the apartment next door were out for the evening. The girl at the end of the hall had taken a sleeping pill and even slept through five minutes of door pounding by the police.

Neither the desk clerk nor the house manager was of much help at first. The desk clerk, a young man with curly brown hair, long eyelashes, and suspiciously red lips, was terribly, terribly bored and terribly, terribly vague about who had entered and left the lobby during the evening. The manager said that the dead man had registered three weeks previously as Gerald Sampson of New York, although he agreed with the desk clerk that the deceased had a pronounced Southern accent.

Lieutenant Max Ritter was convinced that the dead man's name was not Sampson and that he had not come from New York. In the wastebasket of Apartment 26 the Lieutenant had found an envelope addressed to Mr. Paul Wallace, General Delivery, Northbank, and postmarked Baton Rouge, Louisiana. There was no return address on the envelope and no letter inside the envelope or in the wastebasket.

In a dresser drawer, under a pile of expensive shirts, Ritter found a Social Security card in the name of Paul Wallace and a passbook showing a balance of $1706 in a Cleveland bank to the credit of P. L. Wallace. In an envelope stuffed into the inside pocket of a Brooks Brothers sports jacket hanging in a closet, the detective found an envelope containing a dozen newspaper clippings about a young singer named Patty Erryl.

THE KILLER WITH NO FINGERPRINTS

Even in the smudged halftone pictures, Patty was a comely lass, apparently not far out of her teens, brimful of that intangible effervescence which is the exclusive property of youth. In most of the poses her eyes glowed with the roseate vision of an unclouded future. Her blonde head was poised with the awareness of her own fresh loveliness. Patty Erryl was quite obviously a personality. Moreover, Lieutenant Ritter concluded as he read through the clippings, Patty had talent.

Patty had been singing in Northbank night clubs for the past year. Just a month before the sudden demise of Mr. Paul Wallace, she had won the regional tryout of the Metropolitan Opera auditions. In a few weeks she would go to New York to compete in the nationally broadcast finals.

Ritter took the clippings downstairs and reopened his questioning of the bored desk clerk.

"Ever see this dame?" He dealt the clippings face up on the reception desk.

"Ah? Well, yes, as a matter of fact I have." The clerk fluttered his eyelashes. "I saw the pictures in the papers, too, even before I saw the girl, but I somehow didn't connect the one with the other. Yes, I've seen her."

"Did she ever come here to see this bird Wallace?"

"Wallace? You mean Mr. Sampson?"

"I mean the man in Twenty-six."

"Ah. Well, yes, as a matter of fact she did."

"Often?"

"That depends upon what you call often. She's been here three or four times, I'd say."

"Do you announce her or does she go right up?"

"Well, the first time she stopped at the desk. Lately she's been going right up."

"What do you mean, lately? Tonight, maybe?"

"I didn't see her tonight."

"If she comes here regular, maybe she could go through the service entrance and take the elevator in the basement without you seeing her?"

"That's possible, yes."

"Does she always come alone?"

"Not always. Last time she came she brought lover boy along."

"Who's lover boy?"

"How should I know?" Again the clerk fluttered his eyelashes.

"He's a rather uncouth young man whom for some reason Miss Erryl seems to find not unattractive. She apparently takes great pleasure in gazing into his eyes. And vice versa."

"But you don't know his name?"

"I do not. We don't require birth certificates, passports, or marriage licenses for the purpose of visiting our tenants."

"You're too, too liberal. You let in murderers. Did lover boy ever come here without lover girl?"

"He did indeed. He was here last night raising quite a row with the gentleman in Twenty-six. When he came down he was red-faced and mad as a hornet. Right afterward the gentleman in Twenty-six called the desk and gave orders that if lover boy ever came back, I was not to let him up, and that if he insisted I was to call the police. Lover boy had been threatening him, he said. But I think he came back again tonight."

"You think?"

"Well, I had just finished taking a phone message for one of our tenants who was out, and I turned my back to put the message in her box when this man went by and got into the elevator. I only had a glimpse of him as the elevator door was closing, but I'm sure it was lover boy. I shouted at him but it was too late. I tried to phone Twenty-six to warn Mr. Sampson—"

"Wallace."

"Wallace. But there was no answer, so I assumed he was out. Then a few minutes later the phone in Twenty-six was knocked off the hook."

"Did you see lover boy come down again?"

"Now that you mention it, no, I didn't—unless he came down while I was up banging on the door of Twenty-six."

"Or took the car down to the basement and went out the service entrance, maybe?"

"You're so right, Lieutenant. Or he could have been picked up by a helicopter on the roof." The clerk giggled.

"Very funny." Ritter advanced his lower lip. "Any other non-tenants come in tonight since you came on duty?"

"Traffic has been quite light this evening. There was the blonde who always comes to see the man in Sixty-three on Wednesdays. There was a boy from the florist's with roses for the sick lady on Nine, and there was an elderly white-haired gent I assumed to be delivering for the liquor store on the corner."

"Why?"

"Well, he had a package under his arm and it was about time for Miss Benedict's daily fifth of gin, so—"

"What time do you call 'about time'?"

"About an hour ago."

"This was before Wallace's light went up on your switchboard?"

"About twenty minutes before. Now that I think of it, I didn't see him come down either. Of course, with all the excitement—"

"That makes two for your helicopter," the detective said. "Let me know if you think of any more."

Ritter went upstairs again for another look at the dead man and to wait for the coroner who had been summoned from his weekly pinochle game but had not yet arrived. At least this was one case the coroner could not very well attribute to heart failure—"Coroner's Thrombosis," as Dr. Coffee called it—since the cause of death was plainly written in blood.

The dead man had been on the threshold of middle age. His temples were graying and there was gray in his close-cropped beard. The beard, instead of giving him an air of distinction, left him with a hard ruthless face.

His features were regular, except perhaps for his earlobes which were thick, pendulous, and slightly discolored as though they had been forcibly twisted.

Whoever killed Mr. Wallace-Sampson must have really hated him to have done such a savage knife job on him. Why, then, would the victim have admitted a man who was such an obvious and determined enemy? Could the murderer have obtained a key from some third party?

Ritter's reverie was interrupted by the approach of Sergeant Foley, the scowling fingerprint expert.

"Lieutenant," he said, "we got something special here. I think we're stuck with a sixty-four-million-dollar question and with no sponsor to slip us the answer."

"You mean you can't make the stiff?"

"Oh, the stiff's a cinch. We haven't made him yet, but we got a perfect set of prints and he's old enough so he must be on file somewhere in the world. But the murderer—no soap!"

"Sergeant, you surprise and grieve me," Ritter said. "With my own little eyes I see five perfect bloody fingermarks on the bathroom door."

"Finger marks yes," said Sergeant Foley, "but prints no."

"Meaning what?"

"Meaning no prints. No ridges, no pore patterns, no whorls, no radial loops, no ulnar loops—no nothing."

Ritter frowned. "Gloves?"

"We usually get *some* sort of pattern with gloves, even surgical gloves sometimes, although they're hard to identify. But here, nothing—and I mean *nothing*."

"The knife?"

"Same thing. It wasn't wiped. Bloody finger marks, yes—prints, no. The knife, by the way, comes from the kitchenette here."

Max Ritter scratched his mastoid process. He pursed his lips as though rehearsing for a Police Good Neighbor League baby-kissing bee. Then he asked, "Your boys finished with that phone, Sergeant?"

"Yup. Go ahead and call."

A moment later Ritter was talking to his private medical examiner, Dr. Daniel Webster Coffee, chief pathologist and director of laboratories at Northbank's Pasteur Hospital.

"Hi, Doc. Get you out of bed? . . . Look, I got something kind of funny, if you can call homicide funny . . . No, the coroner's a little late, but this one he can't write off as natural causes. A knife job, but good. Like a surgeon, practically . . . No, I don't think there's anything you can do tonight, Doc. I already emptied the medicine chest for you, like always. But if I can talk the coroner into shipping the deceased to your hospital morgue for a P.M. . . . You will? Thanks, Doc. I think you're going to like this one. The killer's got no fingerprints . . . No, I don't mean he left none; he's *got* none. Call you in the morning, Doc."

When Dr. Coffee returned to the pathology laboratory after the autopsy next morning, he handed two white enameled pails to his winsome, dark-eyed technician and said, "The usual sections and the usual stains, Doris. Only don't section the heart until I photograph the damage."

Doris Hudson lifted the lids from both pails and peered in without any change of expression on her cover-girl features.

"Lieutenant Ritter is waiting in your office, Doctor, talking to Calcutta's gift to Northbank," she said. "If you agree that Dr. Mookerji is not paid to entertain the Police Department, I could use him out here to help me cut tissue."

Doris's voice apparently had good carrying qualities, for the rotund Hindu resident in pathology immediately appeared in the doorway and waddled into the laboratory.

"Salaam, Doctor Sahib," said Dr. Mookerji. "Leftenant Ritter is once more involving us in felonious homicide, no?"

Dr. Coffee nodded.

"Hi, Doc," said Ritter. "What did you find?"

"The gross doesn't show much except that the deceased died of shock and hemorrhage due to multiple stab wounds in the cardiac region and lower abdomen. As you know, Max, I won't have the microscopic findings for a day or so."

"Did you shave off the guy's whiskers?"

"That's not routine autopsy procedure, Max. But it's pretty clear that he grew a beard to hide scars. There's old scar tissues on one cheek, on the chin, and on the upper lip."

"He also grows the bush to hide behind." Max Ritter grinned. "Doc, the guy's a con man and a small-time blackmailer. I wire the Henry classification to the F.B.I. last night and I get the answer first thing this morning. His name's Paul Wallace, with half a dozen aliases. He's got a record: four arrests, two convictions. Two cases dismissed in New York when the plaintiffs, both dames, withdrew their complaints. Last four years are blank, the F.B.I. says, at least as far as Washington knows."

"What about the murderer with no fingerprints?" the pathologist asked.

"That's what I want to talk to you about, Doc. Since this Wallace is a crook, maybe the guy that knifed him is another crook he double-crossed. Maybe the butcher boy had a little plastic surgery on his fingers."

"I don't know, Max." Dr. Coffee shook his head, then with one hand brushed an unruly wisp of straw-colored hair back from his forehead. "I've never seen a first-class job of surgical fingerprint elimination. Did you ever see the prints they took off Dillinger's corpse? His plastic job was a complete botch. No trouble at all to make the identification."

"Then how do you—?"

"Give me another forty-eight hours, Max. Meanwhile, what progress have you made running down blind leads?"

Ritter told the pathologist about Patty Erryl and her visits to the dead man's apartment with and without "lover boy"; also about the bored and vague desk clerk's recital, and about his own conclusions.

"This white-haired old geezer with the package under his arm is definitely not delivering gin to Miss Benedict in Seven-oh-two for any liquor store within half a mile," said Ritter. "I checked 'em all.

Could be that his package was the plastic raincoat I found in the bathroom.

"Anyhow, I just come from talking to this Patty Erryl, the opera hopeful." Ritter brought forth his envelope of clippings and spread them on Dr. Coffee's desk. "Look, Doc. A real dish. Not more than twenty. Born in Texas, she says—some little town near San Antonio. Grew up in the Philippines where her father was a U.S. Air Force pilot. He was killed in Korea. Her mother is dead too, she says. I ain't so sure. Maybe Mama just eased out of the picture, leaving little Patty with a maiden aunt in Northbank—Aunt Minnie Erryl. Anyhow, little Patty studies voice here in Northbank with Sandra Farriston until Sandra is bounced off to join Caruso, Melba, and Schumann-Heink. Remember Sandra? Then Patty goes to New Orleans to study with an old friend of Sandra's for a few years, she says. Then she comes back to Northbank to live with Auntie Min and sing in night clubs, under Auntie Min's strictly jaundiced eye. Then all of a sudden she wins this Metropolitan Opera audition tryout—"

"What about lover boy?"

"I was just coming to that, Doc. Seems he's a reporter on the Northbank *Tribune*. Covers the Federal Building in the daytime and the night-club beat after dark. Name's Bob Rhodes. He's the one who pushes her into the opera auditions. Quite a feather in his cap, to read his night-club columns. He thinks he discovers another Lily Pons."

"What has he been seeing Wallace about?"

"I don't know yet." Ritter pushed his dark soft hat to the back of his head. "Seems last night's his day off and I can't locate him. I'm on the point of putting out a six-state alarm for him, but little Patty talks me out of it. She guarantees to produce him for me at eleven o'clock this morning. Want to come along?"

"Maybe I'd better. How does the girl explain her visits to Wallace?"

"She don't know he's a crook, she says. Friend of her dad's, she says. Ran into him in New Orleans when she was studying music down there, then lost sight of him for a few years. When he sees her picture in the papers after she wins that opera whoopdedoo, he looks her up here in Northbank. She goes to see him a few times to talk about her family and maybe drink a glass of sherry or two. That's all. She has no idea who killed him or why."

"What about that stuff you collected from the medicine cabinet in Wallace's bathroom?"

"I got it here." Ritter pulled a plastic bag from his bulging pocket. "It ain't much. Aspirin, toothpaste, bicarb, hair tonic, and this bottle of pills from some drug store in Cleveland."

Dr. Coffee uncorked the last item, sniffed, shook a few of the brightly colored tablets into the palm of his hand, sniffed again, and poured them back. He picked up the phone.

"Get me the Galenic Pharmacy in Cleveland," he told the operator. A moment later he said, "This is Dr. Daniel Coffee at the Pasteur Hospital in Northbank. About a month ago you filled a prescription for a man named Wallace. The number is 335571. Could you read it to me? Yes, I'll wait . . . I see. Diasone. Thank you very much. No, I don't need a refill, thank you."

Dr. Coffee's face was an expressionless mask as he hung up. He pondered a moment, then picked up the phone again. He dialed an inside number.

"Joe? Coffee here. Has the undertaker picked up that body we were working on this morning? . . . Good. Don't release it for another half hour. Dr. Mookerji will tell you when."

The pathologist took off his white jacket, hung it up carefully, and reached for his coat. He took the detective's arm and marched him out of the office. As he crossed the laboratory, he stopped to tug playfully on the tail of the Hindu resident's pink turban.

"Dr. Mookerji," he said, "I wish you'd go down to the basement and wind up that autopsy I started this morning. I need more tissue. I want a specimen from both the inguinal and femoral lymph nodes, and from each earlobe. When you're through, you may release the body. Doris, when you make sections from this new tissue, I want you to use Fite's fuchsin stain for acid-fast bacilli. Any biopsies scheduled, Doris?"

"Not today, Doctor."

"Then I won't be back until after lunch. Let's go, Max."

The office bistro of the Northbank *Tribune* staff was on the ground floor of the building next door. There reporters and desk men could refuel conveniently and could always be found in an editorial emergency. It was whimsically named "The Slot" because the horseshoe bar was shaped like a copy desk with the bartender dealing fermented and distilled items to the boys on the rim—like an editor meting out the grist of the day's news for soft-pencil surgery.

There was a pleasant beery smell about the place, and the walls were hung with such masculine adornment as yellowing photos of prizefighters and jockeys, moth-eaten stags' heads, mounted dead fish, a few Civil War muzzle-loaders, and framed *Tribune* front pages reporting such historic events as the sinking of the Titanic, the surrender of Nazi Germany, the dropping of the first atomic bomb, and the winning of the World Series by the Northbank Blue Sox.

The masculine decor was no deterrent, however, to invasion by emancipated womanhood. A series of stiffly uncomfortable booths had been erected at the rear of the barroom, and from one of them, as Dr. Coffee and Max Ritter entered, emerged a dark-eyed, flaxen-haired cutie who, from the swing of her hips as she advanced toward the two men, might have been a collegiate drum-majorette—except for the set of her jaw, the intelligent determination in her eyes, and the challenge in her stride.

"Hi, Patty," said Lieutenant Ritter. "Where's the fugitive?"

"Fugitive!" The girl flung out the word. "I warn you, I'm not going to let you frame Bob Rhodes. Who is this character you've brought along—a big-shot from the State Police, or just the F.B.I.?"

"Patty," said Ritter, his Adam's apple poised for a seismographic curve, "Dr. Coffee is maybe the only friend you and your lover boy have in the world—if you're both innocent. Doc, meet Patty Erryl, the girl who's going to make the Met forget Galli-Curci, or whoever they want to forget this year. Where's Bob?"

"He's been delayed."

"Look, Patty baby, if you insist on obstructing justice, I'll have lover boy picked up wherever he is and we'll take him downtown for questioning without your lovely interfering presence."

"Don't you dare. If you—"

"Just a minute, Max," Dr. Coffee cut in. "Remember I've never met Miss Erryl before. I may have a few questions—"

The pathologist was interrupted by a crash near the entrance. A man, sprawled momentarily on all fours, immediately rose to his knees, trying to recapture the bottles that were spinning off in all directions.

Patty Erryl sped to his rescue. She caught him under the armpits, straining to get him to his feet. "Bob, please get up. They're trying to railroad you, and I'm not going to let them."

"Come, my little chickadee, there's no danger." Rhodes had re-captured three of the elusive bottles. "There are no witnesses. There is no evidence. I did not kill Fuzzy Face."

"Bob, you've been drinking."

"No, my little cedar wax-wing. Only beer. My own. If only Mr.

Slot would stock my Danish brand. You know I never drink until the sun is over the yardarm. Which reminds me. We have passed the vernal equinox. The sun must be over–"

"Bob!"

"Rhodes," said Max Ritter, "the desk clerk saw you at the Westside last night."

"That near-sighted pansy!" Rhodes exclaimed. "Don't you ever try to prove anything by his testimony. And don't tell me that anything I say may be used against me, because even if this place is bugged I'll deny everything. You've drugged me. You've beaten me with gocart tires. You've kicked my shins black and blue. I'll swear that you've–"

"Stop it, Bob."

"May I ask a question, Mr. Rhodes? I'm Doctor–"

"Sure, you're the learned successor to Dr. Thorndyke, Dr. Watson, Dr. Sherlock, Dr. Holmes, Dr. . . . . Indeed, I've heard about you, Dr. Sanka. Go ahead and ask."

"What were you doing at the Westside Apartment Hotel last night?"

"I was on assignment."

"From whom?"

"I'm not at liberty to say. The highest courts of this state have ruled that a newsman is not required to reveal his sources. Privileged communication."

"This ain't a matter of privileged communication," Ritter said. "This is a matter of murder in the first degree. Look here, Rhodes–"

"Just a minute, Max. Mr. Rhodes, were you inside Apartment Twenty-six last night?"

"No."

"Did you see a man named Paul Wallace last night?"

"No."

"But you know that Paul Wallace was killed in Apartment Twenty-six last night, don't you?"

"Sure. I read the papers even on my day off."

"Did you see anyone go into Apartment Twenty-six last night?"

"No."

"Did you see anyone come out?"

Rhodes hesitated for just the fraction of a second before he said, "No."

"What were you doing on the second floor of the Westside?"

"I was playing a hunch. I'm a great little hunch player."

"You make mincemeat of Wallace's lights and gizzard on a hunch?" Lieutenant Ritter asked.

"Down, Cossack!" said Rhodes. "Down. Roll over. Sit up. Beg . . ."

"Bob, you're not making any sense," the girl broke in. "Lieutenant, I'll tell you why he was at the Westside. He had an awful fight with Paul Wallace the night before last. You see, Bob and I are very much in love, and Bob is terribly jealous. He thought Paul Wallace had designs on my virtue, so Bob told him if he as much as invited me to his apartment again, he would kill him."

"And last night he made good his threat?"

"Of course not. Last night I told Bob he was being silly and he would have to go around and apologize to Paul Wallace. Only he couldn't apologize because nobody answered when he knocked on the door. I guess Mr. Wallace was already dead."

From the expression on Bob Rhodes's face, Dr. Coffee judged that at least part of the girl's story was new and startling to him.

"Patty," said Ritter, "if this guy Wallace was so buddy-buddy with your family, how come your Auntie Min never heard of him?"

"Because I never spoke of him in front of Auntie Min. Auntie is a real spinster. She thinks all men are creatures of the devil. If she ever thought that I went to see Mr. Wallace alone, she'd simply die, even if he is old enough to be my father."

"Is he your father?"

"No, of course not. Lieutenant, why don't you let Bob go home and sober up? You'll never get a straight story out of him in this condition."

Ritter ignored the suggestion. "Getting back to your Auntie Min," he said, "how come she wasn't worried to death about you being alone with that voice coach of yours 'way down south in New Orleans?"

Patty laughed. "He's even older than Mr. Wallace."

"What was his name, Miss Erryl?" Dr. Coffee asked.

The girl hesitated. "You wouldn't recognize it," she said after a moment. "He wasn't very well-known outside of the South. In the French Quarter they used to call him Papa Albert."

"No last name?"

"That was his last name—Albert."

"Address?"

"Well, he used to live on Bourbon Street, but the last I heard he was going to move away."

"To Baton Rouge?"

"I–I don't know where he is now."

"Didn't he write to you from Baton Rouge?"

"No."

"Or to Mr. Wallace?"

"I'm sure I don't know."

"Do you know of anyone who might have written to Mr. Wallace from Baton Rouge?"

"I . . . I . . ." Patty Erryl suddenly covered her face with her hands and burst into tears.

"Lay off the gal, will you, Cossack?" Rhodes stood up, swinging a full beer bottle like an Indian club. "If you have to work off your sadistic energy somewhere, call me any day after dark and I'll give you some addresses which I suspect you already know. You can bring your own whips, if you want, and–"

"Sit down, Mr. Rhodes." Dr. Coffee gently removed the bottle from the reporter's hand. "Miss Erryl, I happened to listen to the broadcast of your operatic audition. I thought you did a first-rate job. I particularly admired the way you sang *Vissi d' Arte*. Do you have any real ambition to sing La Tosca some day?"

The girl's weeping stopped abruptly. She stared at the pathologist for a moment. Then she said, "Why do you ask that?"

"You seemed to have a feeling for the part of Floria Tosca," Dr. Coffee said. "I'm sure you must be familiar with the libretto. You are, aren't you?"

Patty Erryl's lips parted. She closed them again without saying a word.

"Come on, Max," Dr. Coffee said. "Miss Erryl is right. I think you'd better tackle Mr. Rhodes when he's more himself."

"But Doc, he admits–"

"Let's go, Max. Goodbye, Miss Tosca. Goodbye, Mr. Rhodes."

As the police car headed for Raoul's Auberge Française (one flight up) where since it was Thursday, Dr. Coffee knew they would be regaled with *Quenelles de Brochet* (dumplings of fresh-water pike in shells), Max Ritter said, "Doc, I shouldn't have listened to you. I should have taken that wisecracking reporter downtown."

"You won't lose him, Max. I saw some of your most adhesive shadows loitering purposefully outside The Slot."

"You never miss a trick, do you, Doc?" Ritter chuckled. "Doc, you don't really believe that a guy gets that squiffed so early in the day just because he can't apologize to a dead swindler, do you?"

"Hardly, Max. But a man might get himself thoroughly soused if he realized he was seen heading for the apartment of a man with whom he had quarreled the night before and who had since been murdered. My guess is that he spent the rest of the night ducking from bar to bar, trying to forget either that he killed a man or that he had certainly maneuvered himself into the unenviable position of appearing to have killed a man."

As they waited for a light to change, Ritter asked, "What was that crack of yours about Tosca?"

Dr. Coffee laughed. "Pure whimsy. Probably unimportant. I wanted to watch the girl's reaction."

"You sure got one. What's the angle?"

"Max, why don't you drop in at the Municipal Auditorium when the Metropolitan Opera troupe stops by for a week after the New York season?"

"Doc, you know damned well I never got past the Gershwin grade. Who's the Tosca?"

"Floria Tosca is the tragic heroine of a play by a Frenchman named Sardou which has become a popular opera by Puccini. Tosca is a singer who kills the villain Scarpia to save her lover, an early Nineteenth Century revolutionary named Mario, and incidentally, to save her honor. As it turns out, her honor is about all that is saved because everybody double-crosses everybody else and there are practically no survivors. But it's a very melodious opera, Max, and I think you might like it. Listen." Dr. Coffee hummed *E Lucevan le Stelle*. "Da da da deee, da da dum, da dum dummmm . . ."

"You think we got a Patty La Tosca on our hands, Doc?"

"It's too early to tell, Max. Right now, though, I'd say it might be a sort of Wrong-Way Tosca. Instead of Floria Tosca killing Scarpia to save Mario, Mario may have killed Scarpia to save Tosca. Only I'm not sure who Mario might be. I'll know more tomorrow or the next day. I'll call you, Max."

Dr. Coffee was reading the slides from the Wallace autopsy. The Fite stains provided colorful sections. The acid-fast bacteria appeared in a deep ultramarine. The connective-tissue cells were red, and all other elements were stained yellow. He raised his eyes from the binocular microscope and summoned his Hindu resident.

"Dr. Mookerji, I want you to look at this section from the femoral lymph node. You must have seen many like it in India."

Dr. Mookerji adjusted the focus, moved the slide around under the nose of the instrument, grunted, and held out a chubby brown hand.

"You have further sections, no doubt?"

"Try this. From the right earlobe."

Dr. Mookerji grunted again, then twisted the knobs of the microscope in silence.

"Hansen's bacillus?" ventured Dr. Coffee.

"Quite," said the Hindu. "However, am of opinion that said bacilli present somewhat fragmented appearance. Observe that outline is somewhat hollowish and organisms enjoy rather puny condition if not frankly deceased. Patient was no doubt arrested case?"

"The patient is dead," said Dr. Coffee, "but I'll go along with you that it wasn't Hansen's bacillus that killed him. It rarely does. In this case it was a knife." He stared into space as he toyed with the slides in the rack before him. After a moment he asked, "Doris, when is that New Orleans convention of clinical pathologists that wanted me to read a paper, and I replied I didn't think I could get away?"

Doris consulted her notebook. "It's tomorrow, Doctor."

"Good. Doris, be an angel and see if you can get me a seat on a plane for New Orleans tonight. Then try to get me Dr. Quentin Quirk, medical officer in charge of the U.S. Public Service Hospital at Carville, Louisiana. Make it person to person. Then get me Mrs. Coffee on the other line."

In five minutes Dr. Coffee had reservations on the night flight to New Orleans, had instructed his wife to pack a small bag with enough clothes for three days away from home, and was talking to Dr. Quirk in Louisiana.

"This is Dan Coffee, Quent. I'm coming down to your shindig tomorrow after all . . . Sure, I'll read a paper if you want. I don't care whether it's in the proceedings or not. Will you let me ride back to your hospital with you after the show? Fine. I've always wanted to see the place. See you tomorrow then, Quent. 'Bye."

The pathologist had barely replaced the instrument when Max Ritter walked into his office and tossed a pair of very thin rubber gloves to his desk.

"Developments, Doc," the detective said. "I just come from Patty Erryl's Auntie Min's place. She happens to have five pairs of surgeon's gloves in the house. Seconds, she says. Big sale of defective gloves at the five and ten. Forty-nine cents a pair because they're imperfect but still waterproof. She buys six pairs for herself and

Patty to wear when they do the dishes. But there's only five pairs there when I find 'em. She can't remember what happened to the missing pair. She says she thinks Patty threw 'em out because they split."

"So you think old Auntie Min wore the defective surgical gloves to kill Wallace?"

"I don't say that. But this lush Rhodes is at her house practically every night to sell his bill of goods to Patty. If he should have grabbed that sixth pair of surgeon's gloves one night, it might explain why there ain't any fingerprints."

"Max, have you arrested Rhodes?"

"Not exactly. But the chief is getting impatient. I'm holding Rhodes as a material witness."

"Good lord! Well, at least I won't have to face Patty when she starts raising hell to get lover boy out of custody. I'm going to Louisiana tonight, Max. If it's at all possible, don't prefer charges until after I get back. I have a hunch I may pick up a few threads down there. Do you have that letter with the Baton Rouge postmark?"

"Sure."

"And a photo of Patty Erryl?"

"A cinch."

"Wish me luck, Max. I'll call you the minute I get back—maybe before, if I run into something hot and steaming."

Dr. Coffee savored the applause with which the convention of pathologists greeted his paper on *Determination of the Time of Death by the Study of Bone Marrow.* He also savored two days of gastronomic research: *Pompano en papillote* at Antoine's and *Crab Gumbo chez Galatoire,* among other delights. Then he drove northwest along the Mississippi with his old classmate at medical school, Dr. Quentin Quirk.

Except for an occasional mast which poked up above the levees, Old Man River was carefully concealed from the Old River Road. The drive through the flat delta country was enlivened by the pink-and-gold bravura of the rain trees, the smell of nearby water hanging on the steamy air, and the nostalgic exchange of medical school reminiscences—who among their classmates had died, who had gone to seed, who had traded integrity for social status, who had gone on to be ornaments to the growing structure of the healing sciences.

Dr. Coffee carefully avoided mentioning the real purpose of his visit even after the moss-hung oaks and the antebellum columns and wrought-iron balconies of the entrance and Administration Building loomed ahead.

It was Dr. Coffee's first visit to Carville. In spite of himself, he was surprised to find that the only leprosarium in the continental United States should be such a beautiful place. He knew of course that modern therapy had removed most of the crippling effects of the disease, which was not at all the leprosy of the Bible anyhow, and that even the superstitious dread was fading as it became generally known that the malady was only faintly communicable.

Yet as Dr. Quirk gave him a personally conducted tour of the plantation—the vast quadrangle of pink-stucco dormitories, the sweet-smelling avenue of magnolias leading up to the airy infirmary, the expensive modern laboratories, the Sisters of Charity in their sweeping white cornettes, the gay parasols in front of the Recreation Hall, the brilliantly colored birds, the private cottages for patients under the tall pecan trees beyond the golf course—Dr. Coffee wondered how it was possible for the old stigma to persist in the second half of the Twentieth Century. When he settled down to a cocktail in Dr. Quirk's bungalow, however, he remembered what he had come for.

"Quent," said Dr. Coffee, "I've seen Hansen's bacillus only twice since we've left medical school, while you've been living with it for years. Didn't we read something in Dermatology 101 about leprosy affecting fingerprints? Some Brazilian leprologist made the discovery, as I remember."

"That's right—Ribeiro, probably, although several other Brazilians have also been working in that field—Liera and Tanner de Abreu among them."

"Am I dreaming, or is it true that the disease can change fingerprint patterns?"

"Definitely true," said Dr. Quirk. "Even in its early stages, the disease may alter papillary design. The papillae flatten out, blurring the ridges and causing areas of smoothness."

"Do the fingerprint patterns ever disappear completely?"

"Oh, yes. In advanced cases the epidermis grows tissue-thin, the interpapillary pegs often disappear, and the skin at the fingertips becomes quite smooth."

Dr. Coffee drained the last of his Sazarac, put down his glass, and gave a rather smug nod.

"Then I've come to the right place," he said. "Quent, you may have a murderer among your patients—or among your ex-patients."

"Murderer? Here?" Dr. Quirk got up and pensively tinkled a handful of ice cubes into a bar glass. "Well, it is possible. Over the years we have had three or four murders at Carville. When did your putative Carvillian commit murder?"

"Last Wednesday night," said Dr. Coffee, "in Northbank. The murderer left bloody finger marks but no distinguishable prints. I suspect the victim might also have been a one-time patient of yours. There was Diasone in his medicine chest, and at autopsy I found fragmented Hansen's bacilli in the lymph nodes and in one earlobe. Did you know a character named Paul Wallace?"

"Wallace? Good lord!" Dr. Quirk shook Peychaud bitters into the bar glass with a savage fist. "That no-good four-flushing ape! Yes, Wallace has been in and out of here several times. Whenever he gets into trouble with the law, he tries to scare the authorities into sending him back here. 'You can't keep me in your jail,' he says. 'I'm a leper. You have to send me to Carville.' But I wouldn't take him back any more. He's an arrested case. Last time he tried to dodge a conviction, I sent him back to serve time. I knew he'd end up in some bloody mess. Who killed him?"

"Somebody who must have loathed his guts enough to cut them to pieces. It was a real hate job—by a man with no fingerprints."

Dr. Quirk shook his head. "I can't imagine—"

"Quent, did you ever see this girl before?" Dr. Coffee opened his brief case and produced a photo of Patty Erryl.

Dr. Quirk squinted at the picture, held it out at arm's length, turned it at several angles, squinted again, brought it closer, then slowly shook his head.

"No," he said. "I don't think—" Suddenly he slapped his hand across the upper part of the photo. "Sorry," he said. "Change signals. Her hair fooled me. I never saw her as a blonde before. That's Patty Erryl."

"An ex-patient?"

Dr. Quirk nodded. "She came to Carville as a kid. Her father was an Air Force officer in the Far East. She was raised out there—Philippines, I think; one of the endemic areas, anyhow. When her father was killed in Korea, her mother brought her back to the States. The girl developed clinical symptoms. Her mother brought her to Carville and then faded out of the picture."

"Did she die, too?"

"I'm not sure. Maybe she remarried. Anyhow, she never once came to Carville to visit Patty. Patty responded very well to sulfones and

when she was discharged as bacteriologically and clinically nega-
tive, an aunt from somewhere in the Middle West came to get her."

"That would be Auntie Min of Northbank," said Dr. Coffee. "How
long ago was Patty discharged?"

"Two or three years ago. Do you want the exact date?"

"I want to know particularly whether Paul Wallace was a patient
here while Patty was still in Carville."

"I'm not sure. I'll check with Sister Frances in Records." Dr. Quirk
poured fresh Sazaracs.

"No hurry. I suppose you know that Patty is quite a singer."

"Do I! When she sang in the Recreation Hall, radio and television
people used to come down from Baton Rouge to tape her concerts."

"How far away is Baton Rouge?"

"Oh, twenty, twenty-five miles."

"Did Patty's voice develop spontaneously, or did she have a coach?"

"Well, I guess you could say she had a coach of sorts."

"Papa Albert?"

Dr. Quirk's teeth clicked against the rim of his cocktail glass. His
eyebrows rose. "You come well briefed, Dan."

"Where does Papa Albert live? Baton Rouge?"

Dr. Quirk laughed briefly. "For twenty-five years," he said, "Carville has been home to Albert Boulanger. He was a promising young
pianist when the thing hit him. This was before we discovered the
sulfones, so he was pretty badly crippled before we could help him.
Hands are shot. He can play a few chords, though, and he's still a
musician to his fingertips."

"Fingertips with papillae and interpapillary pegs obliterated?"

Dr. Quirk looked at the pathologist strangely. He muddled the ice
in the bar glass, and squeezed out another half Sazarac for each of
them. He took a long sip of his drink before he resumed in a slow,
solemn voice.

"Patty Erryl was a forlorn little girl when she came here," he said,
"and Albert Boulanger sort of adopted her. He taught her to sing
little French songs. When she began to bloom, he fought off the
wolves. He would invite her to his cottage out back to listen to opera
recordings evening after evening.

"She was an early case. She could have been discharged in three
years, except that she wanted to finish her schooling here. I think,
too, that she appreciated what Papa Albert was doing to bring out
the music in her. He was like a father to her. And since she scarcely
knew her own father, she was terribly fond of the old man."

Dr. Coffee drained his glass again. "I suppose your records will show that Albert Boulanger was here at Carville last Wednesday night."

"I'm afraid not." Dr. Quirk frowned. "He had a forty-eight-hour pass to go to New Orleans last Wednesday. He wanted to see his lawyer about a new will. The old man hasn't long to live."

"I thought people didn't die of Hansen's disease," Dr. Coffee said.

"Boulanger has terminal cancer. He found out just two weeks ago that he's going to die in a month or two."

"Could I speak to him?"

"Why not?" Dr. Quirk picked up the phone and dialed the gate. "Willy, has Mr. Boulanger come back from New Orleans? . . . Yesterday? Thanks." He replaced the instrument. "I'll go with you," he said. "Papa Albert has one of those cottages beyond the golf course. We won't move him to the infirmary until he gets really bad."

Albert Boulanger must have been a handsome man in his youth. Tall, white-haired, only slightly stooped, he bore few external signs of his malady. Only the experienced eye would note the thinning eyebrows and the slight thickening of the skin along the rictus folds and at the wings of the nostrils.

As Dr. Coffee shook hands, he saw that Papa Albert had obviously suffered some bone absorption; his fingers were shortened and the skin was smooth and shiny.

"I stopped by to bring you greetings from Patty Erryl in Northbank," Dr. Coffee said, "and to compliment you on the fine job you did on Patty's musical education."

Papa Albert darted a quick, startled glance at Dr. Quirk. He apparently found reassurance in the MOC's smile. He coughed. "I take no credit," he said. "The girl has a natural talent and she's worked hard to make the best of it."

"I hope she wins the opera finals," the pathologist said. "Did you get to see her when you were in Northbank on Wednesday?"

Papa Albert looked Dr. Coffee squarely in the eyes as he replied without hesitation, "I've never been in Northbank in my life. I was in New Orleans on Wednesday."

"I see. Did you know that Paul Wallace was killed in Northbank last Wednesday night?"

"Paul Wallace is not of the slightest interest to me. He was a blackguard, a swindler, a thoroughly despicable man."

"Do you have a bank account in Baton Rouge, Mr. Boulanger?"

"No."

"But you did have—until you sent about $1700 to Paul Wallace."

"Why would I send money to a rotter like Wallace?"

"Because you love Patty Erryl as if she were your own daughter. Because you'd do anything to stop someone from wrecking her career just as it's about to start."

"I don't understand you." Papa Albert wiped the perspiration from his forehead with the back of his hand. He coughed again.

"Mr. Boulanger, you and I and Dr. Quirk know that there are dozens of maladies more dreadful and a thousand times more infectious than Hansen's disease. But we also know that the superstitious horror of the disease is kept alive by ignorance and a mistaken interpretation of Biblical leprosy which equates the disease with sin. Despite the progress of recent years there is still a stigma attached to the diagnosis.

"Suppose, Mr. Boulanger, a blackmailer came to you or wrote to you making threats that suggested a newspaper headline such as 'Girl Leper Barred from Met After Winning Audition.' Wouldn't you dig into your savings to prevent such a headline? And if the blackmailer persisted, if his greed increased, I can even envision—"

"Dr. Coffee, if you want me to say that I'm happy that Wallace is dead, I'll do so gladly and as loudly as I can. But now . . ." Papa Albert had begun to tremble. Perspiration was streaming down his pale cheeks. "Now, if you will excuse me . . . Dr. Quirk has perhaps told you of my condition—that I'm supposed to get lots of rest. May I bid you good evening, Doctor?"

He tottered a little as he walked away.

The drainage ditches were aglitter with the eerie light of fireflies as the two doctors left Papa Albert's cottage.

"What do you want me to do, Dan?" Dr. Quirk asked.

"Nothing," Dr. Coffee replied, "unless you hear from me."

Max Ritter was at the Northbank airport to meet Dr. Coffee.

"News, Doc," he said, as the pathologist stepped off the ramp. "Rhodes has confessed."

Dr. Coffee stopped short. "Who did what?"

"Rhodes, the lush, the lover boy, the star reporter and the talent scout. He signed a statement that he killed Wallace."

Dr. Coffee managed a humorless laugh. "Tell me more," he said as they passed through the gate and headed for the parking lot.

"While you're away I took a gander at the phone company's long-distance records. I find two calls in one week from Patty Erryl's number to the same place in Louisiana. Who makes the calls? Not me, says Auntie Min. Must be a mistake, says Patty. Not two mistakes, says Ritter. Then Rhodes comes clean. *He* makes the calls.

"Patty is terrified of this Wallace character, but she runs to see him every time he raises his little finger. Why? Well, Rhodes phones a newspaper pal in Louisiana to smell around a little, and he finds out Wallace is blackmailing Patty. Seems when she was studying music down there she got mixed up with a crummy bunch and got caught in a narcotics raid. She's let off with a suspended sentence but the conviction is a matter of record. Wallace finds out about it and starts putting the screws on her, so Rhodes kills him. So I lock him up."

"That poor, love-sick, courageous, gallant liar!" said Dr. Coffee as he climbed into Ritter's car. "Let's go right down to the jail and let him out."

"But Doc, Rhodes confessed!"

"Max, Rhodes is making a noble sacrifice, hoping, I'm sure, that he can beat the rap when he comes up for trial. He's given you a confession he will surely repudiate later if it doesn't endanger Patty. He's confessed so that you will not run down those long-distance phone calls and discover they were from Patty to the Public Health Service Hospital in Carville, Louisiana."

"The phone company didn't say anything about Carville. The number was a Mission number out of Baton Rouge exchange through Saint Gabriel."

"Exactly. All Carville numbers go through Baton Rouge and Saint Gabriel, and the exchange is Mission."

And Dr. Coffee told Ritter about Carville, Hansen's disease, and Papa Albert Boulanger.

"I'm positive, Max, that Papa Albert is the white-haired man with the package under his arm—the man the clerk at the Westside saw get into the elevator shortly before Wallace was killed on Wednesday," he said. "I'm also sure that he was paying blackmail to protect Patty.

"When Papa Albert found out two weeks ago that he didn't have long to live, he decided that before he died he would get Wallace out of Patty's life forever. Northbank is only two hours from New Orleans by jet. He could have come up by an early evening plane, killed Wallace, and been back at his New Orleans hotel by midnight.

He'll have an alibi, all right. Who wouldn't perjure himself for a man with only a month or two to live."

"But Doc, if he's going to die anyhow, why doesn't he just give himself up, say he did it for Patty, and die a hero?"

"Because that would undo everything he's been willing to commit murder for. That would connect Patty with Carville. And let's face it, Max, the stigma of Carville is still pretty strong poison in too many places."

"Not for Rhodes it ain't. Or don't you think he knows?"

"He knows. But he's an intelligent young man and he's in love with Patty."

"I still don't see what Rhodes was doing at the Westside the night of the murder if he didn't kill Wallace."

"He'll deny this, of course, but I see only one explanation. Papa Albert didn't have Wallace's address—Wallace has been getting his mail at General Delivery. My guess is that Boulanger called Patty, probably from the airport, to get the address. And Patty, realizing after she had hung up what the old man was intending to do, sent Bob Rhodes out to the Westside to try to stop him. Rhodes got there too late."

"Do you think we can break Boulanger's alibi, Doc?"

"I'm sure you could build a circumstantial case. You could dig up an airline stewardess or two who could identify him as flying to and from New Orleans the night of the murder—he's a striking-looking old gent. You could subpoena bank records in Louisiana to show that he withdrew amounts from his savings account approximating Wallace's deposits in Cleveland. Maybe the desk clerk at the Westside could identify him. But you'll have to work fast, Max. Otherwise you'll have to bring your man into court on a stretcher."

"You really think he's going to die, Doc?"

"Sooner than he thinks, I'd say. The metastases are pretty general. The lungs are involved—he has a characteristic cough. The lymph nodes in his neck are as big as pigeons' eggs. With luck he may last long enough to hear Patty sing in the finals—La Tosca, I hope. Unless, of course, you start extradition proceedings."

The detective swung his car into the "Official Vehicles Only" parking space behind the county jail.

"I dunno, Doc," he said as he switched off the ignition. "Maybe we ought to let God handle this one."

"Q"

Phyllis Ann Karr

Blood Money

A tale of the Seventeenth Century, a tale of death and ruin, of greed and hate, of bloodshed and revenge and—money . . .

Were I five years younger, dear husband Hal, I would have killed myself for bringing such shame upon your memory. But to-day, let me be content to set all the matter down in this paper, and bury it in the earth above your grave. And pray you, also, be content with this much, for there has been enough of bloodshed.

That your father was a hard man, who should know better than you? Had his lordship your father been willing to lay aside his quarrel with Camden, this six years past come Shrovetide—had he bethought himself that his only son's life hung in the balance—had he summoned Camden, who was the nearest surgeon—but no, having sworn to ruin Camden's repute, he must needs send to Saltash for Trevane, for sottish, worse-than-useless Trevane—and that when your pressing need was for physic that same night! And so now we lie apart, with cold earth and sod and stone between us, when you might have been still in my bed.

I pray you, Hal, do not judge me in haste. I have a horror of judgements which cannot be undone. This present disgrace took root when you and I were little more than children, in 1616 when your father sued and won his unjust judgement against Thomas Penhallow, and, when Penhallow would have appealed, the Justice replied to him in the words King James had used to Star Chamber, that "it is better to maintain an unjust judgement, than ever to be questioning after sentence is passed." So that Penhallow was ruined, losing house and lands and all, and it was rumoured his child starved and his wife left him because of it, too.

Penhallow had reason enough to hate your father, Hal, but he dropped from sight, and for fifteen years his lordship had no thought of him save to gloat now and again over those words of his late Majesty, words which could be turned to such convenient use.

But some while after you were buried, your father went to work on Master Carnsew and Sir Edward, and by wearing them down he was able, last year, to buy out both their shares in the Wheal Nancy mine. And one day going to see his new mine, and standing to look on at the men who were drawn up out of the shaft, he met with one who, on stepping into the light of day, stood gazing back at his lordship. Then your father peered more closely, and saw beneath the grime and ore dust and coating of years, and knew this man to be Thomas Penhallow.

We searched and made enquiry (for after Harkness refused to stop longer in Wilharthen House your father had made of me, though a woman, a sort of secretary; a clever economy it was for him, seeing he need pay me no more than food, gowns, and chamber in Wilharthen, which he must have provided me in any case; nor could I leave him like Harkness, having nowhere to go). But all we learnt from the enquiry was that Penhallow had been three or four years in the Wheal Nancy, working as a tributer, for a share of the ore he brought to surface, and a good man for finding out new lodes; and the mine captain thought he had come from the Great Pelcoath when it filled with water, but how long he had been at Pelcoath, or where he lived before that, the mine captain could not say.

Your father privately fed a hope that now Penhallow had seen his old and powerful enemy, he would leave of his own will; but when the man did not do so, his lordship began to cheat him of his earnings. Your father had learned well enough, Hal, the arts of juggling accounts and corrupting assayers. To my shame, I also helped him cast up his columns of false figures—there are so many little persecutions a man may put upon his daughter-in-law day by day, she living alone under his roof.

But Penhallow did not leave—only his pile of ore grew less, which diminished your father's profits a little. Then, in the next fortnight there was a cave-in that shut up the new tunnel, and although no men were trapped therein, yet no ore could be got from it for three days while they dug it out again. At the last, his lordship went again to see how he might have more tin out of the miners, when Penhallow's core, having come up after their morning's time below, and playing at quoits, a quoit flew astray and narrowly missed your father, who would believe not otherwise but that it had come in malice from Penhallow's hand.

Whether indeed Thomas Penhallow meant your father some bodily mischief, or your father merely chose to believe it was so, his lordship now made up his mind he must see to the man he had wronged fifteen years ago, before that man saw to him. There was a certain worthless fellow called Ned Curnow working at the Nancy, or rather signed on to draw his month's pay, for little ore he ever brought to surface. They said that some traces in his speech and bearing shewed him to be a gentleman or gentleman's son fallen into low estate, and scarcely a day passed but Curnow was in mischief of some sort, and often serious mischief.

The mine captain pointed him out to your father, that same day of the quoit, and remarked he wished to turn this Curnow out of the mine. His lordship questioned the captain more closely, and ended by telling him to have the fellow come round to see him at Wilharthen House.

Curnow did not come round until two mornings after, and being let in by Bosvannion (our new steward, Hal; old Parsons died a fortnight after you), and finding us in the parlour, he bowed, and looked at me as a man looks at a woman, past my thirtieth year as I was, and still in the mourning I have meant never to lay aside. Then, taking an apple from the bowl on the table, he sat in the oaken armchair, which used to be your favourite, and put his feet on the settle.

Three weeks before, this vagabond had been whipt through the streets of Saltash, and stood in the pillory, and cared not who knew it, and yet he bore himself as if Wilharthen were an ale-house, and your father his drinking companion. Only to me, Hal, did Curnow shew respect. I sat on and sewed. Your father had brought me far enough into his confidence that, though he did not tell me in so many words all that was in his heart, he cared little whether I went or whether I remained.

His lordship told Curnow of the enquiries he had made. "It was only by the grace of Sir Edward Chilwidden," said he, "that you were not banished to the galleys when you would not say the name of your home parish, and it is only the lightest thread holds you from the Stannary Gaol now."

"Send me up, then," said Curnow, "to galleys or gaol, whichever you will."

The rogue had washed his face, I think, before coming up, and perhaps even his hair, which fell long and golden on his shoulders; but his beard was untrimmed and the rags he wore left the dust of the mine on all they touched, and he was like a man who has lost all joy and desire and hope, so that he no longer cares how long he lives or when he dies.

I too, Hal, I had lost all joy, all desire and hope, and there have come lines into my face, and silver hairs amongst the chestnut. I would look very seldom in my glass but that it was your gift to me.

So your father talked for some minutes to Curnow, sounding him, as I have seen him sound the mettle of a mare before buying, or the honesty of a judge before bribing, whilst Curnow sat and ate his apple. The colour of Curnow's eyes was between green and grey, and he looked at your father as I think he might look at a long deep shaft in the mine.

At length his lordship came to the point, and offered Curnow fifteen pounds for doing away with, for killing Thomas Penhallow.

Curnow put back his head and laughed. "So I am to murder a man," he said, "and be paid for 't, too. How if I were to go to the magistrates with this tale?"

His lordship replied that "I have the magistrates in my purse, and the judges, too."

Curnow threw the core of his apple into the fire. "I misdoubt it," said he, "if you pay them in proportion as you offer to pay me."

Then they haggled over the money as if Penhallow had been a pound of fish or a pile of ore, and at last Curnow settled for twenty-five pounds. His lordship gave him ten, and told him to return when he had done it, and to come at night. Curnow bowed to me again in leaving us, and looked once more into my eyes, as a man looks at a woman. I dropt my eyes to my seam. (Your father had money enough, Hal; I could have sewed with good thread, that was not forever knotting and breaking.)

I had no power to stop this thing, Hal, but what great difference was there, after all, between how your father had dealt with Thomas Penhallow fifteen years ago and how he would deal with him now? In any case, whatever we keep hid from outsiders and strangers, it is no life to go about in ignorance and suspicion of those under the same roof with you, those on whom you depend, and I judged it better I should know, than only suspect.

This was why I sat up with your father into the night, to see the play run out to its end. His lordship had sent the steward on some errand to Launceston, and ordered Betty to her room an hour before sunset, to stay there all the night as punishment for some fault he pretended she had made in sweeping her kitchen, all so that we would be alone. And I much thought he meant to settle all likelihood of Curnow ever telling of the crime he had committed.

There had come no word nor even rumour from the mine during the day, and we did not know whether Curnow would return on this

night or another—or indeed, I thought, ever. Your father sat and
studied over his accounts. You remember how he loved his accounts,
Hal; as others love their coin, and more, for there was ever the hope
of catching some mistake I had made in casting them up, for which
he might take me to task. I nodded over my book, and as the hours
passed I rose to pour out a glass of wine from the silver bottle which
had been your mother's pride.

"I would advise you against it, Margery," said your father grimly.

I smelled the wine. It was hippocras, sleep-heavy with many
spices. I brought back the glassful and set it at his elbow, rather
than my own. He did not drink. "Why did you not find some means
of killing Penhallow by your own hand?" I asked.

"Penhallow would not have trusted himself near enough my
hand," said your father. "Nor would I have trusted myself near his."

"Perhaps Ned Curnow will not trust himself near your hand again,
neither," said I, measuring my words.

"I took the man's measure," said his lordship. "There is fifteen
pounds in the balance. He will come."

I thought that your father had but applied his own scale to Curnow, while that insolent man with neither hope nor desire nor fear
in his grey-green eyes had likely taken better measure of his lordship. But I did not speak this thought, and so we waited.

Somewhat after midnight a storm broke, and, thinking Curnow
would not come, I might have sought my bed; but every moment I
delayed would lengthen out into another moment, and yet another,
and so I sat on, scarce thinking, with my book open in my lap.

Your father had laid aside even his accounts, and all was still,
excepting only the thunder and rain without. A mouse ventured
into the middle of the floor. Your father said, "We must find another
cat," and at the sound of his voice the mouse scurried away.

Close on to one, Curnow came, knocking at the door in the pattern
they had arranged. His lordship sent me with a rushlight to bring
in his hireling. Curnow was wrapped in a ragged sodden cloak, and
trailed mud and filth wherever he stepped, yet on seeing me, he
gave me a greeting which shewed he had indeed had gentle breeding
once.

When we were come again into the parlour, his lordship stood
with the silver bottle in one hand already and a fresh glass in the
other. "Have you done it?" he asked.

Curnow unwrapped the cloak and tossed it down on the bench.
Beneath it he carried in one hand his miner's pickaxe of iron. The

rain had wetted him through, cloak and all, but had not utterly rinsed away the blood and bits of hair from the flat-headed end. Curnow stepped forward to shew it his lordship at closer hand.

His lordship looked closely at the blood, and nodded. "There is your fifteen pounds, safe in the purse," said he. "But drink you a glass of hippocras before you go, to warm you against the weather."

"Tom Penhallow told me much about you before he died," replied Curnow, "and there is one thing which I owe his soul."

And turning the pickaxe to its sharpened end, he drove it into your father's skull. The poisoned wine mingled with the blood and streams of filthy water, and the silver bottle took a great dent as it fell and struck the floor.

Curnow let fall his pickaxe with your father's corpse, and turned to me. He smiled. "Here is enough of murder for the day, my lady," he said. "But do not follow me, lest you take a chill in the storm."

I smiled at him then as a woman smiles at a man. "There will no one come until the morning," I said. "Time enough to take off your clothes and dry them by the fire."

Hal, your father never did but one good work in the whole of his life, and that was the begetting of you, and that he undid again the night he let you die for his stubborn heart. Yet he was your father, and my father-in-law, and murdered, and he had at least the bowels to leave me better provided for by his death than he had in his life. Let his slayer go out into the night and the storm, and by morning was it likely they could find so much as his trail?

Forgive me, Hal, my husband, but how else could I keep Ned Curnow until the morning, when he could be taken, save in my bed?

Lloyd Biggle, Jr.

Have You a Fortune in Your Attic?

Grandfather and the Great Fiddle Mystery ... Was the old violin, stored in the Peterson attic lo these many years, a genuine Stradivarius? The trouble was, Grandfather knew nothing at all about violins ...

Detective: GRANDFATHER RASTIN

It was a sight Borgville had never seen before and most likely would never see again, and I almost missed it.

It had been raining hard all morning, and for want of anything else to do I was down in the cellar getting in some target practice with my air rifle. I had a couple of windows open, and when I heard something that sounded like a herd of cows stampeding along the sidewalk, naturally I went to look.

It was Doc Beyers' wife, and she was *running!*

Mrs. Beyers prides herself on being the most sedate woman in Borgville—though as Grandfather says, she really hasn't much choice. There's so much of her to move around that it's only a question of doing it sedately or staying put. She even holds her laughs down to chuckles because of what she'd have to move if she cut loose with anything more violent than that. If I'd known she was going to be running in front of our house, I'd have set up some chairs and charged admission.

I watched her until she started up our walk, and then I headed for the stairs. I got to the front hall just as she came stumbling across the porch. My Grandfather Rastin had seen her coming, and he was waiting at the front door. He helped her out of her raincoat, and she gasped, "Elizabeth . . ." and collapsed onto the sofa.

"Take it easy," Grandfather said.

"Elizabeth . . ."

"Elizabeth will keep for a couple of minutes. She's standing outon her porch now, looking over this way, so she can't be in very bad shape. Wait till you get your breath back."

For the next ten minutes Mrs. Beyers panted on the sofa, and was hushed up by Grandfather every time she opened her mouth. I came close to dying of curiosity, but Grandfather sat down and rocked as if it was an ordinary social call. He always says the first lesson a man has to learn from life is patience, and in eighty years he'd learned it pretty well.

Finally Mrs. Beyers got a grip on her breathing, and Grandfather let her talk.

"Elizabeth found a violin in her attic!" she said.

Grandfather nodded. "You don't say. That'd be . . ."

"It's a Strad—Strad—"

"Stradivarius? You don't say. That'd be . . ."

"It's worth a fortune."

"You don't say. That'd be Old Eric's fiddle. I heard him play it many times, when I was a boy. I often wondered what happened to it."

"It's a godsend, what with Elizabeth needing money for Ellie's wedding. She wants you to come and see it."

"I've seen it," Grandfather said. "Many times. Old Eric was quite a fiddler in his day."

"He lived to be a hundred and two," Mrs. Beyers said.

"A hundred and three. And he loved to tell about the time . . ."

"Will you come and see it?"

"I suppose."

We got our raincoats and went back to Elizabeth Peterson's house with Mrs. Beyers, all three of us walking very sedately.

Elizabeth Peterson has been a widow for more years than I am old, and in a friendly sort of way half the women in Borgville hate her. She's the example everyone holds up to them. She has no regular income at all, and has to work at anything offered to her at Borgville wages, which aren't much; but somehow she manages wonderfully well.

Lately, though, she'd been worried. Her daughter Ellie, the prettiest girl in Borgville, was graduating from high school and getting married. Her fiancé was Mark Hanson, whose father is our Village President, and President of the Borgville Bank, and the richest man in town. Naturally, Mrs. Peterson wanted her daughter to have the prettiest wedding and the biggest and best reception in the history of Borgville, if not the whole state of Michigan; but she didn't have any money.

So I wasn't surprised to find her hardly touching the floor as she paced up and down her porch waiting for us. Even I had a vague notion that a genuine Stradivarius might be worth a lot of money.

"Do you think it really is?" she asked Grandfather, all out of breath, as if she, rather than Mrs. Beyers, had been doing the running.

"Of all the things I'm not an expert in," Grandfather said, "it's violins. But I'll take a look. How'd you happen to find it?"

"It was more a matter of remembering it than finding it. It's been up there in the corner of the attic for years, and I guess I just forgot it was there. The funny thing is, I knew all the time it was valuable. It's a tradition in the Peterson family. My husband told me once that when he was a little boy playing in the attic, his mother would tell him not to go near Grandpa Eric's fiddle, because it was a valuable instrument. It never occurred to me that the value could be measured in money."

"It's the usual way of doing it," Grandfather said.

"Anyway, yesterday at the church social Miss Borg gave a talk about people finding fortunes in their attics—in old stamps and books and things; so afterwards I asked her—just as a joke—about old violins, and she came by today, and—come in and see it."

Miss Borg was still there, standing by the big round dining-room table. She's a little old lady with white hair, and she looks nothing like the terror she is teaching history at Borgville High School. The violin was on the table, and she was gazing at it as if it were the Holy Grail in Tennyson's *Idylls of the King,* which is one of the numerous epics the students at Borgville High have stuffed into them.

The violin looked like something that might possibly raise nine cents at a rummage sale. The case was a battered old thing of wood. The hinges were missing, and it had been held together with a couple pieces of rope. The one string left on it had snapped, and the whole contraption was falling apart. There were loose pieces in the bottom of the case, and on the violin there was a big crack along one side, which meant that whatever else it might do, it would never hold water. There was loose hair all over the place, except on the bow where it belonged.

Miss Borg said when she was a little girl she heard the Peterson family legend about Old Eric's valuable violin, but she doubted that anyone, including Old Eric, ever realized just how valuable it was. She shined a flashlight down into the violin, and said, "Look!"

Grandfather looked, and then I looked. Pasted inside the violin was a piece of paper, brown with age, and on the paper were some letters. The ink had faded, and some of it was illegible, but with Miss Borg's help I was able to make out: ... *adivarius Cremon* ...

"That's the label," Miss Borg whispered. "See—it says so right here." She had a thick book called *Biographical Dictionary of Musicians,* and under "Stradivari, Antonio," it said, "His label reads: 'Antonius Stradivarius Cremonensis. Fecit Anno. . . .' "

Grandfather scratched away at his head. "I guess it might say that. The only way to tell whether or not it's genuine is to take it to an expert. I suppose if it's a valuable instrument it could be fixed up."

"A violin maker could take it all apart and put it together again," Miss Borg said. "It would be as good as new. Better. An old instrument is always better than a new one."

"Maybe," Grandfather said. "My advice would be not to get excited about it until you hear what an expert has to say."

Mrs. Peterson wasn't listening. "What do you think it's worth?"

"I've heard that Stradivarius violins bring as much as fifty thousand dollars," Miss Borg said. "Or more. Of course some are worth more than others. Even if it isn't one of the best ones it should bring quite a lot. Five or ten thousand dollars, at least."

"Five or ten thousand!" Mrs. Peterson said.

"Since it's Saturday, you won't be able to do anything with it before the first of the week," Grandfather said. "First thing Monday morning."

"Five or ten thousand!" Mrs. Peterson said again. Most likely she'd just moved the wedding reception from the church basement to the big room above the Star Restaurant.

"Maybe there's someone in Jackson who'd know about it," Grandfather said. "On Monday. . . ."

Mrs. Peterson still wasn't listening. She looked again at the violin—looked at it as if she was seeing it for the first time—and then she sat down and started to cry. Grandfather dragged me out of there, and on the front porch we met Hazel Morgan, Dorothy Ashley, and Ruth Wood, all coming to see the violin. Half a dozen others were on their way, from various directions. It was then I noticed that Mrs. Beyers hadn't come in with us. She was out spreading the Good Word. . .

Grandfather hadn't anything to say on the way home, or even after we got there.

As soon as it stopped raining he went over to Main Street to borrow the Detroit paper from Mr. Snubbs, who runs the Snubbs Hardware Store; and the rest of the day, whenever I mentioned the violin, he hushed me up.

"Whether or not a violin was made by Stradivarius is just not the kind of question I can settle," he said. "I refuse to waste any energy even thinking about it."

"Miss Borg shouldn't have spouted off about all those dollars before they find out for sure," I said.

"Miss Borg should be shot."

On Saturday night all the stores in Borgville stay open late so the farmers can spend the money they were too busy to spend all week, and almost everyone comes to town. That night the talk up and down Main Street was about Elizabeth Peterson's violin. Suddenly everyone in town remembered hearing a grandfather, or an uncle, or some elderly person down the street tell about what a remarkable fiddler Old Eric Peterson was, and what a valuable violin he had.

The queer thing was that my Grandfather Rastin, who usually remembers such things better than anyone else, was acting skeptical about the whole business.

He and some other old-timers were sitting on the benches in front of Jake Palmer's Barber Shop, and when Grandfather suggested that it might be better to get an expert's opinion before sticking a price tag on the violin, Nat Barlow got pretty hot about it.

"Everyone knows it's valuable," he said. "My father heard Old Eric say so himself. Anyway, Old Eric played dances all over this part of the state, even some in Detroit, and everyone said he was the best fiddler they'd ever heard. Why wouldn't he have a valuable violin?"

"Is Sam Cowell in town tonight?" Grandfather asked.

"Haven't seen him," Nat said.

"How much would you say his car is worth?"

Everyone laughed.

"That pile of junk?" Nat said.

"There isn't a better driver in Borg County than Sam Cowell," Grandfather said. "Seeing as he's such a good driver, why wouldn't he have a valuable car?"

That shut Nat up for the next hour or so.

"I've been trying to remember a few things about Old Eric," Grandfather said. "He loved to talk about the time he played for Ole Bull, and Ole Bull. . . ."

"Who—or what—is Ole Bull?" someone asked.

"He was a famous Norwegian violinist. One of the greatest." Grandfather said. "He was touring the country giving concerts, and Old Eric went way off to Cincinnati, or Chicago, or somewhere to hear him. He took his fiddle along, on the chance of picking up some money along the way, and after the concert he got to meet Ole Bull. He introduced himself as another Norwegian fiddler, and Ole Bull asked him to play. Old Eric . . ."

The crowd wasn't much interested in Ole Bull.

"They tell me a Wiston reporter was over to see Elizabeth this evening," Bob Ashley said. "There'll be a piece about the violin in the Wiston newspaper."

"Got your oats in yet, Bob?" Grandfather asked.

"I don't suppose a Stradivarius violin turns up every day," Bob said.

That was when Grandfather headed for home, looking mighty disgusted. I caught up with him and asked for his version of the Peterson family legend.

"I never heard of any legend," he said. "Old Eric may have told his family something about that violin, and whatever he told them was so, because Old Eric was no fool. If it was a Stradivarius violin he'd have known it, and so would everyone else in Borgville, which makes it seem odd that I never heard anything about it. On the other hand, I do remember *something* about Old Eric's fiddle, but I haven't been able to recollect what it is."

After Sunday dinner the next day, we sat on our front porch and watched the procession to Elizabeth Peterson's house. Those who hadn't seen the violin yet wanted to see it, and a lot of those who'd seen it wanted to see it again, and traffic on our street was heavy.

Then Mark Hanson came by. He was home from the University for the week-end, and on his way to an afternoon date with Ellie. Mrs. Beyers met him in front of our house, and made some crack about him marrying an heiress, and he shrugged and came up on the porch to talk to Grandfather.

"Family tradition to the contrary," he said, "I don't think that violin is worth a button. And it can't possibly be a Stradivarius. It has a very odd shape—too short and too wide. Did you notice?"

"One violin looks just about like another one to me," Grandfather said.

"I talked to Mr. Gardner—he's the orchestra director at Wiston High School. He says thousands of violins have a Stradivarius label, but all it means is that the violin maker *copied* a Stradivarius violin, or tried to. This one isn't even a good copy."

"What does Ellie think about all this?" Grandfather asked.

"Oh, she agrees with me, but we're both worried about her mother. The truth will be a terrible blow to her, and there doesn't seem to be a thing we can do about it. Mr. Gardner is coming over this evening to see the violin. Most likely one look is all he'll need."

"If it's the wrong shape, as you say, then anyone who knows violins would see that right away. When is he coming?"

"He wasn't sure—sometime after eight."

"I'll be over," Grandfather said. "I'd like to hear what he has to say."

"Glad to have you," Mark said. "But please don't tell anyone else he's coming. What he has to say may not be good news, and I don't want a big audience there."

Mark went after Ellie, and the two of them walked back up the street hand in hand, Ellie looking pretty in a new spring dress and Mark admiring her as a fiancé should. By that time I'd gotten tired watching the procession, so I went off to play baseball; but I made a point of being on hand when Grandfather went over to Peterson's that evening.

News has a way of getting around in Borgville, and there was a good crowd there—enough to fill the parlor, anyway. Mrs. Peterson bustled about, happy and excited, trying to feed everyone. The Peterson family legend got another kicking around, and every now and then someone would go into the dining room for another look at the violin.

It was nearly nine o'clock when Mr. Gardner came up the street, driving slowly and looking for house numbers, which very few houses in Borgville have. He had to be introduced to everyone, and he went through the motions of this in a very abrupt way, as if he wanted to get on with the business at hand. I noticed when I shook hands with him that his hands were white and soft, and sometimes he would bow to a lady and show the bald spot at the top of his head.

"It's in here," Mark said finally, and led him into the dining room. Miss Borg and Mrs. Peterson and Ellie went along. The rest of us crowded up to the big arch that separates the dining room from the parlor, and watched.

Miss Borg tried to give Mr. Gardner the flashlight, so he could see the label, but he waved it away. "I don't care what's written inside," he said. He picked up the violin, and it came out of the case trailing loose parts. He looked at it, turned it over for a glance at the bottom, and put it back.

There wasn't a sound in the house. In the parlor everyone had stopped breathing.

I will say this for him—he didn't prolong the suspense.

Mrs. Peterson's face went suddenly white. "You mean—it isn't worth anything?"

"Worth anything?" Mr. Gardner snorted. Grandfather snorts sometimes, when he's real disgusted, but this was a different kind of snort. A nasty kind. "It's worth something, I suppose. If you had it fixed up, which would cost—oh, maybe fifty dollars, if you include a new case—then you might be able to sell it for twenty-five. My recommendation is that you burn it—there are enough bad violins around. One less would make the world a better place—a better place for violin teachers, anyway."

He left without waiting to be thanked—though Mrs. Peterson was in no condition to thank him anyway. Everyone else left right after him, except Miss Borg, who was indignant, and Grandfather, who seemed very thoughtful.

"The idea!" Miss Borg said. "Why, he didn't even look at the label!"

"If you don't mind . . ." Mrs. Peterson said. Then she started to cry, and it wasn't at all like the crying she'd done when she thought the violin was worth a lot of money.

"Don't burn it just yet," Grandfather said to Ellie. "I want another look at it myself."

Ellie nodded, and Mark showed us to the front door.

"Well," I said to Grandfather as we crossed the street, "I guess the wedding reception is back in the church basement."

He didn't seem to hear me. "I finally remembered something," he said.

"Something about the violin?"

"It was such a long time ago. I was only a boy, you know, when Old Eric died. But it seems . . ."

He went straight up to the rocking chair in his bedroom, where he usually takes his problems, and he was still rocking when I went to bed. I couldn't see how rocking would turn Mrs. Peterson's piece of junk into a valuable violin, but I didn't ask him about it. There are times when it is better not to bother Grandfather with questions, and one of them is when he's in his rocking chair.

In the morning it seemed as if all his rocking was wasted, because Sheriff Pilkins dropped in while we were still at breakfast, to ask Grandfather if he'd heard anything about a burglary the night before.

"Not yet, I haven't," Grandfather said. "Where was it?"

"Elizabeth Peterson's house," the Sheriff said. "Someone stole a violin."

Grandfather and I yelped together. "Violin!"

"Yep. She had this violin on her dining-room table, and when she came down this morning it was gone. Naturally she can't remember the last time she bothered to lock her doors. Funny thing, though—the burglar wasn't really stealing it. He was buying it. He left her an envelope full of money."

"How much money?" Grandfather asked.

"A thousand dollars."

Grandfather whistled, and I dropped the toast into my cereal. "Last night Mr. Gardner said that violin might be worth twenty-five dollars if she spent fifty dollars fixing it up," I said.

"So I heard," the Sheriff said. "There are some funny angles to this case. How many people knew she had what might be a valuable violin?"

"Half of Borg County," Grandfather said.

"Right. And how many of them knew this Mr. Gardner said the violin was practically worthless?"

"Those that were there last night, and whoever they managed to tell before they went to bed. Maybe about a fourth of Borg County."

"That leaves a lot of people who didn't know."

"You won't have any trouble narrowing down your list of suspects," Grandfather said. "There aren't very many people around here who'd have a ready thousand dollars for a speculative flutter on a violin."

"Tell me something I don't know."

"How is Elizabeth taking it?"

"Not very well. She's pretty blamed mad about the whole thing. She's sure now that the violin is worth a fortune, and someone is trying to do her out of it."

"It's just possible that taking a thousand dollars for that violin is more of a crime than stealing it."

"That's what I think myself. But Elizabeth is certain the thief wouldn't have left the thousand if he hadn't known it was worth a lot more. She wants her violin back, and hang the money. Which is why I'm here. You didn't chance to notice any suspicious-looking characters hanging around last night, did you?"

"Borgville doesn't have any suspicious-looking characters," Grandfather said.

"They're all suspicious-looking to me. Look—I know you can come up with information I can't touch. Let me know if you find out anything."

Grandfather nodded. "I'll go have a talk with Elizabeth, and look around."

So Grandfather went to Peterson's, and I went to school. Miss Borg intercepted me in the hallway, and asked me if I'd heard the news. She seemed excited about it—in fact, until I could get to a dictionary I thought she was excited to the point of being sick, because she said she felt vindicated.

I didn't go home for lunch, so I don't know how Grandfather spent the day. Sheriff Pilkins passed the time working, which is something he has no natural aptitude for, and when he came to see Grandfather that evening he was looking glum.

"I have a list of suspects," he announced.

"Good," Grandfather said. "Then you're further along than I am."

Normally it would cheer the Sheriff up to find he's ahead of Grandfather in anything, but this time it seemed to make him mad. "Lucy Borg," he said, "was pretty irked at what Gardner said about the violin. She could have taken it with the idea of getting another expert opinion on it."

"Somehow I can't see Lucy burgling a house. And where would she get a thousand dollars?"

"Then there's this Gardner—he could have lied about the violin, and then stolen it so he could sell it himself. Elizabeth favors this theory."

"Why?"

"Who knows why a woman thinks anything? Gardner supports a big family on a schoolteacher's salary, and he wouldn't have been able to lay his hands on a thousand dollars on a Sunday night. Then there's Pete Wilks, who lives on Maple Street right behind Peterson's. He took an unusual interest in that violin."

"He had an old violin of his own," Grandfather said. "He was interested in finding out if his might be valuable. There is also the question of where he would get a thousand dollars. The money complicates things."

"It sure does. My favorite would be Mark Hanson. It's common knowledge that the Hansons tried to give Elizabeth money for the wedding, and she wouldn't take it. Mark could have used this as a back-handed way of making her take the money, and the Hansons are one family that could come up with a thousand dollars in a hurry. The only trouble is, they didn't do it. Mark was with Ellie until nearly midnight, and then his folks drove him back to Ann Arbor and stayed there overnight."

"So where does that leave you?" Grandfather asked.

"Nowhere!"

"I have an idea or two. Let's go see Elizabeth."

Mrs. Peterson met us at the door, and she didn't waste any time showing what was on her mind. "Did you get it back?" she asked the Sheriff.

Sheriff Pilkins sputtered all over the place. I guess law officers don't like blunt demands for quick results. They'd rather talk about all the progress they're making, which they can do without getting any results at all.

"Did you think over what we talked about this morning?" Grandfather asked.

"I certainly did," Mrs. Peterson said. "I want the violin."

"Give me the money, then, and I'll try and get it back for you."

The Sheriff stared at Grandfather. "Where are you going to get it?"

"The law isn't involved in this," Grandfather said. "Party unknown bought Elizabeth's violin for a thousand dollars. The transaction isn't satisfactory to her, so she's going to take the violin back and return the money—if I can arrange it, that is."

"Baloney!" the Sheriff shouted.

"I don't see that there's much you can do about it."

The Sheriff didn't seem to, either, and he stood there glaring at Grandfather. I'm not one who cares much for art, but I never get tired of watching the way his face changes color when he and Grandfather meet head-on.

Finally he stomped down off the porch, muttering something about accessories, and withholding information, and interfering with legal processes. Mrs. Peterson came back with an envelope and handed it to Grandfather.

"You understand," Grandfather said, "that if Gardner turns out to be right about the violin you've made a bad deal for yourself."

"We went through all that this morning," she said. "I want the violin."

"I'll get it for you if I can."

Grandfather stuffed the envelope into his shirt pocket, and the two of us went home.

I'd like to tell you all about Grandfather's system for tracking down a thief, but I can't. I expected him to make a mysterious telephone call as soon as it got dark, and then head for a meeting in some alleyway. Instead, he sat down and read all evening, and he was still reading when I went to bed.

In the morning, when I went down to breakfast, the violin was lying on *our* dining-room table.

"Where'd you get it?" I asked.

"You're most as bad as Pilkins. What difference does it make? Elizabeth will be satisfied, the person who took it is satisfied, and beyond that what happened is nobody's business."

After breakfast he took the violin over to Elizabeth Peterson, who was very happy to have it back–that is, she was happy until later that day, when Mr. Hanson drove her to Jackson to see a violin repair man there. This man told her even more emphatically than Mr. Gardner that the violin was nothing but junk, and he didn't think it would be worth twenty-five dollars even if it was fixed up.

The violin went back to the Peterson attic, and Mrs. Peterson started all over again to try to figure out how to pay for a big wedding and reception without any money, and Sheriff Pilkins stopped by three times a day the rest of the week in the hope of prying the name of the violin thief out of Grandfather.

Other than that, nothing happened. That is, I thought nothing happened, but on Friday, Jimmy Edwards, whose mother works in the telephone office at Wiston, asked me how come Grandfather was getting all those long distance telephone calls.

"What long distance telephone calls?" I asked.

"How would I know if you don't?" Jimmy said. "All I know is, Mom said your Grandfather has been getting calls from all over–New York, Los Angeles, Chicago . . ."

"I don't know," I said, "but I'm sure going to find out."

But I didn't. All Grandfather did when I asked him was grunt and shrug. All Friday evening he grunted and he shrugged, and all Saturday morning, until about ten o'clock. Then a big limousine

such as had never before been seen in Borgville drove up in front
of our house. A chauffeur in a fancy uniform popped out and opened
the rear door, and a tall, gray-headed man got out and walked up
to our house.

Grandfather met him on the porch.

"You're Mr. Rastin?" the man asked.

Grandfather nodded, and shook hands with him.

"Where is it?" the man asked.

"Across the street," Grandfather said.

They headed for the Peterson house, with me tagging along, and
Grandfather introduced the man to Mrs. Peterson—his name was
Edmund Van Something-or-other—and sent Ellie chasing up to the
attic after the violin.

We sat down in the parlor and waited.

"Has it been in your family for a very long time?" Mr. Van asked.

"It belonged to my husband's great-great-grandfather," Mrs. Peterson said.

"You don't say. Treasures are often preserved in this way. My
first Stradivarius violin . . ."

Ellie bounced in, all out of breath, and carefully placed the violin
on a coffee table beside Mr. Van. She untied the knots and took off
the top of the case, and then she scooted back out of the way, as if
she expected Mr. Van would be throwing the violin at someone as
soon as he saw it.

He did look at the violin. He looked at it once, with an expression
of disgust such as I never hope to see again. Then he picked up the
loose lid of the case, and held it on his lap looking at the violin bow
that was hooked onto it.

"François Tourte!" he said.

"The label is under that little doohicky that screws in and out,"
Grandfather said.

"Under the frog. Yes. It really has a label?"

He unscrewed something or other, fished a magnifying glass out
of his pocket, and said, speaking very softly, "This bow was made
by François Tourte in 1822, aged seventy-five years. Splendid!
Tourte never branded his bows, and rarely labeled them."

"Is it genuine?" Grandfather asked.

"Unquestionably genuine."

"I had no way of knowing. A label, of course, can be stuck onto
anything."

"Unfortunately true. Even a violin such as that one—" he made a face, "–could have a Stradivarius label. But craftsmanship cannot, as you say, be stuck on. One look at the shape of the head–Tourte. It still has the original frog–Tourte. The thickness of the shaft, the narrow ferrule–all unmistakably Tourte. And it's in remarkably fine condition. The grip is a little worn. The slide, too, but not badly. The man who owned this bow knew its value. I stand by my offer. I'll pay four thousand dollars for it."

He looked at Mrs. Peterson, and for a long moment she couldn't find her voice.

"You want to buy the violin?" she stammered.

Mr. Van winced. "Not the violin. The bow. This bow, Ma'am, was made by François Tourte, who was to the violin bow what Stradivarius was to the violin. And more. There were great violin makers before Stradivarius, but Tourte created the modern bow–its design, its materials, to some extent its mechanics. Without the Tourte bow, string instrument technique as we know it would be impossible, and the work of the great instrument makers would to a considerable extent be wasted. Will you sell the bow for four thousand dollars, Ma'am?"

"It's a very good offer," Grandfather said.

Mrs. Peterson still didn't seem to understand. "You mean–the violin . . ."

Mr. Van clapped his hand to his forehead. "The violin I do not want, but I'll buy it if I must. What is it worth? Five dollars? Ten? I'll give you four thousand and ten dollars for the violin and the bow."

"Oh," Mrs. Peterson said. "You just want the bow. I'll sell that, and keep the violin as a–a memento."

"Splendid!" Mr. Van whipped out a check book and began to scribble. He presented the check, shook hands with everyone present, and walked back to his car carrying the lid of the case with the bow still hooked onto it. He carried it the way I've seen couples carry their first baby when they bring it home from the hospital.

Mrs. Peterson sat down and gazed at the check for a long time. "I don't know how to thank you," she said. Then she started to cry, and Ellie looked as if she wanted to cry, too, and it was as good a time as any for Grandfather and me to get out of there, which we did.

"Sheriff Pilkins will have a fit," I said, when we got back to our porch.

"It'll do him good," Grandfather said.

"He'll say anyone who stole something worth four thousand dollars belongs behind bars, and he'll threaten to put you there if you don't tell him who it was."

"Let him threaten," Grandfather said. "That was one crime that will stay unsolved permanently."

"How'd you know the thing was valuable?"

"Something I remembered Old Eric saying. He played for Ole Bull, and he had a bow that was better than anything Ole Bull had. Ole Bull tried to buy it from him. I figured if the bow was good enough back in the eighteen sixties, or whenever it was, for a great violinist to want it, it might still be worth something. But none of these local experts thought to look at the bow. The violin was unbelievably bad, and it distracted their attention. So when I got the chance I looked at the bow, and I found that label. I told Professor Mueller, at Wiston College, and he said a Tourte bow might be worth a fair amount of money, and the person who'd pay the most for it would be a collector of old instruments."

"Why not a violinist?" I asked.

"A bow can be made today that plays just as well as that one. Maybe a little better, for all I know. It's the same as with postage stamps. An old stamp may be worth hundreds of dollars, but you can buy one at the post office for four cents that will do just as good a job of getting a letter through the mails. Professor Mueller got the word around to some collectors, and this man made the best offer, so I told him to come and see the bow."

"Then Old Eric knew the bow was valuable, rather than the violin, but after he died the family legend got things twisted."

"I suppose."

"That still doesn't explain who stole the violin."

"Like I said, that's one crime that won't ever be solved," Grandfather said.

"I'm not so sure," I said. "I think I can figure it out myself. Someone thought the violin just *might* be worth something in spite of what Mr. Gardner said. So he went to Mr. Hanson, and said, 'Look, we should get this violin to a genuine expert, but of course there's a good chance that it really isn't worth anything, so why not do it this way. You put up a thousand dollars, and I'll steal the violin and leave the money. If it turns out to be worth more, we can give Mrs. Peterson the difference. If it turns out to be worthless, she'll still have the thousand dollars for the wedding. She wouldn't accept the money as a gift, and now that Mr. Gardner has said the violin is junk she wouldn't sell it to us for a thousand dollars, because she'd figure that would be the same as a gift. But if we steal it, and leave the money, she'll think the thief didn't know it was junk and she's made a good deal for herself.' The only trouble was, Mrs. Peterson thought otherwise, and called in the Sheriff and messed everything up."

"Not bad," Grandfather said. "It only goes to show that you can't figure out in advance how a woman will react to anything."

"And of course there was only one person who had any reason to think the violin—or the bow—might be valuable even after Mr. Gardner said it was nothing but junk."

Grandfather grinned. "Right again. I stole it myself."

Brian W. Aldiss

The Lonely Habit

There are different types of British crime writing—as, of course, there should be. In contrast with the quiet, sedate type of crime story, here is an altogether different kettle of fish—a monstrous story, but so effectively told that you may find it strangely moving; an under-the-surface study that will disturb you, that will even give you the shudders . . .

People with my sort of interest in life are very isolated—that is, if they're intelligent enough to feel that kind of thing. My mother always says I'm intelligent. She's going to be annoyed when she hears I'm arrested for—well, no need to be afraid of the word—for murder.

We'll have a good laugh about it when I get out of here. That's one thing I do admire in myself. I may be intelligent, but I still have a sense of humor.

I dress well. Not too modern, to keep me apart from the younger set, but pretty expensive suits and a hat—I always wear a hat. Working for Grant Robinson's, see. They expect it. I'm one of their star representatives, and popular too, you'd say, but I don't mix with the others. And I would never—well, never do it to one of them. Or to anyone I know or am in any way connected with.

That's what I mean about intelligence. Some of these—well, some of these murderers, if you must use the word, they don't think. They do it to anyone. I do it only to strangers. Complete strangers.

Quite honestly—I say this quite honestly—I would not think of doing it to anyone I knew, even if I'd only just been introduced. My way, it's much safer, and I think I might claim it is more moral too. In the war, you know, they trained you to kill strangers; you got paid for it, and were even given medals. Sometimes I think that if I gave myself up and really told them *my* point of view—I mean really and sincerely from the heart—they would not, well, they'd give me a medal instead. I mean that. I'm not joking.

The first man I ever did it to, that was in the war. It was like a new life opening up for me. Since then, I suppose I've never done more than two a year, but how my life has changed! They talk a lot of nonsense about it, all these criminologists, so called. They don't know. But the bad habits it's cured me of!

I used to sleep so badly, I used to be nervous, used to drink too much, and all sorts of bad habits you mustn't mention. I read somewhere it weakened your eyes. And a funny thing, after I did that first fellow, I never had asthma again, and it used to trouble me a lot. Mother still sometimes says, "Remember how you used to wheeze all night when you was a little chap?" She's very affectionate, my mother. We make a good pair.

But this first fellow. It was an East Coast port—I forget the name, not that it matters so much, although I sometimes think I wouldn't mind going back there, you know, just for sentiment. Of course, I suppose your first—well, your first, you know, *victim* (there's a daft word!) is very much like your first love affair, if you go in for that sort of thing.

All the others, however many of them there have been, have never come up to that first one. It's never been quite the same. I mean, they've been lovely and well worthwhile from my point of view—but not a patch on that first one.

He was a sailor, and he was drunk, and I was in this convenience on the sea front. Terrible night it was, raining like fury, and I was sheltering in there when this chap reels in, quite on his own. I was in my army uniform—rifle, bayonet, and all—and he knocked my rifle over into the muck.

Really I was more scared than annoyed. He was so big, see, well over six foot, and terribly heavy. He asked me if I had a girl friend and of course I said no. So then he came at me—I mean, there wasn't much room. I thought it was some sort of sexual assault, but afterwards I thought about it over and over, and I came to the conclusion that he was just attacking me. You know these stupid people: they just like to use their fists, given the chance, and I think he was attacking me because he thought I was standing there with a purpose and that I had abnormal ideas. Which of course was not so. Happily I am very very normal.

Obviously I am tremendously brave too, because I was not scared when he came at me, although I had been before. My brain went very clear, and I said to myself, "Vern, you can kill this drunk with your bayonet!"

A great and tremendous thrill ran through me as I said it. And when I stuck the bayonet into him, it was as if I had guidance from Above, because I did not hesitate or miss or strike in the wrong place or not strike hard enough, or anything that anyone else might have done. At that time, I really did think I had received guidance from Above, because I was praying a lot in that period of my life; nowadays, the Almighty and I seem to have lost our old rapport. Well, times change, and we must accept the changes they bring.

He made a loud noise—very much like a sneeze. His arms went up and he fell all over me, pushing me against the door as if he was embracing me. Again that tremendous thrill went through me. Somehow it has never had the same power since.

I hung on to him, and he kicked and struggled to be fully dead. It was a bit alarming, because I wasn't sure if he was really a goner; but when he was finally still, I stood there grasping him and wishing he had another kick left in him.

The problem of disposing of him came next. When I pulled myself together and thought, that one was easily solved. All I did was drag him out of the place, through the rain, to the sea wall. I gave him a push; over he went, into the sea. It was still pouring with rain.

This is a funny thing. I saw that he had left a trail of blood all the way to the edge, but I did not like to stop and do anything about it because I hate getting wet; I hated it then and I'm still the same.

Perhaps that may sound careless of me. Perhaps I trusted to Providence. The rain poured down and washed all the stains away, and I never heard anything more about the matter.

For a while I forgot about it myself. Then the war was finished, and I went home. Father was dead, no great loss, so Mother and me set up together. We'd always been good friends. She used to buy my vests and pants for me. Still does.

I got restless. The memory of the sailor kept returning. Somehow, I wanted to do it again. And I wondered who the sailor had been—it seemed funny I didn't even know his name. In a book I once read it talked about people having "intellectual curiosity." I suppose that's what I had, intellectual curiosity. Yet I've heard people say that I look rather stupid—meaning it in a complimentary way, of course.

To recapture that first thrill I bought a little bayonet in a junk shop and took to looking into conveniences. I don't mean the big ones that are so noisy and busy and bright. I like the quaint old Victorian ones, the sleepy ones with drab paint and no attendants and hardly any customers. I am an expert on them. To me, they are beautiful—like old trams. Call me sentimental, but that's how I feel about them, and a man has a right to express himself. They arouse artistic promptings in me, the real ones do.

It was pure luck I found the one in Seven Dials. Most of the area was demolished, but this fine old convenience has been left, dreaming in a side alley. It is still lit by gas, and the gas-lighter man comes round every evening and lights it. That was the place I chose to—well, to repeat my success in, if you like.

It wasn't only a question of art, oh, no. In my job you have to be practical. I found that the inspection cover inside this place would come up easily. A ladder led down to another cover, eight feet below the first one. There were also pipes and things. When you opened this second cover, you were looking right into the main sewer.

It was as good as the seaside!

For my purpose this unhygienic arrangement could not have been better. I mean, when you've done with the—well, with the man's body—it must be disposed of. I mean, finally disposed of, or they'll be round after you, you know, the way they are in the films—like the Gestapo, you know, knocking at your door at midnight. Funny, here I sit in this cell and I don't feel the least bit scared. I didn't do it, really I didn't.

It's a very lonely habit, mine. When you're sensitive, you feel it badly at times. Not that I'm asking for pity. I reckon a lot of these chaps—well, a lot of *them* was lonely.

So I did it again. It was a sturdy little man this time—said he was some sort of a scout for a theatrical agent or something. Very soft-spoken, didn't seem to worry about what I was going to do. Most of them are really worried—wow! This scout, he just shed a tear as I let him have it, and did not kick at all.

Some hobbies start in a funny way—casually, if you like. I mean, as I got him down to the lower cover—I threw him down, of course—all the stuff came out of his inner pocket. I gathered it up and stuffed it in my own pocket before slipping him into the sewer, where the water was running fast to bear him away.

Frankly, it was a waste of effort. The glow just wasn't there. No inspiration and no relief. It just didn't come off. At the time I resolved never to do the trick again, in case—you never can be sure, you know—in case they found out.

Once back home with Mother, I made an excuse to slip up to my bedroom—naturally, we have separate rooms now—and I looked at what I had in my pocket. It was interesting—a letter from his sister, and two bills from his firm, and a clipping from a newspaper (two years old and very tattered) about a general visiting Russia, and a card about a pigeon race, and a little folder showing all the different shades of a shiny paint you could buy, and a union card, and a photograph of a little girl holding a tricycle, and another of the same little girl standing by herself and laughing. I stared at that photograph a lot, wondering what she could be laughing at.

One time I left it lying about and Mother found it and had a good look at it.

"Who's this then, Vern?"

"It's the son of a chap I work with—daughter, I mean."

"Nice, isn't it? What's her name?"

"I don't know her name. Give it here, Mum."

"Who's the chap? Her father, I mean, which is he?"

"I told you, I work with him."

"Is it Walter?" She had never met Walter, but I suppose I had mentioned his name.

"No, it's not Walter. It's Bert, if you must know, and I met his little girl when I went round to his place, so he thought I'd like a photo of her, because she took to me."

"I see. Yet you don't know her name?"

"I told you, Mother, I forgot it. You can't remember everyone's name, can you? Now give it here."

She can be very annoying at times. She and my father used to have terrible rows sometimes, when I was small.

As I said, mine is a lonely way of life. I began to dream of those hidden pockets, warm and safe and concealed, each with their secret bits and pieces of life. Everywhere I went I was haunted by pockets. I wished I had emptied all the pockets of that scout—wished it bitterly. You hear people say, "Oh, if I could have my time over again." That's how I felt, and I began wasting my life with regret.

Another man might have turned into a miserable little thief, but that was not my way. I've never stolen a thing in my whole life.

The third fellow was a disappointment. His pockets were almost empty, though he had some race-course winnings on him that I was able to use towards some little luxuries for Mother.

And then I suppose my luck was in, for the next three I did gave me something of the relief I found with my first—well, my first *partner*, you might say, to be polite about it. They were all big men. And what they had on them, hidden in their pockets, was very interesting.

Do you know, one of those men was carrying with him a neatly folded copy of a boys' magazine printed twenty years earlier, when he must have been a boy himself. You'd wonder what he wanted that for! And another had a nautical almanac and a copy of a catalogue of things for sale in a Berlin store and a sickly love letter from a woman called Janet.

All these things I kept locked up. I used to turn them over and over and think of them, and wonder about them. Sometimes, when the men were found to be missing, I could learn a little more about them from the newspapers. That was fun and gave me a great kick. One man was something big in the film world. I think that if life had been different for me, I might have been a—well, a detective. Why not? Of course, I am much happier as I am.

So time went on. I got very careful, more careful after each one. I mean, you never know. Someone may always be watching you. I remember how my dad used to peep round doors at me when I was small, and it gave me a start even when I hadn't done anything wrong.

Also, I got more curious. It was the intellectual curiosity at work, you see.

Now this brings us up to date, right smack up to date. Today!

See, I mean, it's been eighteen months since I—well, since I had a partner, as I sometimes think of it. But you get terribly lonely. So I went back to the Seven Dials one, and this time I said to myself, "Vern, my son, you have been very patient, and as a result I've got a little treat for you with this one."

Oh, I was very careful. I watched and watched, and was sure to pick on a type who obviously wasn't local, just passing through the area, so that there would be nothing to connect him with the Seven Dials.

He was a businessman, quite smart and small, which suited me well. Directly he went in the convenience I was after him, strolling in very slowly and naturally.

This fellow was in the one and only cubicle with the door open—the door hinge was broken, so the door wouldn't close really. But I don't change my mind once it is sort of cold and made up, so I went straight over to him and held my little bayonet so that it pricked his throat. He was much smaller than me, so I knew there wouldn't be a nasty scene; being fastidious, or squeamish you might say, I hate anything nasty like that.

I said to him, "I want to hear about a big secret in your

life–something you did that no one knows about! Make it quick, or I'll do you in!"

His face was a vile color, and he did not seem to be able to talk, though I could see by his clothes he was a superior man, rather like me in a way. I pricked his throat till it bled and told him to hurry up and speak.

Finally he said, "Leave me alone, for God's sake! I've just murdered a man!"

Well, that's what he said. It made me mad in a freezing sort of a way. Somehow I thought he was being funny, but before I could do anything, he must have seen the look in my eyes, and he grabbed my wrists and started babbling.

Then he stopped and said, "You must be a friend of Fowler's! You must have followed me from his flat! Why didn't I think he might be clever enough for that! You're a friend of Fowler's, aren't you?"

"I've never heard of him. I've nothing to do with your dirty business!"

"But you knew he was blackmailing me? You must know, or why are you here?"

We stood and stared at each other. I mean, I was really as taken aback by this turn of events as he was. For me this whole thing was meant to be a–well, I mean it was a sort of relaxation; I mean, it really is *necessary* for me, else I'd probably be flat on my back with asthma and goodness knows what else, and quite unable to lead a normal life, and the last thing I wanted to do was get mixed up with–well, with murder and blackmail and all that.

Just as I had reached the conclusion that maybe I ought to let this one go, he started to draw a gun on me. Directly his hand went down, I knew what he was after–just like in those horrible films that they really should ban from showing where they go for their guns and shoot those big chaps kak-kak-kak out of their pockets!

So I let him have it, very cold and quick, a very beautiful stroke that only comes with practice.

This time I could not wait for any sentimental nonsense. I opened the inspection cover and dropped him down, and then climbed down after him. I took his gun because I wished to examine the beastly thing before disposing of it. And then I slipped my hand into his warm inner pocket.

I found an open envelope containing a strip of film together with some enlargements from the negatives. Those photographs were positively indecent–I mean, really indecent, for they showed a girl, a grown girl, with no clothes on whatsoever. I did not need telling they were something to do with this blackmailer Fowler. They just showed what sort of a mind *he* had! The world was well rid of him, and this beauty who had tried to shoot me.

In an agony of embarrassment I slipped those vile things into my pocket to be examined later, opened the other hatch, and tipped him into the fast-flowing water. Then I shut down everything, wiped my face on my handkerchief, and walked out into the alley.

Two plainclothes men were waiting for me outside.

I was just so astonished I could not say a word. They said they wished to question me about the shooting of Edward Fowler, and before I knew what was what, before I could even telephone Mother, they were taking me away in a police car.

Everyone says the police aren't what they were. This time, they really have made a big mistake! But I have got a solicitor coming to sort things out for me, and at least I was able to send a message to Mother telling her that I was fine and not to keep lunch waiting for me.

I didn't tell them a thing—I mean, I can still keep my wits about me. I keep on saying I never heard of any Edward Fowler, and that's all I say.

Of course, the little pistol and those revolting photographs are going to be rather difficult to explain.

But I'm innocent—absolutely innocent! You can't tell me otherwise.

"Q"

Vincent McConnor

Just Like Inspector Maigret

Meet a new armchair detective—George Drayton, 73 years old, retired book publisher, devotee of mystery stories—as he becomes involved in his "first case." Old George Drayton's "armchair" is his favorite morning-bench or afternoon-bench in the private park of Knightswood Square; and in following George's park-bench private-eyeing you will get an intimate glimpse of an old (and old-fashioned) Square in the heart of London—in a story charmingly and lovingly told . . .

Detective: GEORGE DRAYTON

The green park in the heart of London, to the passing eye, had not changed in half a century. But to George Drayton, born 73 years ago in a vast bedroom overlooking Knightswood Square, it had been altered in every possible way. Nothing was as it used to be.

He was the second person to enter the Square, fog or shine, every morning. Purdy, the gardener, was always the first, and Mrs. Heatherington the third. Actually she was fourth because her ancient Pekinese, Kwong Kwok, darted through the gate ahead of his mistress. That was how it had been for more than 30 years. Except that the gardener was never there on Sundays or bank holidays. On those days George Drayton was the first.

Every resident of the long rows of identical mansions surrounding Knightswood Square possessed a key which unlocked all the gates in the shoulder-high iron fence. A discreet sign near each gate warned that this was a private park.

George Drayton sniffed the morning air as he stepped out under the white-pillared portico and let the massive front door close itself behind him. He stood for a moment on the broad top step, eyes darting across the sunny Square in search of Purdy. A blue veil of smoke curled at the far northern corner. The gardener would be burning yesterday's accumulation of twigs and dead flowers. He daily raked every path and walk, picked up each fallen leaf and broken branch. Before dusk they were always neatly piled for burning the following morning.

The sun had climbed above the chimneys on the opposite side of the Square, dropping a curtain of haze across the elegant Regency façades so that all he could see was a blur of white columns against shadowed brick. It was going to be a pleasant August day. He would sit on his morning-bench under the protecting branches of the oak tree. There were several favorite benches he occupied, depending upon time of year and weather, but never the same bench, morning and afternoon.

George started down the shallow marble steps to the sidewalk and was careful not to drop his books or leather cushion. He carried three books into the park every morning. Today there was a new novel from his own publishing house and two detective novels.

"Morning, sir." Fitch, the caretaker, squinted up the basement steps where he was polishing the brass hand-rail. "Another fine day, sir."

"Splendid." He kept walking or Fitch would come charging up the steps for a chat that could delay him at least ten minutes. On those unfortunate mornings when it was impossible to escape, Mrs. Heatherington and Kwong Kwok always reached the Square ahead of him.

He hesitated at the curb and peered up and down for any moving vehicles. There was only the milkman pulling his small cart at the far end of the street. George walked more briskly as he crossed to the narrow pavement which edged Knightswood Square. Reaching the curb he slowed his steps again and headed for the nearest gate. He rested the cushion and books on the gate post as he felt in his pocket for the key. There was always a moment of panic when he was unable to find it among the jumble of loose objects. Blast! He would have to go all the way back to his flat. Fitch couldn't help him. None of the caretakers were permitted to have keys. Then his fingers touched cold metal and a sigh of relief escaped from his lips.

George unlocked the gate and stepped into the Square. He had made it ahead of the Pekinese.

Before closing the gate he removed his key from the lock and dropped it back into his pocket. Then, in a final burst of speed, he headed for the shaded morning-bench under the oak tree. He placed his leather cushion on the bench and sat on it, arranging the books beside him.

As he filled his first pipe for the day he let his eyes wander over the familiar mansions around the Square. George knew who lived behind every window. He also knew who slept late, who was ill, dying, or convalescent, and which wife had left which husband. His charwoman, Mrs. Higby, kept him informed. Twice a day she reported all the latest news of Knightswood Square. At the moment she complained that nothing much was happening. There had been little worth talking about since last year's murder. That sort of thing didn't happen often enough to please Mrs. Higby.

She came to him for several hours, every day but Sunday, and also did daily work in two other mansions on the Square. Late morning, while he sat in the park, Mrs. Higby would straighten the flat and cook his lunch. He always made his own tea but she would return, after finishing her other jobs, and prepare his supper before catching a bus home to Putney.

Each day as she served his lunch and supper she reported, with relish, the news of the day. He looked forward to Mrs. Higby's gossip because, otherwise, he would never know what was going on behind his neighbors' windows. It had been exasperating, last winter, when she was kept to her bed with the flu. He had hired a woman through an agency but she had known nothing about the other residents of the Square. It was as though his morning and evening papers had not been delivered for three weeks.

Purdy wheeled an empty barrow past, without a word, touching an earthy finger to his leather cap. He never paused for conversation until late in the afternoon.

George watched as the gardener settled down to work, digging at the roots of a rosebush. Then he turned to look across to the south side of the Square, but there was no sign of Mrs. Heatherington and her Pekinese.

He checked his watch. 9:36. Six minutes late! Very likely packing for her holiday. She was taking an afternoon train from Victoria Station to Brighton where her daughter-in-law would be waiting to drive her across to Hove. The old lady spent two weeks every August with her son and his family in their pleasant Georgian house overlooking the distant seashore. Mrs. Higby had described the place to him, in detail, many times; she had heard all about it from her friend, Mrs. Price, who came in twice a week to char for Mrs. Heatherington.

A blur of movement caught his eye at the opposite side of the park and he turned his head to see someone on a bicycle. As his eyes adjusted to the distance he saw that it was Willie Hoskins who, once a month, washed every window facing the Square. Each flat had its regular day for the window cleaner.

Willie braked his bicycle in front of Number 26, hoisted it across the pavement, and propped it against the railing of the basement areaway.

Then he lifted a bucket from the handlebar and carried it up the steps to the front door. George could see the flash of color as the sun caught in Willie's red hair, noticed the yellow rubber gloves tucked under the wide leather belt that circled his waist, the faded blue shirt and trousers as the boy went into the house. Boy? He was a married man of 23 with a wife who, according to Mrs. Higby, regularly had him up before a local magistrate on charges of drunkenness, nonsupport, and knocking her about.

The tenants of the Square frequently threatened to dispense with Willie's services, but he would disarm them with his great smile, flashing white teeth and tossing his curly head. It was suspected that Willie was not averse to tossing some of the ladies of Knightswood Square between washing windows. "He's a complete rascal, he is!" Mrs. Higby would say. "Always leave the front door wide when he does any windows where I be."

George turned to look, once again, for Mrs. Heatherington. She was just coming down the front steps of the mansion where she had a second-floor-front flat. The Pekinese was pulling on his leash, furious at being late, eager to get into the park. He yanked his mistress across the street and when she had unlocked the gate, sprang onto the grass jerking the leather leash out of her hand. The small beast darted to a favorite bush as the old lady closed the gate and dropped the key into her handbag. She crossed to the busy dog and bent stiffly to retrieve his leash. Then, finally, she stood for a moment surveying the Square.

That was when George Drayton looked in another direction. He had no idea whether Mrs. Heatherington could see him from that distance, but he didn't want her to think he was observing her. So he always looked away.

He noticed Willie Hoskins washing a window on the third floor of Number 26—Colonel Whitcomb's flat. A reflection of sunny sky gleamed from two panes he had already finished, but the others were dull with a month's accumulation of London soot. As he watched the window cleaner work he could hear the scuffling sound of Mrs. Heatherington's footsteps approaching down the walk, and as she came nearer he sensed the soft padding of the Pekinese. He turned to look and found that they were much closer than he had anticipated.

The Pekinese stalked past with majestic disdain but his mistress nodded and smiled. George Drayton bowed as usual. They never spoke. In fact, he had never heard Mrs. Heatherington's voice except when she talked to the dog.

George watched them head for the north gate. The old lady paused for a moment to speak to the gardener. Usually she only nodded to Purdy. Probably telling him that she was leaving on holiday. The gardener touched his cap as she continued on her way out of the Square, toward the Old Brompton Road. She would have final errands to do. Small presents for her grandchildren. Very likely a visit to her bank to withdraw money for the two-week holiday.

He wondered how old the dog might be. A Pekinese, named Kwong Kwok, had accompanied Mrs. Heatherington back from China, more than 30 years ago, when she returned to London after the death of her husband. Ever since there had been a Pekinese named Kwong Kwok, but it was impossible that the original dog could have survived so many years. The dog was a constant topic of conversation among the charwomen. To them and to George Drayton all Pekinese looked alike.

The first pram of the day, guided by a uniformed nanny, rolled into the Square as George picked up his small pile of books. Soon there would be dark clots of nursemaids and prams. Older children would avoid them and keep to the far side of the park where they could run and shout without glares and reprimands from the easily disturbed nannies.

He decided to put off reading the novel from Drayton House. Since his retirement, eight years ago, they had sent him a copy of each new book but, too frequently, he only became upset when he read the pretentious trash his nephew was publishing. No point in getting into a temper on such a beautiful day. He put the book aside and hesitated, deciding between the new Simenon and the new Christie. This would be a perfect morning to read about Paris. Simenon it would be . . .

As he turned to the first page he glanced across the Square to the dirt-encrusted windows of the third-floor flat where last year's murder had taken place. They still remained curtained. The Clarkson flat had never been rented. And the murder remained unsolved.

For two hours he lost himself in a rain-drenched Paris. Inspector Maigret sat in a small café, drinking calvados, listening to neigh-

borhood gossip as he watched a house across the street where a man
had been murdered. Home for lunch with Madame Maigret in the
apartment on the Boulevard Lenoir, then back through a cold drizzle
to the café with its view of the bleak street. Drinking toddy after
toddy. Smoking his pipe . . .

George put down the book and filled his own pipe. Why couldn't
he sit here and through pure deduction, like Inspector Maigret, solve
last year's murder? Except that New Scotland Yard had put their
best men on the Clarkson case and they had been unable to find
any trace of the murderer.

As George lighted his pipe he noticed Mrs. Higby, parcels clutched
in both arms, dart up the front steps of his building. Another hour
and she would have the flat in order and his lunch waiting. Wouldn't
she be surprised if he announced the name of the Clarkson murderer
as he ate his noon chop!

He turned again to study the curtained windows of the murder
flat. The victim, young Mrs. Clarkson, had been separated from her
husband, but not divorced. Harry Clarkson had an alibi for every
minute of the afternoon when his wife was killed. They had found
her partially clothed body, sprawled across the bed, one silk stocking
twisted around her throat and another stuffed into her mouth. The
newspapers said that she had not been attacked sexually.

Clarkson had testified, at the coroner's inquest, that he had not
seen his wife in several months. His solicitor sent her a monthly
check and, regularly, tried to persuade her that a divorce would be
wise; but she had refused to discuss such a possibility. Her char told
the police that Mrs. Clarkson entertained many male visitors. She
had never seen any of them but, every morning, she had to clean
all the ashtrays. Unfortunately, she had no idea how much money
Mrs. Clarkson kept in the flat, so there was no way of knowing
whether there had been robbery as well as murder. The dead
woman's purse, containing a few shillings, was found on her dressing
table.

The police reported there had been no fingerprints. All the locals
were questioned—caretaker of the building, milkman, florist, laun-
dryman, greengrocer, window cleaner, postman, delivery boy from
the chemist shop. Every name in Mrs. Clarkson's address book had
been traced and interrogated. Nobody knew anything.

A distant chime of bells brought George Drayton out of his dream
of murder. Twelve o'clock. He would finish the Simenon after lunch.
As he got to his feet he glanced, once again, at the Clarkson flat.

Maigret would have solved the mystery easily, sitting here in the Square, looking up at those curtained windows. But he, George Drayton, didn't have a suspicion of an idea—in spite of all the detective novels he had read and published.

He gathered up his books and leather cushion and headed for the gate. As he walked down the path he noticed that the gardener was already wolfing a sandwich, perched between the handles of his barrow. George looked for Willie Hoskins but the window cleaner had disappeared. All the windows of Colonel Whitcomb's flat gleamed in the noon sunshine, reflecting bright rectangles of blue sky.

Instead of a chop there was cold salmon for lunch which he ate with appetite. He had all his meals at a small table in the study, surrounded by overflowing bookshelves and facing tall windows which overlooked the Square.

Mrs. Higby had her usual morning collection of gossip. "That young American couple what sublet Number 29 are leavin' for Paris next week."

Yes, Maigret would have solved the Clarkson murder without difficulty. Except that now the case was more than a year old and the clues would have long since vanished.

"The old gent in Number 12 is boozin' again. Mr. Mortan, the super, had to help him out of his cab last night. Carry him in to the lift an' up to his flat. I've a lovely bit of Leicester for you."

He studied the curtained windows of the Clarkson apartment, across the Square, as he ate the cheese. Curious that someone—the caretaker or the dead woman's solicitor—wouldn't have those unsightly windows washed.

"Mrs. Heatherington's off this afternoon on holiday. Her an' that ol' dog. This year she's told Mrs. Price, her char, not to come in while she's away. Paid her two weeks' wages, she did. Told her to have herself a bit of a rest. Such a fine lady, Mrs. Heatherington."

After lunch George placed his cushion on an afternoon bench near the northwest corner of the Square, his back to the sun. He filled his pipe again and as he smoked he watched the renewed activity around him.

The gardener was pruning some kind of shrub near the rose arbor. Most of the noisy older children had not reappeared. Probably having an afternoon nap. Several of the nannies had returned with their prams. Or were these different nursemaids? Some of them sat dozing in the warm sunlight.

He noticed that Willie Hoskins was now washing the windows of Mrs. Heatherington's flat. Odd that the old lady would want them cleaned the afternoon she was going away. Except that she had given her char a holiday, so there would be no one, these next two weeks, to let Willie Hoskins or anyone else into the flat.

George opened the Simenon and immediately returned to Paris. He became so absorbed in Maigret's progress that he was no longer aware of the others in the Square. Squealing children ran past him unheeded. The distant chime of the bells on the quarter hours did not penetrate to his inner ear. He was conscious only of the sounds and voices of Paris, just as Maigret heard them.

A sudden pentrating scream, shrill and sharp, pulled him back to London and Knightswood Square.

Some of the nursemaids still sat beside their prams. The gardener was sweeping one of the walks. No one in the Square seemed to have noticed the scream he had heard. Or had he heard it? And was the sound human or animal? Perhaps one of the older children playing in the distance? The sound was not repeated.

George raised his eyes to the windows of Mrs. Heatherington's flat. Apparently the window cleaner had finished and gone on to his next job. One of the windows had been left open and the curtains had not been drawn together.

He took out his watch and checked the time. 4:27.

Mrs. Heatherington would have telephoned for a cab and left for Victoria Station long before this. Strange he hadn't noticed her departure. He remembered the scene from other years. Luggage brought down by the cabbie. Last of all, the small wicker hamper containing the Pekinese. He wondered if the old lady had forgotten to shut that window and close the curtains in the flurry of her departure.

He saw that he had finished all but a dozen or so pages of the Simenon. The puzzle in the detective novel was nearly solved.

. . . Maigret was moving quickly now. Each of the clues which had seemed so innocent before, had become ominous as the great French detective linked them together.

"Pardon me, sir."

George looked up from his book to see the gardener with a large bouquet of yellow roses in his hand.

"Told Mrs. Heatherington I'd have these for her. Fresh cut. So they'd last till she got to Hove."

"They're very beautiful."

"Said she'd get them before she took off. But I never seen her go."

"Didn't notice her leave, myself. I was reading."

"Guess I'll take them home to the Missus. S'prise the old girl."

Purdy held the bouquet in front of him, carefully, as he started back up the walk.

George reopened the Simenon. As he read on, something seemed to shadow the final pages of the book. The printed words faded together and his thoughts wandered.

Why had Mrs. Heatherington forgotten the bouquet of roses?

And why hadn't she shut that window before she left on her holiday? And closed those curtains?

. . . Maigret had crossed the street and was climbing the stairs to the floor where the murder had taken place.

There had been no fingerprints in the Clarkson apartment because the murderer had, obviously, worn gloves.

It was a dog that had screamed. George was certain of it now.

Could it have been Mrs. Heatherington's dog? Why would the Pekinese make such a sound? It seldom even barked. Of course there were other dogs in the mansions around Knightswood Square.

. . . Maigret was now standing in the dark hall, outside the murder apartment, listening at the door.

Too bad Mrs. Clarkson had not owned a dog. Might have saved her life.

George glanced across to the curtained windows of the Clarkson flat again.

Those dirty windows. Disgraceful.

Dirty windows!

George whirled to look again at Mrs. Heatherington's windows. Something wrong there!

The open window had been completely washed. All its panes sparkled in the afternoon sunlight. And the window next to it reflected blue sky in every rectangle of gleaming glass. But the other two windows were still dull with grime.

Half the windows of Mrs. Heatherington's flat had not been cleaned–

Why?

Had Willie Hoskins seen something inside Mrs. Heatherington's living room? Something that had stopped him in the middle of his job?

And why the devil hadn't the old lady shut that window and closed those curtains before she left to catch her train?

Why had she gone off without that bouquet of roses the gardener had cut for her?

Yellow roses.

Something else yellow—

The window cleaner's gloves! That was it! Willie Hoskins always wore yellow rubber gloves.

No fingerprints.

Why had the Pekinese screamed?

What possible reason—

"Murder!" The terrible word exploded from his throat. "Murder!" He was on his feet, pointing up at Mrs. Heatherington's open window.

Everyone in Knightswood Square had turned to stare. Purdy was running toward him across the grass.

"Up there! Mrs. Heatherington! Hurry, man! Get the police!"

The gardener, without pausing to ask questions, raced toward the nearest gate, at the southern end of the Square.

George Drayton collapsed onto his leather cushion, exhausted and out of breath. All he would ever be able to remember of the next hours would be a blur of strangers.

Arrival of the first policeman.

Cars screeching to a stop.

Dark-suited men hurrying to Mrs. Heatherington's flat.

The ambulance.

A clutter of curious people gathering on the sidewalk.

White-uniformed figures carrying something down the steps.

His bench surrounded. The dark-suited men. Polite questions. How did he know what had happened? What had he seen? Had he heard something? The dog? Questions ran together until they gave him a headache.

He finally managed to get home to the quiet of his flat where he stretched out gratefully on the sofa in his study . . .

Mrs. Higby wakened him. "You're a hero! Saved the old lady's life, you did! They say another hour an' she'd have been a goner. Just like her dog. Poor little beast. His head bashed in—"

"Mrs. Heatherington? Is she—"

"In hospital. They had to operate. But she's goin' to be fine. I just talked to Mrs. Price, her char, and the police told her. They say the old lady's money was stolen. What she took out of the bank for her holiday. Afraid your supper's goin' to be late this evenin'."

The telephone rang.

Mrs. Higby hurried to snatch it from the desk. "Mr. Drayton's residence ... What is it, love? What's happened now? ... Fancy that!" She turned to pass on her information. "It's me chum, Mrs. Price. They've caught Willie Hoskins! Drunk in a Chelsea pub. The old lady's money still in his pocket." Her eyes widened as she spoke into the phone again. "He didn't! Well, I never."

She turned back toward the sofa. "He's confessed to killin' Mrs. Clarkson last year. I always said he was a rascal."

George Drayton smiled. He had solved the Clarkson case. And he had done it without moving from his bench in Knightswood Square.

... Just like Inspector Maigret.

James M. Ullman

Operation Bonaparte

Another adventure of the two industrial investigators, Michael Dane James and Ted Bennett—this time, a "classic" case of an embezzling and absconding financier, hiding out in Rio with $8,000,000 of the stockholders' money . . .

Detectives: MICHAEL DANE JAMES and TED BENNETT

Ted Bennett nodded to the receptionist, deposited a two-suiter in a corner, and strode unannounced into the office of Michael Dane James, business and industrial espionage consultant.

James, a broad-shouldered, middle-aged man of medium height, looked up with a scowl. He settled his horn-rimmed glasses on his pug nose and demanded, "What are *you* doing back in New York? You're supposed to be on assignment in Rio, finding out where Lou Orloff is hiding the eight million he stole."

"I left hurriedly," Bennett explained. He pulled up a chair and lit a cigarette. "Anyhow, I didn't see much point in sticking around."

"You didn't? Well, I do. That stockholders' committee is paying us good money to investigate Orloff's finances." James rubbed a hand over his close-cropped hair and sighed. "Not that the information will help them much. Once a thief like Orloff gets himself and his loot out of the country, the cause is lost. Those poor investors who paid thirty dollars a share for Orloff's stock in its heyday will be lucky to get one cent on a dollar. But Sam Powell, the attorney for the committee, is a good friend of mine. What little help we can give him, I want to give him."

Bennett, a tall, lean man in his late thirties, said positively, "Mickey, I spent two weeks nosing around in Rio. And believe me, we won't learn anything more about Orloff's finances down there than we know now."

"Sure we will, Ted. He's living in a lavish villa, keeping to himself and making only rare public appearances, just as he did in the-

201

States—before his corporate house of cards started tumbling, before the stockholders learned he was looting their company like a bank robber going through a vault, exchanging the company's assets for stock in a pyramid of worthless holding companies under his control, and then selling the assets and stashing the money nobody-knows-where. But a man like Orloff—he won't allow those stolen millions to lie idle. He's probably putting it all into South American real estate, or making a down payment on a fleet of tankers."

Bennett shook his head. "Orloff is not doing any of those things. His tangible assets in Brazil consist of one villa and one Mercedes-Benz automobile. Less than a hundred thousand dollars in value at the very most."

"How can you be so sure?"

"Because," Bennett said, gazing blandly at the ceiling, "the man who has been dodging reporters and living in luxury in Rio for the last five weeks—that man is *not* Lou Orloff . . ."

Thoughtfully Sam Powell chewed on a cigar. A large, bearish man, he peered out of his Manhattan penthouse window. Then he turned back to James and Bennett.

"Well," he drawled, "that *is* a poser."

"It sure is," James agreed. "While everyone snooped around the mystery man living in conspicuous seclusion in Rio, the real Orloff had five weeks to bury himself in some other part of the world."

"He's taking quite a risk," Powell said. "The impersonation was sure to be discovered sooner or later. And that imposter might talk."

"I don't think," Bennett interrupted, "the imposter knows Orloff's true whereabouts any more than we do. The false Orloff gets two thousand dollars deposited to his account in a Rio bank on the first of every month. The money is sent from a numbered account in a Swiss bank. That's his living allowance—and two thousand a month can go a long, long way in Brazil, especially when you're occupying a villa that's already paid for."

"How did you find him out?" Powell asked.

"I began to suspect," Bennett said, "when, despite all the checks I made, I couldn't find that he owned anything of value in Brazil except the house and the car. Supposedly, he'd stolen eight million dollars from your company. Where was it? Moreover, he made no apparent attempt to communicate, by mail, telephone, or any other means, with anyone in any other part of the world. And unlike the real Orloff, who spent most of his time cooking up new swindles, *this* Orloff seemed mostly concerned with sitting around his swimming pool and drinking rum. He's accompanied by the real Orloff's secretary, incidentally, a Miss Irene Conover, a stony-faced old girl who turned up with him in Rio and no doubt keeps cluing him in on how the real Orloff behaved."

"Ted," James put in, "bribed a servant to steal a glass from the supposed Orloff. He took the fingerprints from the glass and compared them with the real Orloff's. They didn't match."

"If that man isn't Orloff," Powell speculated, "then who is he?"

"We already know that," James replied. "Before coming to see you, we ran the false Orloff's prints through the machinery we employ in industrial security investigations. The false Orloff's prints were on file because he'd been in the Army. His name is Herb Vann. Vann was a second-rate actor before the war. After the war he tried to make a go of it as a master of ceremonies in night clubs. He stuck with that for twelve years, without any significant success, and finally quit. He became a traveling salesman, based in Worcester, Massachusetts, handling a line of men's wear. A little more than five weeks ago–a few days after the real Orloff disappeared from New York–Vann disappeared from New England. He'd quit his job and told his employers and friends he was moving to the West Coast."

"He maintained his bank account, though," Bennett said. "Only now it's a lot heftier than it ever was before. The day he dropped out of sight, he added twenty thousand dollars to the few hundred then in the account."

"Vann," James said, "did meet the real Orloff several times. We learned that from a talk with Vann's former booking agent. Vann bore such a decided physical resemblance to Orloff that a number of Orloff's acquaintances, who caught Vann's act, brought the actor to Orloff's attention. Orloff went to see Vann's act and was so impressed with the resemblance that once or twice he hired Vann to perform at parties, imitating Orloff himself. Orloff got a big kick out of it."

"It seems," Powell mused, "we have a problem. We three know that Lou Orloff, who is under a number of State and Federal indictments for fraud, and who stole eight million dollars from the stockholders I represent, is *not* hiding in South America, as the rest of the world believes. If we transmit this knowledge to the authorities, the deception will be exposed, as it should be. But if we do that, the real Orloff, wherever he is, will be doubly on his guard.

If he—and any part of our eight million dollars—is still in the United States, he might move the money out of the country immediately. What little chance we'd have of recovering any of the money would be lost."

James glanced at Bennett. Then he said, "Give us a chance to crack this one, Sam. Let Orloff go on thinking for another few weeks that the impersonation is still undetected. We'd like nothing better than to nail a thief of Orloff's proportions."

"But where on earth," Powell asked, "would you start looking for Orloff? Because by now, he could be *anywhere* on earth."

"Right here in New York," James said, "where the real Orloff was last known to be. That's *one* place we'll begin. Another is Worcester, Massachusetts, where the actor now playing the role of Orloff was last heard of under his own name."

"All right," Powell said slowly. "If you think there's a chance . . ."

"There's a chance," James replied. "I'll go to Worcester, and start tracking Herb Vann. And Ted will start dogging Orloff. I'd do that myself—only one of the people to be checked is Orloff's ex-mistress. And since Ted is a bachelor and I have a wife and family out in Scarsdale, I think Ted should get that assignment."

Patricia Doyle added a jigger of vermouth to the pitcher and stirred. She filled two cocktail glasses and handed one to Bennett.

"Cheers," she said. She sipped and walked to a chair and sat down. Dark-haired and still under thirty, she wore a decorous blue afternoon dress.

"This stockholder's committee you're working for," she said. "Do you really think you can recover any of the money Lou stole?"

"Right now," Bennett conceded, "the prospects don't look good."

"I don't imagine they do. Lou was a very thorough man. When I look back, I can see now that he was planning this all along. He bought the villa in Rio, you know, more than a year ago. I was with him. He asked me not to mention the purchase to anyone. He said the stockholders might get the wrong idea. Actually, he was afraid they'd get the right idea."

"Miss Doyle," Bennett said, "we'd appreciate your cooperation . . ."

The woman chuckled. "It's a pleasure, Mr. Bennett. Between you and me, the last few months I was just someone Lou dragged around with him, as a sort of decoration. Frankly, I wanted to leave him a long time ago, but he wouldn't let me. Oh, I'm a big girl, and when Lou persuaded me to become what the newspapers call his 'companion,' I went into the deal with my eyes wide open. I thought: 'Here's a high-powered businessman, and if you play your cards right, maybe you can persuade him to marry you.' Well, I soon found out how wrong *that* notion was. First, Lou Orloff wasn't marrying anyone, and second, I learned he wasn't a high-powered business-man. He was a high-powered crook. After just three months with him I concluded he'd wind up either an exile, which he is now, or a convict. It was inevitable."

She sipped again at her martini.

"I stuck with him," she went on, "because he solved a lot of my problems—like paying the rent and buying the groceries. He wasn't lavish.

"Actually, he was stingy. But he had to buy me furs and jewelry because it was part of his act—the wealthy, confident, man-of-the-world. He wasn't really confident, though. He was always scared someone was going to rob him. He figured everyone was as big a crook as he was. He didn't trust *anyone*, not even me. I remember once, we were driving through a desert in Arizona and something went wrong with the car. Lou was furious. Not because we were stuck alone out there in the desert, with the temperature more than a hundred and snakes crawling over the highway, but because he was sure, absolutely sure, that when a trooper found us and radioed for a tow truck, the operator of the tow truck was going to pad the bill."

She put her glass down and lit a cigarette.

"It's hard to explain. I hated him because he was cruel, a cheat, and so suspicious of others that he belonged in a mental hospital. But on the other hand—well, I've got to admit it, I had to admire him. He started with nothing—not a thin dime. He spent his early years as a roustabout in the Louisiana and Texas oil fields. He was a huge man, very tough and very strong. He worked out every morning with bar bells. And physically, he was fearless. He earned a lot of medals during the war, you know—I saw the bullet scars. He was a raider out in the Pacific islands, operating behind the enemy lines. And one time he got shot full of bullets, stood up, and killed eleven Japanese with an automatic rifle. They gave him a Silver Star for that."

"The reason I'm here," Bennett said, "is to see if we can trace Orloff's exact movements between New York and Rio. So we can get some sort of lead to the eight million dollars . . ."

Patricia Doyle shrugged. "I couldn't tell you. His secretary, Irene

Conover, handled those details. And Lou never trusted her much, either." She paused. "I can guarantee you one thing, though."

"What's that?"

"Wherever Lou went, he picked up his strongbox first."

"What strongbox?"

"A big metal one. He had some diamonds in it—what he called his 'hard wealth,' something he could use for currency in case the country got blown up by atom bombs, or he had to skip in a hurry. But more important than that, the box contains his personal ledger. I opened that ledger once, and he socked me—smack in the face. At the time I didn't realize what the notations meant. I do now. This ledger shows exactly what he did with the money he stole from your stockholders."

"What did you see when you opened it?"

"He'd trace the sale of some property or stock from your company—up to the holding company on top of all the other holding companies he owned. And then he'd show where the money went after he drew it out of the last holding company."

"Do you remember," Bennett asked, "where the money did go?"

She laughed. "Lou fooled me there. He used code names, I guess. According to the book, all the money he stole went to Napoleon."

"Napoleon?"

"Not 'Napoleon,' exactly. He'd list these sums, then some names of companies and people I never heard of, and finally the code name for where the money was hidden away. And usually the code name would be 'Bonaparte.' Just that one word. He had an awful lot of money in 'Bonaparte'!"

"Where did Orloff keep this strongbox?"

"He moved it around, but always to cities where one of his companies had an office. The last time I remember, Mr. Bennett, he had it hidden somewhere in Kansas City, Missouri. That was maybe two months before he left New York. If that strongbox was still in Kansas City, he went there before he went anywhere else. You can make book on that."

Bennett stepped into a telephone booth on a Kansas City downtown street. He asked the long-distance operator to connect him with the number of a booth in a hotel in Richmond, Virginia.

Michael Dane James answered. "Ted?"

"Yes, Mickey."

"I hope you've uncovered something, because I haven't got much.

Vann came to Richmond from Worcester, to see his mother. He told her he was going abroad for a while. She remembers he had tickets for New Orleans, and that once he telephoned a woman in New Orleans collect. I'd imagine that woman was Orloff's secretary, Irene Conover, who turned up in Rio with Vann. New Orleans must have been where they met."

"Well, I'm on a hot trail here," Bennett reported. "Orloff made an appearance at his Kansas City office the day after he left New York. He had the strongbox under his arm. It was after the building closed, and the watchman had to unlock the door to let him in. The watchman remembers that Orloff went up to his office for a while and then came back down. Orloff was picked up by a man driving a 1960 Chevrolet sedan. Orloff got into the sedan with his strongbox and the two men drove away."

"Anything else?"

"Plenty. The superintendent let me into Orloff's office—it cost a ten-spot. Orloff's furnishings are still there, although they'll be sold soon for nonpayment of rent. I found Orloff's classified telephone book open to the private detective section. He'd checked a little agency just a few blocks from his own office. So I walked over to the agency—and found that it's gone out of business."

"Why?"

"Because the private detective who ran it—a guy named Prentiss—is dead. He was killed in an automobile wreck. His car went off the road somewhere in Arkansas and landed in a ditch. The accident happened the same night Orloff showed up with his strongbox. And Prentiss was driving a 1960 Chevrolet sedan."

"Sounds to me," James said, "as though Orloff and Prentiss left Kansas City together. With Prentiss hired, perhaps, as a bodyguard, since Orloff had his precious strongbox."

"I talked to the detective's widow," Bennett went on. "Prentiss had done some work for Orloff in the past—industrial spying, a few years ago. The widow said she didn't know where Prentiss was going the night he was killed in Arkansas. All she knows is, her husband called from his office, said an important job had come up, and he'd be out of town a day or so. The next word she had of Prentiss was a telephone call from a sheriff in Arkansas, telling her that her husband had been found dead in this wrecked car."

"Anyone else in the car with Prentiss?"

"Nobody was *found* in the car with him. The widow and the sheriff assumed Prentiss was traveling alone, on his way to a job."

"Well," James said, "it's almost sure that Prentiss had a passenger when he left Kansas City—namely, Lou Orloff. You'd better drive to Arkansas and look into the accident further. I'm going to New Orleans, to see if I can discover what happened to Vann after he arrived there."

James hesitated. "We seem," he added, "to be headed more or less in the same direction. Maybe in a day or so we'll both wind up in the same place."

Bennett turned off the highway at the foot of the hill. His rented car bumped up a dirt road a hundred yards or so to a frame house.

He braked and cut the engine.

In a wooded area to his right, a man who had been digging a hole stopped, jammed a shovel into the ground, and started wearily toward Bennett.

Bennett climbed from the car and walked toward the man who was heavy-set and in his forties. The man paused to mop his brow as Bennett neared.

"Howdy," Bennett said. "I'm from an insurance company. I'm investigating an accident that happened in front of your property last month."

Ruefully the man smiled. "I heard about that. Sorry, but I probably can't help you much. My name's Gordon, and I took possession of this place only two days ago. I just bought the property."

"What happened to the former owner?"

"He's an old farmer, Ira Wilson. He moved to Florida, he didn't exactly say where." Gordon dug into a shirt pocket and pulled out a cigar. He bent and lit it. "I'm from Fort Smith, y'see. Always wanted a country place of my own. For vacations and week-ends and retirement . . ."

"Sure. You mind if I see where they found the car?"

"Not at all."

Bennett and Gordon trudged through the woods.

"It's kind of a long time since the accident happened," Gordon observed. "How come you're lookin' into it now?"

"It's a life insurance policy," Bennett explained glibly. "The claim was filed just last week. I haven't talked to the sheriff yet, but I got the accident report from a deputy in his office. Apparently, the accident happened up ahead there, where the road curves.

"That's right. It's easy to find the exact spot, because the car knocked down a tree."

Bennett viewed the fallen tree, which lay at the foot of a steep incline. He took a camera from his pocket.

"This is a lonely spot," Bennett said. "Now I understand what they meant on that accident report—that the exact time of the accident was unknown. A wreck could lie here for hours, especially at night, without anyone seeing it from the road."

"That's true," Gordon said. "There's very little traffic. And now that you mention it, a car's headlights wouldn't sweep down that far."

Bennett took some pictures.

"Well," he said, returning the camera to his pocket and pulling out a notebook, "it does look ordinary enough. That is a steep curve." He began writing.

"They tell me," Gordon said, "there's an accident here at least two or three times a year."

"The deputy said that too. Thanks for showing me around."

Gordon accompanied Bennett back to his car. Bennett waved, drove back to the road, and returned to the Arkansas county seat where the sheriff had his office.

The sheriff was in this time. A stony-faced, alert young man, he said, "I understand you been looking into that fatal accident down by the Wilson place."

"The Gordon place, you mean."

"That's right," the sheriff smiled. "Old Ira Wilson sold out and left for Florida or somewhere. He never did tell anyone exactly where. He must have inherited a fair pile of money, though. Four weeks ago, just before he sold his place to Gordon, Ira bought himself a new Cadillac. With cash."

"Who in his family died?"

"Some old aunt, Ira said. He'd never mentioned her before. But I guess she musta been loaded. About this accident. You think there's something wrong?"

"You never can tell. After all, Prentiss was a private detective."

"I know. The thought occurred to us, too. But there didn't seem anything out of the ordinary. The steering wheel went right through the man when the car hit the tree. It's a bad curve, and it'd been raining. It makes the pavement there a lot slicker than a city man like Prentiss might think. I checked that wreck real close, and so did the state troopers. The only thing we didn't understand was—there was a hubcap missing."

"A hubcap?"

"Off the rear wheel. Couldn't find it anywhere. But most likely, it fell off before the accident and Prentiss never had another one put on."

"This Ira Wilson, who owned the land where the car crashed. Was he home the night of the accident?"

"Well, that's a funny thing," the sheriff said. "We thought he'd be home. A state trooper spotted that wreck in the woods right after dawn. We went to Ira's house to learn if he'd heard anything. We didn't really expect he did—there was a lot of thunder that night, and Ira don't hear too good, and besides, his house is a fair distance from the accident scene. But Ira wasn't there. His pickup truck was missing too. That worried us, because he hadn't told anyone he was going on a trip. We figured maybe he went off the road somewhere in that storm, too, and we put out a message on him. But he called in about noon, long-distance from a motel in Louisiana. He said he'd heard about the accident on the radio, and he just wanted us to know he was all right. He'd gone to Bonaparte on business, y'see."

"Bonaparte?"

"Yeah. Bonaparte, Louisiana. About two hundred miles from here. You keep going south on the road where Prentiss got killed, and you'll wind up right in Bonaparte."

Bennett stood before a public telephone in a Bonaparte drug store. He opened the Bonaparte telephone book to the classified pages and thumbed to the "motel" listings.

He started down the list alphabetically. He called each motel, identified himself as an insurance investigator, and asked if an Ira Wilson had registered on April 15 or 16.

At the ninth motel he received an affirmative answer. Bennett told the owner he'd be right over, hung up, went out to his car, and drove to the motel.

"Sure, I recall the man," the owner declared. "You say he filed a claim with your company six months ago? Reporting he's totally disabled?"

"That's right. Said he couldn't even walk without help."

"Well, the Ira Wilson who stopped here was an old guy all right, but he wasn't disabled. If it's the same man, he drove in here by himself in a pickup truck with Arkansas plates. I recall because it was such an odd hour—six in the morning—and he seemed a strange customer for a motel like ours, anyhow. But he had plenty of cash. He peeled a twenty from a real big roll."

"You got any idea where he was coming from? I'd like to find some other people who saw him walking around under his own power."

"I'll tell you about that. I was outside, picking up the morning newspapers, when he came along. I looked in his cab and saw blood on the seat, on the passenger side. I asked him what had happened and he got real sore. He said he'd just driven a friend who was sick up to the sanitarium. Well, I let him have a room. I was suspicious, though, so I called the sanitarium. But they said it was all right, that he had delivered a very sick friend there."

"What sanitarium is that?" Bennett asked.

"It's right up the road. The E. G. Bailey Sanitarium."

"Is Bailey a doctor?"

The motel owner laughed. "No, not E.G. He's got a doctor to run it, but E.G., he just put up the money. He puts up the money for a lot of things in Bonaparte, mister. He's just about the richest man around here."

"What's his main business?"

"E.G.," the motel man said, "is president of the bank."

"Well, thanks," Bennett said. "You've been a big help."

Bennett returned to his car and drove to downtown Bonaparte. He parked in front of E. G. Bailey's bank, which occupied a four-story building in the heart of town.

Bennett stepped from the car. He dropped a nickel into the parking meter and started toward the bank entrance. But when he was ten yards from the door, a man stuck his head from another parked car and yelled, "Hey, Ted."

Bennett turned. Gazing at him from behind the wheel of the car was Michael Dane James.

"I figured you'd get here sooner or later," James went on. "Let's take a ride. I know a place where they'll serve you a plate of soft-shelled crab for a dollar. And beer is only twenty cents a bottle."

James backed the car from the curb and steered up Bonaparte's Main Street.

"How," Bennett asked gloomily, "did *you* get here?"

"You're an ingenious fellow," James conceded. "But you have no monopoly on ingenuity. Why do you think you're working for me, and not the other way around?"

"I never figured that out."

"I'm here," James said, "because the Bank of Bonaparte came to my attention in New Orleans. The actor Vann's trail ended there.

But then I searched for some trace of Orloff's secretary, Irene Conover, who I assumed had been the woman Vann telephoned from Richmond. And sure enough, she'd arrived in New Orleans the day after Orloff disappeared from New York. Registered in a hotel under her own name, too, which indicates that this whole impersonation stunt must have been improvised. But the day after the Kansas City detective wrecked his car in Arkansas, Irene Conover vanished for twenty-four hours. She rented a car and drove off. When she came back, she gave the hotel manager a large sum of cash to be stored in the hotel safe overnight. The sum was so large that the manager noted the printing on the wrappers around the money—wrappers from the Bank of Bonaparte, Louisiana. And once I heard the magic word 'Bonaparte,' I got terribly interested in that bank. It would explain Orloff's mysterious ledger. Every 'Bonaparte' entry would represent a deposit in a dummy account in the Bank of Bonaparte. Because where else could anyone hide millions of dollars in a small town like Bonaparte, except in a bank?"

"I suppose," Bennett said, "you've already subjected E. G. Bailey, president of the bank, to the background check I was about to undertake."

"I have," James said. "E. G. Bailey, years ago, was a wildcatter in the Louisiana oil fields. His partner back in those days was none other than our old friend, Lou Orloff."

"Each, I imagine, went his own way," Bennett said, "Orloff into the intricacies of high finance, Bailey into small-town banking."

"Correct. But Orloff was probably a secret stockholder in that bank. At any rate, he must have set up the dummy accounts there, with his old friend Bailey's knowledge, planning later to transfer the money to South America. And that's why Orloff was heading for Bonaparte after he left Kansas City—to complete the transfer arrangements with Bailey. After which he intended to meet his secretary in New Orleans and then skip to Rio."

Bennett lit a cigarette.

"What else have you been up to?"

"I just opened an account in the bank—as the James Sales Company. Sales of what, I'll leave to your imagination, just as I left it to the bank's. But it was a highly instructive afternoon. My initial deposit was big enough to command the attention of the highest echelon in the Bank of Bonaparte. And among other things I learned that E. G. Bailey has been out of town for three days. He's expected back later today, though, and I have an appointment to meet him at one p.m. tomorrow. But next Monday he's going out of town again. What happened to you?"

Bennett told James how he had followed Orloff's—and Wilson's—trail from Arkansas to Bonaparte.

James turned off the road and parked in front of a white frame restaurant.

"Here we are," James said. "But before we go in—describe for me once more that man Gordon who occupied the farm in Arkansas, the one who bought it from Ira Wilson."

Bennett did so.

"Well," James said, "in the back seat of this car is a manila envelope containing a photograph of E. G. Bailey. And unless I miss my guess, the man you saw on that farm was not a Mr. Gordon of Fort Smith. It was E. G. Bailey, the president of the Bank of Bonaparte."

Bennett reached back, opened the envelope, and looked carefully inside.

"You're right," he said slowly. "Now, that's a funny way for a Louisiana bank president to spend his time—digging holes on a tract of bottomland in Arkansas."

"It sure is," James replied. He opened the door. "And it kind of brings all the pieces in this puzzle into place, too. Let's eat. Then you're going back to New Orleans, while I make inquiries of whatever local authorities handle vital statistics. I want you to buy me something in New Orleans. What you buy, I'm going to sell to E. G. Bailey when I see him tomorrow. It will be the one and only transaction of the James Sales Company. But it may wind up as the most important sale I ever made."

Sam Powell walked out of a hearing room in the Federal courthouse in Little Rock, Arkansas. Bennett and James were waiting in the corridor.

Powell shoved a cigar into his mouth and grinned. "It's going to take time to unravel the details, but we just got a look at Orloff's ledger. It shows there should be at least six million, maybe more, of that stolen money in the Bank of Bonaparte, under dummy names which Orloff and Bailey set up, and which our stockholders now stand an excellent chance of recovering. Not to mention the value of Orloff's diamonds."

James chuckled. "Poor old E. G. Bailey. He sure looked startled the other morning when Ted and I and those Federal marshals stepped from behind the Wilson farmhouse and caught him lugging that strongbox from the woods to his car."

"Poor Lou Orloff, you mean," Powell replied. "He spent a lifetime building up his house of cards. And then . . ."

"Then," Bennett said, "he wound up in a pauper's grave in Bonaparte, Louisiana, as John Doe."

The three men strolled down the hall and into an empty courtroom.

They sat down. The hearing into Orloff's affairs would reconvene in half an hour.

"Orloff's death," James said, "was the direct result of his own greed and suspicion. Orloff was injured in that crash, but he was a strong and fearless man. He'd absorbed a number of bullets, once, and survived to win a medal. So he put the safety of his strongbox first, and his own welfare second. When he crawled out of that wrecked car and saw that Prentiss was dead, Orloff decided to hide his strongbox then and there. He wasn't about to let any stranger he might meet in the next few hours know about that strongbox—especially policemen who might turn up at any time to investigate the accident. And even if he persuaded someone, as he ultimately persuaded Ira Wilson, to drive him to the sanitarium in Bonaparte, he feared he might become unconscious during the ride, and the strongbox might be stolen. He was also afraid of being hospitalized in that sanitarium, perhaps anesthetized for hours or days at a time, with the strongbox lying around for anyone to pick up."

"As I understand it," Powell said, "Orloff pried a hubcap off the rear wheel of the wrecked car and used that as a digging tool to bury the strongbox on the Wilson farm."

"That's right," Bennett said. "Then, the strongbox taken care of, he finally gave some consideration to himself. He stumbled to Wilson's house and bribed Wilson to drive him to Bonaparte, to the sanitarium, where he knew Bailey could arrange to keep his admittance a secret, since Bailey owned the place. But the delay in seeking medical attention, plus his exertions in burying his strongbox, proved fatal. According to the doctor at the sanitarium, who talked readily enough when Federal authorities questioned him, Orloff died less than twelve hours later."

"He died," James added, "without disclosing the spot where he'd buried the box. Orloff did tell Bailey it was somewhere on the farm, though, and ordered Bailey to buy the farm and get Wilson off the property–to forestall Wilson's digging it up by accident. But Orloff had faith, to the end, that he'd recover from his injuries and dig up that strongbox himself."

"So Bailey," Bennett said, "posed as a man from Fort Smith and bought the farm. He also conceived the impersonation 'red herring'–the false Orloff–when the real Orloff died. He realized that unless another Orloff turned up somewhere, the authorities would start tracing Orloff's movements from New York. They might learn about the accident in Arkansas, might start digging up the Wilson farm, too. Bailey conferred with Orloff's secretary. Both knew about the actor, Herb Vann. Bailey paid the secretary to find Vann and arranged for him to assume Orloff's identity in Rio for a few months. The villa in Rio had already been purchased, the secretary had Orloff's passport so everything was set. All that was necessary was for Vann to show up in Rio, with the secretary at his elbow to guide him over the rough spots."

"The purpose of the deception," James said, "was to give Bailey enough time to buy the farm, get Wilson moved off, and start digging for the strongbox on his own. That's how he was spending his time when Bennett showed up to investigate the accident–he was digging. It was a job he wanted to do alone. Like Orloff, he didn't trust anyone to help him. Because the strongbox now meant an awful lot to E. G. Bailey–as much as it had meant to Lou Orloff, when Orloff was alive. The diamonds inside were only a minor consideration. The big thing was, if Bailey could find and destroy Orloff's ledger, he could then transfer all that money from Orloff's dummy accounts into dummy accounts of his own, without fear that the ledger would ever turn up to trap him–a neat little gain of more than six million dollars, and no taxes. No wonder he was willing to spend a little money to maintain Vann as the false Orloff."

"As soon as we realized Gordon and Bailey were the same man," Bennett added, "the whole pattern became clear. Why else would Bailey buy the Wilson farm and spend his time digging alone, except to uncover that strongbox? And if Orloff had buried the box and after five weeks hadn't returned to dig it up himself, it almost certainly meant Orloff was unable to return, that he had probably died in the sanitarium."

Powell smiled. "It was nice of Bailey to find the box so quickly, while you two and those Federal marshals were hiding nearby. Bailey might have spent weeks poking around before he uncovered it."

"Well," James grinned, "we sort of *induced* its quick discovery,

Sam. We staked out the farm that morning because we knew Bailey was going to find the box. He'd been searching with a shovel before. But when I met him back in Bonaparte, as the president of the James Sales Company, I used a little creative salesmanship on Mr. E. G. Bailey. I even made a twelve-dollar profit on the deal, Ted's expenses going to New Orleans and back for this item notwithstanding. I sold Bailey the very thing he needed most—a portable metal detector."

Barry Perowne

The Raffles Bombshell

Another adventure of Mr. A. J. Raffles, the Amateur Cracksman and Cricketer . . . Raffles is the most famous Gentleman Burglar in the annals of English crime-writing—his name is perhaps better known around the world than even that of his French peer, Arsène Lupin, and no early American thief or con man—not Get-Rich-Quick Wallingford or The Gray Seal or Jimmy Valentine or Jeff Peters or The Phantom Crook or the Infallible Godahl—has reached the pinnacle of international fame to stand beside Raffles and Lupin. In this period piece about Raffles, faithful in every detail to its turn-of-the-century tone and background, the great A. J. adds an unusual crime (unusual for him) to his usual second-story work—and adds it with his customary style, which is an appealing kind of English élan.

Criminal: A. J. RAFFLES

It so happened that A. J. Raffles was batting when the open carriage with the four portly gentlemen in it entered Lord's Cricket Ground.

A sibilance of whispers ran around the stands, gay with parasols, blazers, and boaters in the heat-shimmer, and from where I was sitting, on a bench on the pavilion terrace, I heard some woman behind me ask:

"Who are they?"

"The one with the beard and the white Homburg hat," a man's voice answered, "is the King."

"Oh, how exciting! Who's that sitting beside him?"

"That's John L. Sullivan, the great prize-fighter."

"Fancy the King going about with prize-fighters!"

"There's only one John L. Sullivan, my dear," the man said tolerantly. "He's in London on a visit, and the King's very taken with him. I expect he wants to show Mr. Sullivan something of our summer game. Americans don't play it, you know."

"How strange of them! Oh, look, there's a different flag going up the flagstaff!"

The carriage, with its two tophatted coachmen on the box, and its two fine black horses arching their proud necks against the bearing-reins, was standing now just to the right of the pavilion terrace, in a good position to watch the game.

As the Royal Standard shimmered red-and-gold at the summit of the flagstaff, the crowd rose to its feet with a rustle, and the white-flannelled players in their various positions on the great circle of emerald turf faced the carriage and doffed their cricket caps.

The interruption was brief. King Edward VII was a great sportsman, his visit was informal, and with a genial gesture he intimated that play should be resumed.

"There seem to be a lot of policemen about, all of a sudden," said the woman sitting behind me.

"When the King appears, the bobbies pop up everywhere," explained her companion. "Oh, good shot! Well hit, sir!"

Raffles had struck a ball from Kortright, the fastest bowler in the world, firmly to the boundary.

"The King's talking to Mr. Sullivan about something," said the chatterbox.

"He's probably explaining to Mr. Sullivan the technique of that shot A. J. Raffles just made."

"They're lighting cigars," said the chatterbox. "Mr. Sullivan has a diamond ring and stickpin."

"My dear, I beg you," said her companion, "stop staring at the royal carriage. It's simply not done."

"Those poor horses! Why don't the coachmen put nosebags on them to munch in?"

"Evidently the King doesn't intend to stay long—probably just till the Tea Interval, which is due at four o'clock. Now, please, do pay attention to the game."

It was at an interesting stage. Raffles had scored 73, so there was a good chance of his reaching his hundred by teatime. The sun blazed down. Except for the sound of bat meeting ball, and an occasional ripple of handclapping, an increasingly tense hush brooded over the ground as the hands of the pavilion clock crept toward the hour of four.

Suddenly, just as the burly Kortright was making his run up to the wicket to launch one of his thunderbolts at Raffles, a wild scream pierced the silence. Kortright almost fell. Recovering himself, he glared off to his left, towards the stand on the side opposite the royal carriage.

"Oh!" gasped the woman behind me. "Whatever's happening?"

From a swirling of the crowd in the stand over there, I saw a lithe, lightly-built figure break free, vault the low rail, and run out onto the turf. The interloper wore white flannel trousers and a pink blazer. I glimpsed dark glasses under the floppy brim of a white linen hat, but it was the globular object in the interloper's hand which wrenched a concerted gasp of horror from the crowd.

"Oh, my God!" muttered a man sitting beside me. "A nihilist!"

From the globular object, considerably larger than a cricket ball, dangled a length of fuse from which, as the interloper hurled the object, overarm, high through the air toward the wicket, trailed a thin feather of smoke.

The bomb landed in midwicket, between the two batsmen. The interloper came running on towards the King's carriage. Bobbies raced out to head the interloper off. Seeing them coming, the interloper whipped off the floppy linen hat and dark glasses. Long hair, of a honey colour in the sunshine, rippled down over the interloper's shoulders as, flinging up her hands, she cried out, "Your Majesty—"

Her further words were lost to me, for the bobbies were on her. Crowd and players alike were struck to immobility—all save one. Raffles, his bat raised, was running toward the bomb, which lay with its fuse smoking and rapidly sputtering on the turf.

"Leave it, Raffles!" I was on my feet, shouting at him, in panic. "Don't touch it! Stand back!"

But Raffles slammed down his bat on the fuse. It must have been quickmatch, for it still sputtered fiercely. Raffles threw aside his bat, snatched up the bomb with one batting-gloved hand, jerked the fuse right out of it with the other.

Dropping the little that remained of the fuse, Raffles trod it out with his nailed cricket boot, and, seeing a bobby approaching at the double, lobbed the now harmless bomb to him as casually as if it had been a cricket ball.

A collective sigh of relief went up from the crowd.

"What was she shouting about?" asked the chatterbox behind me, as a group of bobbies hustled the bomb-thrower, quite a young woman, away to some waiting Black Maria. "It sounded like 'Women of England' and 'concubinage.' What's concubinage?"

"It's a form of—uh—subjugation," replied the chatterbox's escort, sounding embarrassed. "By God, though, that was quick thinking by Raffles—a jolly good show! Listen to the people clapping for him!"

"There's a gentleman from the King's carriage gone over to speak to him," said the chatterbox. "Oh, look, the gentleman's taking him to meet the King! D'you think Mr. Raffles will be knighted or something?"

"Hardly that," replied her escort. "Still, congratulations are in order—though, of course, Raffles may merely have been thinking that he didn't want a hole blown in the turf before he'd scored his hundred."

"Sir," I said, turning my head to look the fellow in the eye, "as a personal friend of A. J. Raffles, I resent that remark. No such thought would have entered his head. His action was instinctive—and typical of him."

"I beg your pardon," the young fellow said, with a flush. "I confess the remark was unwarranted. I gladly withdraw it. Uh, come, Daisy dear, I think perhaps we'd better go to tea now."

The couple sidled off, the fellow shamefaced, his chatterbox companion looking back at me curiously.

I glanced across at the royal carriage. Raffles, standing beside it, still wearing his batting-pads, doffed his cap as the King shook hands with him and introduced him to John L. Sullivan. Knowing Raffles as I did, I knew he would not fail to note, as he shook hands with the great pugilist, Mr. Sullivan's diamond ring and stickpin; but I also knew that, King Edward himself having made the introduction, Mr. Sullivan's belongings would remain taboo as far as Raffles was concerned.

A hand gripped my arm. It was the man who had been sitting beside me.

"Did I hear you say, sir," he asked, "that you're a personal friend of A. J. Raffles?"

"I am indeed, sir."

"In that case, I should appreciate it if you would introduce me to him. I see that His Majesty's carriage is departing and the Tea Interval is now upon us. If you could arrange for me to meet Mr. Raffles during the interval, I should be most grateful. I have a proposal to make to him."

Though he had been sitting beside me all afternoon, I had not until now taken much note of the man. Impeccably dressed in grey cutaway and grey topper, he was tall and thin, with a sallow, haughty face and a ribboned monocle.

"A proposal?" I said cautiously.

"I am Lord Pollexfen, of the Pollexfen Press. Sir, just listen to this crowd!"

As umpires and players were coming to the pavilion, which Raffles already had entered by a side door, the crowd in the stands was chanting, to rhythmic handclaps, "We—want—A. J. Raffles! We—want—A. J. Raffles!"

"You are hearing, sir," said Lord Pollexfen, "the Voice of Britain! Within an hour, newsboys will be crying on the London streets the name of A. J. Raffles—a name already well-known as standing for all that is finest in English sporting life. To-morrow he will be the subject of laudatory editorials in every newspaper in the land. For some time I've been seeking a name for a project I have in mind. Sir, I have found that name!"

His monocle glittered compellingly at me.

"The iron is hot," said Lord Pollexfen. "Will you please tell your friend Mr. Raffles that I should like to discuss with him immediately the launching of a magazine—a monthly magazine of the highest class—a magazine, edited by himself, to be called *A. J. Raffles' Magazine of Sport.*"

To cricketers the world over, the Long Room at Lord's is little short of a shrine. And it was in this historic chamber, with the sunshine from its open windows mellow on panelled walls and priceless trophies, that the foundations of *Raffles' Magazine* were laid.

He himself determined my own role in the project. Keen of face, his dark hair crisp, his blazer and muffler sporting the colours of the noted I Zingari Club, he put a hand on my shoulder.

"I'd like to point out, Lord Pollexfen," he said, "that my friend here, Bunny Manders, is himself a skilful journalist. While I'm prepared to figure as Editor of the proposed magazine, my sporting engagements occupy most of my time. I should need the practical conduct of the magazine, under my general guidance as regards policy, to be in capable hands—and I can think of no more capable Assistant Editor than Bunny Manders here. How d'you feel about that, Bunny?"

It was true that, on Raffles' advice, I dabbled in freelance journalism as a cover for the more lucrative activities in which I was his confederate.

"I shall be happy to cooperate," I said.

To this, Lord Pollexfen made no objection, and he proceeded to suggest that an honorarium for Raffles would be appropriate, and for my own services an emolument in the nature of a salary. Though delicately enough phrased, the actual sums mentioned by the Press baron were nothing to write home about, but Raffles accepted them with casual inconsequence.

When the peer had gone off to arrange about office space and staff for us in the Pollexfen Press Building in Covent Garden I said that I felt we might have made a better bargain.

"Why strain at sprats, Bunny," Raffles said, "when there may be mackerel in the offing?"

"You have some idea, Raffles?"

"That depends, Bunny."

"On what?"

"On the girl who threw the bomb. You heard what she was shouting about. It may have possibilities." Raffles' grey eyes danced as he offered me a Sullivan from his cigarette-case. "She'll be up in front of the magistrate at Marlborough Street to-morrow morning. We'll be there."

In addition to her honey-coloured hair, the girl in the dock at Marlborough Street Magistrates' Court next morning proved to have other attractions. She had spent the night in a cell, but evidently someone, possibly her solicitor, had wisely brought her more appropriate attire in which to appear before the magistrate than the trousers she had worn at Lord's.

Her name was Mirabel Renny, and she was a fine figure of a girl, standing there in the dock, though her proud bearing and defiant expression were at variance with the moving plea which her solicitor, quite a young man, made on her behalf.

"My client, Your Honour," he said, "as the only girl in a family dominated by her father and five large, athletic brothers, naturally occupied a subordinate place. As Your Honour is doubtless aware, pernicious literature about the social and political status of the female sex has been filtering into this country from the United States. Some of it chanced to fall into the hands of my client, who, in her girlish simplicity, was so unduly moved by it as to leave her country home and come to London. Here she lodged at a Ladies' Hostel in Fulham, where she fell in with some elder persons of her sex who likewise had been infected by these imported fallacies."

The girl opened her mouth, as though about to rebut her own solicitor's statement, but the young lawyer continued hastily, to forestall her.

"No doubt in a pathetic attempt to emulate her brothers' athletic prowess," he said, "my client has acquired, Your Honour, a taste and aptitude for outdoor pastimes—golf, croquet, tennis, archery, horseback-riding, to name but a few. Taking advantage of these admittedly hoydenish proclivities of my client, the elder persons at the Ladies' Hostel prevailed upon her to be the instrument of yesterday's lamentable demonstration at Lord's Cricket Ground—a demonstration which she now deeply regrets."

I saw the girl's hands, lightly sun-tanned, clench hard on the rail of the dock. Again she opened her mouth, but her solicitor hastened on.

"If Your Honour pleases," he said, "any actual damage to the turf at Lord's, the immemorial headquarters of our summer game, would have been viewed with repugnance by my client, with her sporting inclinations, however little they may become her in other respects. Indeed, as Inspector Harrigan has stated in evidence, the bomb-casing could not possibly have been fragmented by the detonation of its contents, consisting as these did merely of small fireworks—Chinese crackers or squibs."

This was news to Raffles and myself, who had arrived while the hearing was in progress, and we exchanged a surprised glance.

"In view of the fact, Your Honour," pleaded the solicitor, "that the bomb was designed only as a means of attracting attention, and that my client now bitterly regrets the incident, I ask Your Honour to exercise leniency in this case."

The magistrate, after addressing some stern remarks to the defendant in the dock, said, "The fine will be ten guineas, with two guineas costs. Next case!"

"Come on, Bunny," said Raffles.

To my astonishment, he sought out the functionary who collected fines and paid the girl's fine. As he returned his wallet to his pocket, Miss Mirabel Renny and her attendant solicitor came to the desk, and the functionary, indicating Raffles, said that the fine had been paid.

Though Raffles was now wearing an immaculate town suit,

with a pearl in his cravat, the girl immediately recognized him.

"Why, you're the man who was batting at Lord's when I—" She broke off. Her fine eyes flashed. "How dare you," she said hotly, "presume to pay my fine? I'm not in need of charity from *men!*"

"No charity is involved," Raffles assured her. "The amount will be deducted from your first month's salary."

"Salary?" she exclaimed. "What d'you mean? What are you talking about?"

"The post of Contributing Editor on a magazine now in the fruitful planning stage," said Raffles. "If such a post, with the opportunity it provides for the dissemination of opinion, should happen to appeal to you, Miss Renny—"

No question about it. She jumped at it. And, as the next few weeks proved, Raffles could not have made a happier choice of young sportswoman to help in carrying out the editorial policy on which he had decided.

As he explained to Mirabel Renny and myself, before he went off to join cricketing house parties at some of the stately homes of the country, "Sport is in the English blood—which biologically, as far as I know, is no different in women from what it is in men. So we want to produce a well-balanced magazine which will equitably represent the interests and views of those of both sexes who have a taste for active pastimes."

Mirabel's enthusiasm knew no bounds. She threw herself heart and soul into executing the role he assigned to her. She was a dynamo of activity. Our office in the Pollexfen Press Building looked out on Covent Garden, from which rose the clip-clopping hoofbeats of the horses drawing tumbrils ablaze with flowers, while market porters bustled about with tall, round towers of fruit-baskets balanced on their heads in the sunshine.

We were untroubled by Lord Pollexfen, as Raffles had insisted on full editorial control. Raffles himself was active in the background on our behalf and, thanks to his influence, marvellous literary material came in, for merely token fees, from some of the greatest names in the world of sport.

What with this, and with Mirabel's aptitude and energy, my own task in putting together our first issue was far from onerous. Usually, at about noon, I would suggest that I take her to lunch, for she looked charming in the blue skirt and white shirtwaist, crisp and businesslike, which she wore to the office. But it was rarely that she would leave her work.

"You go ahead, Mr. Manders," she said. "I shall just have a sandwich and a cigarette."

She made out that she smoked Sullivans, like Raffles, but I knew this was just a gesture of emancipation, as cigarettes made her cough. But I would leave her to it and saunter across the Strand, bustling with hansoms in the sunshine, for a leisurely lunch and a few rubbers of whist at my club in the Adelphi, dropping back to the office at about four o'clock for a last supervisory look round before returning to my Mount Street flat to take a tub and dress for dinner. It was not a bad life, the editorial life.

I sent Raffles a card, care of the Vice-Chancellor of Oxford University, whose guest he was while playing cricket there, to let him know when the foundry proofs, the final proofs of our first issue fully made-up, were due from the printers, the McWhirter Printing & Engraving Company, in Long Acre. He turned up, looking tanned and fit, the same morning as the proofs arrived and was very pleased with them.

"A great job, Bunny! You and Mirabel have done wonders. Our first issue's a corker. It'll open a new era in sporting journalism."

There was a knock on the door. Lord Pollexfen strode in.

"Ah, good morning, Raffles," he said. "Good morning, Manders. Mr. McWhirter, the Master Printer, tells me he's delivered your foundry proofs. I'd like a look at them before deciding how many thousands of copies to venture on as a printing order."

Raffles handed him the proofs, and I offered him a sherry-and-bitters, which Raffles and I were drinking as a mid-morning refreshment. The peer shook his head, pushed his silk hat to the back of it, and, still standing, screwed his monocle into his eye to examine the proofs.

"A splendid Contents page, gentlemen," he said. "Such names! John L. Sullivan—Lord Lonsdale of the Lonsdale Belts—Sir Harry Preston on the subject of Tod Sloan, the great jockey—Vardon on golf—Prince Ranjisinjhi on tiger-shooting! Excellent! Outstanding!"

"We owe those contributions to our Editor," I said, indicating Raffles, who was sitting on the edge of my desk, swinging a leg idly.

"I foresaw something of this, of course, when I approached him," said the Press baron. "I knew what I was doing. I always do." He turned the pages. His smile faded. "What's this? What are these interpolated effusions by *women?*"

"Those are articles," Raffles said, "obtained by our Contributing Editor from various eminent ladies with active tastes."

"But good God, man! John L. Sullivan's article on boxing followed by some female whining about the exclusion of her sex from witnessing the bouts staged at the National Sporting Club? This is monstrously out of place, Raffles!"

"I'm sorry to hear you say that, Pollexfen," said Raffles.

"And here again—the great Harry Vardon on golf immediately followed by some woman bleating about the need for a more socially acceptable kind of garment as a first step to eradicating the insult to her sex in their being obliged to drive off more favoured tees than the men. What provocative nonsense! What does the idiotic woman mean—'a more socially acceptable kind of garment'?"

"It's shown there in the illustrations," Raffles said. "One illustration depicts the hampering effect on the golf swing of ankle-length skirt and petticoats in a high wind. The contrasting illustration shows the healthful freedom, both physical and psychological, provided by a garment, a form of trousering, specially designed by our own Contributing Editor."

"This disgraceful illustration," the peer said angrily, "appears to have been posed for by that young woman in the other office. I've seen her before somewhere. Isn't she the one who threw the bomb at Lord's?"

"Indeed yes," said Raffles. "Our Contributing Editor."

Lord Pollexfen threw the proof down on my desk. "I will *not* publish a magazine polluted through and through with this kind of subversive stuff. It's entirely contrary to the policy of the Pollexfen Press, which is to keep women contented in their homes. I'm deeply disappointed, Raffles. This issue will have to be remade, omitting the offensive material. And call that young woman in. I intend to dismiss her instantly."

"I'm sorry, Pollexfen," Raffles said quietly. "*I* engaged Miss Renny. As a matter of principle, I will neither dismiss her nor alter one word of this first issue of my magazine."

"Then, by God, you must look elsewhere for a publisher!"

"In that case, Manders and I will publish the magazine from our own resources. Shall we not, Bunny?"

"Certainly, Raffles," I said, wondering uneasily what resources he was talking about, as we both were overdrawn at the bank.

"I warn you," said the Press peer, glaring haughtily through his monocle. "A. J. Raffles is not the only name to conjure with on the sports horizon. I shall seek a superior name for my sports magazine—and use the entire financial resources of the Pollexfen Press to crush any amateurish attempt at a rival publication."

"That is your privilege," Raffles said courteously.

"I also decline," barked the peer, "to be responsible for expenses incurred to date, including McWhirter's bill, and I shall require vacant possession of this office by six p.m. today."

He stalked out, slamming the door.

Raffles chuckled. "In chivalric terms, Bunny, there goes a male rampant, mounted on a prejudice, in a field ensanguined. Of course, this was inevitable."

"You expected it?" I said, astonished.

"I counted on it, Bunny." He offered me a cigarette from his case. "Well, now, first things first. We're without premises. We're overdrawn at the bank, but the manager's a cricketer and a good friend. He won't mind our using the bank as an accommodation address. Got a pencil handy? Take down this announcement."

Lighting my cigarette and his own, he paced thoughtfully.

" 'Owing,' " he dictated, " 'to the refusal of the original publisher to permit the expression of female opinion, and therefore withdrawing financial support, prospective contributors to *A. J. Raffles' Magazine,* which hopes soon to publish under less prejudiced auspices, are notified that unsolicited contributions should be submitted to The Editor, *Raffles' Magazine,* care of County and Confidential Bank, Berkeley Square, London, accompanied by a stamped, self-addressed envelope for return if unsuitable.' That's the conventional wording, I think, Bunny?"

"Well, more or less," I said.

"Good," said Raffles. "Run it in the Personal columns of all evening and daily newspapers till further notice. Now, another thing: as eligible bachelors, we both get plenty of invitations to dine out—"

"You in the best houses," I said, "myself at the second best."

"Comparisons are invidious," said Raffles. "Accept all the invitations you get. I shall do the same. And we owe no duty to Pollexfen, so there's no need to make it a secret, in mixed company, that we've parted from him, and the reason for it, and are trying to get out the magazine by using our private means. Now, let's call Mirabel in and see if she's prepared to stand by us in this crisis."

One flash from Mirabel's eyes, when she heard that we were now to go it alone, made it plain where she stood. So, for better or worse, I rented a bleak little office for us just off Drury Lane.

Money being tight, I was glad enough to dine out frequently, and it seemed to me, when I recounted our trouble with Lord Pollexfen, that the mirth of the men at the table was offensively raucous, but that some of the ladies looked at me sympathetically as they withdrew to the drawing-room and whatever ladies talk about there, and left us men to our port.

My leg was pulled unmercifully by some of these hearties, but my real worry was the Master Printer, Mr. McWhirter. We were in a galling position. We had a fine magazine made up and ready to print, but there was not a hope of a single copy coming off the presses of that canny Scotsman until his bill for services to date was paid.

"We shall have to call on somebody, Bunny," Raffles said.

"Who, for instance?" I asked gloomily.

"A certain barrister who's a member of one of my clubs, Bunny. His name's Sir Geoffrey Cullimore, K.C. He's a blustering brute who makes at least fifty thousand a year by reducing men to jelly in the witness-box, and women to tears."

"Then what's the use of calling on a man like that?" I said.

Raffles gave me a wicked look. "His wife has a valuable necklace, Bunny."

My heart lurched.

The Cullimore mansion was in Eaton Square, and Raffles, masked, shinned up the porch pillar to pay his call, by way of the window of the master bedroom, at two a.m. on a moonless night. I myself waited below on the porch ready to reel out, in evening-dress and opera hat, and, enacting the role of a gentleman who had dined too extensively, confuse with maudlin inquiries the bobby on the beat if he should make an inopportune appearance.

Fortunately, he did not show up at all, and when Raffles rejoined me, removing his mask, he had the necklace-case in his pocket.

"It's locked," he told me. "I'll pick the lock at Kern's place."

Ivor Kern, the fence we did business with, a young-old man with a perpetual, cynical half-smile, had an antique shop in King's Road, which was not far off. Under the flaring gaslight in Kern's cluttered sitting-room over the shop, Raffles picked the lock of the necklace-case and threw it open.

It was empty.

Raffles was as shocked as I was, but Kern's smirk widened.

" 'Emmeline Cullimore,' " he said, reading the name embossed on the leather necklace-case. "Well, as it happens, *I* can tell you where that necklace is. It's just across the road in the very secure safe of a pawnbroker friend of mine."

"How d'you know?" Raffles said grimly.

"Because jewellery offered to him in pledge," Kern said, "he usually brings over to me for an expert valuation before making an advance. A lady wanted to pledge a necklace with him this morning. She wore a veil and said her name was Doris Stevens, but he recognized her because she lives nearby, in Eaton Square. She was Lady Cullimore. I valued the necklace at two-thousand-and-seventy pounds. He gives ten per cent of value on pledges, so he let her have two-hundred-and-seven pounds on it. Bad luck, Raffles—you can't win every time."

We parted in silence, I to my flat in Mount Street, Raffles to his set of rooms in The Albany, just off Piccadilly.

To my surprise, he showed up at the office in Drury Lane next morning, and seemed to be in very good spirits.

"I have news for you, Bunny," he said, as he poured himself a sherry-and-bitters. "I dropped in at the bank on my way here. Yesterday afternoon, just before closing-time, a lady made a deposit to the credit of *A. J. Raffles' Magazine*. She wore a veil, and signed the paying-in slip in the name of Doris Stevens. It was a cash deposit, in five-pound notes, with two sovereigns, of exactly two-hundred-and-seven pounds."

"Good God!" I said. "What d'you make of this, Raffles?"

His grey eyes danced. "One wonders, Bunny." He took out his wallet. "I cashed a cheque for a hundred for incidental expenses—to keep our announcement running in the Personal columns, and to pay Mirabel's salary, and so on, with a little ready money for ourselves. We shan't need much, as we're dining out so frequently nowadays."

I accepted my share, and was glad of it. But the McWhirter problem remained. He was badgering for his bill to be paid, and it obviously was quite useless to offer him, on account, the mere £107 remaining to the magazine's credit, and expect him to print thousands of copies of our first issue on the strength of it.

I pointed this out to Raffles one morning about a week after the curious incident of the veiled lady.

He nodded regretfully. "We're stymied, Bunny. The only thing we can do is go and see Lord Pollexfen. It's no use prevaricating. We must be realistic. Come on, let's go and take our medicine."

"A damned bitter draught," I said, as we put on our hats and walked round to Covent Garden, ablaze with the flower-barrows in the lovely sunshine. "If he *does* agree to take over the magazine again, it'll be on his conditions—no female opinion, Mirabel to be sacked."

Significantly, we were kept waiting for some time in the ante-chamber of the Pollexfen Press Building before we were admitted to Lord Pollexfen's sanctum, which was almost as large as the Long Room at Lord's.

The peer, without rising from his massive desk or inviting us to be seated, screwed his monocle into his eye.

"Well?" he said haughtily.

"I hear rumours in Fleet Street," Raffles said, "that you're going ahead with your plans for a sports magazine."

"I informed you of my intention of doing so. I've found a suitable name for its bannerhead. What I say I will do, Raffles, I *do*."

"Frankly, Pollexfen," Raffles said, "we've run into certain difficulties—McWhirter and one thing and another. We've found the business side of producing a magazine a considerable encroachment on our time and—candidly—on our personal resources."

"I warned you," the peer said coldly. "Publishing is not for amateurs. If you're here to seek a return to our former relationship, I'm not interested. My alternative plans are afoot. Now—"

"You expressed some interest," Raffles said quickly, "in the literary material I obtained from personal acquaintances—Mr. John L. Sullivan—Prince Ranjisinjhi—"

The peer, his monocle fixedly regarding Raffles, withdrew his hand slowly from the bell on his desk.

"I could, I think," Raffles said, "persuade those gentlemen, as a personal favour to me, to allow the transfer of their material to your own magazine, if you—oh, the devil! Manders and I aren't business men. We've sunk more than we can afford into the magazine. If you'd care to consider acquiring its literary assets for a reasonable sum—"

"What d'you call a reasonable sum?" snapped the peer.

"Well, if you'd take over McWhirter's bill to date," Raffles said, "and—well, we'd like to get back a crumb or two of what we've spent. We could, of course, go to the City for finance—I have friends there—if we decide we *must* go on. But—"

"It interferes with your hedonistic way of life," Lord Pollexfen said sarcastically.

Raffles shrugged. "I don't know what we have left of the funds we personally put into the magazine's bank account, Pollexfen, but if you care to pay a sum equal to the current balance, you can take over the magazine's literary assets and all the work done so far—lock, stock, and barrel—and we'll be free of the whole thing," he added, with a gesture of weary disgust.

The Press baron hesitated. But he knew our present balance could not possibly be greater than the amount of McWhirter's bill, and he said, with abrupt decision, "Very well. I'll do that. Naturally, I shall require your bank manager to vouch for the amount currently standing to your magazine's credit."

"Won't you take my word for it?" Raffles said coldly.

"I'm afraid not." The peer struck a bell on his desk. The door opened. "Call my brougham," said the peer, with hauteur. "Where's your bank, Raffles?"

"In Berkeley Square."

"Then let's get the matter over and done with."

As, to the clip-clopping of the horse, the three of us rode in the brougham through the turmoil of the sunny streets, I knew Raffles must be inwardly raging, as I was myself. If only Lord Pollexfen had accepted Raffles' word for what stood to the magazine's credit, then Raffles might have named a reasonably substantial sum. As it was, we were about to be humiliated, and the Press peer's whole attitude betrayed his awareness of the fact.

"This is Lord Pollexfen," Raffles told the bank manager, when we were shown into his office. "He's acquiring the literary assets and so forth of *Raffles' Magazine*, Mr. Harper, for a sum equal to the magazine account's present balance—are you not, Pollexfen?"

"That is the agreement," the peer said haughtily.

"I can tell you the balance in a trice," said the bank manager, opening a large ledger.

I could have told him in less than a trice. Our balance was £107.

"At the conclusion of yesterday's business," said the manager, running a finger down the page, "the sum standing to the credit of *A. J. Raffles' Magazine of Sport* was precisely seven-thousand-five-hundred pounds, sixteen shillings and—"

My knees felt weak. The room spun round me. There seemed to be long silence. Then there was a scratching sound. It was made by Lord Pollexfen's pen. He was writing a cheque. He tore it out and threw it on the desk.

At the door, he turned, lean and tall, his monocle glittering.

"The name of A. J. Raffles," he said, "will never again be mentioned in any periodical published by the Pollexfen Press."

The door slammed.

A few minutes later, as Raffles and I were leaving the bank, I noticed a heavily veiled lady at the counter. Raffles gripped my arm, checking me. The lady pushed a sheaf of banknotes across the mahogany to the attentive clerk.

"To be placed," said the veiled lady, in a voice so low, almost furtive, as scarcely to be audible, "to the credit of *A. J. Raffles' Magazine.*"

We walked on out into the sunshine.

That night, we took Mirabel Renny and a friend of hers called Margaret, a fine, forthright type of girl, like Mirabel herself, to dine at Frascati's palatial restaurant in Oxford Street.

"I'm afraid, Mirabel," Raffles said, as the wine waiter brought champagne bottles in a silver ice-bucket to our table, "that you won't be entirely pleased by the reason for this dinner. Perhaps we'd better admit the truth right away. The fact is, we've sold the magazine."

"*Sold* it?" she said incredulously.

"For seven-thousand-five-hundred pounds," Raffles said. "To Lord Pollexfen."

"Pollexfen? But—but that means—"

"It means you're sacked, I'm sorry to say," Raffles admitted. "So this cheque I'm handing you is—in lieu of notice."

Mirabel's fine eyes flashed. "*Men!*" she said. "I might have known this would happen, Margaret. The moment things get difficult, men think only of themselves. They're selfish, through and—" She looked again at the cheque. "But—but this is for *seven-thousand-six-hundred pounds!*"

"Bunny and I owed the magazine account a hundred," Raffles explained. "I've already apologised to Bunny for omitting to tell him that I've kept in close touch with the bank all along regarding the state of the magazine's account."

"The privilege of an Editor-in-Chief," I said, a shade wryly.

"But, of course," said Raffles, "Bunny shares equally with me the seven-thousand-five-hundred from Pollexfen—which has nothing whatever to do with this cheque, Mirabel. This money came from other sources. What marital injustices or male insensitivities may explain this money, I just don't know. But you need have no hesitation in using it to start a magazine of your own, Mirabel, to further the Cause you have at heart. This money came entirely from women—unknown women in this country, Mirabel—that their voice, at last, may be heard in the land."

She gazed at him. She blinked. Tears came into her eyes.

They were the tears of sheer, incredulous happiness, but Raffles, embarrassed by them, quickly unwired a champagne bottle. The cork popped.

"We must admit," he said, as he poured the bubbly fizzing into our glasses, "that we owe much to Mr. John L. Sullivan, Prince Ranjisinjhi, and those other great names who provided priceless literary material. But let's drink now, above all, to those anonymous others, those nameless ones who so hopefully submitted," said A. J. Raffles, raising his glass, *"unsolicited contributions!"*

HISTORICAL NOTE

Though Mr. Manders' account of the above adventure makes no mention of the fact, it may be of journalistic interest to note that Lord Pollexfen's plans for a sports magazine excluding the name of A. J. Raffles were forestalled shortly thereafter by the appearance, from a rival publishing house, of *C. B. Fry's Magazine of Sport*, which flourished in the golden years of the Edwardian heyday.

Mr. C. B. Fry, perhaps the most famous of A. J. Raffles' cricketing contemporaries, and also at that time holder of the world's record for the broad jump, was ably assisted in his Editorship by young Mr. Bertram Atkey, whose later tales of the Exploits of Winnie O'Wynn, long-running in *The Saturday Evening Post* of the 1920's, were dramatized by the eminent actor, Mr. William Gillette, the theatre's greatest Sherlock Holmes.

And finally, Barry Perowne's real name is Philip Atkey, and Philip Atkey-Barry Perowne is Bertram Atkey's nephew.

Ellery Queen

Uncle from Australia

All of us would like to have a rich uncle from Australia—but a rich uncle from Australia can turn out to be an altogether mixed blessing . . . a classic situation—with a difference . . .

Detective: ELLERY QUEEN

"How did you happen to call me, Mr. Hall?" asked Ellery. He had been annoyed at first, because it was half-past ten and he was about to bed down with his favorite book, the dictionary, when his phone rang.

"The security hofficer at the 'otel 'ere gave it to me," said the man on the line. His salty cockney accent savored of London, but the man said he was from Australia.

"What's your problem?"

It turned out that Herbert Peachtree Hall was not merely from Australia, he was somebody's uncle from Australia. Uncles from Australia were graybeard standards of the mystery story, and here was one, if not exactly in the flesh, at least in the voice. So Ellery's ears began to itch.

It appeared that Mr. Hall was all of three somebodies' uncle from Australia, a niece and two nephews. A migrant from England of thirty years' exile, Hall said he had made his pile on the nether continent, liquidated it, and was now prepared—ah, that classic tradition!—to give it all away in a will. The young niece and the two young nephews being his only kin (if he had any kith, they were apparently undeserving of his largess), and all three being New York residents, Hall had journeyed to the United States to make their acquaintance and decide which of them deserved to be his heir. Their names were Millicent, Preston, and James, and they were all Halls, being the children of his only brother, deceased.

Ever the voice of caution, Ellery asked, "Why don't you simply divide your estate among the three?"

"Because I don't want to," said Hall, which seemed a reasonable reason. He had a horror, it seemed, of cutting up capital into bits and pieces.

He had spent two months getting to know Millicent, Preston, and James; and this evening he had invited them to dinner to announce the great decision.

"I told 'em, 'Old 'erbert,' I says, 'old 'erbert 'as taken a fancy to one of you. No 'ard feelings, you hunderstand, boys, but it's Millie gets my money. I've signed a will naming 'er my heir." Preston and James had taken his pronouncement with what Hall said he considered ruddy good sportsmanship, and they had even toasted their sister Millie's good fortune in champagne.

But after the departure of the trio, back in his hotel room, the uncle from Australia had afterthoughts.

"I never 'ad trouble making money, Mr. Queen, but maybe by giving it away I'm asking for some. I'm sixty, you know, but the doctors tell me I'm fit as one of your dollars—can live another fifteen years. Suppose Millie decides she won't wait that long?"

"Then make another will," said Ellery, "restoring the *status quo ante*."

"Mightn't be fair to the girl," protested Hall. "I 'aven't real grounds for suspicion, Mr. Queen. That's why I want the services of a hinvestigator, to muck through Millie's life, find out if she's the sort to bash in 'er poor rich uncle's 'ead. Can you come 'ere right now, so I can tell you what I know about 'er?"

"Tonight? That seems hardly necessary! Won't tomorrow morning do, Mr. Hall?"

"Tomorrow morning," said Herbert Peachtree Hall stubbornly, "could be too late."

So for some reason obscure to him—although his ears were itching like mad—Ellery decided to humor the Australian. The hour of 11 P.M. plus six minutes found him outside Hall's suite in the midtown hotel, knocking. His knock went unanswered. Whereupon Ellery tried the door, found it opened to his hand, and walked in.

And there was a bone-thin little man with a white thatch and a bush tan stretched out on the carpet, face down, with a brassy-looking Oriental paperknife in his back.

Ellery leaped for the phone, told the hotel operator to send up the house doctor and call the police, and got down on one knee beside the prone figure. He had seen an eyelid flicker.

"Mr. Hall!" he said urgently. "Who did it? Which one?"

The already cyanosed lips trembled. At first nothing came out, but then Ellery heard, quite distinctly, one word.

"Hall," the dying man whispered.

"Hall? Which Hall? Millie? One of your nephews? Mr. Hall, you have to tell me—"

But Mr. Hall was not telling anything more to anybody. The man from down under was down, down under, and Ellery knew he was not going to come up again, ever.

The following day Ellery was an inquisitive audience of one in his father's office at police headquarters. The director was, of course, Inspector Queen; the cast were the three Halls—Millicent, Preston, and James. The banty Inspector put them through their paces peevishly.

"All your uncle was able to get out before he died," snapped the Inspector, "was the name Hall, which tells us it was one of you, but not which one.

"This is an off-beat case, God help me," the old man went on. "Murders have three ingredients—motive, means, opportunity. You three match up to them pretty remarkably. Motive? Only one of you benefits from Herbert P. Hall's death—and that's you, Miss Hall."

Millicent Hall had a large bottom, and a large face with a large nose in the middle of it. She was plain enough, Ellery concluded, to have grasped at the nettle murder in order to achieve that luscious legacy.

"I didn't kill him," the girl protested.

"So say they all, Miss Hall. Means? Well, there are no prints on the knife that did the job—because of the chasework on the handle and blade—but it's an unusual piece, and establishing its ownership has been a cinch. Mr. Preston Hall, the knife that killed your uncle belongs to you."

"Belonged to me," coughed Preston Hall, a long lean shipping clerk with the fangs of a famished ocelot. "I presented it to Uncle Herbert just last week. Father left it to me, and I thought Uncle Herbert might like to have a memento of his only brother. He actually cried when I gave it to him."

"I'm touched," snarled the Inspector. "Opportunity? One of you was actually seen and identified loitering about the hotel last night after the dinner party broke up—and that was you, James Hall."

James Hall was a bibulous fellow, full of spirits of both sorts; he worked, when one of the spirits moved him, in the sports department of a tabloid.

"Sure it was me," James Hall laughed. "Hell, I stayed around to have a few belts, that's all, before tootling on home. Does that mean I am the big bad slayer?"

"This is like coming down the stretch in a three-horse race," complained Inspector Queen. "Millicent Hall is leading on motive—though I'd like to point out that you, Preston, or you, James, could have knocked the old boy over to teach him a lesson for not leaving his money to *you*. Preston's leading on means; I have only your uncorroborated word that you gave the letter knife to Herbert Hall; what I *do* know is that it's yours. Though, again, even if you did give Hall the knife, you, Millie, or you, James, could have used it in that hotel room. And James, you're leading on opportunity—though your brother or sister could have easily sneaked up to your uncle's room without being seen. Ellery, what are you sitting there like a dummy for?"

"I'm thinking," said Ellery, looking thoughtful.

"And have you thought out," asked his father acidly, "which one of the Halls their uncle meant when he said 'Hall' killed him? Do you see a glimmer?"

"Oh, more than a glimmer, dad," Ellery said. "I see it all."

CHALLENGE TO THE READER

Who killed Uncle Herbert from Australia?
And how did Ellery know?

"Old 'erbert was right, dad," Ellery said. "Millie, drooling over the prospect of all those Australian goodies, couldn't wait for her uncle to die naturally. But she hadn't the nerve to murder him by herself—did you, Miss Hall? So you held out the bait of a three-way split to your brothers, and they willingly joined you in the plot. Safety in numbers, and all that. Right?"

The three Halls had grown very still indeed.

"It's always disastrous," Ellery said sadly, "trying to be clever in a murder. The plan was to confuse the issue and baffle the police—one of you being tied to motive, another to the weapon, the third to opportunity. It was all calculated to water down suspicion—spread it around."

"We don't know what you're talking about," said the drinking Hall, quite soberly; and his brother and sister nodded at once.

The Inspector was troubled. "But how do you know, Ellery?"

"Because Herbert Hall was a Cockney. He dropped his aitches; in certain key words beginning with a vowel, he also added the cockney aitch. Well, what did he say when I asked him which one of the three had stabbed him? He said, 'Hall.' I didn't realize till just now that he wasn't saying 'Hall'—*he was adding an aitch.* What he really said was 'all'—all three of them murdered him!"

Edward D. Hoch

Captain Leopold Gets Angry

It started out as a nasty case—children in danger. And that kind of case always hit Captain Leopold in his gut, hit him even harder than murder...

Captain Leopold and Lieutenant Fletcher have a new associate—Connie Trent, former undercover narcotics agent and now a member (and the best-looking one!) of the Detective Division of the Police Department...

Detective: CAPTAIN LEOPOLD

The children had lingered at the playground through most of the morning, enjoying the sudden July sunshine after three days of rain. The young man who paused to watch their playing might have been basking in the sun himself, enjoying a solitary stroll across the park.

After a moment he called out to one of the nearby children. "Liz? You're Liz Lambeth, aren't you? I know your daddy."

The little blonde girl left the others and came cautiously closer. She was nine years old, with a child's curiosity, and the man had a pleasant, friendly face. "You know my daddy?"

"Sure. Come along. I'll take you to him."

She screwed up her face uncertainly. "He's at work!"

"No, he isn't. He's parked right down the road in his truck. You want to see him, don't you?"

"Yes."

"Well, come with me, then. It's just a little way."

He held out his hand, and after a moment the little girl took it.

The armored car had just pulled up in front of Independent Electronics Corporation when the young man left his parked auto and walked quickly toward the entrance. He paced himself well, so that his route intercepted that of the uniformed man who was carrying a heavy white sack in one hand and a drawn revolver in the other.

"George Lambeth," he said, making it a statement and not a question. The guard turned and slowed his pace. In the armored car the driver suddenly became alert. The young man extended his hand, revealing a child's crumpled red T-shirt. "We have your daughter. She'll be dead in ten seconds unless you give me that money."

"What?" The color drained from the guard's face and he glanced toward his partner in the truck.

The driver had his gun out now and was opening the door. "What is it, George?"

"Five seconds, Mr. Lambeth."

"They've got my daughter," Lambeth told the driver. "They've got Liz."

The uncertain driver raised his gun, but the young man stood his ground. "Shoot me and she dies. My partner is watching from that car across the street, and he has a gun at her head."

"Give him the money, George," the driver said.

George Lambeth handed over the heavy white sack. The young man accepted it with a nod and tossed the red T-shirt on the pavement. Then he turned and walked back the way he had come.

In another minute his car disappeared from view around a corner.

Lieutenant Fletcher brought the report to Captain Leopold's desk shortly after one o'clock. "This looks like another one, Captain. He snatched the nine-year-old daughter of an armored-car guard and threatened to kill her if the guard didn't hand over the Independent Electronics payroll."

"How long ago?"

"Just before noon. The girl was released unharmed a few blocks away. They're questioning her now, but it sounds like our loner again. He lured her into his car near the playground, then bound and gagged her and left her on the floor in the back seat."

Leopold nodded. "How much money?"

"Eighty-seven thousand, mostly in small bills. It seems the company maintains a check-cashing service for employees."

"Description fit last week's bandit?"

"Close enough, and the modus operandi is identical." A week earlier the son of a supermarket manager had been kidnaped and held for ransom—all the cash in the supermarket safe. Then, too, a lone young man—apparently unarmed—had made the demand for money, and calmly carried it away in a supermarket shopping bag.

"Get those guards down to look at pictures. The little girl, too, if she's able to." Leopold felt a surge of anger at the crimes. There was something about the endangerment of children that hit at his gut the way not even a murder could. Perhaps it was because he had no children of his own. Perhaps this made all of them his children.

Lieutenant Fletcher scratched his head. "I'll do that, Captain. But there's another angle we might check out. Connie Trent was at my desk when the first report came in. She has an idea about it."

"Connie? Send her in."

Connie Trent was easily the best-looking member of the Police Department. Tall and dark-haired, with a constant twinkle in her large brown eyes, she'd managed to charm the entire Detective Division after only six months on the job. But it wasn't only her face and figure that Connie had going for her. A college graduate with a degree in sociology, she had joined the force as an undercover narcotics agent. Her cover had been blown after four months when she helped set up the biggest drug raid in the city's history, but she had continued working among addicts as a known member of the police force. Oddly enough, the people she encountered seemed to show little resentment against her former undercover role. It was almost as if they welcomed the relief that arrest sometimes brought.

Connie still carried a snub-nosed Colt Detective Special in her handbag, but she was unarmed when she entered Leopold's office. The tight green dress she wore was hardly immodest, but Leopold observed that it wasn't designed to hide everything either.

"Good to see you again, Connie," he greeted her, extending his hand. It wasn't his practice to shake hands with women, but he felt somehow that a policewoman was different—especially when she was as attractive and feminine as Connie Trent.

"You've heard about the armored-car robbery?" she asked, getting right to business.

"Fletcher just told me."

"It's the same as last week's supermarket job, and I may have a lead for you. I didn't want to say anything till I was certain, but with this second robbery I can't take a chance any longer. Next time this guy might kill a child."

"It's someone you know?" Leopold asked.

"Not exactly." Connie Trent sat down, crossing her long legs. "When I was doing undercover work I met a girl named Kathy Franklin. She was on heroin, and she led me to a lot of the others who were arrested later. I helped Kathy get a suspended sentence, and signed her onto a methadone maintenance program. I've seen her about once a week over the past two months, and she's really straightening herself out. She has a job as a waitress in a bowling alley, down near the Sound.

"Anyway, she has a boy friend named Pete Selby who's still on heroin. I think he's the one who got her hooked originally, though she'd never admit it. I've never seen Pete, so I figure he's been avoiding me. But one night last week when I stopped by to check on Kathy it was obvious Pete had just left."

"How obvious?"

"You know—she was sort of tensed up, and there were cigar butts in the ashtray. I asked her and she admitted he'd been there. In the kitchen there was a shopping bag from the Wright-Way Supermarket. It's way the other side of the city from Kathy's apartment, but there was this bag on the table next to a bottle of rye and two glasses. So when I heard about the robbery the next day I was suspicious. The robber carried the money away in a shopping bag just like that one."

"You didn't report it then?"

Connie Trent shrugged. "You can't convict anyone with just a shopping bag. But he's still on heroin, and that means he needs money. I figure someone would have to need money a great deal to pull anything like these two jobs, with the children."

"She's worth talking to," Leopold agreed. "Want to go there with me?"

"Of course!" Connie said quickly. She seemed honored by the invitation, which surprised Leopold.

"Let's go, then. Fletcher, you talk to the guards and the little girl, see if you get anywhere with the pictures on file."

Kathy Franklin lived in a fourth-floor walkup apartment near downtown.

The area was part of a much-delayed urban renewal program that had left the blocks around her building barren and scarred as if by war.

Here and there a single sickly tree grew, revealed after years of hibernation by the demolition work around it; but for the most part the setting was depressing even on a sunny July afternoon.

Leopold stepped over a shallow puddle of water that had accumulated from the recent rains and followed Connie up the steps of the building. As they climbed to the fourth floor he wondered for the first time if Kathy Franklin was black or white, and he found out when a pretty white girl opened the door to Connie's knock.

"Oh! Come in," she said, her voice a bit reluctant as she stepped aside.

Connie introduced Leopold and explained why they had come. "Today an armored car was robbed, Kathy. By the same person who robbed the supermarket last week."

"I don't know anything about that," Kathy Franklin said, a little too quickly.

Leopold cleared his throat. "We want to ask you about Pete Selby."

"I haven't seen him in months." Too quickly again.

"Miss Franklin, the man who committed these crimes is a particularly vicious person. He endangered the lives of two children. Now you say you haven't seen Pete Selby in months, but you admitted to Miss Trent that you'd seen him just last week."

She shot Connie a deadly glance. "I forgot about that time. He was only here a few minutes."

"He brought a shopping bag with him, from a supermarket that was robbed."

"I asked him on the phone to bring me a loaf of bread and some milk. Are you going to arrest him for that?"

"What about today?" Leopold asked, ignoring her question. "Where was he this morning, just before noon?"

"I told you I haven't seen him, and I meant it." She was suddenly nervous, grabbing for an open pack of cigarettes that slid from her grasp; the cigarettes spilled across the carpet. She cursed and bent to retrieve them.

Connie was on the floor helping her, and Leopold drew back. He wasn't getting anywhere. Perhaps a woman had a better chance with her.

"Look here, Kathy," Connie began, reaching for the last of the cigarettes. "If Pete is involved in these crimes you have to tell us. Can you imagine how you'd feel if one of those child hostages was killed?"

"I don't know anything," Kathy insisted. "Not a thing."

"Where's Pete living these days, Kathy? Is he shacked up with another woman?"

"*No!*" she screeched from the floor, still on her knees. "He's with Tommy Razenwood!"

"Where?"

"I don't know. They have an apartment somewhere."

Then, as if suddenly remembering Leopold's presence, Kathy got to her feet and lit a cigarette. "I don't know anything about it," she told him. "I don't see Pete any more."

"If he's still on drugs he needs money. Is Razenwood on the stuff, too?"

"I don't know. I know nothing about Razenwood."

Her face was frozen into an expression that told Leopold they had pressed it to the limit. If there was more information to be had, they weren't going to get it from her this afternoon. "All right," he said with a sigh. "Come on, Connie. We'd better be getting back."

The policewoman nodded, then reached out to touch Kathy on the arm. "If you hear anything, Kathy, you have my number. Please call me."

Downstairs Leopold asked, "What do you think?"

"Oh, she's still seeing him. There's no doubt about that. But she may just be covering up his usual drug activities. Until we get an identification from that armored-car driver or the supermarket manager, it's all guesswork."

He had to agree. "Let's get back downtown. Maybe Fletcher had some luck with the witnesses."

Fletcher came into the office almost at once, holding a group of files and mug shots. "We got it, Captain! The driver picked him out, and the manager and the little girl confirmed it."

"Let me guess," Leopold said. "Pete Selby."

Fletcher shook his head. "I struck out on Selby. He was the right age and build, but the wrong face. I was running through some of the people arrested with him in drug raids, though, and I hit a bull's-eye. A guy named Tommy Razenwood."

"Razenwood." Leopold took the picture and studied it. "He and Selby are rooming together somewhere. If we find one we'll find the other." The young man in the photo was grim-faced and sleepy-eyed. His age was 23, the same as Selby's, but he had only one drug arrest, for LSD. There was no evidence that like Selby he was on heroin.

"No known address," Fletcher pointed out.

"Kathy Franklin knows where they're holed up. I'm sure of it." He pressed a buzzer on his desk. "And if anyone can get through to her, Connie can."

"You sorta like her, don't you, Captain?"

"Connie? She's an intelligent young woman."

Fletcher winked. "I wasn't talking about her brains."

Connie Trent appeared at the door and smiled at them both. "Something else, Captain?"

Iore of the same, I'm afraid. The witnesses identified Selby's roommate, Tommy Razenwood, as the man we want. Do you think you could talk to Kathy again and tell her this, convince her it's Razenwood and not Selby we're after? I'm sure she knows where they are, and at this point she's the only lead we have."

"I'll do what I can, Captain."

After she'd left, Leopold said, "Fletcher, I think we'd better put a twenty-four-hour watch on Kathy Franklin's apartment. If Connie doesn't get anywhere, I still want to know if Selby shows up there again."

"What orders if he does show?"

"Follow him. Tommy Razenwood is the one we're after now."

The next morning, at an hour still too early for most activity, a boy on a bicycle was starting out to deliver the morning newspapers on a quiet residential street near the north edge of the city. His name was Jim MacIves and he was twelve years old. He lived in the big white house on the corner with his parents and his two sisters.

This morning, as usual, he'd been the first one up. His father could sleep another hour before the alarm would ring to rouse him for his job at the bank. By that time young Jim would be back home and ready for breakfast.

The car was waiting at the first intersection, and the young man opened the door to call out, "Got an extra paper I can buy, kid?"

Always thankful for another sale, Jim said, "Sure," and wheeled up next to the car.

That was when the man grabbed him around the neck, yanking him off his bike.

Jim tried to fight back, to break the grip on his throat and keep from being pulled into the car, but the man was too strong. The boy felt something hit him on the side of his head and the strength went out of him. He slipped to the pavement, feet tangled in his bike. The man stepped quickly from the car to lift him inside.

"What's going on there?" a voice shouted from the ground floor of one of the houses. Even in his dazed condition Jim recognized old Matthews, who always sat by the front window waiting for his paper, even at seven in the morning. "Leave that boy alone!"

Matthews came running up, his slippers slapping on the sidewalk, and the young man straightened to face him. He hit the old man on the side of the head, but harder than he'd hit Jim. Then, as Matthews fell forward on his face, the young man seemed to panic. He kicked the bicycle aside and jumped back in his car, and in a moment he was gone.

Jim tried to shake the pain from his head and stand up. The first thing he thought of was poor old Matthews, who'd come running out to save him.

But it was too late for Matthews now. Looking at him there on the sidewalk, Jim could see he was dead.

Captain Leopold came back to headquarters that afternoon feeling old and tired. Perhaps it was the surge of fresh anger that had swept through him at the sight of the dead old man. Or perhaps it was just the senselessness of it all. Why did it have to happen? Why did people like Tommy Razenwood have to go through their lives robbing and killing?

Connie Trent came in, very quietly, and took the chair that Fletcher usually sat in. "I heard about it," she said simply.

He nodded. "That makes it murder now."

"You're sure it was Razenwood?"

"I'm sure. The boy is the son of a bank manager. Razenwood was after another big haul. And he probably would have made it if that old guy hadn't gotten involved."

"The boy identified Razenwood?"

"Right away. Picked the photo out from a handful I showed him." He stared at the picture on his desk, as if trying to conjure up the physical presence of Tommy Razenwood. "What about Kathy Franklin? Did you talk to her again?"

Connie nodded and crossed her long legs. "Kathy promised to call me here tonight, before eight. She's talking to Pete about turning Razenwood in. I think the decision will be easier after this killing."

"I hope so."

"Do you have someone watching her place?" Connie asked.

Leopold nodded. Then, because his eyes were on her legs, he said, "You should get married and settle down, Connie. This is no life for a woman as good-looking as you."

She wrinkled her nose at him. "Is that an offer?"

"Just an observation," he said, realizing he was sounding like an old fool.

They waited until eight o'clock for Kathy's call, with Connie growing increasingly nervous. Fletcher had been out all day, checking known pushers for a line on Selby, but they'd heard nothing from him. It was as if the case had come to a dead end, with only the reporters keeping the phone lines busy, trying for a fresh morning lead on the story.

Then, at 8:15, Kathy Franklin phoned.

Connie motioned Leopold to pick up the extension as she talked. "Hello, Kathy! I was beginning to worry that we wouldn't hear from you."

"I said I'd call, and I'm calling."

"How does it look? Did you talk to Pete?"

A hesitation. Then, "Yes." Very softly.

"Well?"

"We'll do it."

Connie managed to smile at Leopold. "Fine. Where is he?"

"One thing first," Kathy said. "Pete insists on it. Tommy has a lot of friends in town and they might find out what we did. Pete doesn't want to go through life wondering if his next fix might be poisoned. He wants plane tickets out of here for both of us."

Connie looked questioningly at Leopold. He hated to let a junkie off the hook, but at this point they had no evidence against Selby. And they had plenty against Razenwood. He nodded, and Connie said, "Agreed. Where do you want to go?"

"Latin America. He wants two tickets to Mexico City, and then we'll go on from there. Who knows? Maybe it'll be a new life for both of us."

"I hope so," Connie said. "You'll get the tickets when you deliver Tommy Razenwood to us."

"Pete says he can do it tomorrow night. I'll phone you tomorrow and let you know where. Get us out of here on the midnight flight."

"Don't fail us, Kathy. You know it's murder now, and you could both be accessories. It's jail or Mexico, and the choice is yours."

"I know."

Connie hung up and sat facing Leopold. "She'll come through."

"I hate the thought of that guy walking around free for another twenty-four hours."

"We have no choice, unless Lieutenant Fletcher comes up with a lead."

"We can always hope for that," Leopold said.

But there were no leads from Fletcher. Both Selby and Razenwood seemed to have vanished from the face of the earth. No one had seen them at their usual haunts, and even the pushers insisted they did not know their whereabouts.

"It's a blank wall," Fletcher said the next afternoon.

"Then Kathy Franklin is our only contact. Let's hope she comes through."

"You got the tickets for her?"

Leopold nodded. "Connie has them. But she doesn't turn them over until we have Razenwood."

"So we just wait for the call?"

"There's nothing else we can do. I think the case has been publicized enough to have every parent on guard. We're watching the bus and the train stations, and the airport. Of course if he wants to get in his car and drive down to New York there's no real way we can stop him. That murder might have scared him, though. I don't think he'll try another kidnaping."

All through the early evening Connie Trent waited for Kathy's call. When it finally came, just before seven, the voice on the other end was breathless. "Look, Tommy's got a gun. He's planning to leave town tonight, but he's coming here first to pick up Pete's car."

"He'll be at your apartment?"

"Downstairs, in the street. The car is a blue '69 Ford, license number 8M-258. I'll walk out with him to the car, then you can grab him. Be careful, though. He'll use the gun if he has to."

"We'll be careful," Connie said. "You just get out of the way when the police move in. He has a habit of taking hostages, and we don't want you to be one of them."

When she'd hung up, Leopold buzzed for Fletcher. "I want cars blocking both ends of the street, and I want men on foot nearby. It's a bad place for a stakeout, because there are no other buildings."

"I'll handle it, Captain, but we can't move in too early. If he sees too much activity he'll get suspicious and stay away."

"Use unmarked cars, and plainclothesmen. Keep the uniforms out of sight. I'll go in your car."

"What about me?" Connie asked.

"If he starts shooting it might be a dangerous place for a woman."

"I was the one who gave you the lead, Captain—remember?"

"All right," he said with a sigh. "You can ride with us, but you stay in the car." He supposed he had to start treating her like a man sometime.

The summer night was hot and humid, with a forecast of possible thunderstorms in the area. It was the sort of night that would have brought the people of Kathy Franklin's neighborhood into the streets for a breath of air, if there were still any people there. As it was, only one old woman sat on the steps in front of the apartment house, staring up the street at the piles of rubble and the sickly trees. Perhaps, thought Leopold, she was remembering the way it had looked before urban renewal. Or imagining how it might look in the future, after she was gone.

"What do you think?" Fletcher asked as they drove by the building. "Want me to get her out of there?"

"No. He could be watching."

"From where?" Connie asked. "There's not another building within three blocks."

"Let's wait. It's getting dark. Maybe the old woman will go inside."

Because there was no place for cover, the unmarked cars had to remain some blocks away with their motors running, ready to move in. Fletcher's car drove through the area twice, and then they transferred to another vehicle that wouldn't look familiar. This time the old woman was gone from the steps, and the street was quiet.

"It's after nine," Fletcher said. "Still think he'll come?"

Leopold watched the street lights going on, casting their harsh white glow over the shadowed jagged foundations. Before he could answer, a blue Ford turned into the street and parked in front of Kathy's building.

"That's the car!" Connie said.

"Right." Leopold dropped a hand to the pistol on his belt, then took it away. "But it's Kathy driving. And it looks as if she's alone."

"Think he's already inside?" Fletcher asked.

"I don't know. Let's wait and see what happens. She said he'd be leaving in that car. Maybe he's not here yet."

They had fifteen minutes to wait before Kathy reappeared on the steps with a man. He stood in the shadows, glancing both ways on the street, before finally hurrying down to the car. She went with him to the car door and closed it after he slid behind the wheel. Then she moved back a few steps, waving goodbye to him.

"Let's move!" Leopold shouted into the police radio. "All cars!"

The Ford started from the curb, moving slowly at first. It seemed to hesitate and almost stop, then Fletcher rounded the corner and the Ford took off. Two blocks away the police cars screeched into position, cutting off his escape.

"He's stopping!" Connie said. "We've got him bottled up!"

"Stay here and keep down. Come on, Fletcher."

Then they were out of the car and running, their guns drawn. The Ford hesitated between them and the police at the end of the street, and Leopold shouted, "Police, Razenwood! You're surrounded!"

Suddenly he gunned the engine and veered to the left, over the curb, smashing through a board sign and across the rubble of a vacant lot.

"He's getting away, Captain!"

Leopold fired two quick shots and started to run. On the next block they were firing, too, and he saw the Ford's rear window shatter. The car hobbled across the brick-strewn lot and suddenly burst into flames as more bullets found their mark.

"He's trying to get out," Leopold shouted, racing forward. But the flames were too hot. The entire car was enveloped in fire, and there was no chance for anyone to get out alive.

Fletcher ran up then, and Connie, and presently Kathy came across the lot to where they stood. "Oh, my God," Kathy cried, "did you have to do it like that?"

"One way's as bad as another," Leopold said grimly.

They went back to Captain Leopold's office for coffee, and he sat glumly staring at Tommy Razenwood's file on the desk before him. "I don't like it to end this way, either, damn it! But the man was a kidnaper of children and a murderer! Maybe he didn't deserve any better."

"I didn't say a word," Fletcher mumbled. "How do you like your coffee, Connie?"

"Black, thanks."

Fletcher came back in a moment with her coffee. Then he reached across the desk to pick up the files on Razenwood and Selby. But Leopold reached out to clutch them a moment longer. "What about it? What do you two think?"

"You fired first, Captain. If you hadn't, maybe the others might have held their fire. But, hell, I'd have done the same thing. You can't fool around with killers."

Leopold barely heard the words. He was staring at the file on Pete Selby, seeing the notation under *Known Habits:*

Nonsmoker, nondrinker, addicted to heroin, frequents race tracks.

He read the words again. They seemed to have some meaning he couldn't quite comprehend. "You can't blame yourself," Connie was saying.

Nonsmoker, nondrinker, addicted to heroin.

"Maybe I could have handled it differently," he replied, wondering why the words of the report fascinated him so. It wasn't even Razenwood's file, but Selby's. The file belonged to the wrong man.

Wrong man.

"Connie?" Go slow now. Take it easy.

"What is it, Captain?"

"You told me about your visit to Kathy Franklin that first time, when you suspected she was seeing Selby. Remember?"

"Yes."

"You knew he'd just left because Kathy was tensed up and there were cigar butts in the ashtray and they'd been drinking. But Pete Selby doesn't smoke or drink, not according to his file."

"Maybe he just started," she said with a shrug, but Fletcher was leaning forward, studying the file.

"And you mentioned the shopping bag, too. If a man has just robbed a supermarket and carried the money away in a shopping bag, would he bring the bag home and give it to his roommate?"

"He'd get rid of it as soon as he was finished with it," Fletcher said.

"Exactly! And if the bag was at Kathy's apartment it means the money was probably brought there, too."

"But we know it was Tommy Razenwood who stole the money. The manager identified him, and so did everyone else. You mean he gave the money to Selby to take to Kathy's apartment?"

Leopold shook his head. "Remember the cigar butts? There's a much more likely explanation. Razenwood took it there himself. He was probably hiding in the closet when you arrived, Connie. Kathy was willing to admit that Selby had just left because it wasn't true."

Fletcher almost spilled his coffee. "Damn it, Captain, if the Franklin girl was in on the robbery with Razenwood, why should she finger him for the police and fly off to Mexico with Selby?"

"Why, indeed?" Leopold asked. He was already on his feet. "If we hurry, we can just about catch that midnight plane before it takes off."

Kathy Franklin was at the gate, just handing in her tickets, when Leopold reached her. "I came to say goodbye, Kathy."

She whirled, pale as death. "What—?"

"Where's your traveling companion?"

Then he saw Tommy Razenwood, standing to one side with a magazine partly obscuring his face. Tommy saw Leopold at the same moment and seized Kathy. In an instant he had his arm at her throat, with a knife in his free hand.

"Tommy!" she screamed.

"Out of the way, cops! Try to take me and she dies!"

Leopold stood his ground. "Kathy's not some nine-year-old child, Tommy. Kill her if you want, but we're taking you."

He moved then, as Fletcher came in from the other side. Razenwood shoved Kathy into Leopold and tried to run, but Fletcher brought him down with a waist-high tackle that sent the knife flying from Razenwood's grip.

Then they had the handcuffs on him, as Connie grabbed Kathy.

"No Mexico trip after all," Leopold told her. "You made me kill the wrong man."

"He would have knifed me!" She turned to spit at Razenwood, who had ceased to struggle in Fletcher's grip.

"So it was Pete Selby who died in the burning car," Connie said.

Leopold nodded. "A dark street, a closed car, a man fleeing after she'd fingered him as Razenwood—that's all it took to start us shooting. She'd already made sure of that by warning us he had a gun and would use it. Of course Pete Selby was fleeing because he was carrying heroin, not because he was a murderer. Razenwood had taken Selby's place in Kathy's bed, so they figured it was only right for Selby to take his place in the morgue."

Two uniformed police officers appeared then, to help them get their prisoners out of the terminal. The scattering of midnight travelers turned to stare at the proceedings. "How'd they know the car would burst into flames like that and prevent easy identification of the body?" Fletcher asked.

"I imagine it was soaked in gasoline, with a few extra cans in the trunk. Selby hesitated as he started the car, remember. He may have smelled the gasoline."

It was in the police car going downtown, with Razenwood seated between Leopold and Fletcher, that Leopold asked him a question. "What if our bullets had missed, Tommy? What if Selby had stopped the car and tried to surrender before it caught fire?"

He lifted his eyes and stared straight ahead. "That wouldn't have happened, cop. I was on the roof of the building with a rifle, just to make sure he didn't. I don't know if it was you or me who drilled the trunk and set off that gasoline. But I guess it didn't make any difference to Selby."

"No," Leopold agreed, "I guess it didn't."

E d w a r d   D .   H o c h

T h e   T h e f t   o f   N i c k   V e l v e t

*Nick Velvet's 19th caper—and in at least two respects you will find
the exploit different from the 18 previous adventures. But as before,
Nick is still accepting assignments to steal only the valueless—that
is, things valueless to most people and certainly not worth Nick's fee
of $30,000, and Nick is still forced to detect before he can collect . . .*

Criminal-Detective: NICK VELVET

"It's for you, Nicky," Gloria yelled from the telephone, and Nick
Velvet put down the beer he'd been savoring. It was a lazy
Sunday afternoon in late winter, when the snow had retreated to
little lumps beneath the shady bushes and a certain freshness was
already apparent in the air. It was a time of year that Nick especially
liked, and he was sorry to have his reverie broken.

"Yes?" he spoke into the phone, after taking it from Gloria's hand.

"Nick Velvet?" The voice was deep and a bit harsh, but that didn't
surprise him. He'd been hearing that sort of voice on telephones for
years.

"Speaking."

"You do jobs. You steal things." A statement, not a question.

"I never discuss my business on the telephone. I could meet you
somewhere tomorrow."

"It has to be tonight."

"Very well, tonight."

"I'll be in the parking lot at the Cross-County Mall. Eight o'clock."

"How will I know your car?"

"The place is empty on a Sunday night. We'll find each other."

"Could I have your name?"

The voice hesitated, then replied. "Solar. Max Solar. Didn't you
receive my letter?"

"No," Nick answered. "Your letter about what?"

"I'll see you at eight."

The line went dead and Nick hung up the phone. He'd heard the name Max Solar before, or seen it in the newspapers, but he couldn't remember in what context.

"Who was that, Nicky?" Gloria appeared in the doorway, holding a beer.

"A land developer. He wants to see me tonight."

"On Sunday?"

Nick nodded. "He needs my opinion on some land he's buying near here. I shouldn't be gone more than an hour." The excuses and evasions came easily to Nick's lips, and sometimes he half suspected that Gloria knew them for what they were. Certainly she rarely questioned his sudden absences, even for days at a time.

He left the house a little after 7:30 and drove the five miles to the Cross-County Mall in less than fifteen minutes. There was little traffic and when he reached the Mall ahead of schedule he was surprised to see a single car already parked there, near the drive-in bank. He drove up beside it and parked. A man in the front seat nodded and motioned to him.

Nick left his car and opened the door of the other vehicle. "You're early," the man said.

"Better than late. Are you Max Solar?"

"Yes. Get in."

Nick slid into the front seat and closed the door. The man next to him was bulky in a tweed topcoat, and he seemed nervous.

"What do you want stolen?" Nick asked. "I don't touch money or jewelry or anything of value, and my fee is—"

He never finished. There was a movement behind him, in the back seat, and something hit him across the side of the head. That was the last Nick knew for some time.

When he opened his eyes he realized he was lying on a bed somewhere. The ceiling was crisscrossed with cracks and there was a cobweb visible in one corner. He thought about that, knowing Gloria's trim housekeeping would never allow such a thing, and realized he was not at home. His head ached and his body was uncomfortably stretched. He tried to turn over and discovered that his left wrist was handcuffed to a brass bedstead.

Not the police.

But who, then? And why?

He tried to focus his mind. It seemed to be morning, with light seeping through the blind at the window. But which day? Monday?

A door opened somewhere and he heard footsteps crossing the floor. A face appeared over him, a familiar face. The man in the car.

"Where am I?" Nick mumbled through a furry mouth. "What am I doing here?"

The man leaned closer to the bed. "You are here because I have stolen you." The idea seemed to amuse him and he chuckled.

"Why?" The room was beginning to swim before Nick's eyes.

"Don't try to talk. We have no intention of harming you. Just lie still and relax."

"What's the matter with me?"

"A mild sedative. Just something to keep you under control."

Nick tried to speak again, but the words would not come. He closed his eyes and slept . . .

When he awakened it was night again, or nearly so. A shaded lamp glowed dimly in one corner of the room. "Are you awake?" a girl's voice asked, in response to his movement.

Nick lifted his head and saw a young brunette dressed in a dark turtleneck sweater and jeans. He ran his tongue over dry lips and finally found his voice. "I guess so. Who are you?"

"You can call me Terry. I'm supposed to be watching you, but it's more fun if you're awake. I didn't give you the last injection of sedative because I want someone to talk to."

"Thanks a lot," Nick said, trying to work the cobwebs from his throat. "What day is it?"

"Only Monday. You haven't even been here twenty-four hours yet." She came over and sat by the bed. "Hungry?"

He realized suddenly that he was. "Starving. I guess you haven't fed me."

"I'll get you some juice and a doughnut."

"Where's the other one—the man?"

"Away somewhere," she answered vaguely. She left the room and reappeared soon carrying a glass of orange juice and a bag of doughnuts. "Afraid that's the best I can do."

"How about unlocking me?"

"No. I don't have the key. You can eat with your other hand."

The juice tasted good going down, and even the soggy doughnuts were welcome. "Why did you kidnap me?" he asked Terry. "What are you going to do with me?"

"Don't know." She retreated from the room, perhaps deciding she'd talked too much already.

Nick finished three doughnuts and then lay back on the bed. He'd been lured to that parking lot and kidnaped for some reason, and he couldn't believe the motive was anything as simple as ransom. The man on the telephone had identified himself as Max Solar, and asked if Nick had received his letter. Since kidnapers rarely gave their right names to victims, it was likely the man was not Max Solar.

"Terry," he shouted. "Terry, come here!"

She appeared in the doorway, hands on hips. "What is it?"

"Come talk. I feel like talking."

"What about?"

"Max Solar. The man who brought me here."

She giggled a bit, and her face glowed with youth. "He's not Max Solar. He was just kidding you. Do you really think someone as wealthy as Max Solar would go around kidnaping people?"

"Then what is his name?"

"I can't tell you. He wouldn't like it."

"How'd you get involved with him?"

"I can't talk any more about it."

Nick sighed. "I thought you wanted someone to talk to."

"Sure, but I wanted to talk about *you*."

He eyed her suspiciously. "What about me?"

"You're Nick Velvet. You're famous."

"Only in certain circles."

Their conversation was interrupted by the opening of a door. Terry scurried from the room and Nick lay back and closed his eyes. After a moment he heard Terry return with the man.

"What in hell is this bag of doughnuts doing on the bed?" a male voice demanded. "He's conscious, isn't he? And you've been feeding him!"

"He was hungry, Sam."

There was the splat of palm hitting cheek, and Terry let out a cry.

Nick opened his eyes. "Suppose you try that on me, Sam."

The man from the car, still looking bulky even without his tweed topcoat, turned toward the bed. "You're in no position to make like a knight in shining armor, Velvet."

Nick sat up as best he could with his handcuffed wrist. "Look, I've been slugged on the head, kidnaped, drugged, and handcuffed to this bed. Don't you think I deserve an explanation?"

"Shut him up," Sam ordered Terry, but she made no move to obey.

"You kidnaped me to keep me from seeing the real Max Solar,

right?" Nick was guessing, but it had to be a reasonably good guess. The man named Sam turned on the girl once more.

"Did you tell him that?"

"No, Sam, honest! I didn't tell him a thing!"

The bulky man grunted. "All right, Velvet, it's true. I don't mind telling you, since you've guessed it already. Max Solar wrote you on Friday to arrange an appointment for this week. He wanted to hire you to steal something."

"And you kidnaped me to prevent it?"

The man named Sam nodded. He pulled up a straight-backed wooden chair and sat down by the bed. "Do you know who Max Solar is?"

"I've heard the name." Nick tried to sit up straighter, but the handcuff prevented him. "How about unlocking this thing?"

"Not a chance."

"All right," Nick sighed. "Tell me about Max Solar."

"He's a conglomerate. He owns a number of companies manufacturing everything from office machines to toothpaste. Last year while I was in his employ I invented a computer program that saved thousands of man-hours each year in bookkeeping and inventory control on his export and overseas operations. The courts have ruled that such computer programming cannot be patented, and I was at the mercy of Max Solar. He simply fired me and kept my program. For the past year I've dreamed of ways to get my revenge, and on Friday Terry supplied me with the perfect weapon."

Nick listened to the voice drone on, wondering where it was all leading. The man did not seem the type to resort to kidnaping, yet there was a hardness in his eyes that hinted at a steely determination.

"I'm a secretary at Solar Industries," Terry explained. "My office is right next to Max Solar's, and often I help his secretary when my boss is away."

Sam nodded. "Solar dictated a letter to Nick Velvet, asking for a meeting today. Terry brought me a copy, with a suggestion for revenging myself on Solar."

"You knew who I was?" Nick asked the girl.

"I had a boy friend once who told me about you—how you steal valueless things for people."

Sam nodded. "I figured up in the suburbs you probably wouldn't get Solar's letter till Monday—not the way mail deliveries are these days—but just to be safe I used his name when I phoned yesterday.

See, I had to kidnap you and hold you prisoner till after the ship sails."

"Ship?"

"Solar was hiring you to steal something from a freighter that sails from New York harbor in two days."

"It must be something important."

"It is, but only to Max Solar. It would be worthless to anyone else."

Nick thought about it.

"That's not quite correct," he said.

"What do you mean?"

"You can revenge yourself on Solar by holding me prisoner, or you can hire me to steal this object and then sell it back to Solar."

"Why should I hire you? I have you already!"

"You have me physically, but you don't have my services."

"He makes sense," Terry said. "I hadn't thought about that angle. If Nick steals the thing, you can sell it to Solar for enough to cover Nick's fee plus a lot more. You'd be getting back the money Solar cheated you out of."

Sam pondered the implications. "How do we know you wouldn't go to the police as soon as you're free?"

"I have as little dealing with the police as possible," Nick said. "For obvious reasons."

Sam was still uncertain. "We've got you now. In forty-eight hours Max Solar will be in big trouble. Why let you go and take a chance on ruining our whole plan?"

"Because if you don't, you'll be in big trouble too. Kidnaping is a far more serious crime than blackmail. Unlock these handcuffs now and hire me. I won't press charges against you. I steal the thing, collect my fee, and you sell it back to Solar for a lot more. Everybody's happy."

Sam turned to Terry. When she nodded approval he said, "All right. Unlock him."

As soon as the handcuff came free of his wrist Nick said, "My fee in this case will be thirty thousand dollars. I always charge more for dangerous assignments."

"There's nothing dangerous about it."

"It's dangerous when I get hit on the head and drugged."

"That was Terry. She was hiding in the back seat of the car with a croquet mallet."

"You knocked me out with a croquet mallet?"

Terry nodded. "We were going to use a monkey wrench, but we thought it might hurt."

"Thanks a lot." Nick was rubbing the circulation back into his wrist. "Now what is it Max Solar was going to hire me to steal?"

"A ship's manifest," Terry told him. "But we're not sure which ship. We only know it sails in two days."

"What's so valuable about a ship's manifest?"

They exchanged glances. "The less you know the better," Sam said.

"Don't I even get to know your names?"

"You know too much already. Steal the manifest and meet us back here tomorrow night."

"How do I find the ship?"

"A South African named Herbert Jarvis is in town arranging for the shipment. He'd know which ship it is." Terry looked uneasy as she spoke. "I could go through the files at the office, but that might arouse suspicion. They might think it odd I took today off anyway."

"Shipment of what?" Nick asked.

"Typewriters," she said, and he knew she was lying.

"All right. But there must be several more copies of this ship's manifest around."

"The copy on the ship is the only one that matters," Sam said. "Get it, and we'll meet you here tomorrow night at seven."

"What about my car?"

"It's in the garage," Terry said. "We didn't want to leave it at the Mall."

Nick nodded. "I'll see you tomorrow with the manifest. Have my fee ready."

The house where he'd been held prisoner was in the northern part of the city, near Van Cortlandt Park. It took Nick nearly an hour to drive home from there, and another hour to comfort a distraught Gloria who'd been about to phone the police.

"You know my business takes me away suddenly at times," he said, glancing casually through the mail until he found Solar's letter.

"But you've always told me, Nicky! I didn't hear from you and all I could imagine was you were hit over the head and robbed!"

"Sorry I worried you." He kissed her gently. "Is it too late to get something to eat?"

In the morning he checked the sailing times of the next day's ships in *The New York Times*. There were only two possibilities–the *Fairfax* and the *Florina*–but neither one was bound for South Africa. With so little time to spare, he couldn't afford to pick the wrong one, and trying to find Herbert Jarvis at an unknown New York hotel might be a hopeless task.

There was only one sure way to find the right ship–to ask Max Solar. He knew that Sam and Terry wouldn't approve, but he had no better choice.

Solar Industries occupied most of a modern twelve-story building not far from the house where he'd been held prisoner. He took the elevator to the top floor and waited in a plush reception room while the girl announced his arrival to Max Solar. Presently a cool young woman appeared to escort him.

"I'm Mr. Solar's secretary," she said. "Please come this way."

In Max Solar's office two men were seated at a wide desk, silhouetted against the wide windows that looked south toward Manhattan. There was no doubt which one was Solar. He was tall and white-haired, and sat behind his desk in total command, like the pilot of an aircraft or a rancher on his horse. He did not rise as Nick entered, but said simply, "So you're Velvet. About time you got here."

"I was tied up earlier."

Solar waited until his secretary left, then said, "I understand you steal things for a fee of twenty thousand dollars."

"Certain things. Nothing of value."

"I know that."

"What do you want stolen?"

"A ship's manifest, for the *S.S. Florina*. She sails tomorrow from New York harbor, so that doesn't give you much time."

"Time is no problem. What's so valuable about the manifest?"

"A mistake was made on it by an inexperienced clerk. All other copies were recovered and corrected in time, but the ship's copy got through somehow. I imagine it's locked in the purser's safe right now. I was told you could do the job. I want this corrected manifest left in its place."

"No problem," Nick said, accepting the lengthy form.

"You're very sure of yourself," the second man said. It was the first he'd spoken since Nick entered. He was small and middle-aged, with just a trace of British accent.

Solar waved a hand at him. "This is Herbert Jarvis from South Africa. He's the consignee for the *Florina* cargo. Two hundred and twelve cases of typewriters and adding machines."

"I see," Nick said. "Pleased to meet you."

"You want some money in advance? Say ten percent—two thousand?" Solar asked, opening his desk drawer.

"Fine. And don't worry about the time. I'll have the manifest before the ship sails."

"Here's my check," Jarvis said, passing it across the desk to Solar. "Drawn on the National Bank of Capetown. I assure you it's good. This is payment in full for the cargo."

"That's the way I like to do business," Solar told him, slipping the check into a drawer.

As Nick started to leave, Herbert Jarvis rose from his chair. "My business here is finished. If you're driving into Manhattan, Mr. Velvet, could I ride with you and save calling a taxi?"

"Sure. Come on." Downstairs he asked, "Your first trip here?"

"Oh, no. I've been here before. Quite a city you have."

"We like it." He turned the car onto the Major Deegan Expressway.

"You live in the city yourself?"

Nick shook his head. "No, near Long Island Sound."

"Are you a boating enthusiast?"

"When I have time. It relaxes me."

Jarvis lit a cigar. "We all need to relax. I'm a painter myself. I've a lovely studio with a fine north light."

"In Capetown?"

"Yes. But it's just a sideline, of course. One can hardly make a living at it." He exhaled some smoke. "I act as a middleman in buying and selling overseas. This is my first dealing with Max Solar, but he seems a decent sort."

"The *Florina* isn't bound for South Africa."

Jarvis shook his head. "The cargo will be removed in the Azores. It's safer that way."

"For the typewriters?"

"And for me."

After a time Nick said, "I'll have to drop you in midtown. Okay?"

"Certainly. I'm at the Wilson Hotel on Seventh Avenue."

"I need to purchase some supplies," Nick said. He'd just decided how he was going to steal the ship's manifest.

The *Florina* was berthed at pier 40, a massive, bustling place that jutted into the Hudson River near West Houston Street. Nick reached it in mid-afternoon and went quickly through the gates to

the gangplank. The ship was showing the rust of age typical o
vessels that plied the waterways in the service of the highest bidder

The purser was much like his ship, with soiled uniform and need
ing a shave. He studied the credentials Nick presented and said
"This is a bit irregular."

"We believe export licenses may be lacking for some of your cargo
It's essential that I inspect your copy of the manifest."

The purser hesitated another moment, then said, "Very well." He
walked to the safe in one corner of his office and opened it. In a
moment he produced the lengthy manifest.

Nick saw at once the reason for Max Solar's concern. On the ship's
copy the line about typewriters and adding machines read: *212 cases
8 mm Mauser semi-automatic rifles.* He was willing to bet that Solar
Industries was not a licensed arms dealer.

"It seems in order," Nick told the purser, "but I'll need a copy of
it." He opened the fat attaché case he carried and revealed a portable
copying machine. "Can I plug this in?"

"Over here."

Nick inserted the manifest with a light-sensitive copying sheet
into the rollers of the machine. In a moment the document reappeared. "There you are," he said, returning it to the purser. "Sorry
I had to trouble you."

"No trouble." He glanced briefly at the manifest and returned it
to the safe.

Nick closed the attaché case, shook the man's hand, and departed.
The theft was as simple as that.

Later that night, at seven o'clock, Nick rang the doorbell of the
little house where he'd been held prisoner. At first no one came to
admit him, though he could see a light burning in the back bedroom.
Then at last Terry appeared, her face pale and distraught.

"I've got it," Nick said. She stepped aside silently and allowed
him to enter.

Sam came out of the back bedroom. "Well, Velvet! Right on time."

"Here's the manifest." Nick produced the document from the attaché case he still carried. "The only remaining original copy, showing that Solar Industries is exporting two hundred and twelve cases
of semi-automatic rifles to Africa."

Sam took the document and glanced at it. For some reason the
triumph didn't seem to excite him. "How did you get it?"

"A simple trick. This afternoon I purchased this portable copying machine from a friend who sometimes makes special gadgets for me. I inserted the original manifest between the rollers, but the substitute came out the other slot. It works much like those trick shop devices, where a blank piece of paper is inserted between rollers and a dollar bill comes out. The purser's copy of the manifest was rolled up and remained in the machine. The substitute copy that I'd inserted in the machine earlier came out the slot. He glanced at it briefly, but since only one line was different he never realized a switch had been made."

"Where did you get this substitute manifest?" Sam wanted to know.

"From Max Solar. I also got an advance for stealing the thing, which I'll return to him. I'm working for you, not Solar. And I imagine he'll pay plenty for that manifest. The clerk who typed it up must have assumed he had an export license for the guns. But without a license it would mean big trouble for Solar Industries if this manifest was inspected by port authorities."

Sam nodded glumly. "He's been selling arms illegally for years, mostly to countries in Africa and Latin America. But this was my first chance to prove it."

"I'll have my fee now," Nick said. "Thirty thousand."

"I haven't got it."

Nick simply stared at him. "What do you mean?"

"I mean I haven't got it. There is no fee. No money, no nothing." He shrugged and started to turn away.

Nick grabbed him by the collar. "If you won't pay for it, Max Solar will!"

"No, he won't," Terry said, speaking for the first time since Nick's arrival. "Look here."

Nick followed her into the back bedroom. On the rumpled bed where Nick had been held prisoner, the body of Max Solar lay sprawled and bloody. There was no doubt Solar was dead.

"How did it happen?" Nick asked. "What's he doing here?"

" I called him," Sam said. "We needed the thirty thousand to pay your fee. The only way we could get it was from Solar. So I told him we'd have the manifest here at seven o'clock. I left the front door unlocked and told him to bring $80,000. I figured $30,000 for you and the rest for us."

"What happened?"

"Terry arrived about twenty minutes ago and found him dead. It looks like he's been stabbed."

"You're trying to tell me you didn't kill him?"

"Of course not!" Sam said, a trace of indignation creeping into his voice. "Do I look like a murderer?"

"No, but then you don't look like a kidnaper either. You had the best reason in the world for wanting him dead."

"His money would have been enough revenge for me."

"Was it on him?"

"No," Terry answered. "We looked. Either he didn't bring it or the killer got it first."

"What am I supposed to do with this manifest?" Nick asked bleakly.

"It's no good to me now. I can't get revenge on a dead man."

"That's your problem. You still owe me thirty thousand."

Sam held his hands wide in a gesture of helplessness. "We don't have the money! What should I do? Give you the mortgage on this house that's falling apart? Be thankful you got something out of Max Solar before he died."

Ignoring Nick, Terry asked, "What are we going to do with the body, Sam?"

"Do? Call the police! What else is there to do?"

"Won't they think we did it?"

"Maybe they'll be right," Nick said. "Maybe you killed him, Terry, to have the money for yourself. Or maybe Sam killed him and then sneaked out to let you find the body."

Both of them were quick to deny the accusations, and in truth Nick cared less about the circumstances of Max Solar's death than he did about the balance of his fee, and he saw no way of collecting it at the moment.

"All right," he said finally. "I'll leave you two to figure out your next move. You know where to reach me if you come up with the money. Meanwhile, I'm keeping this manifest."

He drove south, toward Manhattan, and though the night was turning chilly he left his window open. The fresh air felt good against his face and it helped him to sort out his thoughts. There was only one other person who'd have the least interest in paying money for the manifest, and that was Herbert Jarvis.

He headed for the Wilson Hotel.

Jarvis was in his room packing when Nick knocked on the door. "Well," he said, a bit startled. "Velvet, isn't it?"

"That's right. Can I come in?"

"I have to catch a plane. I'm packing."

"So I see," Nick said. He shut the door behind him.

"If you'll make it brief, I really am quite busy."

"I'll bet you are. I'll make it brief enough. I want thirty thousand dollars."

"Thirty . . . ! For what?"

"This copy of the ship's manifest for the *S.S. Florina*. The only copy that shows it's carrying a cargo of rifles."

"The business with the manifest is between you and Solar. He hired you."

"Various people hired me, but you're the only one I can collect from. Max Solar is dead."

"Dead?"

"Stabbed to death in a house uptown. Within the past few hours."

Jarvis sat down on the bed. "That's a terrible thing."

Nick shrugged. "I assume he knew the sort of men he was dealing with."

"What's that mean?" Jarvis asked, growing nervous.

"Who do you think killed him?" Nick countered.

"That computer programmer, Sam, I suppose. That's his house uptown."

"How do you know it's Sam's house? How do you know about Sam?"

"Solar was going to meet him. He told me on the telephone."

It all fell into place for Nick. "What did he tell you?"

"That Sam wanted money for the manifest. That you were working for Sam."

"Why did he tell you about it?"

"I don't know."

"Let's take a guess. Could it have been because the check you gave him was no good? A man with Solar's world-wide contacts could have discovered quickly that there was no money in South Africa to cover your check. In fact, you're not even from South Africa, are you?"

"What do you mean?"

"You told me you're an artist, and since you volunteered the information I assume it's true. But you said you have a studio in Capetown with a fine north light. Artists like north light because it's truer, because the sun is never in the northern sky. But of course this is only true in the northern hemisphere. An artist in Capetown or Buenos Aires or Melbourne would want a studio with a good *south* light. Your studio, Jarvis, isn't in Capetown at all. It would have to be somewhere well north of the equator.

"And if you lied about being from South Africa, I figured the check drawn on a South African bank is probably phony too. You reasoned that once the arms shipment was safely out to sea there was no way Solar could blow the whistle without implicating himself. But when he learned your check was valueless, he phoned you and probably told you to meet him at Sam's house with the money or he'd have the cases of guns taken off the ship."

"You're saying I killed him?"

"Yes."

"You are one smart man, Velvet."

"Smart enough for a two-bit gunrunner."

Jarvis' right hand moved faster than Nick's eyes could follow. The knife was up his sleeve, and it missed Nick's throat by inches as it thudded into the wall. "Too bad," Nick said. "With a gun you get a second chance." And he dove for the man.

He remembered the address of Sam's house and got the phone number from a friend with the company. Sam answered on the first ring, sounding nervous, and Nick asked, "How's it going?"

"Velvet? Where are you? The police are here."

"Good," Nick said, knowing a detective would be listening in. "You did the right thing calling them. I don't know why I'm getting you off the hook, but tell them Solar's killer is in Room 334 at the Wilson Hotel on Seventh Avenue."

"You found him?"

"Yeah," Nick said. "But he didn't have any money either."

It was one of the very few times Nick Velvet failed—that is, failed to collect his full fee.

"Q"

Edward D. Hoch

The Spy at the End of the Rainbow

The 27th adventure in detection and espionage of Rand, the head of the Department of Concealed Communications, known as the Double-C man ... An urgent assignment brought Rand to the End of the Rainbow. Now, what should one expect to find at the end of the rainbow? A pot of gold, of course. But Rand found something else. Not gold-colored, but red, green, white, blue, orange, yellow, indigo, violet, and black—strangely enough, the colors of murder...

Counterspy-Detective: JEFFERY RAND

Rand was in Cairo looking for Leila Gaad when he first heard about the End of the Rainbow. It had been nearly two years since they had fled the city together by helicopter with half the Egyptian Air Force in pursuit, but a great many things had changed in those two years. Most important, the Russians were gone. Only a few stragglers remained behind from the thousands of technicians and military advisers who had crowded the city back in those days.

Rand liked the city better without the Russians, though he was the first to admit that their departure had done little to ease tensions in the Middle East. There were still the terrorists and the almost weekly incidents, still the killings and the threats of war from both sides. In a world mainly at peace, Cairo was still a city where a spy could find work.

He'd come searching for Leila partly because he simply wanted to see her again, but mainly because one of her fellow archeologists at Cairo University had suddenly become a matter of deep concern to British Intelligence. It was not, at this point, a case for the Department of Concealed Communications, but Hastings had been quick to enlist Rand's help when it became obvious that his old friend Leila Gaad might have useful information.

So he was in Cairo on a warm April day. Unfortunately, Leila

Gaad was not in Cairo. Rand had visited the University to ask about her, and been told by a smiling Greek professor, "Leila has gone to the End of the Rainbow."

"The end of the rainbow?" Rand asked, his mind conjuring up visions of pots of gold.

"The new resort hotel down on Foul Bay. There's a worldwide meeting of archeologists in progress, and two of our people are taking part."

It seemed too much to hope for, but Rand asked the question anyway. "Would the person accompanying Leila be Herbert Fanger, by any chance?"

The Greek's smile widened. "You know Professor Fanger, too?"

"Only by reputation."

"Yes, they are down there together, representing Cairo University. With the meeting in our country we could hardly ignore it."

"Are the Russians represented, too?"

"The Russians, the Americans, the British, the French, and the Chinese. It's a truly international event."

Rand took out his notebook. "I just think I might drop in on that meeting. Could you tell me how to get to the End of the Rainbow?"

Foul Bay was an inlet of the Red Sea, perched on its western shore in the southeastern corner of Egypt. (For Rand the ancient land would always be Egypt. He could never bring himself to call it the United Arab Republic.) It was located just north of the Sudanese border in an arid, rocky region that all but straddled the Tropic of Cancer. Rand thought it was probably the last place on earth that anyone would ever build a resort hotel.

But that was before his hired car turned off the main road and he saw the lush irrigated oasis, before he caught a glimpse of the sprawling group of white buildings overlooking the bay. He passed under a multihued sign announcing *The End of the Rainbow,* and was immediately on a rainbow-colored pavement that led directly to the largest of the buildings.

The first person he encountered after parking the car was an armed security guard. Rand wondered at the need for a guard in such a remote area, but he followed the man into the administrative area. A small Englishman wearing a knit summer suit rose from behind a large white desk to greet him. "What have we here?"

Rand presented his credentials. "It's important that I speak to Miss Leila Gaad. I understand she is a guest at this resort."

The man bowed slightly. "I am Felix Bollinger, manager of the End of the Rainbow. We're always pleased to have visitors, even from British Intelligence."

"I haven't seen all of it, but it's quite a place. Who owns it?"

"A London-based corporation. We're still under construction, really. This conference of archeologists is something of a test run for us."

"You did all this irrigation work, too?"

The small man nodded. "That was the most expensive part—that and cleaning up the bay. Now I'm petitioning the government to change the name from Foul Bay to Rainbow Bay. Foul Bay is hardly a designation to attract tourists."

"I wish you luck." Rand was looking out at the water, which still seemed a bit scummy to him.

"But you wanted to see Miss Gaad. According to the schedule of events, this is a free hour. I suspect you'll find her down at the pool with the others." He pointed to a door. "Out that way."

"Thank you."

"Ask her to show you around. You've never seen any place quite like the End of the Rainbow."

"I've decided that already."

Rand went out the door indicated and strolled down another rainbow-colored path to the pool area. A half-dozen people were splashing in the water, and it took him only a moment to pick out the bikini-clad figure of Leila Gaad. She was small and dark-haired, but with a swimmer's perfect body that glistened as she pulled herself from the pool.

"Hello again," he said, offering her a towel. "Remember me?"

She looked up at him, squinting against the sunlight. "It's Mr. Rand, isn't it?"

"You're still so formal."

Her face seemed even more youthful than he remembered, with high cheekbones and deep dark eyes that always seemed to be mocking him. "I'm afraid to ask what brings you here," she said.

"As usual, business." He glanced at the others in the pool. Four men, mostly middle-aged, and one woman who might have been Leila's age or a little older—perhaps 30. One man was obviously Oriental. The others, in bathing trunks, revealed no national traits that Rand could recognize. "Where could we talk?" he asked.

"Down by the bay?" She slipped a terrycloth jacket over her shoulders.

"Bollinger said you might show me around the place. How about that?"

"Fine." She led him back up the walk toward the main building where they encountered another man who looked younger than the others.

"Not leaving me already, are you?" he asked Leila.

"Just showing an old friend around. Mr. Rand, from London—this is Harvey Northgate, from Columbia University in the United States. He's here for the conference."

They shook hands and the American said, "Take good care of her, Rand. There are only two women in the place." He continued down the walk to the pool.

"Seems friendly enough," Rand observed.

"They're all friendly. It's the most fun I've ever had at one of these conferences." Glancing sideways at him, she asked, "But how did you manage to get back into the country? Did they drop you by parachute?"

"Hardly. You're back, aren't you?"

"But not without the University pulling strings. Then of course the Russians left and that eased things considerably." She had led him to a center court with white buildings on all sides. "Each building has nine large suites of rooms, and you can see there are nine buildings in the cluster, plus the administrative complex. Those eight are still being finished, though. Only the one we're occupying has been completed."

"That's only eighty-one units in all," Rand observed.

"Enough, at the rates they plan to charge! The rumor is that Bollinger's company wants to show a profit and then sell the whole thing to Hilton." They turned off the main path and she pointed to the colored stripes. "See? The colors of the rainbow show you where you're going. Follow the blue to the pool, the yellow to the lounge."

The completed building, like the others, was two stories high. There were four suites on the first floor and five on the floor above. "How are you able to afford all this?" Rand asked.

"There's a special rate for the conference because they're not fully open yet. And the University's paying for Professor Fanger and me." She led him down the hall of the building. "Each of these nine suites has a different color scheme—the seven colors of the spectrum, plus black and white. Here's mine—the orange suite. The walls, drapes, bedspreads, shower curtain—even the ashtrays and telephone—are all orange." She opened a ceramic orange cigarette box. "See, even orange cigarettes! Professor Fanger has yellow ones, and he doesn't even smoke."

"Who's in the black suite?"

"The American, Harvey Northgate. He was upset when he heard it, but the rooms are really quite nice. All the black is trimmed with white. I like all the suites, except maybe the purple. I told Bollinger he should make that one pink instead."

"You say Professor Fanger is in yellow?"

"Yes. It's so bright and cheerful!"

"I came out from London to check on the possibility that he might be a former Russian agent we've been hunting for years. We arrested a man in Liverpool last week and he listed Fanger as one of his former contacts."

Leila Gaad chuckled. "Have you ever met Herbert Fanger?"

"Not yet," he admitted.

"He's the most unlikely-looking spy imaginable."

"They make the best kind."

"No, really! He's fat and over forty, but he still imagines himself a ladies' man. He wears outlandish clothes, with loud colors most men wouldn't be caught dead in, even these days. He's hardly my idea of an unobtrusive secret agent."

"From what we hear, he's retired. He used the code name Sphinx while he was gathering information and passing it to Russia."

"If he's retired, why do you want to talk to him?"

"Because he knows a great deal, especially about the agents with whom he used to work. Some of those are retired now too, but others are still active, spying for one country or another."

"Where do I come in?" she asked suspiciously. "I've already swum the Nile and climbed the Great Pyramid for you, but I'm not going to betray Herbert Fanger to British Intelligence. He's a funny little man but I like him. What he was ten years ago is over and done with."

"At least you can introduce me, can't you?"

"I suppose so," she agreed reluctantly.

"Was he one of those at the pool?"

"Heavens, no! He'd never show up in bathing trunks. I imagine he's in the lounge watching television."

"Television, this far from Cairo?"

"It's closed-circuit, just for the resort. They show old movies."

Herbert Fanger was in the lounge as she'd predicted, but he wasn't watching old movies on television. He was deep in conversation with

Bollinger, the resort manager. They separated when Rand and Leila entered the large room, and Bollinger said, "Well, Mr. Rand! Has she been showing you our place?"

"I'm doubly impressed now that I've seen it."

"Come back in the autumn when we're fully open. Then you'll really see something!"

"Could I get a room for tonight? It's a long drive back to Cairo."

Bollinger frowned and consulted his memory. "Let me see . . . The indigo suite is still vacant, if you'd like that."

"Fine."

"I'll get you the key. You can have the special rate, even though you're not part of the conference."

As he hurried away, Leila introduced Fanger. "Professor Herbert Fanger, perhaps the world's leading authority on Cleopatra and her era."

"Pleased to meet you," Rand said.

Fanger was wearing a bright-red sports shirt and checkered pants that did nothing to hide his protruding stomach. Seeing him, Rand had to admit he made a most unlikely-looking spy. "We were just talking about the place," he told Rand. "What do you think it cost?"

"I couldn't begin to guess."

"Tell them, Felix," he said as the manager returned with Rand's key.

Bollinger answered with a trace of pride. "With the irrigation and landscaping, plus cleaning up the bay, it will come close to seven million dollars. The highest cost per unit of any resort hotel."

Rand was impressed. But after a few more moments of chatting he remembered the reason for his trip.

"Could I speak to you in private, Professor, about some research I'm doing?"

"Regarding Cleopatra?"

"Regarding the Sphinx."

There was a flicker of something in Fanger's eyes. He excused himself and went with Rand. When they were out of earshot he said, "You're British Intelligence, aren't you? Bollinger told me."

"Concealed communications, to be exact. I know this country, so they sent me to talk with you."

"I've been retired since the mid-sixties."

"We know that. It took us that long to track you down. We're not after you, but you must have a great many names in your mind. We'd be willing to make a deal for those names."

Fanger's eyes flickered again. "I might be interested. I don't know. Coming here and talking to me openly could have been a mistake."

"You mean there's someone here who—"

"Look, Rand, I'm forty-seven years old and about that many pounds overweight. I retired before I got myself killed, and I don't know that I want to take any risks now. Espionage is a young man's game, always was. Your own Somerset Maugham quit it after World War One to write books. I quit it to chase women."

"Having any luck?"

"Here?" he snorted. "I think Leila's a twenty-eight-year-old virgin and the French one is pure bitch. Not much choice."

"Exactly what is the purpose of this conference?"

"Simply to discuss recent advances in archeology. Each of five nations sent a representative, and of course the University thought Leila and I should attend, too. There's nothing sinister about it—of that I can assure you!" But his eyes weren't quite so certain.

"Then why the armed guards patrolling the grounds?"

"You'd have to ask Bollinger—though I imagine he'd tell you there are occasional thieving nomads in the region. Without guards this place would be too tempting."

"How far is it to the nearest town?"

"More than a hundred miles overland to Aswan—nothing closer except native villages and lots of sand."

"An odd place to hold a conference. An odder place to build a plush resort."

"Once the Suez Canal is back in full operation, Bollinger expects to get most of his clientele by boat—wealthy yachtsmen and the like. Who knows? He might make a go of it. Once it's cleaned up, Foul Bay could make a natural anchorage."

They had strolled out of the building and around the cluster of white structures still in various stages of completion. Rand realized the trend of the conversation had got away from him. He'd not traveled all the way from London to discuss a resort hotel with Herbert Fanger. But then suddenly Leila reappeared with another of the male conferees—a distinguished white-haired man with a neatly trimmed Vandyke beard. Rand remembered seeing him lounging by the pool. Now he reached out to shake hands as Leila introduced him.

"Oh, Mr. Rand, here's a countryman of yours. Dr. Wayne Evans, from Oxford."

The bearded Dr. Evans grinned cheerfully. "Pleased to meet you,

Rand. I always have to explain that I'm not a medical doctor an
I'm not with the University. I simply live in Oxford and write book
on various aspects of archeology."

"A pleasure to meet you in any event," Rand said. He saw tha
Fanger had taken advantage of the interruption to get away, bu
there would be time for him later. "I've been trying to get a straigh
answer as to what this conference is all about, but everyone seem
rather vague about it."

Dr. Evans chuckled.

"The best way to explain it is for you to sit in at our mornin
session. You may find it deadly dull, but at least you'll know a
much as the rest of us."

"I'd enjoy it," Rand said. He watched Evans go down the walk
taking the path that led to the pool and then changing his mind an
heading for the lounge. Then Rand turned his attention to Leila
who'd remained at his side.

"As long as you're here you can escort me to dinner tonight," sh
said. "Then your long drive won't have been a total waste."

He reacted to her impish smile with a grin of his own. "How d
you know it's been a waste so far?"

"Because I've known Herbert Fanger for three years and neve
gotten a straight answer out of him yet. I don't imagine you di
much better."

"You're quite correct," he admitted. "Come on, let's eat."

He checked in at the indigo suite he'd been assigned and foun
it not nearly as depressing as he'd expected from the color. Like th
black suite, the dominant color had been liberally bordered in white
and the effect proved to be quite pleasant. He was beginning t
think that the End of the Rainbow might catch on, if anyone coul
afford to stay there.

Over dinner Leila introduced him to the other conferees he hadn'
met—Jeanne Bisset from France, Dr. Tao Liang from the People'
Republic of China, and Ivan Rusanov from Russia. With Fanger an
Northgate and Evans, whom he'd met previously, that made si
attending the conference, not counting Leila herself.

"Dr. Tao should really be in the yellow suite," Rand observe
quietly to Leila. "He would be if Bollinger had any imagination."

"And I suppose you'd have Rusanov in red?"

"Of course!"

"Well, he is, for your information. But Dr. Tao is green."

"That must leave the Frenchwoman, Jeanne Bisset, in violet."

"Wrong! She's white. Bollinger left indigo and violet empty, though now you have indigo."

"He implied that was the only suite empty. I wonder what's going on in violet."

"Nameless orgies, no doubt—with all you Englishmen on the premises."

"I should resent that," he said with a smile. She put him at ease, and he very much enjoyed her company.

After dinner the others split into various groups. Rand saw the Chinese and the Russian chatting, and the American, Harvey Northgate, walking off by himself. "With those other suites free, why do you think Bollinger insisted on giving the black one to the American?" Rand asked Leila as they strolled along the edge of the bay.

"Perhaps he's anti-American, who knows?"

"You don't take the whole thing very seriously."

"Should I, Mr. Rand?"

"Can't you find something else to call me?"

"I never knew your first name."

"C. Jeffery Rand, and I don't tell anyone what the C. stands for."

"You don't look like a Jeffery," she decided, cocking her head to gaze up at him. "You look more like a Winston."

"I may be Prime Minister someday."

She took his arm and steered him back toward the cluster of lighted buildings. "When you are, I'll walk along the water with you. Till then, we stay far away from it. The last time I was near water with you, I ended up swimming across the Nile to spy on a Russian houseboat!"

"It was fun, wasn't it?"

"Sure. So was climbing that pyramid in the middle of the night. My legs ached for days."

It was late by the time they returned to their building. Some people were still in the lounge, but the lights in most suites were out.

"We grow tired early here," she said. "I suppose it's all the fresh air and exercise."

"I know what you mean. It was a long drive down this morning." He glanced at his watch and saw that it was already after ten. They'd strolled and chatted longer than he'd realized. "One thing first. I'd like to continue my conversation with Fanger if he's still up."

"Want me to come along?" she suggested. "Then we can both hear him say nothing."

"Come on. He might surprise you."

Fanger's yellow suite was at the rear of the first floor, near a fire exit. He didn't answer Rand's knock, and they were about to check the lounge when Rand noticed a drop of fresh orange paint on the carpet under the door. "This is odd."

"What?"

"Paint, and still wet."

"The door's unlocked, Rand."

They pushed it open and snapped on the overhead light. What they saw was unbelievable. The entire room—ceiling, walls, floor—had been splashed with paint of every color. There was red and blue and green and black and white and violet and orange—all haphazardly smeared over every surface in the room. Over it all, ashtrays and towels meant for other suites had been dumped and scattered. Fanger's yellow cigarette box was smashed on the floor, with blue and yellow cigarettes, green and indigo towels, even an orange ashtray, scattered around it. The suite was a surrealistic dream, as if at the end of the rainbow all the colors of the spectrum had been jumbled with white and black.

And crumpled in one corner, half hidden by a chair, was the body of Herbert Fanger. The red of his blood was almost indistinguishable from the paint that stained the yellow wall behind him. He'd been stabbed several times in the chest and abdomen.

"My God," Leila breathed. "It's a scene from hell!"

"Let's phone the nearest police," Rand said. "We need help here."

But as they turned to leave, a voice from the hall said, "I'm afraid that will be impossible, Mr. Rand. There will be no telephoning by anyone." Felix Bollinger stood there with one of his armed security guards, and the guard was pointing a pistol at them both.

Rand raised his hands reluctantly above his head, and at his side Leila Gaad said with a sigh, "You've done it to me again, haven't you, Rand?"

They were ushered into Bollinger's private office and the door was locked behind them. Only then did the security guard holster his revolver. He stood with his back to the door as Bollinger took a seat behind the desk.

"You must realize, Mr. Rand, that I cannot afford to have the End of the Rainbow implicated in a police investigation at this time."

"I'm beginning to realize it."

"You and Miss Gaad will be held here in my office until that room can be cleaned up and some disposition made of Herbert Fanger's body."

"And you expect me to keep silent about that?" Rand asked. "I'm here on an official mission concerning Herbert Fanger. His murder is a matter of great interest to the British government."

"This is no longer British soil, Mr. Rand. It has not been for some decades."

"But you are a British subject."

"Only when it pleases me to be."

"What's going on here? Why the armed guards? Why was Fanger murdered?"

"It does not concern you, Mr. Rand."

"Did you kill him?"

"Hardly!"

Rand shifted in his chair. "Then the killer is one of the others. Turn me loose and I might be able to find him for you."

Bollinger's eyes narrowed. "Just how would you do that?"

"With all that paint splashed around, the killer must have gotten some on him. There was a spot of orange paint on the carpet outside the door, for instance, as if it had come off the bottom of a shoe. Let me examine everyone's clothing and I'll identify the murderer."

The manager was a man who reached quick decisions. "Very well, if I have your word you'll make no attempt to get in touch with the authorities."

"They have to be told sooner or later."

"Let's make it later. If we have the killer to hand over, it might not look quite so bad."

Rand got to his feet. "I'll want another look at Fanger's room. Put a guard on the door and don't do any cleaning up."

"What about the body?"

"It can stay there for now," Rand decided. "If we find the killer, it'll be in the next hour or so."

Leila followed him out of the office, still amazed. "How did you manage that? He had a gun on us ten minutes ago, and you talked your way out of it!"

"Not completely. Not yet. His security people will be watching us. Look, suppose you wake everyone up and get them down by the pool."

"All right," she agreed. "But what for?"

"We're going to look for paint spots."

The American, Harvey Northgate, refused to be examined at first. And the Russian demanded to call his Embassy in Cairo. But after Rand explained what it was all about, they seemed to calm down. The only trouble was, Rand and Leila could find no paint on any of them. It seemed impossible, but it was true. Rand's hope of reaching a quick solution to the mystery burst like an over-inflated balloon.

It was Bollinger himself who provided an explanation, when the others had been allowed to return to their beds. "I discovered where the paint cans and the rest of it came from. Look, the side exit from this building is only a few steps away from the side exit to that building still under construction. Just inside the door are paint cans, boxes of towels and ashtrays, and even a pair of painter's coveralls."

"Show me," Rand said. He looked around for Leila but she was gone. Perhaps the day really had tired her out.

The resort manager led Rand to the unfinished building. Looking at the piles of paint cans, Rand had little doubt that this was the source of the vandal's supplies. He opened a box of red bath towels, and a carton of blue ashtrays.

"Anything else here?" he asked.

"Just drapes. Apparently he didn't have time for those."

"What about the carpeting? And soap and cigarettes?"

"They're stored in one of the other buildings. He just took what was close at hand. And he wore a painter's coveralls over his own clothes."

"I suppose so," Rand agreed. The splotches of paint seemed fresh, still tacky to his touch. "What I'd like to know is why—why risk discovery by going after that paint and the other things? He had to make at least two trips, one with the paint cans and the second to return the coveralls and probably gather up a few other things to throw around the room. Who knew these things were here?"

"They all did. I took them on a tour of the place the first day and showed them in here."

"Coveralls," Rand mused, "but no shoes. The shoes with the orange paint might still turn up."

"Or might not. He could have tossed them into the bay."

"All right," Rand conceded. "I'm at a dead end. We'll have to call in the authorities."

"No."

"What do you mean, no?"

"Just what I said. The people here don't want publicity. Nor do I."

"They're not archeologists, are they?"

"Not exactly," Bollinger admitted.

"Then what were Leila and Fanger doing here?"

"A mistake. Cairo University believed our cover story and sent them down for the conference. Fanger, a retired agent himself, knew something was wrong from the beginning. Then you came, and it scared one of them enough to commit murder."

"You have to tell me what's going on here," Rand said.

"A conference."

"Britain, America, France, Russia, and China. A secret conference in the middle of nowhere, policed by armed guards." He remembered something. "And what about the violet room? Who's in there?"

"You ask too many questions. Here's a list of all our guests."

Rand accepted the paper and scanned it quickly, refreshing his memory:

First Floor: Red–Ivan Rusanov (Russia)

Orange–Leila Gaad (Egypt)

Yellow–Herbert Fanger (Egypt)

Green–Dr. Tao Liang (China)

Second Floor: Blue–Dr. Wayne Evans (Britain)

Indigo–Rand

Violet–

White–Jeanne Bisset (France)

Black–Harvey Northgate (U.S.)

"The violet suite is empty?" Rand questioned.

"It is empty."

Rand pocketed the list. "I'm going to look around."

"We've cut the telephone service. It will do you no good to try phoning out. Only the hotel extensions are still in operation."

"Thanks for saving me the effort." He had another thought. "You know, this list doesn't include some very good suspects–yourself and your employees."

"I would never have created that havoc. And my guards would have used a gun rather than a knife."

"What about the cooks and maids? The painters working on the other buildings?"

"Question them if you wish," he said. "You'll discover nothing."

Rand left him and cut through the lounge to the stairway. He was anxious to check out that violet suite. It was now after midnight, and there was no sign of the others, though he hardly believed they were all in their beds.

He paused before the violet door and tried the knob. It was unlocked, and he wondered if he'd find another body. Fanger's door had been left unlocked so that the killer could return with the paint cans. He wondered why this one was unlocked. But he didn't wonder long.

"Felix? Is that you?" a woman's voice called from the bedroom. It was the Frenchwoman, Jeanne Bisset.

"No, just me," Rand said, snapping on the overhead light.

She sat up in bed, startled. "What are you doing here?"

"It's as much my room as yours. I'm sorry Felix Bollinger was delayed. It's been a busy night."

"I . . ."

"You don't have to explain. I was wondering why he kept this suite vacant, and now I know." He glanced around at the violet furnishings, deciding it was the least attractive of those he'd seen.

"Have you found the killer?" she asked, recovering her composure. She was a handsome woman, older than Leila, and Rand wondered if she and Bollinger had known each other before this week.

"Not yet," he admitted. "It might help if you were frank with me."

She blinked her eyes. "About what?"

"The purpose of this conference."

She thought about that. Finally she said, "Hand me a cigarette from my purse and I'll tell you what I know."

He reached in, found a case full of white cigarettes ringed in black, and passed her one. "Is the house brand any good?" he asked. "I used to smoke American cigarettes all the time, but I managed to give them up."

"They're free and available," she said, lighting one. "Something like Felix Bollinger himself."

"You were going to talk about the conference," he reminded her.

"Yes, the conference. A gathering of do-gooders trying to change the world. But the world cannot be changed, can it?"

"That all depends. You're not archeologists, then?"

"No. Although the Russian, Rusanov, knew enough about it to fake a few lectures after Fanger and Miss Gaad turned up. No, Mr. Rand, in truth we're nothing more than peace activists. Our five nations–America, France, Britain, China, Russia–are the only ones who have perfected nuclear weapons."

"Of course! I should have realized that!"

"We are meeting here—with funds provided by peace groups and ban-the-bomb committees in our homelands—to work out some coordinated effort. As you can see, we're no young hippies but sincere middle-aged idealists."

"But why only the five of you? And why out here in the middle of nowhere?"

"A larger meeting would have attracted the press—which would have been especially dangerous for Dr. Tao and Ivan when they returned home. We heard of this place, just being built, and it seemed perfect for our purpose."

"Do you remember who actually suggested it?"

She blushed prettily. "As a matter of fact, I did. I'd met Felix Bollinger in Paris last year, and—"

"I understand," Rand said. "You sent out some sort of announcement to the press to cover yourselves, and Cairo University believed it."

"Exactly."

"Which one of you did Fanger recognize?"

She looked blank. "He didn't admit to knowing any of us."

"All right," Rand said with a sigh. "Thanks for the information."

He left and went in search of Leila Gaad.

He found her finally in her room—the last place he thought of looking. The orange walls and drapes assaulted his eyes, but she seemed to enjoy the decor. "I think I've found our murderer," she announced. "And I've also found a concealed communication for you to ponder."

"I thought this was going to be one case without it. First tell me who the killer is."

"The American—Northgate! I found this pair of shoes in the rubbish by the incinerator. See—orange paint on the bottom! And they're American-made shoes!"

"Hardly conclusive evidence. But interesting. What about the concealed communication?"

She held a little notebook aloft triumphantly. "I went back to Professor Fanger's room and found this among his things. He was always writing in it, and I thought it might give us a clue. Look here—on the very last page, in his handwriting. *Invite to room, confirm tritan.*"

"Tritan? What's that?"

"Well, he spelled it wrong, I guess, but Triton is a mythological creature having the body of a man and the tail of a fish–sort of male version of a mermaid. That would imply a good swimmer, wouldn't it? And seeing them all around the pool, I can tell you Northgate is the best swimmer of the lot."

"Fanger was going to confirm this in his room? How–by flooding the place?"

"Well. . ." She paused uncertainly. "What else could it mean?"

Rand didn't answer. Instead he said, "Come on. Let's go see Northgate."

The American answered the door with sleepy eyes and a growling voice. "Don't you know it's the middle of the night?" Rand held out the shoes for him to see, and he fell silent.

"Going to let us in?"

"All right," he said grudgingly, stepping aside.

"These are your shoes, aren't they?"

There was little point in denying it. "Yes, they're mine."

"And you were in the room after Fanger was murdered?"

"I was there, but I didn't kill him. He was already dead. He'd invited me up for a nightcap. The door was unlocked and when I went in I found him dead and the room a terrible mess. I was afraid I'd be implicated so I left, but I discovered later I'd stepped in some orange paint. When you got us all out by the pool to search for paint spots I panicked and threw the shoes away."

Rand tended to believe him. The real murderer would have done a better job of disposing of the incriminating shoes. "All right," he said. "Now let's talk about the conference. Jeanne Bisset has already told me its real purpose–to work for nuclear disarmament in your five nations. Did Fanger have any idea of this?"

"I think he was onto something," the American admitted. "That's why he wanted to see me. He wanted to ask me about one of the others in the group–someone he thought he knew."

"Which one?"

"He was dead before he could tell me."

"What damage could a spy do at this conference?" Rand asked.

Northgate thought about it. "Not very much. I suppose if he was in the pay of the Russians or Chinese he could report the names of Rusanov and Dr. Tao to their governments, but that would be about all."

"I may have more questions for you later," Rand said.

"He was probably killed by one of the Arab employees," Northgate suggested as Rand and Leila headed for the door.

Back downstairs, Leila said, "Maybe he's right. Maybe it was just a robbery killing."

"Then why go to such lengths with the paint and the other things? There was a reason for it, and the only sane reason had to be to hide the killer's identity."

Leila took out one of her orange cigarettes. "Splashing paint around a hotel room to hide a killer's identity? How?"

"That's what I don't know." He produced the dead man's notebook again and stared at the final message: *Invite to room, confirm tritan.* It wasn't Triton misspelled. A professor at Cairo University wouldn't make a mistake like that.

His eyes wandered to Leila's cigarette, and suddenly he knew.

Dr. Wayne Evans opened the door for them. His hair and beard were neatly in place, and it was obvious he hadn't been sleeping. "Well, what's this?" he asked. "More investigation?"

"The final one, Dr. Evans," Rand said, glancing about the blue suite. "You killed Professor Fanger."

"Oh, come now!" Evans glanced at Leila to see if she believed it.

"You killed him because he recognized you as a spy he used to deal with. He invited you to his suite to confirm it, and when he confronted you with it there was a struggle and you killed him. I suppose it was the beard that made him uncertain of your identity at first."

"Is this any way to talk to a fellow countryman, Rand? I'm here on an important mission."

"I can guess your mission—to sabotage this conference."

Evans took a step backward. He seemed to be weighing the possibilities. "You think I killed him and messed up the room like that?"

"Yes. The room was painted like a rainbow, and strewn with towels and things from the next building. But just a little while ago I remembered there were cigarettes strewn on that floor too, next to the broken ceramic box they were in. There were no cigarettes stored in the next building. I think while you were struggling with Fanger he ripped your pocket. The cigarettes from your suite tumbled out, just as the table was overturned and his own cigarette box smashed. Your cigarettes and his cigarettes mingled on the floor. And that was the reason for the entire thing—the reason the room had to be splashed with paint and all the rest of it. To hide the presence of those blue cigarettes."

Dr. Wayne Evans snorted. "A likely story! I could have just picked up the blue ones, you know."

"But you couldn't have," Rand said. "Because you're color-blind."

That was when Evans moved. He grabbed Leila and had her before Rand could react. The knife in his hand had appeared as if by magic, pressed against her throat. "All right, Rand," he said very quietly. "Out of my way or the girl dies. Another killing won't matter to me."

Rand cursed himself for being caught off guard, cursed himself again for having Leila there in the first place.

"Rand," she gasped as the blade of the knife pressed harder against her flesh.

"All right," he said. "Let her go."

"Call Bollinger. Tell him I want a car with a full petrol tank and an extra emergency can. I want it out in front in ten minutes or the girl dies."

Rand obeyed, speaking in clipped tones to the manager. When he'd hung up, Evans backed against the door, still holding Leila. "Can't we talk about this?" Rand suggested. "I didn't come to this place looking for you. It was only chance—what happened, I mean."

"How'd you know I am color-blind?"

"Fanger left a notation in his notebook. *Invite to room, confirm tritan.* He was simply abbreviating tritanopia—a vision defect in which the retina fails to respond to the colors blue and yellow. It's not as common as red-green blindness, and when Fanger thought he recognized you he knew he could confirm it by having you up to his yellow room. By a quirk of fate you'd been placed in the blue suite yourself. And when you dropped the cigarettes during the struggle, you had only two choices—pick up *all* the cigarettes, blue and yellow alike, or leave them all and somehow disguise their presence."

"Make it short," Evans said. "I'm leaving in three minutes."

"If you took all the cigarettes you risked having them found on you before you could dispose of them. Even if you flushed them down the toilet, a problem remained. Fanger was a known nonsmoker. The broken cigarette box would call attention to the missing cigarettes, and the police would wonder why the killer took them away. If your color blindness became known, someone might even guess the truth. But splashing the room with paint, using every color you could find, not only camouflaged the cigarettes but also directed attention, in a very subtle manner, *away* from a color-blind person."

Evans reached behind him to open the door. "You're too smart, Rand."

"Not really. Once I suspected your color blindness, I remembered your momentary confusion on those rainbow-colored paths yesterday, when you started down the blue path to the pool and then changed your mind and took the yellow one to the lounge. Of course both colors only looked gray to your eyes."

"Walk backward," Evans told Leila. "You're coming with me."

"Who paid you to spy on the conference?" Rand asked. "What country?"

"Country?" Evans snorted. "I worked for countries when Fanger knew me. Now I work where the real money is."

He moved down the hall, dragging Leila with him, and Rand followed. Felix Bollinger was standing by the door, holding it open, the perfect manager directing a departing guest to his waiting car.

"Out of my way," Evans told him.

"I hope your stay was a pleasant one," Bollinger said. Then he brought a gun from behind his back and shot Evans once in the head. . .

Leila Gaad downed a stiff shot of Scotch and said to Rand, "You would have let him go, just to save me! I must say that wasn't very professional of you."

"I have my weaknesses," Rand admitted.

Felix Bollinger downed his own drink and reached again for the bottle he'd supplied. "A terrible opening for my resort. The home office won't be pleased."

"Who was paying Evans?" Leila asked. "And paying him for what?"

"We'll have to check on him," Rand said. "But I suppose there are various pressures in today's world working against disarmament. In America sometimes they're called things like the military-industrial complex. In other nations they have other names. But they have money, and perhaps they're taking over where some of the governments leave off. When we find out who was paying Evans, it might well be a company building rockets in America, or submarines in Russia, or fighter planes in France."

"Is there no place left to escape?" Leila asked.

And Felix Bollinger supplied the answer. "No, my dear, there is not. Not even here, at the End of the Rainbow."